1934 *Ten Lyric Poems*
1935 *12 Ethical Sonnets*
1936 *15 Poems with Time Expressions*
1937 *Homecoming & Departure*
1938 *Childish Jokes: Crying Backstage*
1939 *A Warning at My Leisure*
1941 *Five Young American Poets: Second Series* (with
      Jeanne McGahey, Clark Mills, David Schubert, and
      Karl Shapiro)
1941 *Stop-Light: 5 Dance Poems*
1942 *The Grand Piano: or, The Almanac of Alienation*
1942 *Pieces of Three* (with Meyer Liben and Edouard Roditi)
1945 *The Facts of Life*
1946 *Art and Social Nature*
1946 *The State of Nature*
1946 *The Copernican Revolution*
1947 *The Copernican Revolution* (expanded edition)
1947 *Kafka's Prayer*
1947 *Communitas: Means of Livlihood and Ways of Life*
      (with Percival Goodman)
1949 *The Break-Up of Our Camp and Other Stories*
1950 *The Dead of Spring*
1951 *Gestalt Therapy: Excitement and Growth in the
      Human Personality* (with Frederick S. Perls and
      Ralph F. Hefferline)
1951 *Parents' Day*
1954 *Day and Other Poems*
1954 *The Structure of Literature*
1955 *Red Jacket*
1957 *The Well of Bethlehem*
1959 *The Empire City*
1960 *Growing Up Absurd: Problems of Youth in the Organ-
      ized System*
1960 *Our Visit to Niagara*
1961 *Ten Poems*
1962 *The Lordly Hudson: Collected Poems*
1962 *Drawing the Line*
1962 *The Community of Scholars*
1962 *Utopian Essays and Practical Proposals*
1962 *The Society I Live In Is Mine*
1963 *Making Do*
1964 *Compulsory Mis-education*

Edited by Taylor Stoehr

PAUL GOODMAN

THE FACTS OF LIFE

STORIES 1940-1949

VOLUME III
of the
COLLECTED
STORIES
EDITED BY
TAYLOR STOEHR

BLACK SPARROW PRESS-SANTA BARBARA-1979

"Eros or The Drawing of the Bow" is reprinted by permission of Charles Henri Ford, editor of *View*.

"Excerpts from a Journal: The Legs of My Dog" is reprinted by permission of John Bernard Myers, editor of *Instead*.

"Two Classical Draft Dodgers" is reprinted by permission from *The New Leader*, September 20, 1947. Copyright © The American Labor Conference on International Affairs, Inc.

LIBRARY OF CONGRESS CATALOGING IN PUBLICATION DATA

Goodman, Paul, 1911-1972.
  The facts of life.

  (His The collected stories ; v. 3)
  I. Stoehr, Taylor, 1931-   II. Title.

PZ3.G6235Co vol. 3   [PS3513.0527]   813'.5'2s   [813'.5'2]   79-9289
ISBN 0-87685-356-4 (paper edition)
ISBN 0-87685-357-2 (trade cloth edition)
ISBN 0-87685-358-0 (deluxe edition)

Contents

Introduction

At the beginning of the Forties it looked as if Paul Goodman's career was assured. Back from four years at the University of Chicago with several dozen new stories in his trunk, he was making a splash on the New York literary scene. Two of his books were scheduled for the end of 1941. *Partisan Review* was printing him regularly, *Kenyon Review* and *Poetry* only a little less often, and New Directions included him in its *Annuals* for 1940 and 1941 and in the *Young American Poets* series. Klaus Mann's lavish praise of "A Ceremonial" had been followed by an invitation to contribute a story to *Decision*, his elite "review of free culture," and Goodman was ambitiously thinking of starting a magazine of his own. The University of Chicago Press was interested in his dissertation. When he applied for a Guggenheim, his references included not only academic bigwigs like Richard P. McKeon and Ronald S. Crane, but also the young moguls of avant-garde publishing and criticism, John Crowe Ransom, Philip Rahv, Dwight Macdonald, and James Laughlin. Since he had already been awarded a study grant from the American Council of Learned Societies—chiefly on McKeon's recommendation—he had high hopes for the Guggenheim. He was also looking around for a teaching job. Friends at several colleges would put in a good word for him; at the age of thirty he already had disciples.

But he did not get the job he wanted at Queens; he did not get the Guggenheim; the magazine project fell through; the University of Chicago Press would print his dissertation only if Goodman came up with $895 to pay for typesetting. The fate of his books was still more ominous. *Stop-Light*, his imitations of Japanese Noh plays, came out a week after Pearl Harbor. His antiwar novel *The Grand Piano* coincided with the fall of the Philippines. They got scarcely a review. Meanwhile Goodman was digging his literary grave deeper by composing diatribes against his strongest backers, James Laughlin and John Crowe Ransom, for their support of the war. And he got into a vicious fight with Phil Rahv at *Partisan Review* over the issues of pacifism, the draft, and sedition. He had given one of his "artier" stories to *Decision*, but for some reason—probably political again, but possibly "moral"—Klaus Mann chose not to print "Ravel" (Laughlin took it for the 1941 *Annual*); and Goodman kissed that magazine a permanent farewell when he retaliated by satirizing Mann as Niko Verein in "The University in Exile."

By the middle of 1942 things looked black. Although Laughlin and Ransom continued to publish him in New Directions and *Kenyon*, the *Partisan Review* slammed its door as loudly as *Decision*. Goodman was still writing at least a book a year, and had a backlog of about half a dozen volumes—poems, plays, stories, novels, criticism. Where was he to publish these? And how was he to support his wife and child?

In 1943 his wife left him. His mother had just died; his best friend was killed in an accidental fall from a window during a party. The Guggenheim Foundation turned him down again. That year he published no stories or books, nothing but two poems and an essay written with his brother on "Architecture in Wartime." Some of his friends wondered where he was living, and on what? He managed to get a job at a little progressive school in upstate New York, but was fired at the end of the school year for seducing his students. Instead of becoming famous he was becoming notorious.

He continued to write at a furious pace. Just as in the late Thirties he had flourished in alienation, Goodman now seemed to thrive on adversity. If anything, his troubles improved his style, by giving him something worth writing

8

about. It was impossible to remain aloof from a world that battered him so thoroughly. His response was to offer his views on education, community planning, anarchism, psychoanalysis, religion. He wrote one major book after another: in 1940 *The Grand Piano*, the first volume of *The Empire City*; in 1942 *Don Juan*, a cubist novel about the nature of desire; in 1943-1944 *Communitas*, a book on city planning with his brother Percival; in 1944-1945 *The State of Nature*, the war volume of *The Empire City*; in 1945 *The May Pamphlet*, his political ethics; in 1946-1947 *Kafka's Prayer*, literary criticism, psychoanalysis, and religious thought; in 1947-1948 *Parents' Day*, a novel about the progressive school that fired him; and in 1949 *The Dead of Spring*, volume three of *The Empire City* and the best book he ever wrote. These works took the brunt of Goodman's collision with reality in the Forties, though he also wrote well over one hundred stories, plays, essays, reviews, and prefaces—not to mention the steady flow of poems. His new relation to society is apparent in their topics— political, psychosexual, religious—identified not long before as the prickly areas of his alienation.

After the nadir of 1943 Goodman began to find publishers again, mostly tiny avant-garde houses no one had ever heard of—Vanguard and New Directions were the exceptions. Of the list just presented, only *Don Juan* and *Parents' Day* failed to appear in the Forties, and to make up for them there were two volumes of short stories. By the end of the decade he was perhaps the most-published unknown author in America, as he ruefully put it. "During this period," he wrote to the Guggenheim Foundation in 1949, "very many persons in my ambience, including several close friends, have received aid from you. But very few seem to have done as much work as I, have published as much, or received as little renumeration. Could you answer me, frankly, what it is I do that is wrong?" However others might account for this seesaw of success and discouragement, notoriety and obscurity, it is evident that Goodman's self-image as a writer on-the-outs with society was hardening into a stance—and *that* was becoming his career.

In this context it is interesting to see something new

happening in his stories. During the late Thirties he had kept a watchful eye on the results of his experiments in literary manner and genre, working up a theory of art and alienation. Society was blamed for its failure to provide a usable sourcebook for the imagination, which then turned in on itself, more and more absorbed in the mere formal means of art. His cubist stories were founded on the impossibility of even discussing the subjects that most people thought constituted the real world. In addition to this disaffection, and probably underlying it, was an anxious recognition that he feared the fulfillment of desire even more than he longed for it: in his stories happiness turned out to be the heaviest burden of all. "Alienation," as he summed up succinctly, "is the isolation of the ego from the soul and the world."

In the Forties Goodman seems to have lost interest in this concept of alienation—a good sign that he was no longer alienated, or at least not in the same way. Now he called it "preposterous" to take conventional values "*seriously*, as if such things existed," when the truth was that society "does not exist by fantasies but by natural powers and plenty of good endurance." Society is better than it thinks it is, better even than *he* thought it was. Accordingly his social criticism paid little attention to the notion of the world shared by most people, and leapt quickly to the level of analysis and proposal that those same people branded utopian. To them it was Goodman's notion of "natural powers" that constituted the fantasy.

At the same time that his social thought was unfolding in books like *Communitas* and *The May Pamphlet*, his fiction was developing in somewhat different directions. On the one hand there was his grand project *The Empire City*, explicitly begun as "An Almanac of Alienation" but soon bursting the mold of schematic satire on "that error, America 1940," to become a strange, panoramic inward vision of his times. On the other hand, there was his shorter fiction, now almost completely stripped of the conventional realistic façade—plot, character, setting—so that one hesitates to call some of them stories at all.

At first Goodman tried to fit both his new novel and his

10

stories into the theory of literary manners he had worked out. The larger project was "expressionistic naturalism," a sequence of heroic portraits in which the larger-than-life characters were really only abstractions from "sociological and psychological causes" (that is, the natural powers he saw underlying society). The shorter pieces were called "dialectical lyrics," a Kierkegaardian label for the old-fashioned familiar essay, as in *Mosses from an Old Manse* except that the handling was cubist, with much more emphasis on the formal means than in Hawthorne's sketches.

But as he became more confident about his place in literary history, Goodman lost interest in theorizing about the stages of his career. Much as the theory of literary manners elucidates his earlier work, these new categories are inadequate to the remarkable feats of imagination they christen. *The Empire City* was afloat far beyond its moorings. Already in *The Grand Piano* a "world" had begun to develop. In spite of their origin as mere abstractions from "the true causes of events," Goodman's characters had come to life, they stood for something, not in the sense of representing causes or powers, but in the sense that virtue inhered in their lives. All the characters were heroes, all their acts exploits. Rather than terms like "expressionistic naturalism," one does better to recall the examples of medieval romance and classical epic, *Don Quixote* and *Candide*.

Similarly the short stories of the Forties go beyond their initial conception as further experiments in manner and genre. After a few realistic satires that seem more than anything a reaction to Goodman's sudden re-entry into the life of New York City (ethnic stories like "The Facts of Life" or "The University in Exile") there were "expressionist" sketches like "On the Rocks Along the River" and "The Commodity Embodied in BREAD," overflow from the world of *The Empire City*. "Alcestis," his last purely cubist story, shows how the formal emphasis could get in the way of a serious subject, the issues of war and pacifism. Then came a batch of shorter pieces explicitly identified as "dialectical lyrics," each divided into "gloss" and "scene." In all of these, content was reappearing. Something new was needed to give it scope.

11

The main development began in 1944, after Goodman was fired from his schoolteacher's job. His stories grew polemical in self-justification. "The Knight" indignantly defended his Greek notion of pedagogy: "the teacher patiently hour by hour awakens him, teaches him boldness toward the girls, and sets him free; then they think that the teacher will not have been in love with the boy." In "A Goat for Azazel" Goodman's provocative life-style was summed up as a kind of Dionysian self-sacrifice: "Jimmy dared and did those things that we did not even know we desired."

Whatever one feels about these moral acrobatics (the actions are easier to defend than the exculpations) there is no doubt that his embattled stance was beginning to turn in on itself in peculiar ways. Both these stories have loose, episodic structures, with a few thinly realized characters wandering through moral and psychological fogs too privately conceived to be penetrated without the biographical key. This was the last gasp of verisimilitude. Afterwards we get works more and more essayistic, like "The Father of the Psychoanalytic Movement," a thoughtful elegy for Freud, "The Formulation of Freedom," a snarled inquiry into whether Goodman hadn't betrayed Impulse by making a Principle of it, and "The Emperor of China," a Taoist critique of the will.

As narrative structure gives way to personal exegesis, the mood becomes increasingly self-critical—though it seems always to have surprised Goodman to find himself under attack in his own work. Finally, in "On the Question: 'What is the Meaning of Life?'" he comes to the point all his stories had been circling near: "In every work I return to the one theme, of disparaging the ego; shall I not direct it home, to hatred of myself? and stop escaping into generalities?"

In "Incidents of the Labyrinth" he finds an allegory of the self's search for the soul in the myth of Theseus and the Minotaur.

"There is no Minotaur after all,"
he ended, and he paused in the blank square,
"now to wind up the spool." Why does he stare?
in what glass does his hair stand and the blade fall

12

from the hero hand weaker than a girl?
"I am the Minotaur!"—met dare for dare
in the labyrinthine heart, now everywhere
(so he begins).
        O Theseus, recall
your blood to you and oh, pick up your knife!
at last—the second moment in your life
(but that was long ago and forgot)
you have a rival worthy of Theseus!
but softly, this is for the surgeon cut,
and for pity's sake, an hour's armed truce.

Every thrust and parry of this dialectical lyric betrays self-doubt. As he says, a person who asks questions like "What is the meaning of life?" is not likely to be happy, and one who merely wants to know what sort of question that is, or what sort of person would ask it, is in a still worse way.

One reason Goodman was writing such stories and poems in 1946 is that he had gone into therapy with Alexander Lowen, one of Wilhelm Reich's trainees, and after four or five months of learning the exercises, was continuing self-analysis on his own. All his writing in the Forties bears the mark of psychoanalytic ideas, but after 1946 his work is often best understood *as part of* his own analysis. Some of his stories, like "Little Bert" and "Terry Fleming," are literally attempts to recover childhood memories, and in "Incidents of the Labyrinth" or "The Midnight Sun" he seems to be trying to use the dialectical lyric as a framework for free association. His earlier cubist writing had been highly controlled; now the rhapsodic style, the chanting tempo, are not so much formal devices as propaedeutic exercises, like the Reichian yoga, to open himself to the unconscious. The scenes themselves—wanderings in the labyrinth, voyaging on unknown seas—are obvious analogues of inward search.

It is hard to say how far these investigations got him; after 1947 he made a decisive return to naturalistic fiction, in a few brief stories and especially in *Parents' Day*, a long, self-absorbed examination of the erotic pedagogy that got him fired in 1944. His ongoing self-analysis took narrative

13

form in this "attempt to dispense altogether with the pervasive irony of my other novels . . .[and] to muster the courage to make absolute judgments of value, after (and by means of) analyzing the motives prompting me."

The return to naturalism after a decade of experiment in other manners represents a new stage in the relations of alienation and art. By this time (he was thirty-five years old) Goodman had settled down to a more or less stable life. He had remarried, and along with the eight-year-old child of his first marriage there was a new baby in the house ("Likely and the Dragon" was written for them). Although he had still not achieved any wide recognition, there could be no doubt that he was a mature artist with a serious body of work behind him. In this relatively secure and not uncomfortable position, he again found himself miserable. This time Goodman tackled the problem head-on, by determining to write undisguised autobiography—"analyzing the motives prompting me." It is as if he had decided that all his cubist and expressionist fiction was but a series of dodges, the ego's trick to "ward off the world," "to meet the moment with a formulation of the moment," as he said in the very stories that exemplified the trick.

The interlude of direct self-examination seemed to come to an end in 1949, when he returned to *The Empire City* and wrote his most beautiful and moving book, *The Dead of Spring.* Here was the other side of his self-analysis, probing the unconscious to its most tender reaches. In writing it Goodman plunged himself into a mourning-labor for the failure of all his hopes for happiness. Therapy was not the means to paradise but a way of coping with its loss. For the first time in his life, he found himself unable to write, blocked, clenched in fear and despair. Finally, after a month of struggle, he wrote the death of Laura, "the glancing present."

By the end of the Forties then, Goodman had developed two ways of risking himself in self-analysis: through direct self-examination as in *Parents' Day,* and through the mythic imagination that produced *The Dead of Spring.* During all the rest of his career as a writer of fiction, he oscillated between these two modes, first one voice, then

14

the other. Taking a still more comprehensive view, we can see these as characteristic of the social critic and the artist. Goodman cannot elude these avatars, for they are both in him. He can only give in to them, alternately. This was his way of coping with the old problem of alienation, of the relations of the ego to the soul and the world: accept the world in which natural powers and beautiful human virtues do exist, no matter what other people think; accept the ego as that part of the self which makes daring formulations, about the world; accept the soul from whose depths comes song.

T.S.

THE FACTS OF LIFE

VOLUME
3

The Facts of Life

Childish Ronnie Morris has a wife Martha and a daughter Marcia, aged 9.

Ronnie is middle-aged, as we say of any one ten years older than ourselves, and he has invented a wonderful scheme to milk money from those who make $20,000 a year: he sells them Fine Editions with odd associations, as *The Golden Ass* bound in donkey's hide or *The New Testament* signed by the designer in the blood of a lamb. (He is childish enough to go thru with such a profitable idea, instead of dismissing it like the rest of us fools.) He has a two-masted sailboat; he moves in the circle of his clients. In a business way, he knows Picasso and Thomas Benton, and is the expert at the Club in the trade-secrets of the Muses. In the acts of love, he is medium; he went to Dartmouth; but in fact he is only moderately fixated on the period when he was 5th oar, for he had had an even prior period of ease and lust, which has saved him for philosophy and the arts, rather than the brokerage.

Martha Morris is an Andalusian type. When she arranges flowers she keeps them under control with wires. She drives at high speeds. Her relations with Ronnie are as usual; she is her little daughter's friend, and every Xmas she and Marcia design a gift-volume for Ronnie's clientèle. She is more political than her husband and her position is slightly to the left of the right wing of the left-center: a group that finds no representation in Washington, but used to have thirty seats in Paris. I could write forever, as it would seem, about Martha's teeth as they flash under her

19

nose. Aren't the rhythms delightful, of the description of the upper middle class?

Now little Marcia goes to the University Progressive School where many of her schoolmates have fathers in the embassies, but Marcia too has been to the Near East in search of that lamb. At school they are taught to express themselves freely. Little Marcia, when she does so—she takes after her mother—is delightful!

Marcia has a fight in school today with one of the little gentlemen her contemporaries. He breaks her photographic plate. The fight is about the nature of chickens' eggs. She stamps on his foot. Being a girl, she still has an advantage in mental age and more words to say; she says a sentence in French. He can't punch her in the nose because it is ungentlemanly. He is inhibited from drawing on his best knowledge because it is dirty; but worse, it is gloomily indistinct, and even on these matters she seems to have more definite information, is about to mention it.

"Shut up!" he argues, "shut up! you're just an old-time Jew."

This perplexing observation, of which she understands neither head nor tail, brings her to a momentary pause; for up to now, at least with Harry—tho certainly not with Terry or Larry—she has maintained a queenly advantage. But he has brought her to a pause by drawing on absolutely new information.

Now she does a reckless thing: she dismisses his remark from her mind and launches into a tirade which devastatingly combines contempt and the ability to form complete sentences, till Harry goes away in order not to cry. A reckless, a dangerous thing: because what we thus dismiss enters the regions of anxiety, of loss and unfulfilled desire, and there makes strange friends. This is the prologue to fanatic interests and to falling in love. How new and otherwise real is this observation on its next appearance!

Marcia calls her mother sometimes Momsy and sometimes Martha.

"What did Harry mean," she asks her, "when he called me an old-time shoe?"

"Jew?"

"Yes, he stated I was just an old-time Joo."

Across the woman's face passes, for ever so many reasons, the least perceptible tightening. "Oh oh!" feels Marcia along her ears and scalp; and now she is confirmed and doubly confirmed in the suspicions she did not know she had. When she now has to express herself with colored chalks, new and curious objects will swim into the foreground alongside the pool, the clock will become a grandfather's clock, and all be painted Prussian blue, even tho Miss Coyle is trying to cajole especially the little girls into using warm bright colors, because that is their natural bent.

"Well he was right, you are a Jewess," says Martha. "It's nothing to be ashamed of."

"Said Joo, not Juice."

"A Jew is a boy; a Jewess is a girl."

"Oh! there are 2 kinds!"

It's worse and worse. She never dreamed that Harry was up on anything, but perhaps even his veiled hints conceal something. She feels, it seems inescapable to her, that boys have a power, surely not obvious in school—and the grown-ups even take it for granted! She sees it every day, that these same boys when they become men are superior to the women. Yet men's clothes don't *express* anything, and actresses are better than actors. But just this *contradiction* confirms it all the more, for the explanations of contradictions are in the indistinct region—and everything there is mutually involved. Marcia is already working on a system of the mysteries. Especially when Momsy now tries to tell her some reasonable anecdote about Jewesses and Jews, just like a previous astringent account of the chickens and the flowers.

Martha never happens to have told little Marcia that they are all Jews.

"Is Ronnie a Joo?"

"Of course."

"Are Louis and Bernie Joos?"

"Louis is a Jew but Bernie is a Gentile."

It's a lie, thinks Marcia; they are both the same. (She means they are both effeminate.) Why is Martha lying to her?

"What is ser-cum-si-zhun?" asks Marcia, calling the lie.

This inquisition has now become intolerable to Martha. "Good night, Marcia," she explains.

"Is Rosina a Juice?" Marcia cries, asking about Ronnie's mistress.

"Marcia! I said good night!"

"Tell me! tell me! is Rosina Juice?"

"No."

"Ah!"

"Why Ah!?"

"Good night, Momsy," says Marcia, kissing her.

Since the habits are formed speediest where necessity constrains and yet conscious and deliberate adjustment is embarrassing or tedious, Martha has speedily and long ago learned the few adjustments belonging particularly to Jews of a certain class of money. The other hotel; not on this list; the right to more chic and modernity, but please no associations with Betsy Ross in tableaux or on committees. Of course habits learned by this mechanism are subject to amazing breaches, when submerged desire suddenly asserts itself and the son of Jacob becomes Belmont or Ronnie becomes, as he is, an honorary colonel in the militia. But on the whole, where money is so exchangeable, there are very few special adjustments; for instance, they never even came to Marcia's keen perception, especially since none of the Jews whom she is so often with without knowing it, ever mentions them. Of course, on the other hand, in the more critical social episodes, such as marriage—but forget that. And there are many other meanings, archaically forgotten.

"Since you have to put up with the handicap whether you like it or not," decides Mrs. Ronnie Morris, "why not make an advantage of it, and be proud of it?" And at once she writes out a check for a subscription to *The Menorah Journal*, the *Harper's Monthly* of reformed Jews.

22

"Never heard such a stupid argument in my life!" says Ronnie. He is very angry, like any one who has played the game like a perfect gentleman and then finds that the other side goes too far and calls his daughter an old-time Jew. "What's the use of *pretending* you're a Jew, when you're *not* a Jew?" he shouts.

"We are Jews. Don't shout," says Martha.

"I'll go to school and punch that brat's nose."

Martha says nothing.

"Do I pay $300 a year for him to tell Marcia that she's a Jew?"

"But we are Jews," says Martha, with a new loyalty.

"Since when?" says Ronnie scientifically. "To be a Jew means one of three things: It means first to belong to a certain Race; but there isn't any Jewish race in anthropology. Look at me, do I look like a Jewish race?"

He looks like a highly brushed and polished moujik.

"No. Secondly: it means a Nationality. But even if some Jews think they have a nationality, do I? I went to Jerusalem to pick out a Gentile lamb. Anyway, I can't speak the language. Hebrew isn't the same as Yiddish, you know, even tho it looks the same; but I can't speak that either.

"Third: it's a Religion. So you see," he concludes triumphantly, "it's not a matter of not *wanting* to be a Jew or trying to *hide* that you're a Jew, but you *can't* be a Jew if you're *not* a Jew!"

"Don't be a fool," says Martha. "A person's a Jew if his grandparents were Jews; even one's enough sometimes, depending."

"What sense does that make?"

"Do you think it's by accident," says Martha flatly, "that your mama and papa came to marry Jews and we married Jews?"

She means, thinks Ronnie, when our desire is toward Gentiles, toward retroussé noses and moon-face Hungarians. Does she mean Rosina? She means Bernie. We mean—but there is no time to think of that.

"I'll ask Louis," says Ronnie; for tho he holds sway at the luncheon club, all his ideas come from this poet.

23

"He's taking Marshy to the Picassos tomorrow."

"Let him tell her, then."

"What! are you going to let your daughter find out the facts from a stranger?"

Having slept over it all night, by morning the little girl has contrived the following working theory:

In the beginning, of course, all babies are alike. Her deep-seated conviction on this point has never been in the least shaken by Momsy's anecdotes about the chickens, for it is plain to observe that all babies are alike. (Nor is this the chief reason for her conviction.) But then comes the moment when the thing is cut off the girls. When this takes place, is not yet clear; but it is planned from the beginning, because you can tell by the names; altho sometimes even there is a change of names; with some names you still can't tell; and others are easy to change, like Robert and Roberta or Bernie and Bernice. All of this is an old story to Marcia.

But now, there are some *chosen* ones, who are supposed to be cut but somehow they get off. Why? They are only *partly* cut—and this is ser-cum-si-zhun, because they use a scissors. These are Joos. For a moment, starting from "Louis," Marcia thinks that she can tell by the names, but then when she thinks of "Ronnie" and of "Terry" and "Larry," two boys in school whom she now knows are Joos (in fact, Terry is and Larry is not), she sees that she can't. The *last* names are connected with marrying and have nothing to do with ser-cum-si-zhun.

Now, she sees in a flash, it is *better* to be a Joo, for then you still have the secret power and the thing, but at the same time you can be cleverer like a girl. This is why Larry and Terry are always able to beat her, they have an unfair advantage; but Harry, the dope, is only a boy and not a Joo.

There are also differences among Joos; for instance, Louis is much smarter than Papa. But this *proves* it, for Louis is more like Martha; that is, they cut the *best* amount off him, but not so much from Papa. Anyway, she hates Louis and loves her poor papa. And now an enormous love for poor Harry suffuses her and she begins to tremble and want to go to school; he has so much secret power.

But more important—and, lying in bed, Marcia begins to tremble as she thinks about herself—what is a Juice? and besides all these, there are Gen-tiles. Martha and Marcia are Juice and Bernie is a Gen-tile. Oh! what a mean thing to say about poor Bernie, that he is not even a Juice, but even worse than a girl; he is not even clever. It is nice of Louis to be so kind to him. So it seems that things go in the following order: Boys, Joos, Juices, Girls, Gen-tiles. Except that it is smartest to be a Joo. But what is it! What is it that they did to Marcia to be a Juice? As she lets her fingers move between her thighs, she breaks into a cold sweat, and an urgency of longing loosens her strength. With a violent dismissal, she leaps from bed.

But while she is eating breakfast, an awful emptiness for her boy Harry spreads within her, and she bursts into tears.

Louis, who is quite intelligent, often cannot resist being cruel and supercilious to Ronnie, so that Ronnie feels like punching him in the nose—but then suddenly, at a poignant touch, even suggested by his own monologue, he relapses into natural melancholia. "To me of course," says he suavely to Ronnie, "your Jewish problem doesn't exist. My paternal parent 12th removed was Joseph Karo, the author of the *Shulchan Aruch*, or *Table* of the observances; he had established the lineage back to Joseph son of Eli, so that obviously, if we may lend any credence to the Gentile gospels, we go back to David the son of Jesse and further; but you're a Russian Jew. On my mother's side, I am related to the convert Leo the Hebrew; but that blood thruout is tainted by conversions; my three cousins, Georges de Duchesse, Georges Catala, and Georges Catala-de Duchesse were all converts of Maritain. My cousin Georges Catala-de Duchesse is the Abbot of St. Germain-des-Prés, an *idol*-worshipper, as I told him last summer. It ought to be clear by now, I said, that only Maimonides conceived the relation of God and Man in a way helpful and necessary to the Modern Age. This is my faith. If every Jew would read the *Mishnah Torah*, he would become a perfect snob," cries Louis Parigi with pride, "and would set tradition against tradition and not take the insults lying down or by appealing merely to good sense! Besides, in our poetry both the Parigis and the de Duchesses look for inspiration to the Prophets. My cousin Georges de Duchesse, on the very eve of his baptism wrote his rime royal *Habakuk*; but '*Habakuk*,' as Voltaire says, '*était capable de tout!*' But even in writing my *Anacreontics* I have drawn on the dipsomaniac rhythms of your Chassidim. And by the way, my cousin Georges Catala was married to an 8th remove descendant of the Vilna Gaon, and her suicide was the cause of his conversion, which goes to show what comes of marrying with the Ashkenazim. (Are you also related to the Vilna Gaon, like all the other Lithuanians?) On the National issue, I am like Judah ha-Levi an allegorical Zionist; but the vulgar desire of a temporal habitation—this destroys, as I see it, just our sacred distinction from the *Goyim*"—(he pronounces *Go-yeem* as if he had stepped from a Christian fastness in Aragon where never a Moor or Jew had once set foot); "but God said—but *God* said," says Louis, raising a forefinger, "Make *Succoth*, Booths." At this quotation, suddenly, tears glisten in his eyes and he sinks into the deepest gloom. "Besides," he finishes airily, "except the purity of our Jewish morals, what defense do I have against adultery and sodomy?"

It is especially this breezy ending that makes Ronnie punch him in the nose—almost; yet this happens to be his only heart-felt remark, tho in the form of a wish.

In the afternoon, in front of the impassive checkerboard of *The Three Musicians*, the little girl again bursts into tears. Louis, who has with some skill been pointing out to her only such features of the difficult paintings as she is adequate to, an underfed and melancholy face, a marvelous mother bathed in rose, the fact that in 1920 the colors are no longer blended, and enveloping it all in fanciful anecdotes—he looks at her in stupefaction.

"It's not fair! It's not fair!" she sobs.

They are alone in the room.

"What's not fair?" says Louis.

"It's not fair 'cause it's a myst'ry, and I won't *ever* be able to understand it."

26

The Facts of Life

"Why you've been understanding it very well, Marcia. What you said about the colors I didn't know myself, because you're a painter and I'm not."

"You're *lying* to me—'cause it's a secret myst'ry, and I won't ever be able to understand it 'cause I'm only a girl, even if I'm a Juice."

? ?

"I understand about the colors and the poor boy, but I can't understand it *all*, 'cause they cut my thing off when I was little and Picass' is a man— An' I have nothing left but to be an actress."

He takes her hand, for the tears are rolling down her cheeks.

"—I won't ever be able to make 'em any more with a myst'ry if I live to be a million years old."

She hides her face in her other arm, and she cries with the pent-up anxiety of her 3rd to her 9th years.

A guard comes in and hastily goes out the other door.

On the walls, the impassive objects, which are indeed a secret mystery, stare from side to side.

The tears glisten in Louis's eyes. "This Holy Spirit," he says—he thinks he says—"is given to us and not made by us. It's not my fault if I cannot any more."

"Ah," she says (he thinks), "maybe if it weren't for the Bernies and the Jackies, the prophetic voice of the Lord of Hosts would not prove so disheartened at the 3rd and 4th verse."

"What a despicable argument!" he cries (he thinks), "if I'm finally tired of that boy, why don't I think so right off and not need these thin arguments to bolster up my courage? Stop staring, you," says he to the unblinking middle Musician, "or I'll punch you in the nose."

"Look Marshy," he says reasonably to the little girl whose hand he is holding tight, "you can't expect to make these things right off! You have to develop your power. Just as when you learn to play the piano, you see you have to begin with finger-exercises."

"Oh!" she cries in fright and pulls her hand away. "How could he tell so quick?" she thinks in terror; "Momsy couldn't tell."

27

"See, this one is easy to understand," he says, pointing to those Three Musicians. "You see, this is an oboe."

"What's a Obo?"

"An oboe is a kind of wooden instrument with stops. This part is what the oboe looks like from underneath, which you can't ordinarily see. This is a guitar; he broke it into two pieces in order to make the pattern here with this red business—"

"Can you, Louis?" she seizes his hand, "I mean can you? Can you develop your power by finger-exercises?"

? ?

"Can you? Can you?"

"Certainly. Every day you'll be able to paint a little better."

"Hurrah!"

Two women come in, tittering at a pyramidal creature that is like one of the works of the Six Days.

But the silence is twangling with the music of the guitars of Picasso, with the guitars of Catalonia, with the cubist harmony by which the acrobats drift away.

In the school-field, the 4th year boys, in maroon sweat-suits, are playing the in-tra-mur-al ball-game, while Mr. Donlin is umpiring and keeping order. From time to time some of the little boys have their minds completely on the game. When his side is at bat, Harry is sitting on the lowest bench of the stands and Marcia bounces pebbles on him from above. Outside the iron fence around the field, Timmy and Page McCroskey, who go to Holy Name Academy, are staring at the clean and distinguished boys within. Mr. Donlin looks like a perfect fool, full of manly baby-talk such as, "Gooood try!" or "C'mon *Terry*, let's see what you can do!" Sometimes he loses his temper. One of the boys takes off his clothes and to the amazement of the Irish boys discloses his delicate limbs in another maroon uniform of shorts and a shirt with a big U. Amid a loud chorus, Mr. Donlin has to assert his authority to keep the children from exposing themselves to the cold air.

"Mr. Donlin, Mr. Donlin," mimic the two outside the bars, "kin I take off my drawers?"

28

The Facts of Life

A local merchant-prince, a great contributor to the University, has the exclusive franchise for the manufacture and sale of these many uniforms. Timmy and Page and their friends call the U-school the Jew-school. They are envious of the boundless wealth behind the bars and of the fact that the girls and boys go to school together. "Why doncha let the girls play with youse?" shouts little Timmy. Page, who is a year younger and much bolder, cries, "Mr. Donlin, kin I take off my drawers and show the girls my prick?"

On the large field, which is used for the high-school games, the baseball, thrown by weak arms and tapped by little bats, makes ridiculous little hops and arcs. Terry, distracted by the remark from the fence, drops a little pop-fly and the runners stream across the plate. Mr. Donlin advances to the fence shouting without profanity, go away or he'll punch them in the nose. From a little distance, they shout in chorus: "Jew School Jew School!" and some of the little scholars, who at other times announce proudly that they go to the University P'rgressive School (as if they went to college), now turn pink. "Play ball!" shouts Mr. Donlin in a manly voice.

Now all the little feelings are afire.

Marcia and Harry, however, have heard nothing; but they have now progressed from the first stage of touching-yet-not-touching by throwing things at each other, to the next stage of punching and pulling shoe-laces.

To the Irish boys, so systematically kept in order by their father and by the priest and Brothers to whom even their father defers, there is no way of doubting that non-Catholics enjoy a full sexual freedom. They *know*, in fact, that the Reformation began with fornication; and even more enviable are the Jews, as is proved by the anti-Semitism, otherwise incomprehensible, that forms so large a part of the instruction by the Brothers. And along with this yearning, they observe this wealth and beauty and privilege thru the bars; and so is consolidated that deep sentiment of inferiority which will tomorrow need fire-arms to soothe.

To the little rich boys, on the other hand, it is obvious that freedom lies outside the bars among those wild boys

29

whose dirty language makes them tremble with terror and stirs unconquerable lust in each one when he is alone; who can stay out late and wear hats decorated with paper-clips, and beg for pennies from strangers. So even before the first clash, the rich boys feel physically and morally powerless and would like to be the slaves of the poor ones, and it will require all the machinery of the state to treat them with an iron hand.

But why should I make the case any simpler than is necessary? For Timmy also hates little Page, just as he hates the Brothers in school; and among the U-boys there are the families going up and the families falling down, and the case, for instance, of weedy Tom, whose parents are slipping and climbing at the same time, and who will tomorrow be satisfied and avenged by burning for the lowest hustler, if his name happens to be Woodrow, until with a sinking heart he one day learns that Woodrow isn't a family name, but a war-name, after President Wilson.

Fascinated, Timmy is watching Marcia wrestling with Harry and pulling his hair, while he is trying to concentrate on his team-mate at bat: "Make it be a good one! Make it be a good one!" he cries; and then he suddenly chases Marcia up the stands. Pressed between the bars till he is white, Timmy follows them with his stare, above him, thru the stands. But she jumps down and runs across the field toward the building, and then they both disappear. Poor Timmy stares at the gray door which has just closed.—So in each heart are fixed the types of love, after the girls who seem to be easy, who have the reputation of being available, who are easy and available in idea tho never in fact. The Jewish girls to the Irish boys like Timmy, and the Irish girls to the Jewish boys like Ronnie, and the sailors to Louis. But for the most part, it is just one's own kind that is really available (and really desirable, and absolutely forbidden!), and that we live with in the end, as Ronnie with Martha, and Louis with Bernie; these are no doubt still deeper types of love, tho far too deep to give us any pleasure.

"Knock Knock!" cries Page McCroskey.

"Play Ball!" shouts Mr. Donlin.

"Knock Knock, Mr. Donlin, Knock Knock!" he screams.

30

The Facts of Life

"Don't pay any attention, play ball," says Mr. Donlin.

"Who's there?" answers Larry.

"Cohen!"

"Don't pay any attention!" cries Mr. Donlin.

"Cohen who?" answers a voice.

"Who said it?" shouts Mr. Donlin authoritatively.

"Cohen fuck yourself!" cry Page and Timmy together.

One of the boys throws a stone at them.

"You cock sucker!" says Timmy, casting his eyes about for some resource.

"Shut up, McCroskey," says Terry, "or I'll tell somethin' on you, but I don't want to make you shamed."

"Do you believe that pile o' shit that O'Hara said?" says Timmy wildly.

"Naw, I *saw* it!" says Terry.

"What did O'Hara say?" says Page.

But at this instant a foul-ball jumps out over the fence.

"*H'yaann! H'yaann!*" sing Page and Timmy and run down the block with the ball, grasping off their hats.

"Where's Harry Riesling? He's supposed to be coaching on first," says the beaten Mr. Donlin.

But Marcia and Harry are in one of the empty rooms where they have never been before (it is part of the High School), and she is telling him all about Picass'. He explains to her that he likes Terry and Larry swell, but he hates his big brother; but he promises just not to notice him any more. "He probably hates your papa as much as you hate *him*," Marcia observes judiciously, "so that's something you know on *him*." This insight, this knowledge, casts such an angel light on Harry's usually puzzled countenance that Marcia turns and stares at him. He explains to her that he likes geography and history, but Miss Jensen doesn't make it interesting the way Mr. Bee used to, and that's why he's not smart; and when Marcia tells him that she was in Egypt and the Near-East (as opposed to the Far-East), he is struck with admiration. But how different now is this admiration and his pleasure and pride in her ability to form complete sentences, as if she were a teacher whom he can kiss and lick and not even have to discuss certain things

31

with, from the animosity he felt yesterday when she was so god-damned smart. She draws on the blackboard the dolphins playing at the *Ile de France*'s prow.

"There are geniuses in every race," says Ronnie passionately, with all the energy of his desire for Rosina; "but both per capita and absolutely there are more of them among the Jews."

"I thought you said there was no Jewish race?"

"That's what I thought, but facts are facts and you can't get around it. Einstein Ehrlich Freud."

"Yes, the Jews are always going in for syphilis or psychoanalysis or the 4th dimension," says Martha.

"Picasso—"

"Ha, the same thing!"

"Proust—"

"There you have it!" says Martha triumphantly. "I'm not saying the Jews are not geniuses, but they're *queer*, they're just queer, that's all."

"What about Dali? He's not a Jew."

"Will you please tell me what you're trying to prove by that? I thought you were trying to prove that all the Jews, including yourself, were geniuses."

"No, but you said that Proust and Picasso were Jews."

"*I* said it? *I* said it?"

"I didn't say you said it especially; they *are* Jews, *half*-Jews."

"Oh don't be a fool."

Ronnie says nothing.

"And let me tell you another thing," says Martha, "you Jews are not doing yourselves any favor by putting yourselves forward so much. If Felix Frankfurter is so smart as he's supposed to be, he knows that especially just now there's no place for another Jew on the Supreme Court bench. Every Jew that gets on the Supreme Court makes it just so much harder for us and Marcia. Where do you think I'm going to be able to send her to college?"

"That's a fine way of looking at it!" cries Ronnie. "It's true enough," he thinks; but Martha has always been ahead of him on national and international affairs.

32

The Facts of Life

"You're a Jew, so all right!" says Mrs. Ronnie Morris née de Havilland. "It's nothing to be ashamed of. But why bring it up in public? Who asks you?"

"Who?" says Ronnie bewildered.

"But trust a Jew to put himself forward as if he were something peculiar! If it weren't for the Jews there wouldn't be any anti-Semitism."

"Who?" asks Ronnie.

New York City
1940

On the Rocks Along the River

The air and airs and winds of March were such, more by nipping threats than actual bites, that one felt he was withdrawing from them into himself—especially one who was ahead of the seasons and wore a sweater in March and would wear a shirt in April; but even the overcoated remained on the *qui vive* in their woolen cylinders. No one felt, what was nevertheless the case, how the atmosphere was supporting him all around and rushing in and out of him. But on the 1st and 2nd of April! days unusually warm and brilliant, people suddenly had the sentiment that the atmosphere was supporting them, caressing and almost crowding them, with high pressure both outside and in. The little breezes that blow up the legs were allowed to be noticed and the hair was given to the south wind. People even glanced upward at the swift clouds.

When Mynheer and his five small disciples, whom he was introducing to the structure of the environment (and this was all their education), descended the rocks along the river where fishermen were fishing and hardy boys were already swimming, he noticed, was amazed by, the busy continuum of the air evident close and far. Noticed the tiny and vast motions themselves and the fact that together they crowded all the space there was! A steady airy motion was arriving from the south; but up above, it was evident, a strong east wind was gathering the clouds in mountains. Wisps at the edges of the storm-bank were still dissolving apparently into nothing; yet it was clear how whirlpools of vapor were saturating the darkening blue. In the middle air,

35

gulls and crows were standing motionless—as it seemed! Fearfully accelerating (as a falling body does) the smoke of a pipe sped round up its still spiral and vanished. The surface of the river was everywhere giving itself to the air. Most of the bright splashes fell back into the river in drops, but the tiniest sparkles passed into the atomies of the air. A dead fish on the rock: the stinking gases were powerfully agitating the little air; and the wings of small fleas (the first of the year) were wildly fanning these gases.

These were the Vortices of the gases. The noble Dutchman pointed them out to the five. They became conscious that they themselves were breathing in and out and were shaking the density with speech.

Now among these gases, it could be seen also that the persons—including Mynheer and the boys, and the fishermen, and the lady and gentlemen spectators on the rocks, among whom was Mr. Impetigo (and the Governor of the State walking in obscurity from the other end of the path)—all these were *Flexible Tubes.* They were tubes sucking in not only the atmosphere of the environment but nourishment of all kinds and furnishing a thru passage for it. For except in matters of perception it was especially in these interior passages that these tubes came into contact with the environment which was supporting their vitality and growth. The dense atmosphere caressed the tubes around, and also penetrated them thru and thru; but not, in the interiors, according to the "freedom of the winds," but the atmosphere was accepted and released according to the tubular rhythms of each kind, so that among the rocks and sitting on the rocks the tubes were bringing far-off environment, as well as being immersed in and out in river vapors.

Meantime the Hudson River was everywhere vibrating in green V's and blue W's, and was brightly ripped in rows of X's. It licked the rocks in green Lambdas which were then elongated into white-dotted I's. The south air was everywhere writing on the river the words VIX VIX and IWI.

When Mynheer the pedagogue—led to the idea by the change in the weather and by the perception of the little and vast vortices—saw suddenly that the people, and even he himself, were great tubes, he was so taken aback that he didn't dare communicate the thought to the five. This thought seemed to him to make maxims unedifying and to take the heart out of his desires, and in general to cast aspersions on the educational behavior. But he excused his silence by saying to himself that these tubes were not perceptions at all but were merely interpretations, and the boys could make their own interpretations. Yet the tubes *were* perceptions, for there, lolling on the jagged rock, was the great tube Mr. Impetigo, topped with a Panama hat.

This hat was soaring and settling in the breezes and about to take flight.

For now the south air, struggling with the eastern storm, was steady no longer, but came in gentle gusts, making the whole fabric of space tremulous. Now caught in the contrary currents, a sheet of newspaper rose up a yard on one wind, then turned over into the sunlight and soared a yard on the other wind, and so, veering from blue to white and soaring from north to west, the *Herald Tribune* rose up, smaller and smaller to the view, and became invisible in the empyrean. And in fair exchange, a cold pour from above trickled down and made a naked swimmer tremble. Everywhere the smokes of the pipes were sucked upward faster round their spirals; and the midges fanning the little air rose on the great air.

The Panama hat stood on its rim and Mr. Impetigo raised his left hand—

This great tube on the rock, Mr. Impetigo, was an eccentric. Last week when he had a gas-bill to dispute with the Utilities Company, he refused to deal with any subordinate officials but went over their heads to the president of the board, "where policy is made." And when he had to buy a pair of scissors, he bought a dozen gross, in order to take advantage of the jobber's price; in this way he always had many commodities lying around. In general, Mr. Impetigo understood that every transaction was part of the Imperial economy and he tried to move according to the great principles agitating the whole.

—Suddenly the hat was sailing on the water.

"The hat! the hat!" he cried in the gusts, writhing like the fixed hydra and initiating torn streamers of vibration that in one place among the rocks sounded like "Bhagadvat" and in another "Paraloo."

If I may paraphrase the poem, substituting for drowned Sappho the Panama hat:

> The ripples moved in longs and shorts above it,
> against the crown they broke in many shorts;

and already the straw hat was offshore twenty yards and on its way to the Isles.

But in this emergency, a skilful fisherman whipped his supple rod; the leaded line snaked to the mark. The hook bit; and the Panama hat was raised dripping aloft—while every one along the shore burst into rounds of spontaneous applause, all except that tragic Governor who, moving in solitude of soul and with eyes downcast, never even saw the beautiful spectacle.

They excitedly exchanged vowels in the wind from rock to rock.

And by that unerring fishline in the hands of an expert, Mynheer was moved to the reflection that it did not matter, it was just as well or even somewhat better, that they were all flexible tubes. *This* could not destroy the meaning of maxims nor take the heart out of his desires nor cast aspersions on the educational activity. Indeed he saw with *pleasure* that his five were pretty pink or golden small tubes.

He called them together to report on their observations (and he was in no mood to be critical).

And first, Nosey Parker, the little tube who had the flaring nostrils, said: "There's a damp smell and it's sure gonna rain."

The pedagogue patted the naïve boy on the head.

Big-earned Timmy had gone further afield. "The Sirens," he said, "the Sirens promise to tell you something, but they sing only the vowels, A, E, I, O, and U."

"There are only three sirens," said Mynheer, "and they sing Aaah, Eeeee, Oooh. Augie?"

Augie, concerning whom the others used to joke that he was all eyes, said merely, "It's gettin' dark, let's go home."

On the Rocks Along the River

But the fourth, a muscular and lascivious little athlete, cried out: "Them dead fish gi' me the chills. The wind seeps right thru their open mouth without even a taste."

There is a poem called *Sirens*, which begins:

> Piercing sweet a trio thrilling
> at twilight woo the sailors more than willing
> and on they come with rowing pressed
> while Vesper blazes in the west.

It goes on to say:

> Half on a rock, half in the brine
> a sailor's body lies; the fishes are
> eating his ankles 'neath the water-line,
> shaking the reflex of the Evening Star.

The last of the boys, named Thumbs, said: "I was skimmin' rocks. I make 'em jump seven times!"

Mynheer said: "School is almost over for today; but on the way back I want you to notice how every one is a big tube with the environment slowly passing thru, in one end and out the other."

As if by one impulse, the five stood on the marble ledge and peed in five golden arcs into the sea. A little girl nearby, seeing this for the first time, recreated the famous joke and said: "How practical it is!" or in another version: "What a handy thing to take along on a hike!"

But now it was surely going to storm. The bruised sky was black and blue; and it seemed as if the motion had altogether left the air. I say "seemed" because the vortices were not really dissipated but as if congealed. I say "as if" because they had really collected a terrible potential, like the clenched teeth of death-agony
  —half-way between a wince and a bite, really vibrating at a fearful frequency, too fast to be visible.

The *Herald Tribune*, rain-soaked in heaven, fell on the water with a loud slap.

It was almost quiet. The screaming little girls vanished. Oppressed now by the atmosphere which so lightly used to fill and support them, but which now, the barometer dancing every millimeter, seemed about to *burst* them, the great tubes straggled heavily away from the rocks, the swimmers clutching their clothes and the pedagogue leading away his five senses. Mr. Impetigo put on his already streaming hat. All were heavily straggling away, except for Governor Marengo who was slowly advancing his regardless eyes downcast.

On the flat slate water, in mile-long staffs, immediate bends, and half-mile whorls, the air, alive and startled for an inch above the water but elsewhere congealed, was writing *freely*, like a Chinese poet who in the moment of *release* from the obligation of ideographs (it is the moment of the poetic climax just after the dramatic climax, and he expresses only feelings, the feelings unsettled by the reverse of fortune), draws the great loop and flies back across it, and ends in the jagged lightning and a puncture that leaves a crest of foam.

Nevertheless—amid this compressed air, threatening to burst asunder every large and small tube—along the tangible rocks and the stiff water—here came something Empty: a twilit cloud full of whispers. This alienated region *no longer partook of the nourishment* and was *immune to the pressure*. It was *no longer in the same flow of time*, which I indicate by writing of it in the present-tense.

It is the Governor of the State who, having committed his crime, is in soul-solitude.

His crime closes him in a cloud and protects him like that cloud of invisibility which the Venus shed round her son in the maritime city of Carthage. (For divine love too encloses in a cloud.) Against this preternatural cloud which is walking, the vortices did not even break. Within, the light is dim and there is a whispered conversation.

In absolute silence the rain began to fall and to patter the water.

Alas this criminal! except for these intimate whispers can hear no other voices, which all communicate by shaking the ambient air. To his surprise he finds that he cannot communicate with his dear love, his fiancée, altho it used to seem that they had an affinity for each other's good or evil. (This was a terrible potential across which they spoke in gusts.) Now he has done the deed demanded—but without regrets, for doesn't he have preternatural powers? but none but these.

In absolute silence the rain began to fall and to patter the water. This storm did not break but spread into quiet noise as the sky briefly brightened at sunset.

As he was walking along with eyes on the ground, Governor Marengo noticed the remnants and the relics of the tubular beings.

The characteristic death of tubes is to be either scotched or sectioned. On a flat rock a fisherman had left scotched fragments and sections of sandworms. A section on a rusty hook. A scotched fragment, stuck fast by its liquid, was still (till sunset, says the legend) undulating his feathery feet. Another section was crawling blindly.

A drooling rubber, that had temporarily isolated a virile tube, lay on a rock. Another was drifting in the water.

It is almost another world, rather than another aspect of the world, that we see if we keep our eyes fixed on the ground. The large tubes especially loom perpendicularly when alive and using their implements; cigarettes, gloves, and tackle are employed aloft from the ground. The discarded relics on the flat—bits of silver-paper and paperclips, and strings—re-enter a non-utilitarian existence.

It is the kingdom of the dead. By a small aberration of perception (given the wrong mood), one could see not only relics but remnants—I mean the lifeless penis, the torn-off mouth, re-entering a non-utilitarian existence. (Such things exist on battlefields.)

—As they emerged in the town, Mynheer told his boys to fix their eyes on the street polka-dotted with raindrops and see the orange-peels, etc. In this way Augie, with a cry of joy, found a 50¢ piece.—

Meantime Nurse Mulqueen, the Governor's fiancée, was running swiftly after him along the rocks, afire with love like one whose clothes are in flames.

41

One of the intimate conversationalists in the preternatural cloud is telling a story: "In my early boyhood," he says, "I was afraid that some one would come in when I was masturbating. I held my attention divided, fixed half on the pleasant thrills, but half, and this was the wilder feeling, on the threatened click of the latch, like a sleeping mother listening always for the cry. Later, when I was a criminal, it was already second-nature for me to have an apprehensive heart, and it would have been easy for me to dissociate my soul. Indeed at *any* time, no matter what I was doing, my heart was set to pounding at the click of the latch; I know there was lust in this anxiety. But now at last the calamity has occurred. The doorbell rang; it was no sneaking surprise, you see. I opened the door wide and *Nobody* came in past me—I mean, an empty space charged with Mana."

If I were a sculptor, I should walk along these great rocks and—sneaking up with iron control of my perception to keep it from correcting itself—I'd fix forever in isolation that posture of the rock that made me think it was a person. And if the shore were strewn with these statues! there would be a museum of *my* nightmares like that fixed for the nightmares of all mankind on the hillside of Easter Island.

The Nurse's naïve, most naïve, plan was to overtake her slowly fleeing love and to *rejoin* him, on the grounds that she too had done a deed demanded and was as criminal as he.

It was not the same crime that she had committed, for each one has his or her own crime. (Probably more than one, tho at the given moment it seems that there is only one, so that in order to conceal this one we freely hint that we are guilty of enormities, and do not realize that our friends are stunned by the admissions.)

The Witch was flying along, not in a preternatural empty space, but more like a raging furnace devouring the vortices and space with no residue, as if she were rolling up the world and leaving nothing behind.

But! you might object, crimes committed in such pure love and with the object of bringing to the Governor a kind of peace, are no crimes at all, or at least it is not such that can uncreate the air and rocks. This also was partly true.

42

On the Rocks Along the River

And where she trod the April flowers briefly bloomed—not thickly, but in isolated spots, blue-bells and violets moist with light rain. These little flowers were a *surprise* among the carvings. There was one bluebell or one violet at the base of each figure of nightmare. And its exhalation of odor stirred the little air.

These figures of nightmare were gigantic, the heads of giantesses and giants.

A second intimate conversationalist in the preternatural cloud is saying or rather crooning: "O little Tony, why do you wake up crying in the middle of the night and there's nothing we can do to comfort you? O little Tony! O little Tony, why do you wake up in the middle of the night? O little Tony, why do you wake up crying in the middle of the night and there's nothing we can do to comfort you?"

She is crooning: "Yes, little Tony, it's all right. Yes, little Tony. Yes, little Tony, it's all right in the middle of the night. O little Tony, why do you wake up crying in the middle of the night? Yes, little Tony, it's all right."

[*New York City*]
April 1941

A Parenthesis

For a week and a half Gregory Dido visited among old friends who were now part of the soul (with such attenuated life as remains in institutions even living and post-revolutionary) of an educational institution in the South.

This visit was not idle; it was an inspection, a report. At the same time, away from his city, it was a break in his intimate life.

Thru this breach rose other passions which had been pursuing their ancient careers outside of immediate attention; and especially the passions of a transitional kind, because these found something familiar to themselves in the situation of breach and continuity. Such transitions as erotic adventures, and the wish for reforms. (But underneath all these, flowed as ever the deep currents of the soul.)

Coming from outside, and yet familiar with the living instincts of the governors—for they were all old friends—in a few conversations Gregory was able to unsettle the principles and the heart of the institution; to disrupt, to reaffirm, to purge, and confuse. But this was not presumptuous of him, because it was precisely their and his interest for him to do this. At the same time, the situation itself gave him a disproportionate advantage, so that by comparison with his settled old friends he shone in an heroic freedom and critical tolerance, as a kind of friendly devastator.

And when the young men and women, who like all pupils lived in the soul of the institution by faith, gathered round the conversations at the governors' table to listen, they

45

were amazed by the stranger. Suddenly he recalled to them that their faith in this place was a kind of parenthesis. (Altho his intention was to recall to them only the opening of the parenthesis and by no means to bring the parenthetic passage to a close, for these institutions were the best they had.)

And his own behavior was in parentheses, for he was here for only a week. Knowing it, Gregory Dido looked at these beautiful girls and boys with the simple joy that belongs to the beginning of desire—a joy which as the case is now with us, we can only describe thus in parentheses. He was generous in his signs of affectionate regard for them all; he kissed Jack Shaw and several more; and let his hand rest on a lovely but diffident girl from the mountains named Barbara.

It was even necessary to him to make advances to so many, because this was the proof that after all it was only love, such as it was. But he could not prevent, nevertheless, his spirit from clouding over with pleasure and pain; and the opinions he now expressed at the table had a biting energy and the clarity that came from forgetting his public role.

In the case of Bab, a certain diffidence of hers restrained him to the discussion over coffee of relative and absolute axioms. Yet Gregory, amorous in parentheses, saw her eyes sleep.

Not with impunity! in the presence of so many beautiful objects, he gradually exposed his faculties of sentiment in confident passivity: especially when the flood of stimulated desire did not flow away in perfect lust, but was dammed up by merely teasing difficulties and trickled into esteem, gratitude, psychological notes, contentment with the charming situation; for would not the impatient soul soon combine all these into one fountain of images?

So it fell out. There was a wild, childish adolescent named Peter Gallia, strongly fixed in a way of disobedient naughtiness aged 6—tho the original content had long lapsed. And as soon as the mature man came into the presence of such a sternly carefree poser and grinner, he felt his ease in danger.

Now Peter was wearing a green suede jacket rent below

46

the left shoulder, and thru this rent the paleness appeared—as, to quote Jean, sometimes the ragged playing of a quartet uncovers the beauty of the music. By a curious maneuver Gregory contrived to touch his finger to this parenthesis; and he was lost.

His five days of free pleasure were now given their final form, as was inevitable, of pain. This was the real passion of despair in parentheses, to which all sensibility aspires; that by need gives an illusion of meaning; but in parentheses, because after all it is only love.

In this emergency, the wild boy proved to be a little snob. At the same time, betrayed into an archaic attitude of absolute dependency, he too was unable to withdraw himself from the presence of such an irksome grandeur.

The common scene of his game of electric repellants rushing to fill a vacuum—so that there was an uneasy equilibrium—was the little library. Here Gregory wrote the Marginal Notes on the "Cardinal Virtues." But if when he came the library had no Peter, he could not invent even these parenthetic remarks.

At other times he stood behind Barbara's chair and looked at Peter.

The originally fatal expression, the boy's grin, was of course to be seen no more, but instead a sullen face that for three or four days was more fatal still and amused Gregory to the quick.

He thought of a hundred other voyages, before the Revolution and as early as he could remember—and he had occasion to wonder how it was possible that the beautiful ones should prove to be all cruel. Was it perhaps likely that their cruelty was their beauty? God forbid! it was better to say that there was no trace of cruelty in beauty itself, but that it was the relationship of desire that caused the hellish effect, the promise of which released the energy to exhaust the heart in constrained situations.

There were still, thank God, even for him in his middle years, such correspondences between the things and the inward longings of his heart that in the resulting impasses it was possible for *peace*, which no one seeks, to well up inward and outward both.

To the old man's delight, the boy's friends assured him that in a month Peter would come to his senses.

Naturally, by the time of the last two days of his visit, Gregory's welcome was not what it had been—tho not necessarily less warm. He showed a certain acrimony of suggestions and behavior apt to revivify the youthfulness of chaos: indeed, the fresh breeze was now a little chilling to the bone. The fact was that Gregory was at such a point vis à vis the institution that his only next step could be to join it, and giving up his beautiful advantage, accept the difficulties of the bureaucracy. Could he do *even* this? for, having come as a *transient* visitor, he had established himself in just this transiency. For instance, he alone knew from private conversations what every one in the place was after; the friend of everybody can always learn this *when he is going away soon.* (But then he has to go!)

He had precisely that in-between role or role of demiurge (and not only here, for it was Gregory Dido!), between the governors and the youngsters, between the sexes, between each two individuals, and so forth, that no one is allowed to play in a free established society, whose freedom consists in the fact that each one is condemned to the bitter unease of having to make tentative advances from his own station.

Yet after all! it was really his last night with his old friends.

They relaxed the immediate melancholy of it in plenty of alcohol; and they soon relieved together *all* the tensions of the recent past, such as new ideas, sharp words, or the love of lads with rent jackets. Then, from the vantage-point of this *timeless* satisfaction, they were able to *fix* those conversations and the meaning of some of the actions of the young people, with conclusions taking "all things" into account, and with dramatic narrations, and epigrams. It was possible for them to become definitive in this way, of course, only because there was an ending of some kind at hand; and this was Gregory's last service, for which they were very thankful, namely to provide themselves with a more up-to-date revised code of tentative conclusions than the one they had recently been moving by.

But men who fix the recent past, which is normally a

48

A Parenthesis

movement of the present, as past, are insensibly plunged
into the proper past of submerged memories. This was
Gregory's goal from the very beginning, we saw, when he
made the breach in his intimate life to spend a week and a
half with his old friends. And now they were *all* absorbed in
reminiscences of the war, the establishment, etc. For a
couple of hours there was perfect unanimity among them:
in the society prior to the bureaucratizing of the institutions that they somewhat skeptically revered in common.

Soon, in the same backwards direction always gathering
impetus, every one began to mumble about his ancient
private memories in the mode of communal soliloquies
appropriate to being quite drunk, and appropriate to childish memories, and appropriate to falling asleep on one's
feet.

The next morning Gregory had just had his swim and was
about to pack; his mind was already on business a thousand
miles away; when the door-bell rang. He came out in a
bath-robe, and it was Barbara.

"I wanted to say good-bye and I was afraid I wouldn't have
the chance," she said.

"Thank you!"

"I have a seminar at 11," she added. It was 9.

"Since I'm going away," said Gregory, "will you *kiss* me
good-bye?" This was ridiculous; it seemed to him, as often
happens when something has ended only an hour ago or a
day ago, that all his pleasant week and a half was reviving
round him, in liveliest interest, with a dozen dead little
projects.

But nothing of the kind. For this good-bye kiss led readily
to delicious fornications and sexual give and take of every
kind, having nothing in common with that accursed institution in the South nor with inclinations in parentheses
belonging only to the secret memory.

"To come at the last moment: you have a lot of courage!"
said Gregory Dido, the hero of the so-called Incident of
Eighty-Eighth Street.

"I know from experience," he cried, "how it's nearly
impossible to go thru with what we really want when a
momentary delay and no effort on our part will save us all

the trouble! And then it's too late."

"What do you mean by all the trouble?" she said charmingly.

"Oh, I mean the way people conjecture; or laying yourself open to disappointment; or the alienation of desire from the roundabout environment."

"As for *this* place," said the girl heatedly, "it's completely indifferent to me! I could have died laughing when we sat discussing relative and absolute axioms."

"You see," said Gregory, "I thought I knew what everybody was after; but the fact was that I took the point of view of the institution more seriously than anybody else. I'm always *plus royaliste que le roi.*"

"You see, it took no courage at all, since *not* from the point of view of this institution, I didn't come at the last moment!"

"That's where you're wrong," said the politician sharply; "the place is the most important part of the institution; and by tonight I'll be a thousand miles away from here."

"It's all right," she said.

"No, after all, Barbara, after all—such an act of bravery by which you were able *not* to wait a little longer at the last moment!—I think our joy will last a year or more!"

[New York City]
April 1941

The University in Exile

Some, exiled from all possible lands, lived on a boundary,
on a road or a river or a no-man's plain crossed by shots from
both sides. Others were killed before starting out. There
was no concern but train connections or missed connections, then long hikes; and by "long" I mean five hundred
kilometers often undertaken, sometimes accomplished, by
persons sixty years old. It seemed that the ones successful
in heroic escapes now enjoyed renewed youth, restored
health, freedom of perspective; but this was partly because
they were already a selected group, of those who had been
secretly waiting for a chance to break with their dear habits,
so that the general calamity was their release. Thousands
were put to flight and shot because fleeing. A few were able
to feel

>   for wandering is it
>   that the world is made so wide;

others committed suicide in moral or physical despair.
Jailed, some were so naturalized to conventional opinions
that they were ill with mere shame. Prior collusion with
the rising powers sometimes proved to be the key to escape.
Bribery or foresight or fortitude or ingenuity or callousness
or friends or wealth or luck, or all of these together even
when it seemed that they would be contraries in the same
person, were the virtues of escape. Then, after all, the boat
would be sunk or the general conquest overtake the

51

individual fugitive. Or again, after the excitement of rapid motion had died down a little, there were bad memories, an intolerable present attitude, and no prospects.

2.

The secret object of the dinner party in New York was to get Kaplan the jeweler to contribute five thousand dollars to the University in Exile.

When Niko Verein, the young poet, lecturer, and (already) editor, arrived, the maid Frau Luisa blushed, and her face became radiant. She helped him with his coat.

"Isn't it Niko Verein, the poet?" she whispered to Mrs. Clyde excitedly.

"How did you know?"

"Often he came for dinner when I had my home in Prague. He doesn't recognize me."

Frau Luisa had been the wife of the chancellor of an ancient university. The husband was perhaps dead. But she, for the most part, was content in her new activity which she had intelligently and quickly mastered.

Inside, the conversation was not so much desultory as plain difficult. Almost everyone was haltingly trilingual, and the conversation, manfully launched on the greatest subject, was foundering when it had to be carried on the English phrases that the Germans and Frenchmen knew in common. But Clyde, the host, was strong-minded enough to prevent them from separating into little groups and speaking the languages they knew. He boasted that in his house they learned English.

Under these conditions they were discussing world sociology.

They greeted Niko enthusiastically. What a relief! He represented the interests of all and he spoke all languages beautifully.

Professor Leinhardt despised him as the embodiment of the best official cultural extremism. Jarno couldn't bear any of them, but Verein was the worst. To Mme. Chapelain, his mere presence was a thrust to the heart.

52

"Pardon, pardon, vous ne deviez pas m'attendre. Je viens de donner une causerie chez les aborigines de *Harlem!*" cried Niko, as though it were a bombshell. Everybody laughed.

"De *Harlem!*"

"Vat is Harlem?" asked Frau Doktor Becker.

"We are waiting for Didier," said M. Chapelain sourly.

Mme. Chapelain was anxious. "Où est-ce que ça peut être maintenant?" she asked, holding her watch, which she wore on the inside of her wrist, close to her eyes.

They explained to Doktor Becker what Harlem was, and she, too, had a chance to laugh.

Etienne Chapelain was bursting because he had a far-reaching thesis which, if he could expound it, would no doubt (this is the belief of every third party in an argument) end the sociological argument. If the German ideology, he wanted to say, were as factitious as claimed, would not the reality of human personality corrupt it from within, not in our generation of course? But he absolutely could not move his tongue. His tongue was paralyzed when he tried to express in English anything like an idea. Finally in despair he croaked, "Le luxe—le luxe corrompt toujours."

"Ils ont insisté que Beethoven était un noir," cried Niko; "they say Beethoven was a nigger." He often spoke in French and English concomitantly, rarely in German. Certainly this socially tactful gesture was a mark of unconscious alienation from and contempt for the German refugees. Herr Leinhardt was right to take offense. At the same time the causes of this alienation were worthy of pity. In Europe Niko had been a very important literary figure—but not among the best wits, as he was intelligent enough to perceive; he hadn't yet perceived that it was the same in America too. Meantime he was happy and violently active, much more so than ever before; except that he was nervous and had a hundred tics. His eyes popped, looking for someone who was never there.

When he spoke German it was to quote from Goethe, which at home he would never have dared to do. The more sophisticated practice had not necessarily been better, and Niko's present conversation and even attitude were really immeasurably improved by association with those noble saws; except that it was all spoiled when he passed himself off as the spokesman of the deathless culture.

Speedily the sociological argument degenerated to what was in the headlines, especially since all the linguists had just muttered these words to themselves.

"Ze Grand Mufti even is now an Ahryan," said Professor Leinhardt.

He was ashamed. He and M. Chapelain looked at each other with dumb sympathy. The linguistic difficulty was stultifying; they felt that they not only seemed but were becoming stupid. At the same time, here was a problem in wild mental acrobatics: to use only the vocabulary and ideas of the news reports and yet, by irony or contradictions, to avoid the context of idiocy, or at least to indicate that one's-self was not such an idiot.

The net result was that the Americans thought they were complete idiots.

Meyer Kaplan was a Russian Jew who was a great joker.

"This Hess—you should poddon the expression—" he now began. He was absolutely the first to invent this classic joke about the notorious Hess.

Mrs. Kaplan squealed with joy. (Meyer had invented the joke on the way upstairs and was only waiting his opportunity.) Mme. Chapelain could not, of course, catch the joke, but she recognized Mr. Kaplan's type and she paled with disgust.

None of the foreigners, even Niko, could catch the joke. Clyde chuckled deeply.

"You could never explain it!" choked Mrs. K.

"It would take too long," said Clyde apologetically. The Americans nevertheless couldn't resist laughing on—at the others, of course—while the refugees wore strained smiles.

But Niko brought them all to a pause by appreciatively observing: "A long explanation takes the humor from a joke."

The doorbell rang.

"Didi!" said Madame, with a sigh of relief.

It was Didi. When he came in, hatless and coatless, he was still muttering to himself, "For-mi-dable!" Anyone could have told at a glance, from his color and disarray, that he had just been necking. "For-mi-dable!" he whispered.

"Madam, dinner is served," said Frau Luisa.

Didi, who was nineteen, gulped his cocktail and at once poured another which he took to the table. "C'est formidable."

He was seated opposite the Frau Doktor.

To explain why he was so late, he rapidly told a story, in French, about going through a traffic light and then diving in and out of alleys, like a taxi, to escape a police car. He lent verisimilitude to this by explosions of laughter. In his anxiety, he was betrayed into the pathetic error by which, to conceal the crime present to our consciences, we confess to a lesser one which is as bad, or worse, in the minds of the audience.

"A police car!" cried his mother, terrified.

Fortunately the word was at once seized upon by everybody else.

"How apsurd!" said the Professor. "In America ze police car is a peculiar color; everybody _knows_ it is a police car! Ze—how do you say—ze lawbreaker sees it and away he runs!"

"Don't worry, they have his license number," said Clyde, beginning to be angry, so that, a bad host, he cast terror into the hearts of Monsieur and Madame. He could not help burning when these people criticized American institutions.

"Same in ze hotel!" cried the Professor. "Nobody hass—how do you say—an identification. Why could I not sign _any_ name?"

Clyde became red to the ears when he heard the refugee from the system of tyranny advocating the fingerprinting of non-aliens.

"In America," he said, restraining himself, "we have the principle that a man is innocent until he is proved guilty. This is Anglo-Saxon law."

"Ah so! it iss very interesting to study ze comparative law of different peoples."

"The policeman is there to appeal to if a crime is committed; it is not his business to ferret out the crimes!"

Great! great! thought Jarno. He felt that he could die laughing when he heard this bourgeois discuss legal formalities. But the academic was even deadlier.

"Niko," exclaimed the hostess tactfully, "tell us about your lecture to the aborigines de Harlem."

"My land," said Mrs. Kaplan, "how did Beethoven turn out to be a Negro?"

Helping himself to the wild lamb, Niko, munching, prepared to narrate the story with high spirit when once he would have his fork free to wave in the air.

Frau Luisa, the maid, slowed up the service, to hear as much of the story as possible.

Didi meantime had relapsed into his trance. "Formidable!" he said mechanically. The fact was that whereas in French he was bashful and tongue-tied and could not make love, in English, which he hardly knew, he allowed himself to say anything; and his success was simply astounding! It seemed that the English words retained their primary meanings and the compliments were so clever (it was clever of him to be able to phrase them). Besides—

Absently chewing, Didi began to remember that he had once before experienced a similar freedom of language, when he was a little boy and first went out. It was not only a matter of language, but being away from home. . . .

M. Etienne Chapelain likewise felt that when he tried to speak he was again becoming a child, inadequate to the situation, abashed by his father's authority. For the second time in his life he began to hear, now interiorly, the word Syntax, that made him tremble.

"The climate of New York is O. K. for the boys!" said Mme. Chapelain. "Didi has grown four centimeters. For me it's not so good." She had no appetite. She was puzzled whether the meat was pork, veal, or horse. It was lamb, soaked for three days in buttermilk.

Leinhardt was thinking, as he methodically chewed: "The meat is excellent. And, after all, this small talk—is not so stupid. I have gotten out of the habit of considering such every day topics philosophically. But the kind of knowledge people have of these topics is not altogether erroneous, especially if you take everything into account psychoanalytically. It's really very interesting."

Niko began his story. Luisa was hovering in admiration, half turned toward the pantry.

He glanced at her sharply.

It seemed that someone had asked him, "What about Beethoven's race?" They didn't understand, he explained; what he was trying to show was just that race made *no* difference. "Beethoven was a Negro!" the old man shouted.

Luisa hurried away, to return, as soon as possible, with the broccoli.

Niko leaned forward and whispered to Mrs. Clyde: "The maid isn't colored, is she?"

"No," said the hostess.

"Ah," sighed Niko, smiling happily.

"This I never heard, did you?" he asked. "The theory is that the 'van' in van Beethoven makes him Dutch and his father was in slave trade."

"There was Dumas."

"Ah, Dumas. Yes, Dumas. Everybody knows Dumas père. But this other I never heard. Does it seem likely I shouldn't even have heard of it?"

"Now you hear it," said the Professor drily. "Everyzing you must hear for ze first time."

"Also Pushkin," said Kaplan.

"Pushkin?"

"Pushkin—this is famous," said the Professor.

"But how were there Negroes in Russia?"

"They came as servants to Catherine the Great, isn't it so, Professor? Don't you remember in the paintings there is a little pickaninny with a turban?"

Luisa laughed resonantly, as in the old days, when she, too, had her house and these very people came to dinner.

Kaplan could not swallow, and the tears flooded his eyes.

"I am thinking of my brother Max," he said; "I can just see his face."

Mrs. Kaplan and the host and hostess exchanged glances across the table. Clyde looked at his watch.

"Was there an accident?" said Jarno disdainfully.

"First he was in Berlin. We are jewelers," said Kaplan in

such a tone that the other conversation stopped. "Max couldn't understand anything. From way back my father said he was a shlemihl, I should take care of him.

"So I said, 'Max, go to Vienna.' So I set him up a little business in Vienna. So no sooner was it all ready to open, with a neon sign—I wouldn't say much, twenty feet high—than I said, 'Max, go to Prague.'—"

As soon as the familiar joke pattern established itself, the others—not to be caught short this time—immediately began to laugh in anticipation. Mme. Chapelain could hardly contain her indignation at the tastelessness of telling such a joke.

"In Prague there was not even time to choose a good spot. 'Max,' I said, 'There's nothing here; you had better go to Brussels.'"

The Professor guffawed. Mrs. Clyde was puzzled.

"Brussels was a jewelry center," Kaplan doggedly continued, "and here maybe we could do a little something. But I said, 'Max, pack up and go to Paris.'—"

The others leaned forward for the dénouement.

"And I forgot to tell him to leave Paris!" said Meyer Kaplan in bitter self-reproach.

It was a mad success. Something everybody could understand. The Professor clapped his hands. "He forgot to tell him to leave Paris!" echoed Niko. And even Jarno was forced to smile. Indeed, when Jarno perceived the full malice of the story—told in such company—after the others were subsiding, he laughed out loud.

In a desperate attempt to restore the society to the level that she was accustomed to, or at least to make it clear what that level was, Mme. Chapelain said: "The story is like that what Mme. de Sévigné wrote to Mme. de Grignan concerning the death of Turenne. He was galloping away when St. Hilaire called him back to the fatale spot, like to say: 'Monsieur, arrêtez-vous un peu, car c'est ici que vous devez être tué.' Le coup de canon vint donc. . . . 'Sir, stop a moment, because it's here you must be killed.'"

Mrs. Clyde rang, and they went inside for coffee.

"German Jews!" hissed Kaplan.

His teeth were chattering so violently that he could not

clench the lump of sugar in them.

"Fine ladies and gents, nobody has tsures but you. To you my tsures is a joke. Oh, the donations that in memory of Max I *won't* give you! In the earth I should lie before I give a *cent* to a German charity. This minute I make out five thousand *not* to you!"—

With trembling fingers he opened a check book and wrote a check to the Hartsdale Military Academy.

"When you hear that I gave it to goyim you'll burst a blood vessel! Why shouldn't there be a Max Kaplan Salle d'Armes?

"To *my* charities," Meyer said between his teeth; it was not a new resentment; the bitterness of this charitable rivalry was of old, "to *my* charities you don't contribute; but *I* should feel myself *honored* to help found the University in Exile! Naturally, a Litvak, you're doing me a favor. 'He forgot to tell him to leave Paris'—ha! ha! . . . Maxileh."

He tore up the check he had just written and made out the sum to the Sholom Orphans and Old Folks; for though angry, he was not completely out of his head.

By the wonderful law of opposites, the reflections of Jarno, as he slowly stirred his coffee, were not far from those of Meyer Kaplan.

Jarno had been a Spartacist; he was in America because there was a price on his head. More recently he had embraced the opinions of the Pole Machajski, according to which the class of the intelligentsia is even deadlier than the capitalists, because they are willing to make a revolution to become the new exploiters. Now, here were these professors, journalists, technicians (Chapelain was a chemist) temporarily lost out, yet still struggling in the new environment, plotting a return home not only to privilege but to power. Jarno was also an anti-Semite, not on principle but statistically—he had an especial hatred for physicians and surgeons. As he looked narrowly at these persons who could afford to escape, with their bribes and professional connections, their affidavits and visas, he found it not hard to think of the others who could not afford to escape death. He knew, likewise, the principles by which the American Department of State admitted certain types, rejected other types.

Niko Verein was precisely the type of vermin to whose annihilation Jarno looked forward. If he allowed himself to come to such a dinner party, it was in the spirit of an apprentice exterminator. But he was beginning to fear that the end was not to be in his generation.

Niko was dog-tired; his jaw sagged, and he looked like what he was, no longer one of the Young Poets. So, sometimes for a moment he slipped from his rôle, for which he had only hatred.

But it was impossible; there was too much to do, that is, to save from being *completely undone*. (Such an effort of conservation is not very grateful; it requires infinite pains for an admittedly finite object—which soon enough becomes an object of disgust. Nevertheless!—) Here was M. Etienne Chapelain, for reasons that we know, deriding the syntax of the English language; a single demitasse brûlot had been enough to throw him off his balance. Niko pulled himself to his feet and advanced with a waving demitasse spoon.

Monsieur said: "*He—was given—a book:* 'book,' if you please, is accusatif, in the construction passive. Voilà, accusatif! Tiens, Didi—" he turned to the boy to whom he had never taught syntax or anything else, "On lui a donné un livre: *He—was given—a book!* Ha!"

"What is this accusatif?" asked Clyde, worried.

"In English we say Objective," said Mrs. Clyde.

"Oh, Objective! Direct Object—Indirect Object—"

"We explain 'book' as a Retained Object—un objectif retenu."

"Retenu!" screamed Monsieur at the top of his lungs. "*Objectif retenu!* oh, oh."

"Etienne," cautioned Mme. Chapelain.

"When they squeal *y y* I could cheerfully step on them," thought Clyde. "These squeal, the others growl. If they don't like it—"

Against his deepest, and perhaps his best, inclinations, Niko yet again raised his voice to harmonize western culture against barbarism. "You are judging English by the

60

rules of Latin grammar, M. Chapelain. Still, you are partly right; English is less logical than French but belongs more to the people. We must remember that each language has its own genius; there is living room for all. French is rational and Cartesian; English is irrational but infinitely flexible and Shakesperian." As he said this, poor Niko felt a pang between the eyes.

"What's irrational about it?" said Clyde. "He was given a book—it means, someone gave him a book."

Like a faithful soldier who, wounded and thirsty, and maybe dying, and on a field where at best he is fighting a rearguard action, still briskly salutes, Niko drew back his lips from his fangs in an amiable smile. "It has the rationality of an organism," he said, describing with his hands the shape of a plant.

Professor Leinhardt looked at him. But Niko was the more heroic.

It was 9:30.

The outer doorbell rang.

"Here he is!" cried Nora Kaplan excitedly and sailed out.

Meyer was asleep with his fountain pen clutched in his fist.

Nora returned arm in arm with Max, who was smiling radiantly though his other forearm was in a cast.

"*Max!*" cried Mrs. Clyde, who had casually met him in Berlin and of course did not recognize him, but she had arranged the surprise of the evening.

"*Shh!*" said Niko warningly; he grasped the situation in a flash. "We mustn't wake him up—the shock, the pleasure, the heart—How *are* you?" he said warmly to Max, shaking his hand.

"After so many evasions, we must avoid a malchance," said Monsieur.

"How did you hurt your arm?" asked Didi.

Jarno took command. "Let Max wait inside. His wife will wake him. Then we tell him to prepare for a surprise."

Startled by the quiet, the sleeper awoke.

"Moish!" he said.

"Meyer!" said Max.

"My little brother—" Kaplan exclaimed several times,

embracing him. "You hurt your hand," he said reproach-fully.

The radiant and, to speak frankly, the perfect satisfaction of this reunion was such that M. Etienne Chapelain was reminded of the wonderful promissory verse of Virgil,

Forsan et haec olim meminisse iuvabit.

Overcome with emotion, he said to his wife, "Emma, peut-être qu'un jour le souvenir même de ces choses sera agréable! N'est-ce pas, Emma?"

Jarno sat down and relaxed into his contemplative dissatisfaction.

"Peut-être qu'un jour—" whispered Monsieur. "Maybe that a day—" he dutifully translated.

Kaplan now saw that their laughter, far from being contemptuous, had been a sign of the most intimate kind of sympathy. His ideas underwent a revolution. He wrote out an additional check and gave it on the sly to Leinhardt. "But not a word," he cautioned. "Take it, use it."

"Zees is wonderful!" said Leinhardt, "five zousand dollars!"

"Max!" Meyer called out to his brother, "you have just donated a professor and his assistant to the University in Exile."

"—le souvenir même de ces choses," said Monsieur to himself.

When they left, Mme. Chapelain burst into tears. "Je connaissais Picasso—I used to know Picasso. We'd have dinner at Leo Stein's, then do our duty as the claque for Jean Cocteau's latest clarinetist. When poor Rilke was alive and came to Paris, he rang us on the telephone; am I lying? We didn't discuss whether the spirit of the French language was Cartesian! But even Niko didn't seem then what he now is—you remember he used to sit on the floor? But if you now drop a hint of these things and implore a little response, he pretends that all that never existed.

"And *instead!*" sobbed Mme. Chapelain, "we have dinner with a stockbroker whose name is *Clyde,* whose wife learned pleasant manners from a young ladies' finishing school. We hear the jokes of Mr. Kaplan; and his brother, the itinerant jewler, arrives *with his arm in a plaster cast!* Mr. Meyer Kaplan, mind you, is now asleep in the company. And our little Niko, the same, declares: 'the shock, the pleasure, the heart'!—*this* I shall never forget as long as I live."

But M. Chapelain, who was still entranced by the promissory hexameter, said: "Ne pleurs pas, Emma—don't cry, Emma. It is true that now we have come to spend the evenings with these bourgeois; after all, what did you expect in coming to America? But we also, I am afraid, had our dear habits; even Rainer Maria Rilke was a dear rare habit. It is possible that now, because of this horrible shock, we may come to meet these other persons *anew*, on the level of their humanity. If we were still *there* (là-bas) you could not have spent such four hours without contractation of the skin and flight; the changed circumstances have made the meetings at least tolerable, or at least unavoidable. This is a sign, my dear, that there is more in us, and in them, than ever you suspected. And what follows? two things: the idea of ourselves was in part conventional, no? and there is still something to be found out."

M. Didier Chapelain said to himself: "C'est formidable! Wait till tomorrow!"

New York
1941

Sailors

1. *Round the Bar*

The bars for sailors are decorated with cellophane palm-trees.

When a sailor plunks down a half-dollar on the counter, it is with such an air. It is the most archaic use of money, in simple exchange, prior to the times of accumulation and investment, because these sailors have no economic responsibilities; before 7 A.M. they'll go back to a ship in the Yard; they're taken care of *there*. They count the coins against immediate pleasures, when they take in a movie or down a glass. (They cannot estimate prices because the city is always too strange.) The society has come so far from that archaic money that these young men—many of them are runaway boys—are like children; their little necessities are nothing but little pleasures. How could it be otherwise when *both* their work and their home are so far removed from their market? What a complex society it is that requires these children for its armed forces!

(One or two, like that aerial photographer, know the score and are playing this marvelous dangerous game for their own advantage, exploiting us all!)

Many men and women ashore cannot keep away from the relieving presence of the sailors.

At the great *Royal Palms* there are fifty sailors; eighteen of them are with girls. These are the pleasure-loving girls who cannot keep away from the sailors, or the women who are making money from these children.

But the little pleasures of the sailors are not pleasures at all, but only a way to kill the time, for the absorbing enter-

65

tainments, it seems, are not for the boys who inwardly *need* to be back on a ship by 7 A.M.

Experimentally the man in the tan sweater (who cannot keep away from the sailors) says to a capless boy in blue: "Drinking all alone, sailor?" Offers him a cigarette, and the sailor takes it rather than one of his own from his jumper-pocket. They are therefore now acquainted.

How vivid are at least the blue and the white uniforms of the boys around the bar! On the walls are painted the huge orange Polynesians in the manner of Gauguin.

The sailor's last silver quarter is lying in front of him. "They fucked up my pay till Friday."

(It is true that they weren't paid, because they are about to *leave.*)

"I see," says the man wearily—but he rallies to his duty: "Two more here! . . . on me, boy. My name's Harry," and he holds out his hand.

"Hey?"

"I said my name's Harry," shouts Harry over the two pianos and the screams.

"So what?"

"I said what's *your* name? what do they call *you?*"

"McDougal."

"I mean your *first* name, sailor," says Harry with asperity at last.

How vivid are at least the blue and white uniforms etc.! What can infuse a little comfort into this wan atmosphere?

This sailor doesn't return the pressure of Harry's hand; but Harry patiently lets his hand rest on Mickey's knee. Tho it's midsummer, Mickey is wearing his blues because he's too lazy to launder his whites and they won't let him off the ship dirty; he is hiding his dirty Bob Evans under his jumper.

"I've got one dollar left, while it lasts," says Harry carefully and meaningfully. The woman who has been pressing close against the civilian hopefully, relaxes.

"Didn't you hunt any dear tonight, sailor?"

When the sailors leave the Yard it is often with a desperate intention to have a little pleasure; there is no question of particular preference. They are sometimes *surprised* af-

66

terwards when they take a look. Their pride and honor are involved in what they have to report when they return at 7 A.M. Even so! nevertheless! the lust itself is alive and their pricks stand up at once.

But Mickey says: "Me? I loined the score three months ago! I spend eighteen bucks on this bitch in Boston and when I went to the terlet she pisses away behind my back."

"Three months ago!" repeats Harry bewildered.

Mickey is squeezing his hand even hotly—really spasmodically, because of the happiness of the boys opposite and because of many an envious walk in the bushy park of West Philadelphia when he was fifteen. Yet, groping, Harry simply cannot find any erection there. But ordinarily at the *first handshake* the sailor's penis swells—in those tight pants cut for public love by a jocular tailor!

"Did you say *three* months? Three *months?*"

Round the oval bar, nothing but those white and blue triangles—

Under patient manipulation even Mickey's penis responds a little. "Let's shove off," says the sailor standing up violently.

Around the oval bar are nothing but those white and blue triangles and the marvelous upturned hats. Why do they all come *here?* it is more than forty minutes by train from the Navy Yard. None of them know that there was once a landing station at the foot of this street. Obviously it's an *advantage* if there's a long trip to get to this bar: something might turn up *on the way!* It keeps one from yielding to the temptation suddenly to go back and go to sleep.

They all gather in a circle, far off, like those archaic brothers when they conspired to kill the father.

The fact that they are still together after all makes it impossible for any one of them to venture too far.

Even so! there are at least the blue and white triangles each topped by a circular hat around the oval bar. And at the first handshake the sailor's penis swells—in those tight pants cut for public love by a jocular tailor. What can infuse a little comfort into this wan light?

They'll do *anything* not to have to go back *there* to sleep—so long as they get back at 7 A.M. The lovers of sailors set the alarm-clocks for 5:30, because the boys are so anxious not to be late.

"Do you want to come to my place?" says Harry.

"I gotta get *back!*" cries the other in anxiety.

Harry is a prince of resilience, of pliable insistency. He says: "We'll take a turn in the park."

They are walking the crowded street with pinkies tightly locked. "I don't give a shit *what* they think," says the sailor.

2. *In the Park*

The blue and the white uniforms emerging from or vanishing into the shadows of the park, the blue eclipsed all at once, the white gradually losing its corporeal form.

Just inside the entrance Bat and George are smoking cigars and patiently waiting for little Kenny to return with the communal girl. Experienced men, not kids, at the end of a second four-year hitch, they are about to go back to filling-stations and grocery stores. They are soon on their way to a watery grave.

And here, nervously triumphant, is the boy hero himself, Kenny, his white figure looming and taking form in the shadows. He is not more than seventeen, whatever he told them when he signed up. He buttons a button.

Agnes, stoop-shouldered, trails sweetly behind him.

Two other sailors on the stone coping are sullenly waiting for their buddy who is an hour and a half late; and they are out of cigarettes.

"Where all did you take her?" George whispers good-humoredly mocking Kenny's drawl.

"Up on the rocks by that theah pergola; I leaned her gainst the rahcks."

"Did you get your gun, sailor?" says George, giving the kid his full chance to be proud and laugh.

McDougal is walking five yards ahead of Harry, for he has now decided that this is the best arrangement.

"Where're you goin', sailor?"

"I'm a-huntin' dear."

His blue uniform is immediately eclipsed in the shadows.

Sailors

But Harry and George shake hands warmly. Perhaps George is a little mature, a little outside of Harry's "type"; but the prince of patience has learned indeed, at Columbus Circle and at the *Royal Palms*, what a potent sexual stimulus there is in a word of good sense.

"Ain't people around there?" asks Bat.

"I don' give a shit *who*'s theah—I jest shove it in!" cries little Kenny in extreme self-gratulation.

Aggie is giggling and rousing up George, sitting on his lap. "Do you have tattoos?" she asks.

"Sure! I have a submarine on my chest."

"Ooh, let me see!"

Feeling and peeping in the dim lamplight. "*I* can't see any submarine."

"It's submerged now. . . . Yeah, way down there."

Finally they walk off; and as they do George gives those two waiters such a look.

Bat says: "Did she want anythin'?"

"She saays she loves me."

"Have you got your wallet, kid?"

"Ah kep' my haind on it all the time!"

"Let's shove off," decides one of the sullen boys, the cute one.

"Where you wanna go?" says the other, alarmed. "Let's give him an hour more."

"Where we goin' if he *gets* here?"

"Do you got a cigarette, sailor?" he says pleading to Bat. "No."

Within ten minutes—almost at once—Aggie and George are back, their pink and blue appearing suddenly out of the shadows.

"The place is lousy with flashlights," explains George.

(The fact is that he doesn't want to miss Harry by any means; he has a forty-eight hour leave and Harry will always put him up with a real bed.)

Drawing deep on a five cent cigar, little Kenny is now at the peak of pride and joy: *he* was able, by the impetuousity of youthful desire, to *brush aside* the conventional obstacles and to impose his will. At once a tatter of memory—full of urgency and anxiety and the sentiment of astonish-

69

ing dexterity—flashes within him; his penis swells in its tight place; he wants to come again.

"My dogs are tired," complains Mickey.

They are cutting across lawns and going under bridges.

"We'll be right there," says Harry. After all, these are *his* waters and he knows all the places.

Indefatigably Agnes is now teasing Bat. Is he so strong after all; and whether he could lift her up; and even if he could, how far could he carry her—not more than a few yards.

"Hell, I'll take her back of a bush and let her french me," is Bat's plan.

To Aggie's confusion and extraordinary pleasure Kenny grabs her from behind. But Bat jumps up and picks her up squealing, and the strong man in blue carries off the pink dress into the shadows round the curve among little cries.

"Here he comes now! I to'd you he'd come." It's Van Dongen, the Baron, crossing the street an hour and three-quarters late.

Van Dongen, their buddy, is precise and decided. "C'mon, let's go hunting."

"*Oh* no!"

"What do you mean no?"

"We *hunted.*"

They are really dog-weary; the prospect of plodding the curving paths in the small hours has no charms at all.

"Well I come all the *way* to hunt. I'm a-goin' huntin'!"

"*You* go, sailor. We'll wait here for you again."

"F' Chris sake how long should we wait? when'll you come?"

"If I'm not here by 3 sharp you better shove off."

"F' Chris sake give us a cigarette."

Rather stingily the Baron doles out two cigarettes for each. And his white uniform floats into the darkness.

But *they* are *thankful* for this new determination of 3 A.M. on the formless clock, this division of the endless night into a period with a definite prospect. George begins to get mad as hell.

(He is not really a sailor any more at all; he has been recalled into the reserves because of the Emergency. Just

70

when his name was coming to the top of the list to be appointed a fireman in Camden, they called him back.)

Meantime Harry has come with the reluctant boy into the blackest grove.

"You'll never get it hard," says Mickey, "I'm too drunk."

Whatever it symbolizes, this remark has no factual meaning, for already, before ever he sits down on the pine-needles, his prick is hardening.

Harry passes his hand and the sailor leans his head against the tree-trunk.

"You see, it's hard already," says Harry reassuringly, foolishly interpreting that remark as apologetic.

For an instant, for a single instant in the obscurity, Mickey closes his eyes, energizing the outer obscurity with inner obscurity. Harry unbuttons a black button.

"Wait a minute! what do I get out of this anyway?" cries the youth at *this* moment! And he clutches at the buttons to prevent their opening further, as if they would spring open of themselves.

"Listen sailor—you saw that I had two bits," says the man sharply.

The fact is that he is stunned out of his composure.

Sometimes the sailors ask for money, in deference to a certain idea of their self-respect, or because they have a date tomorrow and need the dough; but not at this moment when the prick is quivering.

(Sometimes *afterwards*; then they are ugly, their unnatural cupidity being then quite unlimited.)

"Well! if there's nothing *in* it—why didn't you say so in the first place!" cries Mickey joyfully, with finality and relish, standing, buttoning the one button.

"No, there's nothing in it for you," says Harry drily. "No hard feelings, sailor—" he says at once, for he expects that there might now be a fight and he dislikes, especially in his shaken condition, to have to lay the boy flat. "Maybe we'll see each other again—" ("Not if I see you first.")

Under a lamp the boy pleads: "Say, brush me off, will ya?"

Harry brushes a few pine-needles off the boy's behind.

"Say, look at that!" cries Mickey, pointing to dirt on his bell-bottoms. "Gee, you sure almost fucked me up."

71

3.

There's a thunderstorm on the Battler's face, and Aggie is in disgrace. She had gotten *insulted,* or at least that's what she said. "I wouldn't even suck Kenny," she said, "and he's only a boy."

"Stow that whore on a 'bus and make your last adoos, an' f' Chris sake let's shove off," says Bat. "I been sucked by nice girls, I don' need to be told off by a Columbus Circle hustler."

Aggie's eyes are blazing.

At the same moment she boards the 'bus, Harry, still overcome with dismay and bewilderment, slumps down next to George.

George offers him a cigar.

But little Kenny, on the horrible subway-ride back to the ship with Bat, is torn with fear and self-reproach for being such a fool. Obviously, he realizes, the reason that this whore fucked him but stalled off the two older men is that she has the clap or worse; she didn't take any account of him because he doesn't know his ass from his elbow; but if she gave anything to George or Bat they'd know how to hunt her down and bash her one. He'll never be able to find her again. Next time, maybe, he won't be such a god-damn smartie-pie.

"F' Chris sake, sailor, didn't you use a rubber?"

"There was so many people theah I couldn't take time; I jest shove it right in. Then I pulled out and put it on anyway."

"That's great."

There's nothing to prevent the boy from having an irrigation when he gets aboard; but he has decided that this burns; so he'll risk it.

The tears are rolling in furrows down Aggie's rouged cheeks. For so long, for so long back, perhaps ever since she was a small girl like the one in the song who kissed the sailor and didn't get the rubber dollie, these sailors, these uniforms so tight-fitting round the hips, and jaunty gait; this frank desire; seemed mysterious and glamorous; the more desirable the more she kept away during those best years when like all the young girls she was afraid of being

Sailors

knocked up by careless love, like the gal in the song—

> Love oh love oh careless love
> love who took me like a flame.

But recently she has come to know them well, and there's the same thing under those pants as under others. Not (God forbid!) that she finds it undesirable, but where is the mystery? Not, again, that just for tonight she hasn't been able to love just Kenny, but now here she is crying bitterly.

"Don't cry," whispers the messenger-boy who has sat down next to her.

"Anything you say, sailor!" says Harry to George; "anything you say!"

"Don't call me sailor."

"—I'll never go out any more, it's bad for my peace of mind. Can you live when you come up against a mad dog—Oh, what's the use. Now you do the steering."

"Listen," says the sailor intensely hissing, "those two dummies there give me such a pain in the can I can't stand it any more. Damn! I hate this outfit like poison. Do you know why the hell they're sittin' on their asses there for three hours?"

"Naturally. They're waiting for a buddy who's pissed off on them and is probably up in the Bronx by now."

"Yeah? that's what they think! They're not sittin' there just to be bored stiff; they're sittin' there because they're froze together, see? An' they're waitin' for the other one because they're afraid to make a move together alone."

? ?

"We're gonna take that lovely pair up to your place an' I'll learn 'em to suck each other off if its the last thing I ever do in my life. My God if I can't vomit when I see them sittin' there like the girlie who says 'Now vat do I do?' Just let 'em let a peep out and I'll bash their puss in. I'll bash their puss in anyway. I'm gonna fuck that brown cutie so hard he won't do nothin' but shit for two weeks."

"Cigarette, sailors?" says Harry.

[Petit Manan, Maine?]
August 1941

73

The Commodity
Embodied in BREAD

*A commodity is therefore
a mysterious thing simply because—*
—Capital, Book I, I, 4

—for Ben

At the Super Market, a certain prospective purchaser was frantic, pale and flushing by turns, and alternately clutching and holding out a two-dollar bill, which everyone knows to be unlucky. It was Mr. Impetigo! the same as once bought the dozen gross of scissors to benefit by the wholesale price, and so always had many scissors lying around. He was thrifty on a lavish scale. But today he wanted only a single metal stew pot.

The trouble was—it was really, we shall see, in Impetigo's bad education, his aggressive sociology—the *proximate* trouble was that a little sprocket seemed to have been dislocated in the machinery of the Economy. The Aluminum Company of America (*Alcoa*) had just advertised its new kitchenware: "these utensils will wear forever"; "they will shine on the wall"; "no dirt in the curves of an aluminum pot." The advertisement ran a page in aluminum paint in *The Saturday Evening Post*; and it aroused in Impetigo's breast—as in whose not?—a strong desire to purchase such a pot.

On the *same Tuesday*, however, the Company withdrew all this line from production, distribution, and sale. This was because it was equally essential to set this metal aside for the National Defense.

Here, then, was the *zealous* Mr. Impetigo in a moment of frustration—

He cried, "I want the pot with the Titegrip cover—"

75

The counter girl said, "The Boy Scouts will collect your aluminum on the Fourth of July."

No no! this actual frustration was not what was making Impetigo so frantic, bringing him even to the edge of what is called a "nervous breakdown." After all, he really needed the stewing pot, and such actual impasses lead at worst to physical, not mental, disorders. But it was the horrors of the imagination! Thus, Mr. Impetigo did not drive, but he knew well that the night service at Texaco Gasoline Stations is a refreshing pause for the motorist who, after weary riding through the rain, can *count on* a cheerful greeting. But the fact *also* was that it was forbidden to sell gasoline after sunset and every station was closed and dark. Now imagine—one need not imagine it, it was in a memorable picture—the anxious motorist on the road, his lights glaring in the pelting rain; but he thinks that *round the next turn* (as the ad said) there will be comfort, ha—

Mr. Impetigo was above all an economist. On the one hand he saw with satisfaction that the advertising was becoming keener: the people were responding to it with enthusiasm; there was nothing that everybody did not want and indeed did not absolutely need to have. What a flow of the Commodities this promised! On the other hand, he saw with dismay that the private incomes were inadequate.

The face of the economist went white—

2.

It is a pleasure to turn from this little frenzy to the serene and cheerful confidence of Mr. Tobias Thomas, who was also at the Market on this Tuesday evening.

With a smile of *amusement* Tobias watched the anxiety of Impetigo under his Panama hat.

"Give me a loaf of bread," he said to the girl with easy assurance.

"Here it is, it is eleven cents," said the blonde merchant, producing from the shelf the shining waxen wrapper given form and body by the doughy mass within.

The Commodity Embodied in BREAD

"Is it eleven cents?" asked Tobias, knowing it well, but drawing out even this preliminary with a certain piety.

"Eleven cents."

"*Here* is the money!" said the man quietly, and laid down a dime and a cent on the counter.

Obviously this act, of Exchange, had a certain sacramental character—But no! for look, instead of resting in the moment, or expressing any emotion whatsoever, Tobias leaned confidently across the counter and said in a low voice: "Now, Miss, supposing I wanted to change this bread, eh? Supposing my wife wanted a different brand?"—

This was apparently absurd! The package was Silver-Sup, the same as he bought every day, and that was advertised on the radio by a famous horse. There was no doubt that this was the package.

"You may bring it back if you haven't broken the wrapper," said the businesslike girl.

Ah! Now Toby took up his purchase, whose waxen wrapper, stamped with the name Silver-Sup Silver-Sup and an equine design, was secondarily protected in a manila bag; and he left the Market.

The reader would have thought—is it not so?—that the moment when the man Bought and Paid For the Commodity was the pregnant moment: the moment charged with invisible power to move and keep in motion the two billion human inhabitants of the world and many dumb beasts; to call into being their tools, conveyances, and—in imitation of the First Day itself—their lights. This was indeed a moment! it rested on a mystery. Yet Tobias, though assuming, as we have seen, a decent demeanor in the face of the Exchange, was an orthodox believer and reserved his *unlimited* awe for the consummation of the mystery itself.

There is a form of heresy—perhaps Mr. Impetigo was such a heretic—that rests its faith *in* circulation rather than *by* circulation. Fascinated by the rapid, the accelerating, exchanges—a study which could indeed distract even an acute mind with its intricacy—these persons vainly imagine that such quasi-visible goings-on are the force which keeps us all as we are and which therefore merits our *deepest* meditation. Once I described a hero of this heresy of

Exchangism, the Eliphaz, who sought to turn all his property into money and wrote down his abomination in the *Book of Endlessly Accumulating Zeroes Without an Integer.* But in the end, these persons are Money-changers.

The essential mystery is simple. It does not require of us subtility, like that of Mr. Impetigo, nor heroic inventiveness, like the Eliphaz; but it is for ordinary persons.

On the way home, Tobias once opened the mouth of the manila bag and looked inside. This brown bag had absolutely no primary significance; it was even given away gratis to all who participated in the social acts. There was none too poor to be given a paper bag.

And now, leaning in the doorway of the Apartment house and smoking a pipe in the sunset, Toby saw G. A. Jensen, the Scandinavian janitor with his walrus mustaches. The two exchanged a cheerful greeting. "Good evening," they said. Tobias, the tenant, liked Gustavus Adolphus, who serviced the building and analyzed the Garbage.

But if he knew the truth he might have been disturbed, for the fact was that the Swede was a natural philosopher, with little or no belief whatsoever.

The Apartment house—so named because all the units were enclosed apart—was an imposing structure of six stories with four Apartments on each. The stories were designated by numerals, the Apartments on each by the letters A, B, C, D.

Tobias dwelt with his family in Apartment 3 C in the rear.

These Apartments were rented on the Market, and each painted afresh for its new tenants. When the Lease was signed, they moved in; they scratched the paint with a knife, and the Apartment was then considered out of circulation.

Round the table of Tobias Thomas, besides the master and his wife, were the three children it was necessary for each pair to beget, taking account of accidents.

The eldest, John, understood that when the hermetically sealed package is opened, the goods is out of circulation.

78

The Commodity Embodied in BREAD

The middle child, June, knew that the package was bought for money at the Market.

The youngest was too small to have any understanding, but shouted "bru-le-bullah! bru-le-bullah!" meaning "bread and butter."

Mimi Caffrey Thomas, the wife of Tobias, prepared a shining white platter, with a border of gilt panels containing carmine roses with pale green leaves, to receive decently the whited and rather worthless body of the Commodity after it was taken out of circulation.

Tobias raised aloft the Bread.

—At this reach of inwardness, it is necessary to observe verbal niceties. When I speak of the Bread with a majuscule B, it is the Bread par excellence (*eminenter*) that stood on the counter. There is no doubt that this was the same Bread that Tobias now held in his two hands; for *all* of us may, with our animal hands, *lay hold* on the Commodity in some shape or other. At the same time we must speak, with a b-minuscule, of bread as mere bread. This is to speak physically (*naturaliter*), but there is no help for it, for in the end all language has this natural origin.

Ought we then to refer to the physical bread perhaps as "bread," in quotation marks? No no! this timidity and arrogance (it is both), which *seems* to free our society from material bonds, in reality robs from us the wonder and the glory of our existence, which is just that *we*, as we are, not "we" in quotation marks, somehow do lay hold of the Bread. It seems innocent to say "bread" in quotation marks: it is Docetism. But follow it through! and it is *Exchangism* and the doctrine of the *Book of Endless Zeroes Without an Integer*. It is frenzy and no peace.

In the end we must keep steadily in mind the words of Marx: "The Commodity is therefore a *mysterious* thing."

Again he says: "When it steps forth—" he is referring to the physical table, the physical bread—"when it steps forth as a Commodity, it is changed into something transcendent."

"The existence of the things *qua* Commodities . . . has absolutely no connection with their physical properties and with the material relations rising therefrom."

Tobias tore the wrapper of the loaf of bread, and the exchange-value departed from the Commodity.

This sacrament—this service—this sacrifice of the real being of the Commodity—*sealed* and *revivified* the identification of Tobias and his family with the unity of the imperial Economy.

So long as every one of us can partake of this death, earning by arduous works the *fact* that the Commodity is destroyed for us, the Economy is secure and will not degenerate into chaos. The exchange-value has vanished! By this ever-renewed *fact* the several billions of the world find occupation for their time and the order of the classes is maintained.

At this same instant, the Exchange-value is potentially given again.

In this simple service the family found peace, having bought and in the relevant sense consumed. How different this is from the torment of the Impetigos and the Eliphazes, raging in the Market and their hearts pounding at the late Figures, as if this were the only service! But they do not put their trust in the ultimate Security.

The Eliphaz, intent on changing all the capital into interest, regarded the ultimate consumption, of which we have just seen an exemplary observance, as the original sin!

It was seven P.M., and over the radio sounded the loud whinny of the famous horse himself, whose name was Silver.

The buzzer of the dumbwaiter rang, for the Garbage; and the mother rose to put on the day's refuse, including the waxen wrapper which was now, of course, an insignificant husk.

"Garbage!" sang up the voice of Gustavus Adolphus through the long shaft. The buzzers were sounding also in 1 C, 2 C, 4 C, 5 C, 6 C.

The small child was greedily stuffing a slice of the white bread into its mouth, and Tobias, with fatherly indulgence, was buttering another slice to follow that.

Perhaps I can say something of this physical bread: It had

80

the potential *virtue* of being quantifiable, in pounds and ounces, for the estimation of the Price. Further, it had the convenience (*convenientia*) of being malleable in lumps or loaves, for the purpose of purchase across the Counter and conveyance. It was destructible, tending to harden, rot, or be devoured, so that it presented no temptation (*scandalum*) to Hoarding. At the same time it was rare, so that unlike the air or earth of which it was composed, it offered an incentive (*fundamentum spei*) to be made the embodiment of the Commodity.

Gustavus Adolphus Jensen was a Garbage Analyst.

This science, sorting out the elements into a battery of cans, he pursued partly for the sake of the Economy, reclaiming the precious foils and metals, and the fats and the bones. But mostly he studied the Garbage just to pry and to know.

This, like all learning, gave him *power* over every single Apartment.

He was a natural philosopher and did not judge the bread in terms of its sociological virtues. But not believing this, he fell into superstitions of his own: for instance, he was a believer in the Vitamins.

A little Swede with walrus mustaches, he stood beneath a feeble light in the basement, cautious, often using a tweezers. Slit the manila bags up their backs, picked a pair of spectacles from among the grounds and eggshells, and drew off the serums in syringes. The midges flew toward the light, and Gustav had a little monkey who, curling her tail round a pipe, delighted in snatching the insects from the air.

These were the revealing remnants of private lives.

Sometimes in the Garbage of 1 C he found her golden wedding ring, which he discreetly placed in the mail box.

Something terrifying! 2 C *never sent down any Garbage at all.* But it was only an Exchangist, intent on turning *all* his property into fungible goods and storing it up against the Day.

Every evening Gustav shook his head disapprovingly when he found the wrapper stamped Silver-Sup Silver-Sup. It was his belief that 3 C would be wiser to buy instead the

THE FACTS OF LIFE

ochre wrapper of Lugan's Gluten, on which was plainly stamped the formula "1200 units vit. B1, USP."

—But the great time was Monday morning when descended bales and bales of the *Sunday Times* and nothing else besides!

The monkey had the face of a malicious old person, alert and lively without any curiosity. Sometimes she stood with her long tail drooped over one arm, like the train of a dress. At other times she arranged her tail in a perfect circle on the floor and squatted in the middle of it.

New York City
October 1941

Alcestis

Rescued from death by Force, tho pale and faint.

Breath and gutturals, such groans! hardly human; but the convulsion was apparent only in his face, as yet—in a rubber lip pulled open to the second molar on one side; then incompletely elastic, unstretched no longer hid the point of the canine. The eyes smouldered once. Then—

A comparative calm. He was *a body in a place*; and what he now said was not without reason or at least the form of reason, for it referred to *existent facts*. What he said was perhaps erroneous but *not meaningless*. It was subject to refutation and persuasion; this was worth keeping in mind. He argued that, In the end *the bodies cannot occupy the same place.*

(He was a large man, organic in the least parts and almost proportioned, as are we all who have inherited eons of natural struggles that have allowed very little meaningless to remain in our bodies.)

But what was forcing him out of the place that he could not help but occupy?

Very well for *you* to ask it! he said, but *you* were not aware of the *pressure* in the lungs and the *weight* on the nape.

This did not seem *un*reasonable. It was not always visible bodies of the same apparent kind that crowded each other in the single places. Subtile and penetrating fluids crept in among solid bodies with explosive pressure, and even more subtile was the powerful tug of gravitation that could unbalance even a giant and make him crash.—

But the physiological rigor was again in authority and a crisis was approaching. Two *explosive* expletives broke from his nostrils; it was credible that there was a terrible pressure within—yet it might be self-induced. But no time for speculation! because in a horrible and *alarming* way his *toes* (attention was centered altogether on his toes), the toes of one foot, began to spread apart from each other, to strain upward from stonelike muscles. When they relaxed it was still worse, because they were like the misshapen handfuls of infantile digits in the *Guernica*. Like a jag of lightning the long muscles stiffened, through the thighs and across the back, hunching in the shoulders and pointed in the nape.

This was no longer a joke! What was it he had *explosively* shouted? Stiffening like lightning! Did you catch the words? Two *explosive* expletives! Like lightning!

Especially when now in measured tones—measured in rhythm but edged in timbre, a little explosive in rhythm—he said: "Remaining in the solid space, and I must! I am *hemmed* in by six right trihedrals. In *different* times, no doubt, *many* bodies could occupy a place; but there is no arrangement with me for these changes in succession. The circumstances are *violent*; I am in a way of *violence*." A *gesture* accompanied this.—

But thank God, with a little smile and a gleam of the eyes—so it was possible to see he had pleasant eyes— perhaps with a greedy kind of childish gleam, he looked across to a place at some distance and snapped his fingers delightedly—and this was the end of the gesture! If this was all of it! a simple desire—one would know how to take steps!

For let us dwell, by all means let us dwell, a moment, on the excellent realms of persuasion, which are the affairs of the Soul and of Society, and even the Divine choices are topics for persuasion (though here we invariably persuade ourselves to assent). There are therefore three realms of persuasion, psychological, social, and religious matters. And I confess that we who are expert in persuasion love to exercise our expertness in these three realms of psychology, sociology, and theology. Not that it's easy! on the contrary it is hard to find the right reasons, though there is always some reason or *other*. It is hard to find the right reasons in the troubles of the soul, of love and ease and how to be sure of one's role; it is even hard to do so in the troubles of social exchanges and social status and especially social alteration; and with regard to the Creation, which has made everything what it is in fact, to say prayers of thanksgiving, blessing, and penance is not learnt by one or two disasters.

Yet—by these right persuasions, these wise and often sad persuasions, by these persuasions, a man can meet every contingency, those which we make and those which we are given to make. He can! by persuasions, if he is expert in persuasions—for there is always some reason or *other*. (But I confess that we who are expert in persuasions are sometimes—not bored! for how could one be *bored*, when he is always finding some reason or *other?*—but in a condition of *confident expectation*, that he will surely find some reason or *other*. If a contradiction turns up, this is all the better occasion to turn the problem this way and that!)

What was disquieting if he cried "My place! my place!"—for such must have been the two explosive expletives; or if not these, something or *other*. To tell the truth, it was a little disquieting that a place in a time was not so easily subject to universal considerations; and yet it was necessary, for one was there or not at all.—Nevertheless! how reassuringly he spoke of "changes in succession"; this one could discuss and make some arrangement. And in the end it came to simple desire, a part of psychology and subject to psychoanalysis.

"Right!" he agreed heartily, "in the end I have a difficult personality, subject to fits. Perhaps even medical treatment is called for."

"No self-castigation; this is even worse than recrimination. Let us thrash this thing out together."

"What arrangement are you thinking of?" he asked cooperatively. "By the way, notice my toes."

"You are perfectly right! we have really made no reasonable offer at all, as yet; we are really more to blame than you."

It was impossible to distract one's attention from the toes which he obligingly raised and spread.

"Perhaps," he suggested, "we might begin by—"
A blow fell.
Such a blow fell with the actuality of a creative act; and in the crowded space—for there was only one space after all—spread death.
There were some bodies that used to occupy their places. His foot—just the *other* foot—had strode sideways. Look out!—
A second blow fell. The traitor! had been carrying on the discussion—
Such a discussion was not autonomous! it was used as a device! This was precisely treachery! What persuasion could be hoped for in such a case?
A third blow fell. There only was one crowded space. Next, *teeth*! An agony—
An agony—quite unlike what was customary—seared one and all.
. . . Excuse this pause . . . not so easy . . . to collect one's senses.

Well, now what? (Did a blow fall?) Everything was not quite the same as before. Yet here was that pathetic man, just as before, filling, like everybody else, all the place he was in, though not exactly the *same* place as before. (But did a second and a third blow fall?) His mouth drawn back exposed the third molar. Would it lead to worse? No— (what! also a third blow?)—he relaxed and was able to speak, and he said: "Today I feel as if I had a little bargaining power."
The sentence congealed the blood, not with fright but with a certain tenseness. Yet why? was it not just such a barter that was the form of persuasion? and would one want a co-economist without "a little bargaining power"? And furthermore, the pain was already passing away.
(One or two were lying dead: this was not a persuasible note.)
Why was it is difficult now to take up where one had left off? *Look out!*—
No, on the contrary! it was nothing but the stiffening like lightning. Take it easy.
Easy?! But how to be *quite* easy? when a certain

tenseness—the fascination of looking at the planted foot—

"My good man, we must now take *everything* into account, the past, the present, and the future."

It was necessary to discuss reparations.

Suddenly occurred something remarkable! Which one struck? There was a light and a black. Was it the persuader struck? The confusion made it hard to be sure. One might have heard an edge in that persuasive voice, the rhythm a little explosive. Hold on! at just what topic ought one to begin to talk in these circumstances of violence? There was a light and a black and a light. A second blow fell. Who struck? The blow fell with the actuality of a creative act.

2.

Suppose a man did not believe in the existence of violence.

(I propose this hypothetically because there is no such man; but suppose a man, not in fear but in self-fear, meandered away from violent circumstances, often outflanking them by a treacherous blow of violence.)

Suppose, then, he would suddenly see violence everywhere he looked! I mean not only in war, society, the family, and what he did to himself, but in jarring good reasons, the forced order of universal natural motions, instead of the Music of the Spheres, the

noises of fire, space, and violence!

The persuasive explanation, itself a violent blow, ending with a violent blow. Suppose in his heart he was painstakingly arousing every violent impulse in order violently to constrain it by the violence of a better reason—and nevertheless a blow fell! Suppose the peaceful constitution violently constraining the social institutions was being wrenched by the violent threats of strong interests—and nevertheless the blow of the war fell. Suppose such a man did not really believe that the violence did not exist by which he was treacherously committing violence; then suddenly wherever he looked there was violence!

87

It is easy for us who are expert in reasons to see that there is plenty of violence in the pleasant and constitutional reasons: we are expert in them, we know what *they* are. But then there is the pure violence of the war; in this we *are* not so expert, and we therefore reason (I am reporting what has occurred): "Precisely in the apparent violence of the war there is really nothing but *persuasion*: the war is being urged in order to provide a strong reason, or at least some reason or *other*, in the confusion of society and the soul; nor is this *un*reasonable—" In the midst of this reasoning, a blow fell.

What a release! for a man who did not believe in the existence of violence by which he was treacherously more and more expert in the violence of reasons and especially right reasons, to deal a blow! (sweeping all that away) because he saw that everywhere he looked there was violence. Now he was firmly established in his place! he was assailed by explosive pressure within and by a gravitational tug threatening to bring him down with a crash.

I am *complacent* to deal strong or weak blows, for such blows fall with the actuality of a creative act. The divine choices, by which everything is what it is, is nothing but this *violence*, sweeping all merely possible reasons away. And why should not *I*, at *last*, *imitate* the

noises of fire, space, and violence

of the Creator of the heavens and the earth? And when He still makes each thing, He sweeps all that away, and so He constrains everything in a place.

(Let me whisper: "Hush! there is a secret doctrine that in this way He, who is not a body, has *committed* Himself!")

I believe in the existence of the commitment: my violent savior, the *prince* of peace. (I think that this formula is clear enough.)

("Poor fellow," I persuade myself in a whisper, "if you could see what calm and splendor have been committed in the world, you would not see everywhere you look nothing but violence.")

This wasn't boring now! when I believed in the existence

of the commitment, my violent savior. Dealing strong or weak blows. There was a light and a black and a light. At least there wasn't a confident expectation! A black, a light, a black. "Come Victory!" cried some and others cried "Come Defeat!" A second blow fell. Who struck? A light. Next, teeth. And agony—not like what was usual—seared one and all. Such a blow fell with the actuality of a creative act.

A black.

This was very close to our lives; not boring now. It was not so easy to find some reason or other; at least there was no longer a confident expectation.

A light.

We have committed ourselves: what a release! "Come Victory!" cried some. And others cried, "Come Defeat!"

Such a blow fell with the actuality of a creative act.

("Poor fellow!" I found a moment to whisper to myself, "if you saw what calm and splendor, etc., you would not be lost in this intolerable boredom.")

3.

Hercules appeared
—leading by the hand the queen Alcestis alive

       though pale and faint.

The hero was pacific and resplendent, rosy with wine, and crowned with leaves, and crowned with Victory. He had the gift of speech, such as you might expect from a human being.

The woman was pale and faint and unable to put one foot before the other (so that she moved by bringing each foot alongside, in a kind of a dead-waltz). She was one rescued from death,

      rescued from Death by Force, tho pale and faint.

Now Jove's *great* son gave her over to her *glad* husband

89

(who was no great hero), amid *universal* applause—for who would *hesitate*, at such a *victorious* moment, to applaud to the echo?

The echo of the applause returned faintly from the Thessalian Forests.

Hercules said: "There are beautiful achievements of Force! Be unprejudiced, make no mistake: to win the Victory is not necessarily shameful."

All knelt. As he stood there, crowned, and with the gift of speech, you would have thought that he and not Admetus was the shepherd of the people.

"By Force is won harmony in marriages; it is necessary to conquer the fear of pleasure by Force. And the establishment of a moderate tyranny is the work of Force. This very Thessaly is habitable because the aboriginal beasts were constrained by strength and Force."

The Queen had no strength to speak at all.

"O Admetus! and Alcestis! and people of Pherae!—" he began. The people with a certain edge of timbre cheered to the echo.

The echo of the cheer, etc.

"It was not by Persuasion that I fought with Death!

"He is standing astride the grave.

"I have come in the disguise of a sad person, crying Come, Death! and he—

"Obligingly he tends his hand. *This* is his mistake!"

He cried out and altered the expression of his face, so that the others cried in horror.

The echo of this cry, etc.

But it was only the beginning of a dance. Crowned with leaves the hero danced the Wrestling of Hercules and Death.

Groaned, "Oh, this is now *close* to me. Either I remain in this place or not at all.

"The woman is standing trembling by; how pale and faint she is.

"This is close to my life. Let others set thoughts in motion, that are fatal only in the long run; but as for me, I at every moment know how my dear body is in the place where it is. Then such a joy—

90

"Such a *joy*! next, *teeth*!"

From the onlookers broke a muffled cry.

But Hercules laughed, and relaxed the dance.

No one applauded, and the silence hung heavy, to the echo. The echo of the silence returned enforced from the woods. In this silence sounded the call of birds. They sang, "Look out!" and "Here is the Spring *upon* us!"

"But best of all is Victory!" cried the great son of Jove, and every one applauded him to the echo.

—I for my part have memories that at least in stories the fear of pleasure has been easily persuaded by Eros; and Orpheus with his lute

> made trees
> and the mountain-tops, etc.;

and he *almost* brought back love from hell; and Amphion built a city with a song.

The size of Hercules was nothing extraordinary; but in a unique way he solidified space round him into the very place where he was. This was due partly to his unusually large hands, and also to the firmness of his stance; and his eyes had a possessive awareness of the close-by, almost as if he were short-sighted. Where he stood was a stonelike block of place.

This block of place was no block of stone! (to tug down with a crash). Changing like lightning, it would stand as an immobile block in another position. And if in that motion, one were struck!—

I am no lover of these strong bodies that consolidate the space (rather than freeing and animating it), but it is not hard to imagine that the women and young men were stupefied, as if, seeing so sculptural a figure, they had seen the Medusa. (But the Witch *eats up* the places.)

A few boys and girls drew closer and, as they wished, felt their own places wrenched. Rather close meant very close to one's life! At the same time it was a friendly Violence, our general guardian, and all *our* place was the more secure because no one could come closer to *his*. I do not think "our lives were in his hands," as they say, but rather in his lee!

"Please, friendly Violence! our lives are in your lee!"
—*"Look out!"*

They recoiled; the others blanched. But there was nothing to fear; only that, like lightning, the hero grew stiff.

There is a drawing of the nature of our flesh in which a protuberance of soft flesh is supported from the ground by a crutch; and this crutch, say it is a leg, is itself composed of supporting little crutches, toe-crutches and ankle-crutches; and all the stature of an upright man is a framework of these great and tiny crutches. The tendency of his body is to slump.

Now the giant Atlas is grown from the bedrock itself, and he is as immobile as the world. With blasts of dynamite we chip little fragments of him.

But Hercules is that blast itself.

Momently expecting any calamity, the Thessalians huddled in pitiful fright around their king. But the shepherd-king Admetus reassured them that there was nothing to fear from his guest-friend. He held out a cup, saying, "Please! friendly Violence." Hercules drank.

Alcestis said: "I saw Ixion turning on the wheel and Sisyphus rolling up the heavy stone, and thirsty Tantalus. These are telling sights. All of the huddled dead are brought by here, to learn not to regret what they just lost, such as it was.

"And there was a warrior under a tree in bloom, wearing a sprig of the blossoms in his hat; and swinging a great sword, fought and fought. And because it was in hell, this continued.

"But nothing follows from what I saw, because we are alive."

4.

Most of us are drawing closer to this friendly violence. And more than a few of us will draw as close as we can in order to be wrenched in our places. But in order *searchingly* to be disturbed, Victory is not the best; those who in self-fear need *fatally to* search their complacency must come closer than that to the unexpected blow.

92

In either case there is a moment of inexpectancy; but the victorious blow does not search any deeper than that. But the blow of defeat searches deeper than that! and quickly there is a second blow.

Best of all is to fight a drawn-out losing fight. It isn't boring—to lose slowly—first on far seas; then in the fight of complicated machines controlled by messages, by the pressure of a finger; but the violence comes closer still, to friends' bodies, and lastly to one's own. This is searching, this is deep; a man has *plenty* of time to think over what is befalling so many others on the way. First he says, "Where so many others have involved themselves, why not also I?" and later he can still speak of "the honorable suicide of despair, with clean weapons and no social injury"; but lastly there is only a shout.

The following is still a *comic* incident: A colossal machine, crowded with a thousand men who are tiny by comparison, is simply engulfed; as when the Admiral on the flagship saw the two dreadnoughts sink from single blows and he said, "Something seems to be the matter with our damned ships today." The classic form of this particular joke is the dreadnought going down the ways with flags flying and keeps right on going down.

"De catastrophe à catastrophe nous marchons doucement à la Victoire"—from catastrophe to catastrophe we are going softly on to Victory.

"Something seems to be the matter with our damned ships today."

5. *In Memory of Those Killed in the War So Far*

Today I remind at least myself that several millions have been killed in the war so far. Praised be the Creator of the order of the worlds who has made exist this abrogation of His power.

1. By *"at least myself"* I mean to remind every one who has strong interests in blows both given and received, whether in the aim of gaining victory or suffering defeat.

That it is an *"abrogation of His power"* is proved as

93

follows: A violent end has cut short the natural resources still energetic in each one of those killed, as that such a person can no longer recognize, nor speak German, Polish, Italian, Chinese, my own English tongue.

And let us say *"Praised be"* because we who are alive can recognize that which is, and have a duty to praise it carefully.

2. *"Whether in the aim of victory or defeat"*: Meaning, sad to say, that it has been with a general desire in almost all our hearts for both of these that we have come to the present.

By the expression *"has cut short natural energies"* I contrast the violent with the natural end in which some resources have run themselves out, because this exhaustion exerts a remarkable persuasion elsewhere in the soul, especially when strong desires have run out.

And when I say, let us praise *"that which is,"* I hope it is not in the interests of good or evil for some unknown aim—though this one can find out only progressively; but I am referring to recognizing who and what we are, as, on my part, it has been already a remarkable thing to discover, at a cost not yet fully assessed, something about violence.

3. *"We"*: I say *"we"* not as a collaborator who would prove the necessity and justification of our strong interests, any more than as an adversary to prove their guilt, but simply. It seems that as a whole the war is a delusion; and we share the delusion with one another in fact, so that it is absurd to say even "if so many are involved, why not also I?" But what to do, granting the existence of the war, is not here in question.

By *"persuasion"* also one often won victory and suffered defeat, as when brought to a pause or joyfully seeing a next step; and this was without abrogation of the Creator's right, because it is precisely by proofs from the world that persuasion proceeds, and there is persuasion when everything available is taken into account, so that nothing is cut short. I think that we might have come much closer to our lives by persuasion than we will by this violence, and surely we could have come closer than we did come. If we failed to do so it was that some of us, at least, practiced persuasion as

94

Arts of Peace, and this was no better than to employ it treacherously in Arts of War.

"With no unknown aim I hope, though this we find out only progressively": I am referring, for instance, to this very way of poetical writing wherein is set down whatever presents itself so long as it is molded into the order and emphasis that express my judgment. Therefore I am not ashamed, though reminding myself of several millions killed, to write such sentences as "there is only one place" or "suppose a man did not believe in the existence of violence" or "best of all is victory" or "something seems to be the matter with our damned ships today." At the same time, though I am using my best resources of persuasion, nothing in fact presents itself as searching as our trouble. This is by no means the fault of persuasion itself, which is nothing but the recognition of the order of the world; it is the fault of my resources and their use. And this, because nothing presents itself, is how I know, and not merely feel by sympathy, that "we" are in trouble; and now look, it is necessary to rely on a delusion to search this trouble!

The second and third order of glosses, the gloss on the gloss and the gloss on the gloss on the gloss, expresses less certainty than the text or the first gloss, because it is easier for a poet to find the right thoughts and feeling than to explain what he means. As I proceed to explain I find that I am setting down what is unsatisfactory and objectionable. Thus, *"the necessity of our strong interests"*: the necessity to rely on a delusion: the necessity of a treacherous use of persuasion. And what *"Arts of Peace"*? Great artists came dangerously closer to themselves than that!—as when the musician was undisturbed by the army at the gate; such a musician was not taken by surprise. *"Nothing presents itself"* to say on behalf of the waste of life! Reasoning in this way I have to say a weak thing, that I am in an admitted delusion, and a hard thing, that the dead are dead in vain and nevertheless there is more of the same to come.

If several of us had more closely persuaded ourselves, as by labor, fasts, and so forth, we should at least have the right not to say "we" in speaking of the millions killed, but to say "not I but they." Would this be satisfactory?

But something or other will present itself of general use! for it happens that a strong argument of universal persuasiveness, deeply searched, rallies all mankind, though an instant before there was nothing. At the very worst, disgust with the war will yet persuade us, brothers, deeper than peace or war. Such a disgust is like a hot wind that blows away the fog of our delusion. (One feels its breath sooner and another later.)

These well known facts could not be stated with more authority by the dead themselves if they could speak, for in our commonplace thoughts we share.

[New York City]
[1942?]

Fights

A Statue of "Strength and Weakness"

This allegorical sculpture consists of two figures, Strength and Weakness, represented by a man and a woman. Strength is constraining her on her back, more by his mass and weight than by his power, his knee in her belly and his legs pinning her knees; and his two hands have hold of her wrists and are keeping her hands wide and helpless. And on the face of Strength is a look of intense perplexity.

The meaning of his perplexity is that Strength does not want to exert force on Weakness; yet she is intent on striking him, hoping (for a moment) to exchange blow for blow. On his left shoulder and the right side of his back, Strength is marked with bleeding scratches that she inflicted before he pinned her down.

Being powerful, Strength wants not to strike but to *rule*; he wants, that is, to exert the *persuasiveness* of power. But this puts him in the greatest difficulty when his power is challenged by the violence of Weakness; the difficulty is tellingly expressed by the perplexity on his countenance and even more by the excessive strain of his muscles far beyond what is needed to hold her down, as if he hoped to hurt her merely by forced *inaction,* while at the same time not transmitting this hurtful power to the object, but constraining it within himself, so that the real struggle is the knot of his own muscles! And if the stone could speak, his words likewise would express nothing but ineffectual perplexity, as if to say "Do you give up?" when she will not give up!

But Weakness, on the contrary, wants to strike and be struck just in order to have her own nature made manifest;

97

what she wants is not to be ruled but to be defeated. Therefore on her face is a look of almost exultant wilfulness and
guile—she is waiting her chance. Thus it is Strength who
bears the wounds and the signs of straining, whereas Weakness is as if untouched; and this is a triumph of the artist,
because if he had to express her nature by portraying the
effects of her powers, he would have to resort to the ugliness
of *deficiency*.

So these two remain fixed, by his perplexity and her
wilfulness; and it is this static moment that the sculptor
has seized on for his composition.

2.

It is not only in this moment of spurious external struggle
that Strength is characterized by the struggle among his
own forces, by a dynamic equilibrium of terrible potential if
its parts should ever be loosed together. The artist has
seized on the present struggle to show obvious signs of this
equilibrium, a knot of muscles, a frown. But it is just by
means of those parts of the figure of Strength which are
obviously *not* involved in the unequal external struggle,
that he expresses the *habitual* inner constraint that characterizes Strength. Thus the subtler habit-formed lines of his
face express the day to day perplexity of withholding his
powers in the face of small opponents; and the modelling of
his ankles and toes express an alertness and nervous composure whose meaning is deep just *because* these parts are
unnecessary in the present struggle, since it is clear that by
the weight of his knee and shoulders alone, resting in her
belly and pinning her arms, he is more than able to hold her
down. In these details we are shown the Strength of all his
life, expressed in a particular conflict, but abiding in him in
every case. And his posture, therefore, is almost that of a
dancer rather than a wrestler: there is something fastidious
and almost effeminate in the way he seems to dole out his
force in accordance with the just measure of an idea rather
than the vigour of an instinct. But if we saw him in motion,
it would be an *athlete* and not a dancer, for the gestures of

an athlete are constrained and fastidious when the resistance is weak, but they have terrible speed and power when the resistance increases.

Suddenly we hear him as if saying: "Not yet the time! this is not the time!" to loose his forces. And are we not then overwhelmed by a sentiment of the waste and pathos of his self-constraint? when ever will it be the time?

What is here presented to us, we realize in a flash, is an effigy of *Fear!*

Certainly not fear of something before him, but self-fear. What *crime* is it that he sees within, that restrains him from striking out, or perhaps from striking out *again*? Did he once strike out?

Maybe it is not for any *far-fetched* reason that helpless Weakness is struggling now! She is in *danger*, and she feels this danger pressing close.

This gives a *deep* sense and a *dark* colour to that look of baffled perplexity on the face of Strength!

And if we turn to the woman, we see why it is that the artist has shown her untouched. In this allegorical art where the outward shows the inward, she at least is not *terribly* contorted by guilt. Her wilfulness is—innocence. Her hair is widespread on the ground; her lips and eyes are wide; there is nothing *guarded* here. Willing to scatter her resources—even to blows given and received—for they are what they are; and screaming aloud.

In such a moment, before the perpetration of a fearful crime, the sculptor has fixed these two forever.

3.

What a strange illusion, that the figures of this statue are—in motion!

Is not Strength in the very act of bringing down his great head and shoulders in a kiss? and she of relaxing to this kiss? His hands are *slipping* from her wrists to cover her hands palm to palm; and his knee is *sliding* to rest touching her knee. We see now why he is restraining his weight: it is with the considerateness of a lover, for it is not yet time to

99

lie *full* weight; but it will *soon* be time, when the pleasure is intense enough to transmute force and pain into its greater self. What we took to be a fastidiousness in his posture is nothing but the indefiniteness of beginning to change position. And the perplexity on his face is a sign of passing from one thought to another: one would say that he has just noticed that she is struggling no longer.

The artist has seized on a kind of *lapse* held between such strong contraries that he seems to have dissolved the fixity of sculpture into a motion; the mind cannot rest in this moment presented; it sees the next, and still sees the moment past.

Surely that moment of impasse, when Strength can merely hold on, as if he were himself despairing Weakness, and she is looking only to strike but cannot because he will forever remain too strong—that impasse will resolve itself; for something *new*, as yet unthought of, will well up there. It is not with impunity that, body to body, they have paralysed their own strongest purposes and lie unprepared for whatever wells up.

This Love alone can dissolve the thunderous block of place in which Strength has imprisoned himself.

This gentle violence can alone assuage the crime to which he is paralysed to commit himself.

One would say that they were *lost* lovers, yet completely disengaged (not like those melting loves of Rodin) from the formless rock.

Now notice how the artist has given to Strength, and to the breasts of the woman, a half-erection. In this there is nothing far-fetched; it is what would often occur in persons wrestling.

One would say that they were *lost* lovers, yet completely disengaged from the formless rock.

[*New York City*]
[*1942*]

A Page of Sketches of Fights

Hot Fighters

These two fighters have one mind, to cut each other down. They are going about it hot, doing as much immediate damage as possible, neither one defending himself. Yet they do not much feel their hurt because each is thinking only of destroying the other. Hurt is a blast blowing up the fire. Stung, they hit harder.

They do not frustrate each other. It is even conceivable that both could succeed: for instance, if it is a boxing match, that one might knock out the other and be standing over him with glassy eyes, but when the referee counts four, he himself falls down unconscious.

Each is not much aware of his own body, nor that his legs are braced against the ground. The blows he throws are attracted by, created by, the face to be demolished, and he does not hear his hissing breaths nor feel how his punches have bounded up from the center of the earth. But the impact is glowing loud with joy.

Neither has the aim to inflict damage, but simply to destroy. So naturally they inflict a lot of hurt and damage until, according to their unequal power and skill and luck, one of them is no longer able to carry on his single-minded aim. He is surprised when he is no longer busy cutting the other down. He was not counting on any other possibility. His damaged body has suddenly become a huge thing. And the object before him is fading away, out of reach. A fist

101

looms and hits him—this time he is immensely aware of its slow coming—and he falls.

Looming over him, the face of the victor only momentarily flashes the look of achievement, for it is at once crossed by trying to remember his ulterior purpose in the fight. So the one lies with a look of surprise in his anguish, and the other in his success has a wandering mind.

A Cold Fighter

This time, with the fighter single-minded to destroy is matched a man who is prudently defending himself against being hurt, biding his time till he can coldly smash and cut his opponent down. This man is not single-minded for he is afraid of hurt and death, but he controls his fear by will.

Soon the anger in the fight is streaked with hatred. Perhaps, just as he defends his body with his guard, the cold and deliberate fighter is warding off feeling hurt by taking relish in smashing the other towards his finish. He wants to *damage* him, it is part of his plan. And he is conscious of throwing every blow.

But suppose that for a moment (or for good) he himself is badly hurt and loses control of the fight, while the other still keeps coming single-mindedly to get him. He is in confusion and may be gripped by panicky fear, not knowing what to do and unable to rally spontaneously. For, centered in himself, he has *not* simply been conveying his punches coming up from the center of the earth through his heels across his back to their impact, and now he is out of touch. He crouches as small as he can behind his guard, while the aggressor rains blows on that not impregnable fortress.

But communing with himself behind his guard, he recovers control, he raises his head, and he resumes with a more steely will, like an ax. And finally he has put together enough damaging blows to cut his opponent down, like a tree. Then he stands over him, breathing heavily, safe, clenching and unclenching his fists, beginning to mutter—till at last his passion rises to the surface and he is shaking with rage.

A Page of Sketches of Fights

Heads of Victors

A boy who has fought single-mindedly only to destroy his opponent, and then afterwards his wandering mind finally realizes that he has won: he is grinning and waving his hands in rapturous appreciation of himself, and shouting, "Ma! I won! I won!"

Another boy who fought single-mindedly, but fighting is the only thing in the world that he does honorably and naively, so afterwards his face at once narrows again to the settled suspicous leer of a conceited gutter rat.

Another boy, a deliberate and skillful killer who has maintained all through the fight an impassive countenance; but now he is swept by uncontrollable fear and you can hear the loud clicking of his teeth.

A Coward

A coward, whose blind terror of hurt or death—or simply of the fact that the other is angry with him—has paralyzed his arms so that he can neither strike a blow nor even lift his guard to protect himself. The other slugs him.

His only recourse is to fall down and be passive, screaming in pain even before he is hurt. But this is not a defense, for the other simply mauls and kicks him like a sack. This beating is not cruel so long as the aim is single-minded to destroy him rather than to hurt or damage him. It is ugly when, as a worthless hoodlum might beat a cowardly homosexual, he is vindictively punishing him and taking satisfaction in that; or both are taking satisfaction in that.

But the radical evil in cowardice is that the coward, unable to stand up for himself, has nevertheless adventured into this situation where he has to fight. Doing so, he has not respected, he has violated, his own animal terror, his timorous nature. A man like that should be circumspect.

But it happens that just when he is being beaten up, he may suddenly no longer be paralyzed. In a flash he single-mindedly accepts his terror and, jumping up by surprise, he takes to his heels. He is likely to get away, for his fright is stronger than the killer's will.

Then the tables are turned. The coward is a coward no longer, but simply a weaker but swifter man. He taunts and jeers at his enemy from a safe distance and makes him look like a fool.

A Man Forced Into a Fight

Yet it is a melancholy but common thing in the world (and makes for a melancholy world) that while the one fighter is for some reason single-mindedly bent on destroying a man, that man does not want this fight; he does not believe in it, he does not think that it is worth the hurt and damage involved. He has been forced into it, and it happens that he cannot quit the field.

Even though he guards himself skillfully, he continues to be hurt and damaged. He fights poorly because he does not mean it, to destroy or even hurt the aggressor, but he wants to establish some different relation with him which is incompatible with fighting with him, but which the other will not allow him to establish.

Hurt, he is not stung but made sick. Naturally, doing something that seems to him senseless, he is awkward. It is evident that he is pulling his punches, so that he looks disdainful, too proud to fight or too superior to fight; indeed, he *is* disdainful; except that he is bewildered what to do and he is wincing because he is badly hurt. But even worse, if he happens for a moment to be stung and comes back fighting strong, he is at once paralyzed by prudence, knowing that any damage he now inflicts he will later have to remedy.

So even a strong, wise, brave, and benevolent man is often cut to pieces in this world by the passionate intensity of weakness and ignorance. Somehow he cannot draw on the strength he has. (How then does he "have" it?)

He is felled and on his face are hurt feelings at having been misunderstood. The glee on the face of the victor standing over him fades to its usual spiteful stupidity.

A Page of Sketches of Fights

Arjuna

Is the just man, then, powerless? No, for here finally is a fight—if it can be called so—where though the one fighter is single-mindedly in error bent on destroying a superior man, the superior man is going about his duty and is *incidentally* cutting him down like an executioner. Like an executioner, continually drawing on the power that is in patience, wisdom, compassion, and the joy of life.

This hero is no warrior. He is fastidiously afraid of being hurt, for he has an affectionate love for his body. But he draws courage, as Socrates said, from his idea. The superior man is not fighting in *this* fight (perhaps in some different fight in which he is in agony at midnight, for he is not too proud to fight), nevertheless his fist is a hammer from which the other reels back stunned. And though the inferior man rallies viciously, the right is like an impersonal sledgehammer and fells him.

It was not the hero's wish to degrade his opponent who was so fanatically throwing away his life in despair, unable to prevail against the future of the nature of things; but inevitably the poor wretch takes his defeat as an insult and expires purple with rage, as ignorant in death as he was in life.

The victor is Arjuna, to whom evil does not cling as water does not cling to the shining lotus. He is standing in his chariot with Krishna the charioteer, and they sound their whelks named Fivefold and God-Given.

Heads of Beaten Men

The head of a man who has fought single-mindedly in error, and still in death he imagines that he was worsted by a trick. There is unbelief in his glazed eyes.

The head of another man with closed eyes, smiling, enlightened in death by the precious knowledge that he no longer has to try.

[New York City]
[1960?]

105

Kennst du das Land?

What is the land where lemons bloom, and the rose is red? the land where the orange-trees bloom and the hibiscus is red? Do you think it is always summertime there?

These are flagrant colors; they are the colors of bad popular pictures; there is little in them of nature. Do you think that it is always summertime there?

"Know'st thou the land where lemons bloom?" Aye, I know it well. Ay!

What, is it Spain? . . . It is a country only in the heart. It is the place where each youth plots his manic habit dread, from which he is not released as the time passes.

This is the land where lemons bloom, and the rose is red. Do you think that it is always springtime there?

To such a land went my mother, and there she died on December 22, the day of the winter solstice. And there I too returned in order to bury her body.

Because of an unbearable strain of living desires we could not remain in the same place with each other; but this knot of desires seemed easier to comfort when we were far apart. For then each one was simply tied in knots by desires—and each heart could be separately rent.

Now mama's has been. I am happy now! Happy now! With her now! Now I'm happy with her now!

This is the land where lemons bloom, and the rose is red. Do you think it's not always springtime there?

She it was first let go of the living strain—at longest last and forever and ever. And now I'm happy with her now. I too shall let it go and make the happiness of the little daughter I have. Shall let it go at longest last and forever and ever.

2.

Being in the land where the lemons bloom and the rose is red, I am standing on a bridge, so that of palm-trees rooted below, the crown of fronds is all about me. I press close my eyes to observe these weedy leaves, which I have never seen before. Are they burning with wrath? Not burning with wrath, altho I see them first thru tears. No blame attaches to them.

On the contrary, it is pleasant in this land where lemons bloom. No blame attaches. I think I shall remain here as my mother used to do. Is it not always springtime here?

Pleasant people are walking across the bridge. Our hearts are tied in knots by desires.

The palm-fronds are burning with wrath, altho I see them first thru tears.

3.

The manic habits have the form of understanding without the content of experience. Thus is the soul tied in its own knots. In early youth each one plots the method by which he will disregard the experience given to him and not made by him; and he is not released from this mania as the time passes.

The soul is tied in its own knots; this method is not idle; it is one of the only possible ways of experience of the poor soul. Shall he not grip to it harder as the time passes? Do you have something better to offer him?

Bereft, let us let go of this unbearable strain.

Yes! before my mother died first, it did not seem to me so feasible to die. But now it seems (*God* always willing! for I have not taken leave of my senses and know well who and where I am)—it seems not ununderstandable in itself, and a kind of duty to the little daughter I have, for I am now the oldest of the generations.

Is this the sacrifice that mama made for us? Is this the manic method (forever and ever) by which I am happy with her now?

4.

I came home, to the door. And there within the noisy house—amid the blare of a horn and the bang of a drum and marching song—the grandmother and the little grand-daughter were playing at a parade. I was late to be coming, but they had forgotten about me. Should I now enter and disturb them and put an end to the little parade? My heart was tied in knots by desires, and I could willingly go elsewhere for a while and comfort it. Should I open the door and hear the silence suddenly fall in the disordered room?

They were making a little parade, amid the blare of a horn and the bang of a drum. Their hearts were not, I think, tied in knots by desires. Let go—

Let go the doorknob and do not go in there.

(Know'st *thou* the land where lemons bloom?)

What a noisy house! they are playing at a parade.

I remember, I came home, to the door. And there within the noisy house—with the blare of a horn and the bang of a drum and marching song—the old grandmother and the small girl were playing at a parade. Bereft—let go the doorknob and do not go in there. *Your* heart is tied in knots by desires, etc.

(Do you think it is not always springtime there?)

This I remember, that I came home, to the door. And there within the noisy house—my mother and my daughter were playing at a little parade.

[*New York City*]
January 14, 1943

A Fire on Our Street*

1. Gloss

"I really don't know whether one can look at a fire without a certain pleasure." This is word for word what Stehan Trofimovich said. . . . Of course the very same man who enjoys the spectacle will rush into the fire himself to save a child or an old woman; but that's altogether a different matter.
—THE POSSESSED, III, 2, iii

Not different, but the same. And not altogether different, but the very ecstasy in the burning is the courage for the life-saving—so that a man you would never expect to be a hero, set free by these pleasures inspires us by his deed, rushing into the flames. Another man, who has gotten a more rational and moderate satisfaction from seeing the old junk burn and the lovely fire, calmly and methodically goes to the rescue of the life, concerning which—unlike the house—he does not make comparative judgments: when the scream is heard in the heart of the fire (unless the inhuman sound of the scream unnerves precisely this man). But it is precisely the man who wrings his hands because so much is being lost, and takes no pleasure in the lively fire, who cannot, not will not but cannot, budge an inch.

Note: The familiar essay, once one of the major prose forms in English, has long been moribund, existing only in the essentially imitative efforts of a Chesterton or, much more cheaply, a Christopher Morley. At the same time, through a dissatisfaction with the limitations of narrative and the awkwardness of ideational lyric poetry, both story-writers and poets have, by the incorporation of symbols, arguments, etc., gravitated towards a kind of familiar essay with a stronger formal unity than that of the older rambling, more personal form; for example, the short pieces of Kafka or the *Orators* of Auden. What I have attempted here, then, is a kind of dialectical lyric prose, a form that stems from Hawthorne's *Mosses from an Old Manse.* For a lengthier discussion of the type, see "Literary Abstraction and Cubism," *New Directions* (1942).

111

The fire is burning, the terribly lively flames are leaping into the sky, the upper storey looks already like a Jack o' lantern, and everybody is making a comparative judgment. There are two kinds of comparative judgments: the first is where the terms are held objectively before the conscious mind, and one chooses between them. This is almost the case of our "rational and moderate" man; perhaps he is a Stoic with the maxim *Nil Admirari*, applicable especially to catastrophes, of fire, madness, etc., that astonish everybody else. (But in the face of the ordinary wonders, of flowers, behavior, etc., he allows himself to be indefinitely astonished and delighted, for the Stoic and the Epicurean are the same person.) To him the fire is simply destroying property, economic and sentimental; he hopes that everybody is insured for both; he shrugs his shoulders and bares his teeth (that shine in the bright firelight).

But the second kind of comparative judgment is internal and psychological, made possible by the special presence of astonishment and danger and the surprising fulfillment of hidden wishes, whereby the conscious and unconscious forces in the soul struggle anew and establish, at least temporarily, a new configuration. The second kind of judgment comes to such conclusions as deep delight, heroism, paralysis. Most of the crowd are making this kind of judgment, and it takes the form of passively watching with deep delight—these people who are not used to esthetic contemplations. Some good-naturedly lend a hand to the firemen; others regard the firemen too as part of the spectacle.

A special case is the handful of small boys who are hiding in corners and giggling beyond all self-control: it was they who accidentally set the blaze a-going, and their laughter is the shock of the enormous extension of power starting from such a little stroke of work.

Now one woman becomes a heroine. "Becomes" rather than "is" or "shows herself to be," because these acts of heroism are particular to the circumstances and are not habitual virtues. (But famous Heroes so-called who habitually perform prodigies are rather either Great Men or Wonder-Workers.) Released from a thousand domestic

112

cares which she sees at this very moment going up in flames, this woman feels suddenly a supernormal flood of ability in those things concerning which we do not make a comparative judgment; and she rushes to save, as Dostoyevsky says, the "old woman or the child." The deed inspires us all; it is precisely deeper than the personal interests that divide one from another; there is no place for envy, but all cry out with anxiety and then joy. Thus, when I spoke above of a person whom "you would never expect to be a hero," it was careless language, for every hero is such a hero, by exception; and every hero, drawing on the common power of humanity, performs a simple deed that cannot fail to take every heart by storm. All her senses, it seems, were abnormally alert and unroutinized; and she carried off the rescue with glorious perfection, as if step by step were inevitable. (Heroes rarely fail.)

But let us look again at our rational moderate onlooker, the Stoic who is also an Epicurean. Realizing that life was at stake, he would himself have rushed to the rescue, and carried it off, or failed to, without glorious perfection—except that he, obviously just he, has been unnerved by the inhuman cry for help. Such a cry he had not thought of, it upsets his calculations. Not that it was an inhuman cry; on the contrary, because it was a truly human cry: the old woman who cried out face to face with death. How can this cry, and the sympathy that thrilled in him, have come into his calculations? Next moment the rescue has been effected; but whereas everybody else shouts for joy at their *extra* good fortune, beyond what was calculable, thanks to the heroic deed, he by exception feels guilty. Rightly so: for what right does he have to enjoy his equanimity by exception if he is not in fact prepared? Now then, this is the kind of man who a moment later might perform a deed not of heroism but of self-sacrifice, having just become aware of the possibility of danger to his dear self and unable yet to rationalize the new fact. He is only looking for a way: perhaps he will kill himself to save a cat.

At last the blaze dies away to its embers, leaving the night darker than ever. And as the reflection of the fire fades from their faces, the fire dies also in their hearts. And now is the time for those who have lost their homes to wail for them.

What is the matter with that Russian author, whom one would expect to be an authority on the fires in the street and the fires in the heart, that he makes such errors and writes of "a certain pleasure" as if it were guilty, and of simple humanity as if it were "an altogether different matter"? The original cause of it I don't know; but on the level of ideas it comes from his mistaken conservatism and his catholic orthodoxy. The things we possess, big institutions and little houses, are divine in genus not in species; they are only second nature, made by us as well as given to us, and always subject to a comparative judgment. Divine in genus in the sense, for instance, that men will surely have some kind of society or other, but any special kind can (and even does!) go up in flames; but human life is given in species along with the trees and the bears and the lively fire itself. Everybody knows it and makes this comparative judgment in the face of the fire. It is not original sin, but almost God's ease, if a few grin and the rest give heartfelt sighs of pleasure when the roof caves in.

2. Scene

A few days later the boys venture to play among the retaining walls and the ruins, dancing forever to the famous rime:

> Mama's in the kitchen
> Pappa's in the hall
> So I can leave my thumb-print
> Upon the parlor-wall.
>
> And when the licking's over
> The pain will pass away
> But the thumb-print on the parlor-wall
> Will stay and stay and stay.

They are making forts in the ruins and clubhouses in the debris. Other boys come, but they drive them away with

114

stones, crying "It's our'n! it's our'n!"

"Why's it your'n?"

No one is such a fool as to answer this, but they drive them away with stones.

When you pull up a floor-board, a fire still smouldering underneath leaps into flame, and is the source for a bonfire, small but commemorative, continuous with the original conflagration.

Tying a string to a tin can full of fire, a boy is whirling it in a circle dropping sparks. It means:

> All that is best is easiest
> And all that is easiest is best.

It is easy to enjoy an enormous extension of power by co-operating with the fuel stored in reserve by generations.

> Will stay and stay and stay!

"It's our'n!"

As night falls, there are four and five starry fires, and more than one whirling can, between and roundabout the retaining walls. The policy of the boys does not exclude free fires. (Especially since there is plenty of charred fuel.) When they dance about, you would almost think that they were the fires.

"It's our'n!"

They drive off the others with stones. During the fight they snatch up tops of ash-cans as shields, crying "It's our'n! It's our'n!"

> The pain will pass away
> But the thumb-print on the parlor-wall
> Will stay and stay and stay.

There are ten and twelve starry fires peeping and blazing among the retaining walls. As they hurry from one to another of these, you would think that they themselves were streaks of fire, and that

THE FACTS OF LIFE

All that is best is easiest
And all that is easiest is best.

[New York City]
April 1943

The Dream of a
Little Lady Painter

—for Judith

1. *Interpretation*

Always painting the statues looming and shining in the
night on the plazas; painting her boyhood lost; painting the
child she wills not to have. She does not think about the
objects she paints; she thinks hard about the colors, planes,
and the composition; but when once she tried to think
about the objects, the work was frigid. (Good enough; for it
is only wonder-workers in the art who can think also of the
objects; not that they control the painting with their
thoughts, but that one way and another it is the quick of the
soul; that the colors, planes, and the composition are hidden thoughts, and the objects are already strokes of art.)

"Why do you always paint such statues looming and
shining in the night on the plazas?"

Says, They are nothing but decoration.

The lady is so simple that she has been able to dream a
universal, typical dream, a dream beautiful of itself. She
dreamed,

That on a plaza in a carriage is a baby, her own, a very
swarthy little girl; and growing from its belly, "connected
like a Siamese twin," is the identical little swarthy girl, but
doll-like in size. The two move their hands perfectly in
unison, but as mirror-images: when the girl waves her right
hand, the lively doll waves its left; when the girl scratches
herself with the right hand, the doll scratches with the left.
The dreamer is petrified with horror at having such a monstrous child, tho the little ones seem happy enough, and the
carriage is wheeling gaily round the place. . . . It vanishes,

117

and a small boy is standing there weeping; extremely fair, his hair yellow as corn, and he has enormous round blue eyes, ringed with red from weeping and because he is almost an albino. "Why are you crying, little boy?" "I am crying because I see too much."

The lady herself has very black hair; she is sexually attracted to blond men. She has the utmost horror of having a child, and therefore of becoming pregnant; her sexual pleasure is made anxious by this fear. History of early masturbation. She paints ambidexterously—no, rather she draws with her left hand and paints with her right. It is "in drawing and composition that the art exists"; the lyrical emotion of her works seems to me to consist especially in the painting.

Now look at the statues looming and shining in the night on the plazas; *glooming* and shining, for they seem to turn from the darkness into the moonlight, they vary from dusky brown to glaucous white: some are quite dark, others are of both shades, others are shining white. Those that are white are free in their airy, almost perspective space; those that are dark are in a kind of box, in a place rather than in space. The former are pleasanter, but the others are "closer to the art."

Always painting such statues looming and shining in the night on the plazas; painting boyhood lost; painting the child she wills not to have; drawing them "according to the art" as she thinks a man does (her teacher was a man), but coloring them with tender gradations (contrary to her teacher's precept).—

Painting such statues glooming and shining, at night; for her dear boyhood sake; and her child; and painting herself petrified with horror.

But thanks to the Creator Spirit, that sets free in joy the dammed-up forces in the world, and they flow like the torrents of the spring, there is nothing in her busy enterprise of *loss* or *mourning* or *anxiety*. Comfortably drawing on forces not her own—and the many pictures gaze from the walls, or are stacked in boxes and closets—so long as she does not question them—*always able* to paint such statues, etc.

118

Dream of a Little Lady Painter

2. Scene

Now our plazas had become nothing but the meeting places of arteries of traffic, flowed thru by the streams of automobiles and 'buses and street-cars and streams of pedestrians; and the stations of underground railroads. Above these loomed day and night the statues—as high above Columbus Circle the statue of the Admiral, and the monument of the sunken Maine at the entrance to the Park, ship's prow mounted by a boy, flanked on either side by Neptune and Death. With such plazas as these was lost the community of our city, for the community of a city is its sociable squares and plazas (enclosed, as Sitte showed), where the people gather from the adjacent houses, temples, factories, and markets, to converse, to haggle, to wait, and watch; to loiter, to *flâner*; to orate; to recapture the norm of social life.

But now we have again enclosed our plazas, where the statues loom by day and night, and have set the fountains to playing.

Now our plazas are again like the Scene in Roman Comedy, a public place on which the doors of the characters open: open, not as in tragedies to reveal the hidden secrets of the palace, but for the thousand private awkwardnesses and mistakes to emerge and be aired, and rectified in the social norm—with a great release of glory.

And the smokeless factories are no longer on the outskirts of the town whither they were—no, not banished, but they used to drag us all away from the community of our city. These also have doorways on the square, and the people frequently emerge to air out that kind of labor in a social norm.

And might you not also expect (as in the Roman Comedy) that those statues will cease their always looming day and night, and occasionally relax—the boy come down from the prow to the delight of the pederasts; Neptune ride off in the rainbows; and Death.

[New York City]
May 1943

119

For My Daughter
on My Birthday

This monstrous man has a hundred arms and hands, with which he gathers his needs and exerts his will: from all sides, in all directions; but he goes resolutely forward in control of it all. Indeed, unless he is manipulating his hundred faculties, gathering, sorting, arranging, poising, and striking, he hardly feels that he is moving freely, and not being forced to move. Tie one hand down, tie it behind his back: with what precision and prudent consideration he exercises the rest; one would say that he is so much the stronger for a little restraint. And what if all but two were tied down and he were like an ordinary man! (It makes a difference to have once been able.) What if these last two were tied behind his back: he looks as if he could bite, and hold on tenaciously. Yet he suffers the illusion that except in that loose and hundredfold maneuvering he doesn't exert his own will at all, or that he exerts only his will and not his spontaneous ease, not himself; but perhaps this ease that he imagines is only the twiddling of 500 thumbs—as we say that a man is all thumbs—for it is almost impossible for such a man to achieve the mastery over his too many hands. Sometimes the circumstances are such that the end of one of his little fingers is caught in a trap: then all his muscles are paralyzed and he can hardly lift one fist to defend himself. But beware!

2. *A Sentence of Rabbi Akiba*

> *If I am not for myself, who is for me?—*
> *and if I am for myself alone, what am I?—*
> *and if not now, when?*
> —PIRKE AVOTH

If I am not for myself, who is for me?

What does it mean in action? is it correct to say it first? what does it mean for himself if a man says it first?

1. Taking thought for *himself,* he withdraws his solicitude from the other things, which are wealth and good repute. For the objects of wealth, tho they seem to cater to one's comfort and self-esteem, are not so close after all as the dear self; they are a distraction from the dear self; and they are valued according to a social estimate. And reputation most of all, to keep it and enhance it, requires one to adopt the social estimate. (But desire and the satisfaction of desire are not solicitude for the other things, but for one's own life and its little secrets.)

In this course, however, the external things go practically from bad to worse: then by following it is one not hurting himself after all, for soon he cannot proceed even in elementary safety? No; for he takes *comfort* in his dear self, and he at least is always there, safely or dubiously—so far.

2. And it is correct to say this *first.* But most men proceed in the opposite order and try first to master wealth and good reputation (to keep their reputation before getting wealth, and to get wealth in order to enhance their reputation); they are content with a *convenient* arrangement, where it is not a compromise arrangement, of their wishes and little secrets. To begin in this way is practical and everything conspires to it, in a society whose chief aim is to be safe from one's-self and to rely on the example of the rest to confirm the avoidance. Thus, if one is not for himself first, it is unlikely that he will ever be for himself.

But since the soul springs alive with the reasons of the world, is it not after all better to be for one's-self in *them,* as we proceed in the education of the young? No; for in fact the accomplishments of men have never yet been carried thru save in desire and little secrets, and the perfect artists taking comfort in themselves.

3. Therefore, taking thought first for himself, he takes little account of the other things—not in hostility or contempt or defense, whatever it might seem, but because he becomes every day more and more closely involved and concerned. For suddenly it comes about that the self in which he has become involved has no *position* of comfort—tho there is plenty of comfort in every flashing desire and the revelation of a little secret—no position of comfort, but everywhere concern. In this way it is possible to undo that evil self, that stands in a man's way whether he looks in or out.

But if a man, making a convenient arrangement, etc., devotes himself to the other things, then at every moment he affirms himself by use of himself rather than by concern for himself, so that: might it not be said that it is just this man who devotes himself to the other things and forgets himself who is in fact for himself? Yes! he caters to himself, except to just that deepest wish of himself, which is for the death of that small self.

And if I am for myself alone, what am I?

Nothing. The next moment there is nothing left of the self-centered little self. But there is the revelation of little secrets into modest or enormous powers. They are not the powers of the self, but are strange to it; they have an easy motion that seems like violence. Then desire withdraws from the imagination where it has been confined and heated by the self (as in a stewpot), and in place of such contrary desires burn the simpler powers from which desires began when the self conceived them as its desires.

I know it only partially, and partially only intermittently: then I cannot tell just what has occurred here. Whether the energy of the soul is finally exhausted, that used to be for one's dear self; and this is plausible, because I know—not partially or intermittently—that I am more

123

tired, and there is no quantity of comfort left in a flicker of desire or an expected revelation, but such things go on only by habit and forcing. But whether this is weariness of the soul or just weariness with the self. Or whether the self vanishes into nothing when, by close concern with every contrary motion of itself, finally it becomes a little more expert and its contrary motions harmonize into the simpler floods from which they began.

Now these simpler powers in which the self comes to be not for itself alone, are some original but some are the causes of the anxiety by which the self came to be. (For the self on its hidden side is made of deprivation and anxiety.) Such a cause is being a father. For a man looks in himself for his father—but he finds only himself. But by close concern with his anxiety he finds—perhaps after his child is grown—that he is a father. Or so, again, he falls simply in love, without imaginary concerns for the shape of features, and he is not for himself alone.

Is there an ambiguity? when he is not for himself alone, does it not imply that he is also himself, and his self is not nothing? Yes! for God forbid that I should say that the self, which is the first greatest work of the creative soul, has become nothing at all; but it is stripped of its bulwarks of avoidance.

And now the imagination, like the eyes darkened by sunshine and flaming with the changing suns of the recovery from fatigue, is inhabited by impersonal images, clear and expressible; strange; that speak at once from heart to heart.

And if not now, when?

The sum of powers from the creation of the world, and their restraint and exhaustion which are also forms of effective power, are about to recreate the world at this instant; and he who draws on this strength of nature, can he not ride the whirlwind and cause the grass to spring alive?

Now—now is the instant to stretch one's hand, when the little past that stood in the way, whether one looked in or out, has vanished into this momentary end result of the long process of time: for it is (thanks be to God) by the original creation, and no longer by the sickness of himself—for

124

For My Daughter on My Birthday

we had come a long way to our present-day diseases—that a man has become what he is. Then the causes of the disastrous outcome—and what a strength they had to have brought a hundred hands to the paralysis of non-commitment!—are the strength with which he now stretches forth a single hand, to gather, to sort, to poise, to strike, to extend a hand in friendly greeting.

The Rabbi has exhausted the field of ethics when at this point he commits you to existence itself, saying Now! if not now, when? But supposing he had said this first, then the infatuation in which we are would become actual folly; and supposing he said it after urging a man to be for himself, then the result would have been actual suicide instead of the death of one's-self. And supposing he had failed to say it now, he would have left a man the prey of vastest dreams.

But now is the time of miracles small and great. So small that the difference from before is imperceptible; watching the wonder-worker, you could not tell the difference to the blinking of an eye; yet there is a miraculous difference. So great that a mountain is removed, as is done by faith.

It's as safe, for an hour, to swim on the *high* seas as in the waters of the cove.

—Even if the manly cry is swallowed by the roar of the gulf.

On the *high* seas—
Crying "Swim! swim!"
"Well, and I *did* swim"—especially *because* both hands were tied behind his back!

"No use tying both hands behind my back, because I'll swim anyway"
Or—
"No need now to tie my hands behind my back, because now I've decided to swim"
Or—
"If—maybe?—*one* hand were untied, now I could try to swim?"

125

On the high seas

On the high seas, there is a drop that "sinks into the shining sea"; and there is a swimmer who, by resisting the element, stays afloat for an hour in the light of common day. There is a wreckage that floats easily by; it floats by. There is a ship that would lord it over the deep if there were not a spiritual turmoil aboard it.

"Take me up, sailors, into your great ship, and I'll tell you a story to bring you peace."

South Windham
September 1943

The Knight

Chivalry is Pride Aspiring to Beauty.
—HUIZINGA

Nothing comes from nothing. These superstitious people are pitiful.

With love and loyalty they cling to, they hinder, their man of power and accomplishment; of sweet ease; of patience and instruction and social gayety; who can create something and has a new idea. Their hearts lift when he appears; they are grateful when he remains. Then next moment they are offended to discover that he does not live as they do. Out of their own glossary of banalities they fit interpretations to him; none of these fits; he is suddenly strange and repellent. What! are *they* persons of power and accomplishment; of sweet ease? If their conceptions were adequate to him, would they too not create something and have a new idea? Do they imagine that all the difference in the world comes from no difference at all? And that he will shock them according to their expectations? (This is precisely not to shock them!) But nothing comes from nothing.

Their spokesman steps forth and says: "Admitted you are better informed, have thought more about it, know your mind and have an idea—nevertheless we maintain our opinion." And at once he runs away and hides. Say: "You servile dog! Run away quick before I rub you the wrong way and teach you respect for evidence."

Well! Next winter let them sit without social gayety and sweet ease.

No. Noblesse oblige. (It is too pitiful.) Our man of patience cannot not lend his hand, because noblesse oblige. He can, they cannot, therefore he must: noblesse oblige. For otherwise the work is badly done; it is servilely thought and timidly effected; and it awakens a disgust in every artist heart. If one has an artist heart, noblesse oblige. It is all right, you hateful little brothers, hinder as much as you can; he will nevertheless lend a hand, noblesse oblige.

I think there is resentment on *both* sides, but no matter! No matter! For the hateful little brothers are in need and it is by a law of first nature that they cling with love and loyalty; and on his side, noblesse oblige.

Next moment the resentment is grinding on the resentment, with flashing sparks. "Ha! Is one of *you* a person of power, and has an idea?"

Then he draws a line in the sand. "Cross that line with your idea! Only don't run away—for God's sake, don't hide," he cries with bitter loneliness.

And one steps up, up to the line, and crosses it.

"Now you are on my side!"

Do you think it is only a childish joke? No, no for when the new champion turns round to look where he is, he sees that all the others are in hiding, and he is on the side of the line with his brother. Do you imagine that there is now a sad, drawn out, lonely fight? No, they are laughing.

Every champion is an immortal peer; and they battle in tournaments according to the rules. There is no mortal blow. How could there be a mortal blow when every blow (given or received) is freely drawing on the power of the heavens and the earth? Meantime each one is secretly longing for a mortal blow.

It is now too late either to die or live, because noblesse oblige. Jean therefore said, *"L'ennui mortelle—l'ennui mortelle de l'immortalité."* (One would willingly commit some folly just to live on among the little brothers.)

But they are so superstitious, in what language is one supposed to talk to them? They believe that something excellent is achieved; they do not believe there is a natural cause. Here is a poem and every common word is bent to the expression; but they do not believe that the poet has, perhaps, a different integrity of life and speech than that which has led them to abuse their words in advertisements; they say, "Why need he have a low standard of living?" A

128

teacher sees a beautiful and gifted boy who spends the days broodingly playing dice with himself (and marking down the score); the others pretend not to notice it, but the teacher patiently hour by hour awakens him, teaches him boldness toward the girls, and sets him free; then they think that the teacher will not have been in love with the boy. A man has set himself to reform the communities by returning to the functions of humanity and assuming that first things are first; then they are angry that he will not take part in an agitation that assumes the American economy as a whole. But nothing comes from nothing.

"Why need he speak so closely?"—"Why need he be in love?"

"You servile dogs, run away quick before I rub you the wrong way!"—is this the language in which one is supposed to talk to them?

No, no, noblesse oblige. And on *their* side it is by a law of first nature that they cling to, and hinder, him with love and loyalty.

And so you think, on *their* side, it does not take courage to put up with, with love and loyalty, such a hard man who does not relax his smile as he saps the consolations of habit and arouses secret longings, perhaps best forgotten? Sometimes they would dearly love to stone that smiling knight. Instead, gathering up their cattle and their children they have gone into hiding behind their walls, for here he comes, deadly marauding.

Deadly marauding, grinning, flaming in his nether parts and tongue.

The little brothers are in hiding, cowering behind their walls. It is not gay there. There is not much consolation in their habits. And because there is no idea, there is no patience, because it is hard to be patient without a strong idea. They are becoming short-tempered and because they are longing for the exhilaration of a stroke of power, they are soon degenerating into violence on each other.

Why does he not come with this challenge? deadly marauding. With his affront? flaming in his nether parts and tongue. With his patience? Has he not a new idea to offend them with? Has he not courage to drain from his heart hour by hour in quiet love? Noblesse oblige!

2.

The knight is "in his pride" (as we say a man is "in his cups").

His mind is closed until further notice.

His will is clenched until further notice.

(*God* take care of him, until further notice.)

He is ridiculous. He has begun to live by points of honor.

Now a point of honor is nothing but a principle of a man's integrity that he insists on when he no longer has to struggle for his integrity. For after a while a man of integrity becomes secure in his knightly integrity; he cannot be tempted from it, for nothing is so satisfying as his integrity. His *integrity* is in no danger. Why does he insist on a point of honor? He is preposterous. He is stripped to the naked pride.

His mind is closed until further notice. He feels, until further notice, that he is "alienated." That is to say, he feels that the principles of social existence of *those* people are not possible principles of existence for *him*. Therefore there is no use of listening to them, but the strategy is to attack at all points. (In fact he does not attack.) Good! but attack at all points. Instead, stripped to the naked pride, he has begun to live by points of honor, as if what they said made a difference after all.

God take care of him, until further notice, for he is not going to take care of himself.

He is preposterous, why should we not make a ridiculous analogy of him? He is like a vacuum-bottle, shut off from us all and with his bright armor reflecting back inward to preserve his little heat (as if all heat did not come from the sun and from radioactive fires). Surely some one will carelessly drop this fragile bottle and spill out the tepid soup.

His will is *clenched* until further notice—because the courage is slowly draining from his heart. Oh!

Oh, I ought not to have made a joke of him, for look, his hands are clenched and the tears are starting in his eyes; and this beautiful and gifted boy—this beautiful and gifted boy

130

is so exhausted that he is broodingly spending the days playing dice with himself (and marking down the score). Am I a teacher?

> I stripped to the naked pride
> ride rapidly (I lend you aid
> noblesse oblige along the way).
> My pride aspires to beauty, I
>
> have no peace among these folk
> I cannot serve and will not strike.
> Lord! give me peace at last, as surely
> as Thou hast given me vain glory.

—But in fact you *don't* ride! Instead you broodingly spend your days, etc. (This beautiful and gifted boy—Am I a teacher?)

3.

Dear boy, stop rolling those dice a minute (and marking down the score), and I'll tell you the history of chivalry and of the beasts of the plain.

Long ago when George and Hercules came by here marauding and slew the animals, it is likely that those animals had really bitten the simple folk. For it was by original resolutions—yes, resolutions often made by night and carried out in the light—that the forest was made habitable for us all.

Later! there was a noble Knight demented who used to ride here, and he had terrible enemies and often gave battle. But these enemies, we are told, were nightmares of his own, they existed only in his imagination, and the battles were battles in dreams. But at least the simple folk ran no danger from them, if they could keep out of the way of the Knight's fury.

And now! (for the history has 3 parts), do you know what the situation is on the plain, on this smiling plain traversed, as you see, by easy streams? From right to left it is peopled by monsters, by threats, by subtleties. And none of these exist. They are the hobgoblins and nightmares of the folk themselves, who seem to have grown quite demented. And it is a lucky man indeed who riding freely by and failing to cry out according to the custom in the face of something that does not exist, is not himself taken to be a Giant or a Magic Pitfall, and cunning intentions attributed to him which if only he had them would long ago have made his fortune. Then it would now be necessary to write the reverse of the history of Don Quixote, for a thousand chimeras and oriental chasms exist everywhere except in fact and before a candid gaze.

These people believe in what does not exist. But we shall see that it is because they have trained themselves to believe that what exists does not exist, that they have come to believe that what does not exist exists.

But alas! the wretched knight who would like to perform a serviceable deed finds that he cannot employ the most obvious natural means—such as direct action, or releasing desire, or the use of words to express what is the case—he cannot act, that is, in the only ways that make an act immortal, without becoming involved in the phantasmagoria.

Woe to him if for one moment he even hypothetically recognizes the existence of these fictions and tilts at them! for then there is no end of it and all the courage is drained from his heart. But there is a mystical gesture that I am going to teach you; use it when the occasion arises. Wave your right hand in front of your eyes in mock despair, so, and say "Oof," as a man does when the madness has become too thick. For it is too thick.

For God's sake, boy, do not, stripped to the naked pride, do not begin to entertain delusions about yourself and your own role, and confound the romance, so that there is *nowhere* a norm of serviceable reason. I have heard tell of a cult of knights gone demented who have a blazon with the motto "Alienation": they are "alienated," they say, from the values of the folk. They are preposterous: they are taking the dreams of these folk *seriously,* as if such things existed, as if such non-things were the cause of the social existence that these people have (such as it is). But nothing

132

comes from nothing. To the degree that society exists it does not exist by fantasies but by natural powers and plenty of good endurance. This is also our society. As for the rest, what kind of man is it who feels he is alienated because somebody else has a bad dream?

No, no, use the little gesture and do not forget to say "Oof."

Do not attack at all points. Do not attack at all. But use, *use* (noblesse oblige) the most obvious natural means, direct action, releasing desire, and the use of words to express what is the case. To them it will seem that you are attacking at all points! How can they fail to imagine that you have cunning intentions which, if indeed you had them, would long ago have made your fortune?

This is the time to use the little gesture and say "Oof."

Others will cling to, and hinder, you with love and loyalty.

After a while their champion will step forth. Challenge him! Draw a line! If he steps across this line—

Now he is on your side.

4. *Sketches for a Romance by an Author with more Heart for it than Myself.*

We rode forth together, the young Welshman and I— except that I do not really ride; but *he* rode and had his adventures, which I am too old for, whilst I mainly sat, here and there, and exchanged thoughts and gossip.

He kept his blazon hidden.

But I carried a sad shield and a sadder motto, though my heart is calm I swear, and God forbid that I should utter a complaint in this providential world that continues to reward me for virtues that I all unconsciously acquired, by the way, when I believed that I was solely bent, with all my ardor, toward my single goal. (And that ardor itself, that burnt my soul, has perhaps had its own reward, though I mistook it often for punishment.) But my blazon was—a Wintry Sun; and my motto was *J'aurais servi: I would have served.*

133

THE FIRST ADVENTURE: THE THREE DAMSELS BEWITCHED

There were three maidens who lived together in an apartment and daily went to business. Their names were Leah, Clotilde and Hermione.

These three closely attached themselves to Davor, not only because he was gifted and handsome, but also because although he was as young as themselves, he was not under a spell. But they were entranced in a deep spell.

They were wasting away in their little apartment, and each time he came to dinner he noticed that they ate less and less of the food, and one of the girls was losing her eyesight.

Clotilde wanted with all her heart to be a dancer, and she worked at modelling dresses.

Hermione wanted to be a dress-model, and she was a typist.

Leah wanted above all to be a housewife, and she worked far into the night as a bookkeeper.

Continually, with bright eyes they talked of their several ambitions. They grieved that the time was passing. And they complained bitterly of the peculiar hazards of their daily jobs with respect to their chosen careers.

Thus, to keep the slimness of a model, Clotilde was undermining the strength necessary for a dancer. By bending over her typewriter, Hermione was distorting the posture necessary for a model. And even in the evenings, Leah could not see her little son.

"What!" cried Davy, "if you have a child and you want above all to make a home, why don't you make a home?"

"The worst of it is," said Leah, whose husband was a sailor in distant seas, "the worst of it is that my husband does not know that my eyes are going bad because of my job, and I am afraid to write to him that I wear glasses, because maybe he will stop loving me."

One of the chief things that stood in the way of Hermione's becoming a model was the following: As a model she would make what seemed to her a munificent salary;

134

but she had been strictly brought up and she felt, in the bottom of her child heart, that she was worth only enough money to pay for her board and lodging; therefore she worked as a typist.

"Look," Davy said sharply to Clotilde, "have you ever tried to make a living in a dance-company?"

"Yes I have. But what I want is to get some money so that I may study seriously."

"Are you saving any money?"

"No. You see, to be a model I have to spend so much on clothes, to look the part."

Obviously these young ladies were demented.

They were under a spell.

Before it is possible to go directly to what one has at heart, one must deviate into a means to the end, which to be sure does not lead to the end but contradicts it. For otherwise! if one did not deviate, there would be the *danger* of attaining what one has at heart.

But noblesse oblige! the young Welshman slept with Clotilde and then she became a dancer after all.

And Hermione, who desired to exhibit herself and therefore hid herself in a deformed posture—when she knew of the seduction of Clotilde, now took her friend's job and exhibited herself after all.

And weak-eyed Leah inherited the apartment and brought home her little son.

Thus in glory ended the First Adventure.

THE SECOND ADVENTURE: THE CLOISTER OF THE ÉLITE
OF THE BELIEVERS IN MAGIC

We came to a great University where old friends of mine did their research and made programs for the nation; and I thought it would be salutary if Davor became acquainted here, in this pleasant square shaded by maples.

(I say "old friends of mine" because I remembered that there was once in them a spark of life. They often do not act as though *I* were a friend of *theirs*, but I do not live by points of honor.)

Now these professors gave themselves out to be scientists of society. "Let us hope that they are physicians of society, for a physician follows close after nature"; but I was dubious, because in their dress and manners my friends looked, not like naturalists, but like small financiers.

In fact this maple-shaded square proved to be the cloister of the élite of the believers in magic.

They believed in the miracle that our social world continues to exist and even to change without a chain of proximate causes. And they believed in the influence of the invocation of Names. It was because of the Names of certain social relations that a Mister made profits.

They did not (like Karl Marx) follow the harried people into the market; and one did not hear them mention the lust and the anxiety by which a man takes leave of his heart in the morning to go to work.

Was it a mere short-cut in formulation? No such a thing! for these Names formed a great *system* of Names to keep our society in being; and in this system there was no loophole for the direct action of men.

For the direct action of a man and his brothers and sisters who one day come to their senses and—initiate a chain of proximate causes. Eh?

No fear! no fear! Direct action unmediated by a name has no place in social science. Therefore no fear!

In their personal contacts with each other, my friends had become great experts at avoidance. They had invented the remarkable categories of Private Life and Professional Life; and with regard to the folk, they spoke of the Primary Environment and the Secondary Environment. Therefore, having *taken* leave of their hearts (morning and evening!) they easily came to take leave of their senses.

Oh, when a true man is found in error, he is paralyzed, because his thoughts go very deep and close; he blanches and his hair stands on end; he tosses a sleepless night and alarms his bedfellow. This was not to be much observed at the University.

136

The Knight

But Davy, as soon as he saw that the manners of my old friends imitated those of small financiers, began to draw heavily on the excellent sherry.

For us, Professor T. had set to making tea.

It was not *altogether* my friends' fault that they were superstitious, for the common people themselves had come to imagine that they really acted according to their Names and affiliations; so that the science of the Names really seemed to describe the subject-matter of the Names.

These names were magical and could call up the reality! (But will it come? will it come? as Hotspur asked.) My dear friend Dr. L., a director of the policy of the nation, was now exclaiming: "If we find the right propaganda, the slogan that satisfies the aspirations of the masses, we can accomplish thus and so."

At this I began to wave my right hand in front of my eyes.

I waited in vain for Davor to say "Oof"; for by now he had drained a bottle and a half and he was making funny faces. He began to hiccup.

"It is astonishing," said L. to me sotto voice, "to see a young American so personally disturbed by the Situation."

"He is partly Welsh."

"Ah, so."

—"You told me," cried Professor T. testily, "to let the water come to a boil. But how does one know when the water comes to a boil?"

With a little click Davy came to his senses and he said "Oof."

ADVENTURE THE THIRD: A DRAGON

When a man had graduated from the University and was a Doctor of the Double Dementia—to believe in the things that do not exist and to be trained not to see the things that do exist—then he was a fit teacher for the children and the adolescents.

"Let us stop awhile at this School," I suggested, "where the youth is famous for its beauty and intelligence, and is

137

not yet demented."

"Is it again manned by old friends of yours?" said the Welsh youth disrespectfully; and when I shamefully admitted that it was—for I too had been a teacher—the young man said "Giddap."

But how can I help it if with obsessional repetition I seek out my old friends and try to revivify friendliness? This is the nature of our chivalry. Aspiring to beauty, to the glow and pause, more original, I think, than the feelings of childhood—and perhaps it is the lively safety of Mother Earth herself—we band together for comfort and reminiscence; without rivalry, for none can have an adventure that is not his own.

I saw that the girls and boys of my old school were taking their endogamic sexual pleasures as of yore; and that a warmth of affection glowed in their loyalty to each other and their school.

"But it must be distracting to formal studies," I said sympathetically to my former colleagues, for I knew what a teacher was up against. "The method—is to *use* these forces." And from my trunk I produced a little Latin primer that I had prepared, stories of rapine and dirty jokes, a delight to translate accurately at the age of 15.

I saw in their eyes that I should be lucky to get out of here half alive.

"There are no such goings-on as you mention."

"What! What?" I took it for granted that they were demented; nevertheless I was surprised. "Ah! perhaps when one of you appears, the lovers disengage, the boys put their hands in their own pockets, and there is a lull in the conversation. Believe me, you miss something. If you would sit down and welcome a caress, soon they would no longer notice your presence (an experience also not without its pathos)."

"A teacher who loses his distance loses his authority."

"Good God, men! some of you have been touched by the creator spirit; all of you have achieved something or other. Isn't this enough *natural* distance?"

"There are certain confidences that a teacher ought not to

allow himself to receive. It regularizes the aberrations and gives them a right. We aren't fools, we know what goes on. But if we behave as if no such things existed, they'll pass away and not hinder a normal adjustment."

"You wicked non-teachers! you retarders! Will you strengthen the illusion that they have already that there is a secret satisfaction that they'll learn about later, if they bide their time, that is if they bide your time. For surely *they* cannot believe that you are so demented as to turn away from their felicity without having something of your own that is better. But you have no such thing and there *is* no such thing! And alas, when they grow up to realize it, they won't have their easy ways either.

"You by no means know what goes on, what gayety and mutuality, the emulation of what is possible and the pasture of the soul; and all of this under the most beneficent sign that there is in all the heavens, the recognition of the desires within. Under this sign one is borne *steadily* onward, with increasing power, to victory. But if you dampen this influence—by resentment, eh?—then you doom them to fiascos like your own.

"*Resentful* persons are not teachers. Aren't you ashamed to envy the exploits of boys? (Is this the proper distance?)

"But when you train yourselves not to see what exists, then indeed you begin to see what does not exist."

—They believed, they believed that the lads and the maidens were racing in a field of deep pitfalls, of incorrigible habits and arrested fascinations; but that there was only a strait and tortuous path on which, creeping along, one could arrive whole at the goal of exclusive matrimony where one would be protected by trained anxiety and romantic illusions. Above all, they believed that there was a nightmare dragon marauding, flaming in his nether parts and tongue, ready to destroy whoever slipped on the slimy way.

But in fact it is only a rough field where every smart kid can leap, tumble and spring up again. And Eros is ever serviceable in harness, to pull him out (though he will also take wing for short flights).

If there are games so pleasant that they want to play on, do you therefore forbid the games? God forbid. Let them play the more vigorously at the next games! Those who love to play the most have the most power to play. If your final game is best, they will want to play most at that. (Does what is true to nature need your protection?)

"Is it logical to do what you do? To assure the goal you cramp their speed all along the way. Answer me, I challenge you! *in what other part of education do you reason the same way?* rather than let each course set fire to the next.

"But you *purposely* dampen their ardor in order to end in joylessness."

? ?

The hateful little brothers had all run away. They were in hiding. And when one stuck out his head—suddenly I saw that *I* was the dragon.

Next moment I was on the alert. For there was this beautiful and gifted boy—(you see I am subject to obsessional repetitions). He was broodingly rolling dice with himself and marking down the score.

"Which of you," I cried indignantly, "is responsible for neglecting him during the eleven years he has been with you, and he has come to this?"

For answer they began to throw stones, and I was lucky to come out of it alive.

But I shall return again, and I hope next time in numbers.

COMPLAINT OF THE STONED KNIGHT

"Give me air! air! But no matter, let me die quickly, before I again breathe the same air as these persons.

"For I have heard the deepest reasons that came to me in love and service, that came to me with the same authority not my own with which I wrote the book of community plans (and I am the author of *Nestor*)—I have heard reasons called rationalizations of base motives I am not even aware of!

"Please! do these gentlemen imagine that ideas that meet

140

the test of need, and cast light, and lead to patient service,
are conjured up as means for one's personal convenience?
And that poems of love are formalized by less than the
whole heart?

"They said I was intelligent and *therefore* could think up
a clever defense—these fools who have never known, it
seems, the fascination of the better reason, that brings heart
and soul to a pause.

"Well! from now on my mind is open to all comers. There
is no nonsense so abject that I am not ready to entertain
it—if certain persons I could name are generally regarded as
honest."

THE FOURTH ADVENTURE: THE BLAZON

Meantime, pursuing his adventures elsewhere than
among my friends, and getting more gratification from
them along the way, Daffy too ended up in a ditch alongside
the road. He was thus able to confirm the formula that "Life
is simple but hard." Not complex (as my friends imagined),
not easy (as no one is fool enough to imagine), but simple
and hard.

And while he was lying there, more dead than alive, there
passed by two members of the petty bourgeoisie.

Now a grand bourgeois is an ancient who shows how the
strong and original virtues can be bent to the purpose of
accumulation. A petty bourgeois has never known original
virtue at all, but what he imagines to be virtue is the effect,
and the means, of somebody else's accumulation, rather
than the cause of his own. To a grand bourgeois abstinence
is a virtue and daring is a virtue. But what a petty bourgeois
imagines to be virtues are emulation and timidity.

"So young," says one, "and already on the skids." He
clicked his tongue against his teeth. "This is the boy who
has been under an evil influence." And he whispered something to his friend which I might in turn whisper to the
reader, but by no means entrust to paper.

The other thought that it was indeed Balinese. "Let's get
out of here," he said, "before a policeman comes and we

141

have to appear as witnesses."

(In this way it is possible to die unattended in New York City or along the roadsides of northern New Jersey.)

"Well, he must pay the penalty."

"The wages of sin is death."

Now when the first said "Pay the penalty," Daffy's right eye opened wide and flamed. And when the other said "The Wages of Sin," then his other eye opened and he leaped to his feet and seized them by the lapels of their coats.

"You dogs!" he shouted, half between sleep and waking, "how dare you speak of me in such a language of exchange and hire? I know you for what you are by the words you use, petty bourgeoisie!

"Now do you think I am afraid or ashamed that my behavior has led me and must still lead me to disaster? In the present case my hopes were indeed a little sanguine and imprudent, but even at the best I know that in the end desire is death (just as the repression of desire is death).

"No, no! this *chain*, this bond, this *bondage*, of cause and effect, of *consequence*, is what I glory in and give *thanks* for—" he was panting and gasping, but each has his own way of praying. "It is the nature that reveals to me something more than I merely desired. It is my share in nature. Because a man like myself does not learn much from what he desires until he sees the consequences.

"Say that the Scorpion stings itself to death and I'll honor you—"

This was the blazon of Davor and this was his device. The emblem was a Scorpion deadly-ringed, and the motto was *Fatum Sui*, "His Own Doom." Nevertheless! isn't it better, I challenge you, that he carry this misery along the open road where at every crossing he is touched by strokes of joy, than to sit broodingly rolling the dice with himself and marking down the score?—until, God willing, we come upon a physician with as much love as I have for him, and more wisdom.

Lord bless Davy Drood and gently heal
the sharpened corners of his smile.

The Knight

Thou canst from no matter what
by life the strength of life create

and sweet ease. Though boy-horrifying
memories are ever crying,
Thou makest them the riches of
victory and quiet love.

THE FIFTH ADVENTURE: THE GIRL FROM THE MOUNTAIN
CONVENT

"Why are you so quiet, Davor? Whose medal are you
wearing? And where is the golden scorpio, your ill-luck
charm?"

—For a young knight will often wear an ill-luck charm, to
remind him that the disasters that befall him are those that
belong to his own nature, till he is sure of his integrity.

"I am in love," he said. "The medal is a superstitious
medal that belongs to the girl Joanna—see, it is St. Christopher. And do you know?"

"What must I know?"

"*Although* or *because* she believes in these ancient al-
legories, she has never even heard of the other folk-tales
that have made our people demented. She seems to love me
almost as I am. Shall I not love her for it—as well as for
herself?"

"What do you say, she has not heard of them? Is she an
imbecile?"

"No, no. She was brought up in a convent in the mountains, and those sisters taught her nothing, either false or
true, except hunting, music and the saints' lives. Now
suddenly she appears in our society—a virgin, but very
desirous, very desirous once it occurs to her—and she does
not take alarm at the terrible hobgoblins, and she fails
completely to see the things that do not exist. We love each
other by the side of the road—very desirous. Shall I have a
child with this wicked innocent?"

"Wait until she finds out your true nature!" I warned him
prudently. "Wait until the others have told her that you

143

speak the truth just in order that people may imagine it is not the truth, and that when you love it is just in order to do harm; wait until she is persuaded that strong ideas are rationalizations."

"No no no no. They have already got to work on her. But when they whispered—"

"Yes—"

"Why, this I had already told her. And when they attributed to us the subtility and malicious intentions which if indeed we had them would long ago have made our fortunes—"

"Yes, yes—"

"She said to them, for she is keen! 'Poor folk! All of this hatred, resentment and superstition is nothing but disguised love and loyalty that you cannot help have for the honor and freedom of these knights! Then why do you make yourselves miserable by indirection? Why do you not go directly to what it is you desire?—if that's possible; for he tells me, what I have not yet noticed, that life is hard, though simple. (But I have found it easy and simple.)'"

"Let her have your child, the fool, and she'll find that it's hard."

—But the tears started into my eyes, and they are in my eyes forever, now also when I am writing about it. For I too once met and loved and married and had a child with a dear lady whose blue eyes likewise did not see the things that do not exist, and she loved me almost as I am. Many times I compared her with Saint Harmony my patroness; and she was the heart of many of the songs I used to sing.

But although or because we were not demented as the others were, we became demented in our own way; and we made what was simple complicated and harder than was necessary. And the end of it was meaningless words and the deeds of fools and the disquiet of our daughter.

ADVENTURE THE SIXTH: THE TOURNAMENT

Stare, looking for an answering sign of comprehension. There is an angry stare returned. Now stare is *grinding* against stare.

The smiles have deepened into frowns, and frown is pushing against frown, till they are tangled in a cloud. (Is there a beam of a smile in this thunderous cloud?)

In vain you wave your right hand across your eyes. It is a true conflict and it will not vanish.

Then at this moment draw a line; and say—*if* it is the case; but if it is not the case, what are you doing here in this tournament of knights?—say: "*I* am not afraid of anything. What are *you* afraid of?"

And supposing he also is not afraid of anything, but will follow where his nature and his best reasons mislead him, just as they have misled you both into this ignorant battle: then he crosses the line.

"Now you are on our side!"—what a childish joke!

The joyous peal of this childish joke is ringing, is *ringing* in my memory. Surely there is the sunny beam of a smile in the thunderous cloud. And the rush of the happy feelings of my eighth to tenth years is reforming from all sides forever. (How could there be a mortal blow?) God blast the dismal customs that drained the courage from that joy! so even now, except in violent danger, it does not rush into my heart and I am already sad. I know that these persons still imagine the right is on their side, and still I see them purposely dampen ardor; *still* they are in the wrong, and I . . . But let me not mar the description of the true combat with the further mention of such persons.

Do you imagine that there is now a sad, drawn out, lonely fight? No, they are laughing. They fight in the tournament according to the rules, and there is no mortal blow.

The rules are direct action and releasing desire and the use of words to say what is the case.

Every blow, given or received, is the actuality of a natural power; how then could there be a mortal blow—given or received?

Every blow is a resolution made by night, that looks eerie in the light. Nevertheless, act it out.

Such a blow, given or received, pauses in the air.

Soon it is storming at every heart.

We others perhaps once receive an immortal blow. We do

not deal out immortal blows. These champions are in the *habit* of dealing out (and of receiving!) the immortal blows.

Will not their combat, blow by blow, be a sacred dance, blow by blow actualizing the powers of the heavens and the earth?

The combat, blow by blow, of the true champions is the proportion of the violence of the heavens and the earth. The blood that is spilled by direct action revives the courage of all mankind.

This is the tournament, this is the sacred dance, this is the prayer of thanks.

When something is said that is the case: it is *evidence.* You cannot pass it by; you must not discount it; you will not go on as though it had never been said. But now you may see how a true man is found in error! He blanches, his hair stands on end, and he cannot lift his arm—when he realizes that the experience of his first to his thirty-third years has misled him into this ignorant combat.

Meantime each one is secretly longing for a mortal blow. Too late! It is now too late either to die or live, because noblesse oblige. *This* is the mortal boredom of immortality. One would willingly commit some folly just to live on among the little brothers.

5.

In the rush, standstill and violence of the powers of the heavens and the earth; and the streaming of time both outside and inside roaring; and desire loosed, released, and always at once fulfilled—but wherever is a blockage and eddy, in deprivation and anxiety the little personalities come into being, longing to die and stream onward and soon achieving it—

the seeing sees whole scenes, either still or in measurable motion; food is what is unlike transformable into what is like; rhythm consists of the patter of speech, of the double and triple gait, and of the climax of orgasms; experience grows out of memories, and love out of habits of desire;

146

there are true reasons; and the ego also develops according to its form.

So long as these forms, these reasons and strokes of love (lovely graces, surely) are preyed on by a little ego person to keep alive his deprivation—he has no life of his own, but how he struggles to die as much as possible!—they have no important meaning; the penurious effort to make them endure is pitiable; they are not the subjects of strong songs of praise;

But let them draw freely for their power of life on the standstill and violence of the heavens and the earth, on desire ever loosed and released—these do not strive either to die or live for they are immortal—then these forms of art, these reasons and these strokes of love have all the meaning that there is; in them we easily achieve immortality; and they are the subjects of strong songs of praise.

Every immortal peer has a sovereign territory. Here, you see, everything is characteristic, the way of tying knots, the acts of love, and the wars. Nothing is fresh and natural; all is blighted by artifice. It is his Style. It seems that it is only in this Style that he can draw freely on the rush and standstill of power. He has tortured himself, by direct acts and saying what is the case, in order to bend himself to this ease.

What! are not the springs of life easily available? Why need he torture himself to our surprise and confusion? (Hush, little brother, are *you* a person of power and accomplishment?) See, here are the springs of life—are they available? Ah, you are vomiting with disgust and paralyzed by anxiety. But if you would closely read these surprises, you would find that which revives courage in your heart.

Some of the peers have a boundless territory. You cannot raise a question, for already you are compelled in every faculty. Others possess only little counties. But each is sovereign in his own and has equal honor; you cannot enter here except under servile conditions, soon relaxed. You breathe the atmosphere of solitary joy, and the flags are gaily flying.

6. *An Outline of the True Theory of Our Friends*

Dear boy, are you lonely? Is it sad to traverse this polity of peers, where there is a commonwealth (the only commonwealth!) but no community, as though one were with statues, though each has an intimate voice? From the dead it is already wonderful to hear speech; but why aren't the living knights fraternal, to give each other comfort and exchange reminiscences?

Therefore let me explain the true theory of our friends and how it is with us.

(For lately a vulgar writer said that the intellectuals are neurotic because of their maladjustment; and if it were so we could not expect them to sit friendly down together. But I challenge this lie.—)

Begin first with an experiment: It is the case that a man is acquainted with many hundreds of persons. Now if you find that one of our friends is acquainted with one or two others of our friends (as we ask a new acquaintance "Do you know so and so?"), then he will prove to be acquainted with fifty or a hundred others. But an ordinary man is likely to know only three or four others. How is this? The acquaintanceship of our friends is less superficial; it probes, it interests itself, it pauses; therefore it rapidly extends to other acquaintances, and these become mutual. Is it that they have, as we say, a "common interest" that gathers them together? No, it is that their selves are more available, and the selves give each other comfort; as selves they are not strange to each other. Examine the "common interests" which indeed they do have: they are the intimate voices and the probing reasons.

Thus potentially, it is our friends who are least alone, whereas other persons less easily come to know each other.

Our friends are simply those who have addressed themselves to something that exists. By "addressed themselves" I mean not with the glancing relation which other persons use, when all the while their hearts are set on conformity, emulation, ambition, according to the conventional norms. I do not mean that our friends habitually address themselves to things that exist, for then they would be true champions, and few of our friends are so. Yet even to have once and for a season been absorbedly devoted to something that exists, makes a great difference: it affirms the integrity of the self. (By contrast those other persons hardly have themselves, for it is by drawing on natural power that one affirms one's-self.) Afterwards, though our friends go astray, it is not possible to go so far astray as the others.

Shall we say that our friends are neurotic? It is precisely the others who are potentially neurotic.

Our friends are not neurotic, but most of them become eccentric. It is easy to see how this occurs. A young person, brighter than the rest, is too bright to be persuaded that something that exists indeed does not exist. He addresses himself to it. Afterwards, by contrast, the rewards of his non-educators have for him less charm. Perhaps he seeks his own rewards (sometimes, alas, in private fancies that exist as little as the normative fancies). Or else he goes from one thing that exists to another that exists. Soon he is a full-fledged eccentric. In this way we see how creative ability, intelligence, strong desire, common sense, are all principles of cumulative eccentricity—so that in the end our friends, too accustomed to waving their hands in front of their eyes, begin to deny that perfectly ordinary goods are good; but it's nothing but short-temper.

Ideally our friends are endogamous, like the true champions. Early undiscouraged from their desires that exist, they are not constrained like the others to love only the strange one who was not banned (and worse, to find in her a kind of infantile memory, from before ever they had a self). But their desires are continuous with the other things to which they have been addressing themselves; this continuum is a rich and ordinary love. Further their selves, available to be touched, band together as we have seen, for comfort and to exchange reminiscences. . . . Now couples are exclusive as the strength of their attention to one another, that is as the degree to which themselves are their things that exist; this *richness* is said to be "romantic love," because it is different from the everyday and it is felt for that which is strange. On the contrary, this richness is nothing but what is left to the *ordinary* love among our friends.

But because we have sinned, we are exiled from one another. Persons that have drawn freely on natural powers, feel themselves alien in the world! and with surly exasperation they protect themselves from their friends. Or they hypothetically assume the reality of nightmares (just to live on a little! just to live on a little!), and soon they are exchanging mortal blows about things that do not exist. And I have even known them to be envious of one another! as if it were possible to have an adventure that is not one's own.

To My Boys and Girls at Broadmeadows.

Quaker Hill—Norwood
August-October 1944

150

The Father of the
Psychoanalytic Movement

"The heavy burden," said Freud, "the heavy burden of psychoanalysis."

To a father a child is sometimes a heavy burden. Nevertheless he bears it and it rarely becomes too heavy. For the first blow of fatherhood is the hardest, when the helpless infancy is reborn also within the heart. After that is but the confirmation of the initial agreement to make all concessions. The father does not break down under the burden but simply wears himself out. If the child rebels, the burden is not heavier but merely harder to manage, like a bulkier box with the same contents.

But on the contrary! if the child does not rebel but precisely fulfills his father's will for him, then indeed the burden is heavier to bear, for the strength of the father is sapped from within. The old man would not have dared to conceive what the young one suddenly in fact does, as a matter of course, by his father's will. So he was trained.

Now further, we speak of a true thought or other gift of the spirit as a man's child; he "fathers" the thought, we say. But the analogy is a bad one. Such a gift is not a heavy burden. Rather, a man who has a true thought or a beautiful idea is borne up by strong wings. Easily he soars above the obstacles that stand in the way of other men. So easily that we often reverse the metaphor and say that the man is supported by the idea—but not as a son is supported by his father, but as an infant is lifted by a nurse, a mother: by a Muse who teaches him to speak and lifts him up with the lightness of infancy when easily one flew (otherwise dumb, helpless, and immobile).

151

What shall we say of our old teacher Sigmund Freud who came to speak of "the heavy burden of psychoanalysis"? He meant to say that the world, whose illness was being threatened by psychoanalysis, was resisting psychoanalysis and bent on destroying it. But this was absurd! for if this idea had spread so far and proved so strong from the beginning, why should it not—*crescit eundo*—be now stronger still? And bear up its professors on strong wings? Certainly when Freud was a young man, starting out, he would not have said, "The heavy burden of psychoanalysis."

Must we not say that our teacher was under the delusion that he was the father of psychoanalysis? (And truly, if any man could ever be called the father of an idea, Freud was the father of psychoanalysis.) That it was precisely because the child was following the father's will for him that the burden was becoming so heavy. In all directions the young ones were in fact doing, as a matter of course, by their father's will (so they were trained) what the old man did not dare to conceive.

What thought did he commit against his own father that he was thus constrained to assume the role of a grieving father? We know that his father said, "You will not come to anything"; then he said defiantly, "I *shall* come to something!"—until the helpless infancy began to be reborn also in his own heart.

No, what *withdrawal* did he feel toward his mother that he was ever unable, like a light infant, to be easily and joyously uplifted by such a smiling Muse?—and if ever a man could be said to be inspired by a Muse, Freud was inspired by psychoanalysis.

"The heavy burden of psychoanalysis"! Obviously we must distinguish between the idea of psychoanalysis and the psychoanalytic movement that consisted of congresses, publications, and the fight for recognition in the universities and asylums. It was the psychoanalytic movement that was the heavy burden. Yes, in these congresses and publications we know well that he was a loving father. Attentive, patient, helpful, encouraging; following the discussion in every detail and proudly summarizing what the boys had done; not without an ironic correction and even an occasional brusque reproof. This was a father! the father of the psychoanalytic movement—who over-protected the psychoanalytic movement—and did not break down under the burden but simply wore himself out.

In congresses and publications. Where, meantime, was the idea of psychoanalysis? It was in the needful patients, in the deep thoughts of ill souls, stammering their distress, their secrets, wounds. It was in the wounds and the ever-productive causes of nature. It was from the wounds of mankind, from discontent and war, and the productive forces in the soul, that sprang alive the idea of psychoanalysis. From dreams. Was Freud the father of these wounds and dreams?

On the contrary, he was a naturalist. And as we are told of Darwin that he sat for three hours with staring eyes while the bee visited the flower, so we may easily think of Freud, the attention crowding into his ears, listening to the voices of the wounds. Not a father, not a teacher, but a pupil and a child.

And as with Darwin, with Aristotle, and the others of the well-behaved observers of nature, one is not surprised that Freud also insensibly finds himself borne up by strong wings, easily, light as infancy. Then he is our guide through hell and heaven, through the fields of vivid dreams and flaming desire, by the salt pools of loss, to the sphinx of death. While he is attentive to the voices of the wounds. Is this "the heavy burden of psychoanalysis"? Also, while the physician heals. Also, bringing liberty and free conscience to all mankind—especially if we resist it! for he knows that the resistance is the way of the cure. Is this "the heavy burden of psychoanalysis"?

But if suddenly (the story goes) Freud, the Professor Ex-traordinary, this naturalist, burst out of the room and cried, *"Warum soll ich solchen Schweinerei aufhören!—why must I listen to such piggishness?"*!

Ah, *then* there is a heavy burden of psychoanalysis! (If true, is not this a revealing anecdote?)

Whipped, as by a scourge, to return to these wounds—to sniff this need; resisting it like the rest, and *still* his atten-tion crowding into his lewd ears. (Many passages confirm this hypothesis.)

153

Making *himself* a heavy burden, when the mother tries to lift him up. Vertigo and vomiting. Ashamed to give himself to this ease.

Imitating the sobriety of his father and nevertheless maintaining a stoical calm and not crying out, but dutifully accepting the kiss. (As he has often seen it dutifully given and accepted in bourgeois homes.)

Meantime, he was the *first* one, and had to analyze himself. (He himself was one of his needful patients.) Against what could his resistance burn if not against psychoanalysis?

The father of the psychoanalytic movement!

Will not the child, in turn, make the burden heavier? not by rebelling but on the contrary precisely by conforming to the father's will for him—doing as a matter of course what the old man did not dare to conceive. (So he was trained.) To try to liberate the war-sick discontented world. To say, *as a matter of course,* and not with sweat on the forehead, "It is highly instructive to learn something of the intensively tilled soil from which our virtues proudly emerge."

How much do we not owe to our dear dead friend and teacher that we can say it as a matter of course! What courage he had! What sadness he bore! *Therefore* let us not too feel guilty in turn, but make of it a brotherly festival.

(I for my part have only pleasure in it, if borne up by the strong wings of speech I can pay my debt to him by a memorial exclamation.)

No no, let us assume, what is certainly the case, that Freud too, attentively listening like a sage naturalist—like a cat, first cocking his ear in a new direction, then turning his head—he too wore a little smile; then he held his breath; then drew deep new breaths and even joyously laughed.

It was only when he came before the public, the psychoanalytic movement, before the congresses and in the publications, and he adjusted his hat and his tie, that suddenly his heavy heart smote him—for our sakes, as he thought! that we, not borne up by strong wings, must nevertheless put up with him, with it. With "the heavy burden of psychoanalysis."

The Father of the Psychoanalytic Movement

Publicly one did not joke about it; privately there was a good deal of laughter at the humorous impasses and witty improvisations. The excitement of being on the right track—yet making it up out of the whole cloth as one went along. Yet it was necessary to wear a hat and tie just as if psychoanalysis were not something childish, just starting out, and much of it no doubt gibberish. What humbug! "The heavy burden of psychoanalysis"!

Come, old teacher, do not feel so conscience-stricken before your young friends. You with your "heavy burden of psychoanalysis"!

Don't joke. Our teacher is sad. The *fact* is, the simple fact, that our teacher has grown very old. "The heavy burden of psychoanalysis"—to an old man *everything* is a heavy burden. I am ashamed. How unbecoming it is for mere boys to scoff at gray hairs. Rather say, Thanks! thanks—father! you *great* man: making ourselves little boys in order that we may see him loom so huge. In order to be lightly picked up.

He raises us high in the air: See!

How far one can see!

Is not the old man himself renewed, as Abraham, a hundred years of age, had a second childhood in little Laughter? Where in this picture is "the heavy burden of psychoanalysis"?

2. (September 24, 1939)

Herewith to many prose-works I prefix *In Memoriam Sigmund Freud:* not to rob the dead, and in love.

The friendly man, our general friend, is dead. Now without a possible addition, in books we read his careful conjectures, first persuasive to the heart surprised, then recognized for even very true. He proved freedom and good conscience to all men (most to those who say the contrary but will be freed tomorrow). First he explored the flowery fields of hell, then the fierce deserts of heaven. An unfinished enterprise. His achievement is to be achieved.

The donkeys braying as he went his way, I'll never name and mar with sarcasm the sorrow for our dead companion.

155

3.

"I shall not publish this essay," wrote the old man in the preface to *Moses and Monotheistic Religion*, "but that need not hinder me from writing it.

"The more so," he went on to say, "since it was already written once before and thus only needs *re*writing."

This is by the author of *Symptoms, Inhibition, and Anxiety*. Is this not high comedy? "The more so since it is already written, and thus only needs rewriting!"

(To be sure, he did publish the essay.)

And the reason he would not publish the essay was that—it might offend (guess who?)—the Roman Catholic Church of Austria! This is by the author of *The Future of an Illusion*.

And then, says he, the Roman Church might—withdraw its support from—the psychoanalytic movement!

It is really necessary to put a dash of ironic anticipation before every phrase in these delicious remarks. This is by the author of *The Interpretation of Dreams*.

And the reason that he could publish the essay after all was that the Roman Catholic Church of Austria proved to be—a broken reed. This is by the author of *On Wit and its Relation to the Unconscious!*

Shame!

Meantime all the world, both west and east, had long been violently ill with the spreading war—though not yet so ill as it was still going to be.

Then some of the young men stormed to the old one and said: We must go down into the streets. The people are ill not in their thousands who come for treatment, but in their hundreds of millions who are about to tear the world apart.

Then Freud said: "At least the present system gives them such an outlet for their aggressive instincts that they do not destroy each other totally." They were *already* fighting the war, organized in a system to destroy each other totally.

"There is a wish to die," he said, meaning especially by this, I think, that *he* wished to die.

"Either you are totally wrong," he said, "or you alone must bear the heavy burden of psychoanalysis!"

156

The Father of the Psychoanalytic Movement

So. A man begins quietly, all unsuspecting perhaps, in a neat office with a few patients. Listening attentively to the voices of their wounds, he is all insensibly touched by the natural things that exist.

Next moment he is a free knight dubbed, wildly marauding (as it seems). On every side he sees monsters with the complacent faces of orderliness, purity, godliness, accumulation that are only masks for the savage resentment of sore wounds. But because he has come to admit the existence of something that indeed exists, he is no longer impressed by the things that do not exist. If there are sore wounds, he, noblesse oblige, will cure them; and he comes all gently, like a raging tempest, as it seems. In the twinkling of a few years, compared with the secular period of the institutions, an endless career lightens before him—a flash of lightning on the blue plain—to free his sisters and brothers! He has found a Royal Road to go into deep places. Muses smile him on. He is the champion of the freedom of the children. There are shouts that he is a black magician and he has invented the nature of children! "Only a Jew has such dreams!" Are not such shouts so many goads to the free knight, to lop more joyously away at the hideous growths that do not exist and, listening attentively to the voices of the wounds, to speak a word that heals as it violates?

Meantime (here is the comedy) our knight has become the Father of the Psychoanalytic Movement. He is famous in congresses for his encouraging summations of what his boys have accomplished, not without an ironic correction and even an occasional brusque reproof. There are schemes for—official recognition. (It is really necessary to begin to insert dashes of sarcastic anticipation.) He is not so eager for the young men to campaign on their own, and be hurt, and hurt each other.

The question is, whether it is possible to be the champion of the freedom of children and the father of the psychoanalytic movement? That is, whether it is possible to be a free knight and a father at all?

It seems to me that Father Abraham was a knightly father. Would any one deny that he was a good father?

"I shall not publish this essay. To be sure that need not hinder me from writing it." The knight is now laying round him within the four walls of his private study.

"The more so since it is already written and thus only needs *re*writing." Rewriting, with the addition of some delicious prefatory notes. This is by the author of *On Wit and its Relation to the Unconscious.*

Father! pleaded some of the young men, lend *your* influence to help us when we go down into the streets.

"Either you are totally wrong," he cried, "or you alone must bear the heavy burden of psychoanalysis."

So. Suddenly wherever one turns, to take a single step, one finds that the freedom and good conscience of mankind, and the joy of the children, have become—a heavy burden. It is not true that the thick-walled institutions do not exist. They exist! Even the Roman Catholic Church of Austria 1938 can be said to exist somewhat, if one exerts only a gentle kind of pressure. Perhaps the brothers and sisters can find refuge there.

(How becoming it is to scoff at the old man!)

Shame!

Shame not on Freud, but shame on the world for bringing our old teacher to this confusion.

The father of the psychoanalytic movement was overprotective toward the psychoanalytic movement. Then just because as a matter of course (so they were trained), some of the young men went down into the streets, he no longer even dared to conceive of it.

4.

(The question, whether it is possible to be a free knight and a father at all.)

Now Abraham was a knightly father.

It is not likely that his boy, the Laughter of his old age, was a heavy burden to him. He did not feel guilty to murder Isaac because this was not his secret wish. Abraham was not overprotective toward Isaac because he did not wish to murder him, because Isaac was not a heavy burden to him.

On the contrary, father of the psychoanalytic movement!

it is easy, in a knightly way, to murder one's child. The example of it is Abraham. All one need to do is to commit, step by step, dividing the steps and subdividing the divisions, the acts leading up to the murder. Thus, when God said: "Take now thine only son Isaac, whom thou lovest, and get thee into the land of Moriah, and offer him there for a burnt-offering on one of the mountains I shall tell thee of"—what did Abraham do first?—It says: "He arose early in the morning."

"He arose early in the morning and saddled his ass, and took two of his young men and Isaac his son; and he cleaved the wood for the burnt-offering, and rose up, and went."

The method by which it is easy, in a knightly way, to murder one's child who is not a heavy burden (one is not over-protective to him): all one need do is to commit the previous act and before that the act previously to that. Thus, "he arose early in the morning": that is to say, he got out of bed, washed, and dressed. That is to say, he awoke. He opened his eyes, first one eye, then the other—and saw that it was early in the morning.

God said, "Abraham!"

And he said, "Here am I."

But if the child is a heavy burden, then the last act burns too vividly before the mind and one cannot take step by step; on the contrary, then one is overprotective and inhibits the previous steps.

It is not the case, when there is a conflict of wishes, that one can will both of them at the same time. This is impossible. But on the contrary, it is easy, in a knightly way, freely, as a matter of course (so one has been trained) to take each step in turn; that is to say, to bring vividly before one's mind the idea of the next step, and thus to do it. This is called willing to do it.

"On the third day Abraham lifted up his eyes and saw the place afar off." That is to say, first he lifted up his eyes, which were presumably a heavy burden, then he saw the place. His eyes were downcast on the ground; then he brought vividly before his mind the idea of lifting up his eyes, *then* he lifted up his eyes, and *then* he saw the place. Is not this easy to do, in a free and knightly way, to think that it is

159

about time that I brought vividly to mind the idea of lifting up my eyes?

"And Abraham said to his young men, 'Abide ye here with the ass, and I and the lad will go yonder.'" See! what a wonderful advantage there is in starting out with three young men! What is extraordinary about it, to go on a trip with three young men? To have some one with, to converse on the way. Avoiding embarrassing silences. For the most part the boys talk to each other. Then afterwards, when the time comes, it is not hard to distinguish from the three the one. This is how to take each step in turn and eventually to murder one's only child. This is called willing to do it.

The boys talked about the things that were of interest to the boys, mainly sports and hunting. The old man concentrated on bringing vividly before his mind the idea of the next step. The ass bore the load of wood. We can judge by this that it was a treeless country with a bare profile of hills.

But *first* it was necessary to awake early in the morning. That is, to bring before one's mind vividly—presumably in the midst of some *other* dream—the idea of opening one's eyes, first one eye, then the other, and seeing that it is early in the morning.

"Abraham!"

"Here am I!"

This is the moment in the other dream that the father presents vividly to his mind the idea it is about time to present vividly to his mind the idea of opening an eye.

"Abraham took the wood for the burnt-offering and laid it upon Isaac his son; and he took in his hand the fire and the knife, and they went both of them together."

Abraham looked at his hand. It was empty. Then he presented vividly to his mind the idea of the knife being in his hand. Thus (in a flash!) he took it. This is easy! This is called willing to do it.

"Father!"

"Here am I, my son."

(Certainly, here he was! Was not this moment too the end result of the long process of time? Each moment had led easily, step by step, up to this step of climbing the mountain step by step.)

160

The Father of the Psychoanalytic Movement

"Behold the fire and the wood; but where is the lamb for a burnt-offering?"

"God will provide Himself the lamb for a burnt-offering!"

The boy was not a knightly father! he found it hard to go just step by step, furthermore carrying a heavy load up the mountain. (Presumably he was trained obediently to carry such a load.) But Abraham was a free knight; he committed it step by step and refused vividly to bring before his mind the idea of anything but the next step, for instance the idea of murdering his only son. Thus, a man is told that he may think of anything in the world except the idea "Q": the ordinary man finds this impossible to do; but if he would give himself freely to the next step, then it is easy to do—in a flash! This is refusing vividly! by giving oneself simply to the next step. It is the psychological method of what is called acting by faith.

Thus, it was easy to write the essay; why was it necessary to bring vividly to mind the idea of publishing it? The more so since it was already written and only needed *re*writing. One did not start in the first place with the idea of writing an offensive essay. But he was the author of *The Future of an Illusion*, and one offensive essay led to another. And the previous act was writing *Totem and Taboo*, a mere anthropological speculation: what was there offensive in that?

There was nothing offensive in bringing vividly to mind the idea of letting one's attention crowd into the ears, to listen to the voices of the wounds; and then—in a flash!— hearing them. This is called willing to do it. To *publish* the essay! To *lend* one's authority to the young men to go down into the streets. To go down into the streets! to liberate the war-sick world—not, at that time, yet *so* sick! Where in this picture is "the heavy burden of psychoanalysis"? But the father of the psychoanalytic movement overprotected the psychoanalytic movement.

Abraham was a knightly father. He did not feel guilty to murder Isaac because this was not his secret wish. He vividly refused to bring before his mind the idea of murdering him, because in a free and knightly way he was willing to take step by step. Borne up by the strong wings of each step by step. "God will provide Himself the lamb for a burnt-offering!"

"And they came to the place that God had told him of. And Abraham built an altar there and laid the wood in order, and bound Isaac his son, and laid him on the altar upon the wood.

"And Abraham stretched forth his hand, and took the knife to slay his son."

He stretched forth his hand, then he took the knife.

He looked at his hand. It was empty. Vividly he presented to his mind the idea of the knife's being in his hand. In a flash the knife was in his hand!

He noticed that his arm was lying by his side, and he vividly brought to mind the idea of stretching forth his hand. That is to say, he vividly brought to mind the idea of a tension in the muscles of his shoulder, first in one muscle, then in another.

That is, first one took a deep breath.

(This is called willing to do it and acting by faith. It is easy to do it, in a fatherly and knightly way, borne up by the strong wings of each act by act, if one commits first the previous act and before that the act previous to that.)

Is not each one of these acts also the end result of the long process of time? *Therefore* one can say, *"Here* am I."

So, in a flash!—for we must not think that just because it is possible to divide the knightly action and to subdivide the subdivisons, that all of it does not happen in a flash! In a flash awaking early in the morning! In a flash one goes down into the streets! In a flash freeing the children! In a flash we shall one day liberate our war-sick world.

"He *took* the knife to slay his son.

"And the Angel of the Lord called to him out of heaven and said, 'Abraham.'

"And he said, 'Here am I.'"

Certainly here he was. But I do not think that Father Abraham lifted his eyes to see where the voice was coming from. I think that his eyes were blinded with free, bitter, knightly, fatherly, guiltless tears.

"'Lay not thy hand upon the lad, neither do thou anything to him.'"

162

Then, "Abraham lifted up his eyes, and looked, and behold behind him a ram caught in the thicket by his horns."

That is to say, first he turned his head and then cleared his eyes (his attention was not crowding into his eyes); then he looked or allowed himself to see; then there was something to see that seized on his attention, *behold!* Shall we not say that his attention crowded into his eyes—away from his memory and other vivid ideas? But before this he was not in any haste to see, but that he slowly lifted his eyes?

Not with any feeling of guilt or as if expecting a reproof—but that it was no longer easy to take any next step, to bring vividly before one's mind any idea at all.

(Now it must come from outside. One is no longer willing to do it.)

That to an old man everything is a heavy burden.

The question is, whether it is possible to be a free knight and an old man at all.

(It seems to me that Nestor was a knightly old man. He did not eye himself according to an unvarying standard.)

"And Abraham called the name of that place Jehovahjirah, as it is said to this day: In the mount where the Lord is seen."

5. *September 25, 1939*

First thru the blooming fields of hell, among
the colored dreams, gay jokes, and gorgeous
mistakes, our guide had conducted us,
to where desire the dragon of my song
was flaming in his nether parts and tongue;
next were we exploring hideous
wastes of heaven, by salty pools of loss,
spiny anxieties, and gulphs of wrong,
even to the secret sphinx, the wish for death:
and here we halted with abated breath
—when suddenly dead, for all our hopes and fears,
is our guide across the air and deep:
this morning a surprise of mournful tears,
a friendly dream now I am asleep.

6.

*"The aged lion, well on his way to being
a couch cover."*
—QUOTED BY HANNS SACHS

Freud was the first of the psychoanalysts and therefore had to analyze himself.

Resisting the analysis, he had no one to vent his hate on but himself.

Therefore Freud said, "The heavy burden of psycho-analysis."*

In this continuing analysis, that lasted too long, finally he came upon the wish to die.

Always eying himself! as if a man could never close his eyes.

He said, *"Ich kann mich nicht acht Stunden täglich anstarren lassen*—I can't let myself be stared at eight hours a day!" and he sat where his patients, his other patients, could not see him. Meantime he devised methods to eye himself also while he was asleep.

But always eying himself according to an unvarying standard, even when he became ill, old, and tired. After a while one cannot any more and comes to speak of "The diminishing of the creative powers that accompanies old age."

Every other person in analysis can burn with resentment against a son of the psychoanalytic movement and ultimately against the father of the psychoanalytic movement. The resentment is burnt out.

Then one dreams at one's ease, no need to watch out, some one else is watching it.

Soon one laughs and (living backwards) learns to smile.

But if Freud did not watch out for himself, who would watch out? His resentment was therefore not burnt out.

"These fools!" he said of his patients. (He himself was one of his patients.)

"Why must I always listen to such piggishness!" said Freud. "The heavy burden of psychoanalysis," he said.

*This excellent reason was suggested to me by Dr. Erich Kraft.

164

"These fools! I can't let myself be stared at for eight hours every day."

Eying himself for twenty-four hours a day for a quarter of a century; finally he saw there—the wish to die. When sleepiness began to overwhelm the eye of judgment , would not this be interpreted (by the eye of judgment) as the wish to die? To close one's eyes.

To relinquish the heavy burden of psychoanalysis.

All the same it is a logical contradiction to say "I wish to die." For the ground of any wish at all is the existence of the desires that express themselves in the wish; their existence cannot be the ground of their non-existence. Further, it is impossible to have a wish without an image, but one cannot imagine *oneself* as dead.

We must think of Freud as methodically eying himself for half a century, as a doctor does, and seeing that he had become old, ill, and tired. Or as a parent keeps an eye on a child who has a tendency to masturbate; what can the child do but get out?

It is possible that there is an universal inertia dragging all life back into matter, but this could not find expression as a wish. Perhaps what Freud meant to say was that there is a wish for a life of unconsciousness, to live *not* under the surveillance of the ego. But this is the A B C of psychoanalysis; why invent something new? To a person not eying *himself,* such a wish is by no means the wish to die, but precisely to live more freely, bringing the ego back into subordination to the instincts. (Also, this is "the strength of the ego.")

This was what Father Nestor did, when he danced with the dogs. It meant that the past with its curse was still blest. And had brought him at last to not less than he was. He did not eye himself any more; and he never had eyed himself according to an unvarying standard.

But we must think now of a man of great faculties and driving power, eying himself according to an unvarying standard (almost a public standard, with a hat and tie). He recognized by sure signs that his faculties were diminished and his power waning: was it not inevitable that he would interpret it, the sense of falling short of the measure, as the wish to die? (Also clinging to life all the harder—so that perhaps it was not apparent till the next year that he was ill.)

This is a mistaken interpretation: what one can one can; but one must not measure it according to an unvarying standard.

A new standard! no longer eying oneself, no longer rallying to the requirement.

To die without saying "I wish to die"! But "my resentment is burnt out."

Not overprotective toward the psychoanalytic movement, but to let the psychoanalytic movement go the way of the psychoanalytic movement.

Meantime the fact was that *everywhere* he looked in all the war-sick world old and tired, the *fact* was that indeed people wished to die. They had organized themselves into armies in order to carry out their wish without loneliness and guilt.

With unerring success millions have achieved their wish. In one city a million and a half. Four millions on one front, twelve millions on another. And thousands and thousands in the sea.

Every single one of these millions the object of grief and mourning. Numbers cannot dullen it.

O naturalist! here are plenty of wounds; what do their voices say?

New York City
March 1945

166

Handball Players

Often, playing handball, I am paired with the weakest player, as if I were the strongest player; and often we two win.

In fact I am a mediocre player, but I have a strong service. Once the play is engaged, my weakness appears. I follow the ball tenaciously and place my own shots cannily, but they are progressively feeble (against a strong player); by the fifth or sixth return I'm a dead duck.

Inhibiting my strength, yet tenaciously keeping the ball in play: as a child agrees not to do whatever it is and nevertheless will not let the issue close (waiting for her **softer nature to reassert itself?) Desiring not to win, but to** fight a *drawn-out* losing fight.

But when I crouch in the corner to serve the first ball, no one is yet in motion, and then, watching where they lie, I can spin the ball to within an inch of any line on the court or at the toes of my opponents. No one is in apparent motion, yet because of the previous serves they are already about to move this way or that, one may easily judge, or they are uncertain: then is the time that they bungle the set-up shot and their confusion is perfected. They are prematurely engaged; I am isolated, motionless, adequate—the world lies open for me to put it at a disadvantage. Against even a strong player, my tricky service, darting every way from the little corner, is worth half a dozen points.

When I am thus isolated, not socially engaged, I do not inhibit my strength and I am a formidable opponent. Woe to those who do not recover their aplomb but become more

167

and more prematurely engaged—really engaged in the memory of the play that is over, but I start afresh, I speed up the tempo—I could sweep them off the court: except that my softer nature reasserts itself and I cannot do them harm. Once I see my own advantage too clearly I am ashamed, and soon I relax both the tempo and my deadly serve. (But strong players, of course, stall and recover their aplomb and then they pound me, tho I hang on tenaciously.)

Playing alone, I dislike to win, to have to win. I like to **prove to my own satisfaction, not my superiority, but my** adequacy to any threat. But I do not like, playing alone, to be guilty of the victory. Perhaps I even prefer to lose, if it is a good contest and I am closely engaged socially, especially if I have shown flashes of power, to make me respected. But the victor is terribly isolated.

2.

Thus I often choose to be paired with the weakest player, especially if he is also the youngest.

Now some strong players crowd their weak partners out of the game. Such persons want too much to win and assert themselves; they are disgusted to see the weak partner bungle the shot that they could have returned with deadly effect. But this is bad policy, for (if the sides are evenly matched) no player can stand against two. Meantime the boy, feeling inferior to begin with, becomes more and more worthless: crowded out of the play in prospect, he is not there when he is absolutely called on; and sure that he is **inadequate, he bungles even when he is adequate. His part-**ner's disgust doesn't help.

Merely as policy, though I do not do it as policy, it is best to allow the weak partner his full court, but to support him close on his weak side. When he feels himself relied on, approved, and supported, then most often, since his weakness has been in part his security of weakness, he plays a little better. Momentarily he enjoys the naturalness of "beginner's luck." If he can confirm this good new habit, he's not such a weak player after all (supported on his weak side).

168

Handball Players

I support him and approve of him like a father. I do it because he is myself: I am the weak player.

Next, in two minutes, because he gratefully listens to me, he has learned the simple secret of never making a random shot without an angle, just to pound the wall with a blundering power like our opponents. See, now it is they who are behind on every play. The boy imagines that he is an adequate player after all. At least—we are a team. He fancies that he is a *strong* player—at doubles.

More and more I withdraw from the volley, leaving most of it to a weak partner! But in this way I have recaptured, even in the midst of the close volley, the isolation and the power that belong to me when I crouch in the corner to serve. My boy is engaged *for* me: shall I not suddenly step in, crowd him from the court, and hit the murderous bounder and uninhibit my strength?

They try to keep the ball away from *me*, as if I had more than this one shot. Obviously they hit it outside the court.

Under these circumstances, when my boy is playing most of the game, my softer nature does not reassert itself; my boy is asserting it for me. We do not relax the tempo; I do not relax my deadly serve; we are not ashamed to sweep them off the court with brutal victory and cry, "O.K., next victims!"

3.

What I like best is not to be closely engaged in the social game at all, not to risk the weak nature and the weak player to the chances of the game that scene by scene recreate the earnest episodes in which I learned to inhibit my strength—but for my favorite, by no means a weak player, to play in there for me, while I coach him, and we win.

He has not yet learned not to follow through and to become weak in the volley, but he pounds it with first nature. And as for the canny cross-purposes by which a child recovers and tenaciously keeps the ball in play—I see to them. And don't I feel the freshness blowing in my dear soul when he crouches, in isolation, and spins out my puzzlers, the low-darting serves, an inch within any line!

Have I done morally to teach the boy, who never earned it

169

by fatal losses, to crouch so cunningly disengaged when all the rest are in premature motion: are they playing the memory that is dead and gone? And *then* he follows through by his own first nature, for it is only a boy!

Yes! why should not at least one exhibit his fearless power? as if he never had father or mother—this is no fatal loss.

Nevertheless there is something too young and terrible in this fearless victory, scouring the court by nature and teaching, freely (not like the poor devils who drive themselves to brutal victory because they have been hurt).

I think that it is only partly in resentment of my dear boy that I feel sadness at his triumph.

Freely victorious, both in isolation and when closely engaged, in despite of my father and mother and all the poor grown-up folk.

The fact is that the ball is no longer in play.

Sitting here on the sidelines disengaged, the more closely engaged for *every* dancing player, I can see how the murderous bound has put an end to the social game; it has destroyed them one and all.

Better, clenching one's will and power, to kill on the serve, immobile and solitary, before one has ever joined at all. To specialize on the serve in order to prevent the play from starting, that will end in our hurt.

"Let me in the next game, fellows," I say. "It looks like Duffy's the best, so pair *him* with the weakest." Ha! and will *he* be able to support and enhearten his partner?

4.

Obviously it is I who must support and enhearten us all, both the weak player in his insecurity and the strong in his disgust, and my own partner—and myself; crying, "Too bad!" or "Partner!" or "Beauty!"

Let's not omit the human cries among the dry noises of the act.

We are not playing against each other. Whom are we playing against? against what are we playing?

Handball Players

We are playing against the wall! No pun; the act of the game is the essence of the game. The competition is our ruse to make us go to the extreme.

Pounding the immovable wall in order to keep the ball in play.

One will not break down a stone wall by pounding it with a rubber ball. (Desire for orgasm.) But at least return to it again and again. Why break the spell of the offering with murderous skill?

Yet unless it is heightened by the excitement of speed, power, and skill, and skill against skill, and will against will, going to the extreme, always within the rules—the rules are just so we may go to the extreme—how should we come to *devote* ourselves to the sacred offering, beyond ourselves and getting out of ourselves, in the social agony.

No fault in the young hero, freely victorious, the fool! that he hits the shot impossible to get; but that the rest of us do not rise to the height to achieve that impossible, and so miraculously offer ourselves in the agony. Doing miracles, forced to do miracles by the difficult demand. God forbid that out of resentment I should be saddened by a pure feat of first nature and second nature. What has a father to do with hurt pride?

Hurling our planet again and again—I am speaking of every ball game. At the immovable wall. The world is returned to us alive, so long as we keep it in play. We try, as far as possible beyond ourselves, during the brief time that the ball is breathing with life, to devote ourselves to the sacred dance. The line divides the court into the Houses of Night and Day. The planet is in play. The wall does not move, but it is consenting. The power is in our own two hands (though one will not break down a stone wall by pounding it with a rubber ball). By my cries I continue to support and enhearten us all. And the young hero, by creating the situation impossible to achieve, has raised us—one and all, not privately—to do miracles.

171

5.

Handball players do not play to win, but they think they play to play. Sometimes they play for a money-prize in order to convince themselves that they are playing to win and are not childishly at play.

Yet they do not play to play after all, but to keep the ball in play. Vainly they pretend that, relaxing from earnest, they are merely playing and not giving an offering to the implacable wall that stands up against them.

Acting—and renouncing the fruit of action, just as Krishna urged Arjuna. This is to act sacredly, there is no guilt in it.

The ball game is not an arbitrary convenience merely to enable us to act; but we act precisely, according to the rules, renouncing the fruit of it (nor is there any fruit of it), in order to keep the ball in play, the wall consenting.

A rubber ball is a similitude of a *live* thing. This is obvious when suddenly it bounds away in freedom, among the legs of the players, across the courts, unwilling to give itself to the power of their hands. Then it dies. (Indeed, when you see an eager, awkward child playing with a rubber ball and "hitting it with all his hard might," you would think that they were both equally live things, bounding to and from each other.)

They play in order to bring to life the little animal; in order to preserve alive the breathing life in it.

The four players, competitively and with their best and sacrificial effort, are generating an immense power to impart to the homunculus and make it leap with life.

To spin our microcosm across day and night and make it wring life from the wall, for it seems to rebound from the wall of its own will.

The sheer wall is the strength of the players that will not fail, relax, or soften—but it returns each blow as hard as it is struck.

Now here is the sheer, immobile, immovable, and impending wall. But there happens to be no other player to make a social game, so the man desultorily pounds the wall himself. It is hard thus to enliven the ball. The man playing

172

Handball Players

with himself is a masturbator; there is no external excitant, nothing unforeseen and distracting the conscious attention, to carry him beyond himself; unless desire and image well from the unknown. Ha! and does he think, desultorily pounding the ball, that he can so carefully control his strength and the enlivening animal? "Return me *that* flicker of Mercury! between the black night and the rising sun."—But he cannot, and it bounds away from him and dies.

At least the wall itself is immobile; it will not move forward against the players, but stands there consenting. (There is nothing unusual behind the blank wall: it is the wall of a building.)

But I used, when I was a child, to have a recurring nightmare: that the walls along the street crumbled as I passed and showered down their bricks upon me. The achievement of this orgasm roused in me a terrible anxiety.

But now the wall stands firm, and the live animal is only a rubber ball, as we develop, figure by figure, faster and faster, the devoted dance of our social game, within the rules, renouncing the fruits of action.

> Casting action upon Brahman,
>   abandoning attachment—
> Evil does not cling to him
>   as water not to the lotus-leaf.

> Rid of attachment, freed,
>   his mind fixed in knowledge,
> acting for worship only
>   —all action melts away.

New York City
May 1945

The Emperor of China

La Gaieté
—BEETHOVEN, *superscription to opus 127*

What does he infer, the Master, the magician, as he sits in his smallness on the swiftest claw of battling tigers? as he aids the whirlwind and therefore, the only one of us, sits still in the storm?

—That it's not the case, if we spend our strength for a free stroke, that there's nothing left for another! Whatever the occasion, there is pleasure for the occasion, if it's our occasion. And there is not a reservoir of force, but force is welling in the soul. And if we use our strength in love, there is still more strength for beautiful collaboration, and even for idiosyncratic strokes—and always we are ready to the present.

To the present: *Ow!* (I am now speaking for the Emperor of China). The wild ducks flying southward rest in the same swamp as on their way northward: the winter upon us. Master, is not this a round, and for me at least not endless? Therefore the little yellowed man, the Emperor of China, is dreaming of immortality, and he has summoned to the court the childlike sorcerer, to mix for *him* the potion of vitality. But will our Master come?

Ah, as he lingers at his ease in the flashing eye of the startled, swifter than anxiety and therefore alone among us masterless, what does the seer see?

—That there is true invention, in nature and social nature and art. It's not the case that what is freely done is only the hopeless palliative for an old wound. The games of children are freely inventing the children, as was not ever known before. Slowly their red stockings flicker across the

175

yard. And smiling our Master waits in the quick of the grievous wound, revelling in the fact that Destiny is Providence.

Is Providence: *Ow!* Yes, who can deny that it has brought us one and all to the present moment? We are rotating into a wound, as the whirlpool spins down into its black heart. That the Destiny of the Emperor of China and of the court of the Emperor of China is the providence of the sadness of all China—who can deny it, as we slowly one by one slide to our death? (But it is said that the people of China is immortal.)

The Master of the Way!—that we see fitfully when the curtain of the world is ripped—what does he know, swimming in the spray-drop (each drop agleam) and sinking with it into the shining sea?

—He knows that what is best is easiest and what is easiest is best. Does it not rest and slide in the accumulated rage of the universe, and set free the next motion of the universe as it trembles open into freedom and the present, as the trembling golden-daisy stretches to the tip of so many trembling petals?—best, easiest, and the latest moment, as our friends will everywhere create small worlds of freedom.

But the ancient court of China turns in its tiresome ritual about the sullen wound. Is turned. And those most ancient and dignified, near the center, are soonest sucked downward to black hell. It is these mandarins of the court who say that the energy of the universe is conserved and that the energy of the soul is conserved: that is, that it dribbles away in use and if a man use it for loving, he will not have it for beautiful collaboration nor to make images of his own idolatry. They say, too, that a man becomes a man by facing away from and forbidding the acts of a child, and not by growing into the glory of the next moment as it comes. So say these circlers of a grievous wound.

But our Master lay seventy years aforming in the womb—in safety from every maiming wound—and he will never be formed a personality like you or me.

In the red-lacquer court they hoard their strength—so they think! But watch close: the ritual is made of thousands and thousands of struggling motions so minute that they cannot see them, but we see them in the delicate tendons taut and in the pitiful eyes. "No strength!" they cry, exhausting their strength as best they can, and meantime they also, like everything in the world, are momently creating new strength that is momently whirling them despite themselves around into black hell. *Ow!* we are so heavily wounded.

Their Emperor is bleeding from the wound. "That sage is an immortal person!" he thinks—the fool! for our Master is not even a person, and we doubt that he is immortal— "Send for him here to mix us a potion of vitality, and perhaps we shall not die the moment after the next motion of the universe."

Ay, send for him! beyond the Great Wall of the Empire— and will our Master come? lying stretched in his vastness around, being the circle of the horizon—who knows what lies beyond him? What is he planning as his thoughts drift across the blue heaven as changeable clouds that are animals and junks, and then they have dispersed?

—That the Silence is overwhelming. That into the silence and the void melt the gongs and ritual and the Great Wall of China, to almost nothing—save from a crevice darts, quick as fire, the apprehensive salamander.

2. *Travel-Song*

As the Small Group, the humanity of the magician, goes up to Pekin—how shall I call it, what seems to be a small band of persons: children, parents, and friends, and some of these are already dead and accompany by their absence? this original humanity, not an individual and not a nation, but the social nature of the magician—as it goes among the trembling grasses, reading by night the calligraphy of the Northern Bear trembling in the moist air: they are dancing a travel-song—

The Easiest, the Best, the Latest Moment.

The Way is the difficult ease. It is hard to do the easy thing: as, to use the strength that one has rather than to strain with the strength that one has not; or to stand out of the way and let play the strength of the world that is crowding to our aid, rather than to hinder it with obstacles; or seeking an end, not to use means that hasten away from the end. These easy things are hard to do. But is the easiest thing to do the hardest thing to do? No, there are many harder things, which we see people in fact set about doing—as, we see people persevere with their last strength in a course which they know to be disastrous.

In general, there is an easy thing to do that is easy to do. This is not, to be sure, the easiest thing (for that requires a wisdom that we do not have); but to do easily an easy thing is already a good step to doing without great difficulty the easiest thing.

And sometimes! the easiest thing to do is the easiest thing to do!—in moments of great stress, as we see people do intricate heroic deeds, releasing the strength of the world that is crowding to their aid; or habitually, in moments of quiet, as an artist draws the easiest line; or revelling in despair, as our dear musician sang so lightly agreeing that he would die.

But always the easiest is the best. It is the Way.

So, demonstrating it by dancing it (for this is the easiest way), the social nature of the magician proceeds up to Pekin.

Now in the opposite direction is coming a herd of sheep tight-huddled. All in one impulse they are fleeing toward their slaughter. Each one of these sheep is nearly alone in its rudimentary mind: it is hardly aware of another as the few flashes of searing odor or want penetrate to its solitude. Yet all are surely bound in one direction and moving as one beast. To such isolated unitary things it makes no difference whether there is a herd of fifty or of one hundred forty million.

But the magical band of children, parents, friends, and the dead has a certain small number: a certain easiest complexity of recognition, mutual aid, mutual need, and rivalry, that releases in social invention the forces of original nature. As on they trembling dance.

The latest is the best: the last motion of nature, as it

trembles thru the present into the next motion after the last. For who can deny that, potentially at least, the present moment is the easiest: it is closest to experience, the most available to use. It crowds upon us, whether we will or no, thru all the senses and in the heart-beat and the muscles taut to ward it off. What are you warding off? do you not recognize it? it is the present moment crowding into being to our aid, accompanied by the forces of all the past. The hostility is spent, exhausted by a touch of death, and all that remains of it (as it seems) is the little living force, no bigger than a salamander, darting, quick as fire, from the crevice. But see this dragon, this present! lying in its vastness around the circle of the horizon enclosing the world.

Dancing to Pekin: that is to say, going on their legs. For they do not roll heels over ears like wheels, or go on wheels, as once I thought to be the motion of Paradise before I considered the nature of earth. For the nature of earth is to be textured: that is, solid and uneven to the touch. By its solidity it offers support in order that its unevennesses may be spanned: so we proceed by making spans and bridges in the roughness. Now if indeed the earth were an endless hard flat plain, then we could expect our locomotion to be wheeled (just as those who go thru the smooth and yielding water have assumed the shape of spindles). But it is hard and rough, and our limbs are light spanners and dividers: the four limbs especially of human beings can make bridges of all kinds in the three dimensions.

And the music of dancing has four gaits: single-time of hopping and jumping, double-time of walking, triple-time of skipping, and quadruple-time of running. All these are native gaits, as you may tell by observing the locomotion of the young. And our social band goes often hopping and jumping, skipping and running to Pekin, waiting up for the aged.

Accompanied, too, by some who are already dead and do not go these gaits; for the gayety of the ego of a natural band is made up somewhat, we know, by the presence of their absence.

3.

The Great Wall of China is complete and all China realizes with horror that it is imprisoned.

We have warded off the natural forces and projected them into things and encysted them in true formulations; now these lie there glowering hostilely at us.

In the court of the Emperor of China they sound the gong of alarm. The Emperor is dreaming of not dying: he is dreaming of that immortal emperor who never died because he never lived.

(The people of China is immortal.)

The Emperor of China and the court of the Emperor of China and the people of China have been hoarding their strength and excreting it shapely brick by brick. This is called building the Great Wall of China—feverishly, slowly—each man alone (one is not physically forced to it)—brick alongside brick, and ordering the rows into a wall, and extending the wall along the survey-lines. This is called hoarding one's strength and building the Great Wall of China.

—So an author orders the letters into a neat word. (First he has projected the threat into a thing, and he denotes the thing in a neat word.) He sets word next to word in lines, he rules line under line to make up a page. (He has now encysted the thing in true formulations.) He arranges these pages in such a sequence. . . . This is called warding off the natural forces! *protecting* himself from anxiety! *hoarding* his strength! building the Great Wall of China.

> The freely run-on speech unsought
> returns in whirlpools to its thought.

In this way it is possible (is it not possible?), building brick by brick, to hoard the strength of the accumulated rage of the universe of the great people, which otherwise might dissipate itself into easy blooms of health, freedom, and joy. But the Great Wall of China is complete!

All China realizes with horror that is is imprisoned.

The natural things lie there, glaring hostilely.

The Emperor of China

Suddenly one is sensible (is one not sensible?) that the whirlpool is turning within and that those nearest the center are sucked round into our wound down into black death. Good-bye to them! one by one.

In the court of the Emperor they sound the gong. The Emperor of China is dreaming of not dying: he is dreaming of that immortal emperor who never died because he never lived.

(The people of China is immortal.)

Must we not say that the force that was building the wall—and each man thought that *he* was building it!—is turning the whirlpool around and down? But the Great Wall of China is complete and all China realizes with horror that it is imprisoned.

See *here!* comes colored, motherly of carriage, and floating a foot above the water, the junk of our silent lord—on the escallops of the whirl and spray. The sails are colored with the feelings Carefree, Omniregardant; her flag is **Super-abounding and her pennons Toothless Smiles. Patience Firmness Duty: these are her carriage, the same as the endurance of the world: who rests in it upborne more** lightly than a babe.

She floats by Non-Attachment. She comes by the Disclosure of the Next Moment.

She pauses in mid-air in the maw of the whirlpool. From the slippery wall of water is thrust a forearm with a despairing clutch.

That which is light rests at ease; that which is heavy is dragged round and down.

Nevertheless our Master makes himself heavy and slowly sinks into the bite of pain.

4.

La Gaya Scienza
—Nietzsche

While the diabolical magician brews the poison potion for the Emperor, he observes silence.

181

While the wizard rests in the wound, he swallows the space about and recreates a Void.

Silence: but the Silence! For there is a secondary silence: when one does not talk aloud or sing, as when a person is alone. This silence is not even refreshing, for one carries on silent wrangles and mutters his composition, and at last, tho alone, he even talks aloud or sings. But deeper than this there is a primary silence that, if one sinks into it, is refreshing, yet still it is not the Silence: this is the silence in which a person listens and does not think of answering, as when we listen to frogs in the marsh, or we look at everything attentively. This silence is relaxing, refreshing, and recreative; and finally we break it with a melody from nowhere— that does not denote the sounds and sights but is as if the same as they. This is a good sign; still, it is not the Silence.

For always we are still forming concepts and judgments, and therefore inwardly saying: "This is the croaking frog"—"there are many of them"—"it is bright"—"their interval is a minor third"—"the dark line of hills"—"the contour." This inward speech, that seems to be only listening and taking in the scene, is betrayed by the motions of the throat: we are saying to ourselves "this" and "is" and "next?"

But how to be silent? and not always forming concepts and judgments. As for me, I am expert in formulations. These I can always make and say, *"there"*—*"that* is what it is"—"it is *only* that, no fear"—"I am safe." "Next?"—"am I safe?"

Building the Great Wall of China; protecting myself from anxiety.

—Yet let me speak no evil of the creator spirit, listening to whom, over my shoulder, and taking in the scene, I joyfully make them, these true formulations. But it is not meant that I should use them to ward off the world. But long ago we suffered a grievous wound and we who are expert in forming concepts and judgments have occupied the world with true formulations.

In the Silence the things are not encysted in formulations.

The Emperor of China

It is before he has learned to speak, as we speak; before his personality is formed, as our personalities are formed.

The images that float across his sky like clouds—they split with fire and there is a crack of thunder: it is indeed raining.

As, in the Silence, our Master who has lain seventy years in the womb, plays with the milk and drool, the shit, the piss, the blood, and the semen.

In the Void, in the quick of the wound, where the wizard has swallowed up the space, he is dancing the creation of the things before they have a name. (We name them because we are expert only in formulations:)

—That the drool and milk, etc. are the Rivers of Paradise.

That when he masturbates he opens high and wide the dome of heaven.

That resting and losing the weight of his body, he divides into territories at his bony joints, and these are the six continents.

That from turds of shit he fashions out the elephants and the bears.

That when he fucks, the electric friction makes the sky blue. The thick lightning.

From the seed the magician is born again, that lay seventy years in the womb. The Master of *La Gaya Scienza!*

As for me, these natural things are no longer so hostilely lowering.

In the Silence, in the Void, they drop lightly into place and tremble open to the most space to the present flowers of May. The wild ducks are flying northward. The moments are flying thick and fast, but they are not flying by, they are not flying by.

In the Silence, in the Void, the natural things drop lightly into place and the moments are flying thick and fast but they are not flying by. The thoughts that drift like clouds across the sky—they split with fire and the magician is born again that lay seventy years in the womb. The Master of *La Gaya Scienza* is dancing us the things that do not yet have a name. Thick and fast the moments are not flying by.

In the hole of the vortex, in the clenched jaws of death,

the hellish wizard is spinning and his skirts fly out. He has made his excrements into missiles and is destroying those who love him. He sucks and will not let loose. They are drowned in the searing piss, beaten by his penis, and jumped on up and down. All things are flying far from him as he spins: he spins alone: his skirts fly out. Can we ever restore to place those things flung far from their center? They are hostilely lowering where they fall. Too late! Our time has been swallowed up by a wizard. Sound the gong.

We were omnipotent when we destroyed it, and now when we would restore it we are not omnipotent; never can we make restitution; *this* is the wound by which we are bleeding to death.

Wifely, high: like the moon rescued from the slime after a fortnight we did not see her and all at once shining in the top of heaven at a bound, such are the full sleeves that offer to the Emperor the cup of vitality. The beverage that is brewed of animal spirits, that is fermented for the duration of the world, and distilled into presentness. The revolution that is frothing at the brim never ceases. And drinking, the natural band will go the wandering steps that do not err.

The Emperor of China sips this poison and straightway he falls down in death agony, croaking.

For the Emperor of China bade the Master of the Way brew for him the elixir of immortality; and drinking it, he is poisoned and dies. Is this the fault of the elixir?—The Master is impassive.

The Emperor of China cries out in his agony: "Ow! I *know* that destiny is providence—my brain is seared with it, as a tongue of fire from the window envelops the house: for it means that, hurrying on, I came back again and again to my grievous wound, and who can deny that that past has brought me to this present crowding into the next and last? Am I supposed *therefore* in the jaws of death to sing, 'Ah! providential!' Wounded: *Ow*—this I did not know I knew. The natural things are now no longer glaring at me so hostilely. Roundabout they lie impassive. Even the Great Wall of China is only a broken wall. What drink is this, that you have poisoned me with? the revolution frothing at the brim does not cease. *Ow. Ow*—I know: it is the same thing

184

to say 'I know' and 'Ow'; isn't it the same thing? Who is this impassive dragon lying around the circle of the horizon with his tail in his mouth? It means that the time is complete. *Ow!* and that immortal emperor, who never died because he never lived: is it *thus* that the people of China is immortal?"

He is dead. What! do they not proclaim another?

The Master says: "Why didn't he drink a second time?"

He says: "Is not every natural force, considered alone, violent? Violent clashes with violent, and there emerges, trembling, what was not known before. This is called 'brotherly conflict' and 'invention.'

"When a man is imprisoned, will not the violence of nature seem to him to be destruction? When a man is imprisoned in himself—the wall is made of formulations and the moat around the wall is a bleeding wound—must not natural violence seem to be the destruction of the world?

"When a man is imprisoned: this is called 'dreaming of immortality.'

"But 'the hounded hare takes pleasure in his leaps, in his dodges, in his speedy course.'"

The mandarins of China say (each man alone and afraid to look at his startled friend): "*Therefore* let us set free the people of China.

"It is said that the people of China is immortal. Perhaps they can teach us to be immortal. Or at least! at least that we, in our yellowed age, may have a little solace in watching the inventive games of the children of the people of China.

"That we may rest from building the Great Wall of China. No longer hoarding our strength and encysting the natural things in formulations.

"In order that the natural things may not glower at us so hostilely.

"To cease to rotate about our grievous wound.

"To dare engage in the conflict of brothers.

"To crowd into the present with the force of the endurance of the world."

New York City
October 1945

185

The Formulation
of Freedom

—for Diana Liben

That I inhibit myself from pursuing something I desire
(youth passing in the street) in order to preserve the public
reputation of a principle of freedom that I have formulated,
urging men to pursue just such desires, condemning men
for inhibiting their pursuit and especially if they inhibit it
on the grounds of public reputation; and furthermore, I
came to the principle as a generalization of my own free
acts, to rationalize and defend them.

Before I persuaded myself that these things were justified
in principle, I did not inhibit myself from their pursuit,
careless enough of my public reputation. But then it was
not necessary to preserve the reputation of my principle, of
my formulation of freedom.

As if the principle would not have to prove its own moral
authority, independently of me; as if indeed my own risk
and fall in pursuit of happiness as demanded by the principle would not rally at least a few to my formulation and
enhance my moral reputation undisgraced.

One would say that I am *using* that principle of freedom
as a means of protecting myself from the free acts of whose
consequences I am afraid—or afraid of the acts themselves.
Yet before I formulated the principle, I overcame the fear of
the acts and their consequences.

Then it seems to be that *formulating* a principle, formulating the principle of freedom! puts me in a different
moral role (role of the grown-ups): I am now inhibited by
the timidity proper to parents and proper towards parents.
Afraid to embarrass my father, my principle—even tho it is

187

the principle of freedom—but preferring to disobey; previously only my disgrace was involved, now it is also his reputation. (Why did my father meddle in the *secret* understanding that I had before he ever came on the scene?) Or on the contrary, afraid for my principle, my child, to embarrass itself by any action whatsoever; clinging to it and refusing to let it go free and act, unwilling for it to exist independent of me—even tho it is the principle of freedom! Ashamed to be disgraced before my father or my child (it comes to the same thing), because I know that he does not dare to do what he urges on the next generation: now willing to be satisfied in *them*, by proxy. Let *them* be free and satisfy me, the child in me, but I am the father and freedom is not for me.

That is, because now it is necessary in principle to be free, I cannot, because this saps from my child-heart the reckless rebellion that overcomes my fear of moral authority. Yes, the recklessness that comes from the secret prior understanding that the child has: that what his mother forbids is what she really desires for him and dares not say it—and this recklessness made me stand out against the authority and be free, except that now the authority has formulated a principle of freedom: and where is the recklessness to come from to stand out against the authority and to do what the authority really desires for me and dares to say it?

The error is in *saying* it, in formulating the principle of freedom. It means, *crystallizing the ego.*—

For the first time I think I have a firm belief: the belief in the freedom of my previous acts of rebellion when I did not have a firm belief. I have rationalized the acts and have a firm belief; justified myself, secure (from anxiety) in my firm belief. That is, my ego is crystallized. But those acts of freedom were the acts of impulse, and by crystallizing the ego, I more strongly repress the impulse; then I am less compelled to do the act and run the risk. *I* am more free (from compulsion) and mankind in me is less free from my tyranny. Thus, just because one has formulated a principle of freedom, there are fewer acts of freedom. (By such means our free societies endure and extend their tyranny!)

Also, that previously the acts of freedom had a certain

mystery and infinity (unconscious compulsion), promising always something I did not know; but this infinity I have not caught in my formulation of freedom. But now I promise only freedom, that is all.

And now I am *committed* to freedom and terrible anxiety. For when the promise was infinite, the responsibility was indefinite: once engaged, I could also still withdraw and avoid the worst penalties. But now I cannot withdraw without destroying my consistency and self-respect; the ego drives me on. If now I act, if I were to act, with firm belief, I cannot help setting a great machine in motion, for I am not inept: this involves greater consequences than what I acted, weakly, on impulse, carefully inhibiting myself. Then am I not justified, committed to freedom, to go slower than when I carefully inhibited myself, and to choose the occasion carefully?

But the principle of freedom is just not to go carefully nor to set large machines in motion for satisfying a simple desire. Why, for such things, does one need to be apt or inept? It is likely that to bide my time and choose the occasion, to preserve the reputation of my principle, is nothing but a rationalization of my fear. Nevertheless I predict that, after a time, recklessly rebellious, I shall indeed choose the occasion and, because I have a firm belief, set in motion a great machine: justified! without anxiety— for one cannot be disgraced acting on principle! and disgraced and succumbing to the anxiety I long for, for in the crisis I shall come to doubt the principle and be left naked.

That I formulate the principle because I am tired of the fight and thereby I reconcile myself to renouncing it and still satisfy the impulses to freedom (which are probably weaker with age). Then secondarily, I find a vast satisfaction in being, and being known as, an expert formulator of the principle of freedom; and why should I jeopardize this security and social prestige by running the old dangers? "I have done my share."

That the formulation of freedom is a sign of resignation and fatigue, and that the formulation of freedom is a sublimation of freedom. That (oh!) this formulation of freedom

189

must *coerce* us to a great act of freedom, choosing the occasion!—

To formulate the principle of freedom just because I am tiring of the fight and losing it (and no wonder then that I do not do a free act), in order to *rally* my better nature to the fight and prevent myself from giving it up. To recapture recklessness, the secret understanding, by proclaiming it as a public principle! no turning back now! Forcing my hand.

But to believe in the justification of the act and *also* to act: this is a blessed integrity of the soul, and where, suddenly, just because I formulate a principle of freedom, am I to get such health and freedom?

I am an artist. With me it is an old story: to meet the moment with a formulation of the moment. What is it to wonder that my darling formulation is not the thing itself? It is a third somewhat between me and the thing. All art is "abstract, because it tries to bring into existence the non-existent by closely copying it" (Rank)—by copying especially its non-existence! The freedom I formulate is not generalized from any freedom I ever knew, otherwise I could not formulate it so artistically; and now when it comes to a new act, imitating the formulation, why this is not the same act as those for which I used to have reckless daring; *this* I could never do. I have always been a free and fearless artist; and when have I ever been a free and fearless man?

Regarded close, my formulation of freedom is a lie. For it implies the achievement, the possibility of achievement, of free happiness (otherwise why should one formulate such a principle?). But the acts of freedom from which I generalized it were always only the acts of free pursuit, not of achievement. The formulation is a desperate dream in which I enjoy the free happiness that I cannot achieve. Then what is surprising if, dreaming it out, having learned to dream it out, and willing it to be true, like an artist (sublimating the impulse), I now have less energy for the mere free pursuit, the fore-pleasure?

Enjoying the security of the expert formulator of freedom: projecting free happiness from me, like an artist: sinking in the daydream that now many others may also sink in: creating thereby a social atmosphere to diminish guilt, and (oh!) *thereby* achieving our free happiness.—

For the formulation of freedom is a device to involve others with me and to socialize and diminish the guilt (band of the brothers). It is the public secret understanding. That is to say, it is a device to say in a general and acceptable way what are my intentions, as the first step in an indefinite erotic approach; hoping that some one will appear for me—and the way smoothed—and I at last gain happiness. But just for this reason, because it is a social device, I must interpret the principle as it might seem to another: this is called protecting the moral reputation of the principle. The formulation of freedom refers to unmixed intentions; but my pursuit of happiness has always been mixed (fearful, rebellious, probably resentful), and now I am ashamed, before my brothers, to pursue on such motives, to jeopardize the social secret understanding and confraternity in which is placed my real desire, and not at all in those reckless pursuits. If it were not my real desire I would not be an expert formulator, free and social.

It means that I am secretly afraid, face to face with my brothers in whom is my real desire, that the formulation of freedom, in which I have the satisfaction of a sure belief, is false. Because I do not believe the formulation of freedom, therefore, having formulated it and seeing it clear, I will not act it: not out of fear but out of desire.—

That perhaps it was a formulation of resentment, by which I hoped to lure my happy brothers to their doom.

Nevertheless! (again I hear the little child who expertly used words to placate the punisher, and nevertheless spoke out his honest say), the formulation of freedom is true! Is there no pity for us, brought up to be fearful and ill—and long pursuing but not achieving happiness—and now aging, nevertheless we tell you plainly and therein spend our last strength (no more left for pursuit), the formulation of freedom?

Let me clutch it to me and cry tears, my formulation of

free happiness. Those who have achieved what they desired no doubt find that achievement gives no lasting happiness; but we who have never achieved it can believe that it would give us lasting happiness—some simple thing, easy, justified by the formulation of freedom.

Would it not give us happiness, since we stand so strongly in the way of achieving a simple thing (especially by pursuing it) that to achieve it would signify the breakdown of every resistance in our soul, all now turned in fury against some easy, justified thing; would it not be the recovery of our blessed health? The formulation of freedom.

This is what we communicate to each other, these tears, in the formulation of freedom that gives us solace and a brotherly and sisterly sympathy too dear to jeopardize by achieving some easy, justified thing.

And that the formulation of freedom is a means of summing up, of consigning to the past, all those free acts from which we have generalized the formulation of freedom. Those unsatisfactory acts. Let them not reappear, like spectres, to tempt us now when we have made *tabula rasa* with the formulation of freedom. To the degree that we are now freed, and look about to achieve some unformulated happiness—in which to have a sure belief.

New York City
November 1945

Little Bert, or The Intervention

His sister Lucy clambered across the stony wall to pick buttercups with longer stems, altho nailed on the apple-tree was the sign "Beware of the Bull." She was 13 and wore a dress of color faded nearly white, and she had formal curls that hung on her shoulders. From out his hiding place, the bull sauntered in her direction, indecisive, like a drunken man on Ninth Avenue. The little boy opened his mouth past his ears and screamed "Help." The outcry made Lucy freeze in fright, but their companion, the farmboy Dan in his overalls, jumped on the stones, took her by the hand, and led her back across—while a flush of admiration and gratitude colored the little boy's cheeks, and a pang of envy smote him between the eyes.

Then sitting near the well that had a hood and a windlass, Lucy was braiding the daisies and long-stemmed buttercups into a garland. She wove daisies into a starry circlet and placed it on Bert's hair where it tickled with embarrassment. Dan watched her with big eyes of desire trembling to his embarrassment.

The grown-up boy and girl walked behind the house and did not reappear at once. Little Bert became fearful and suspicious. His anxiety grew. Sauntering near, as if indecisively, he peered round the corner of the white house, and the two were kissing in the shade. Silently he slipped his arms between them, round her waist. In this way he intervened; he effected a rescue; he shared in the secrecy.

With terrible violent spite Dan twisted Bert's arm behind his back. The tears and sweat started into Bert's face but he would not cry out. But Lucy said, "Let him go, you're hurting him." Dan was confused and abashed. "He didn't hurt me," said little Bert.

Trembling in every joint and his fingers fumbling, Dan turned aside to pee. The trembling communicated itself to Bert and he watched him with open mouth and also with terrible envy.

2.

Auntie Dora, the guardian of the children for their visit at the farm, was at the piano composing *The Lucille Waltz*. Childless as yet, and ultimately childless thru several marriages, she was considered excellent with children because loving and firm, or sentimental and cruel, or perversely lascivious and guiltily vindictive. The piano, of a kind heard no more, was equipped with a special pedal that allowed the upper register to twang like a guitar.

The Lucille Waltz was complete and, however it was, Auntie Dora furiously began to upbraid and beat the girl about her head and shoulders, while Bert cowered behind the wicker chair. "A child is beaten, not I—" What! it was Lucy that was being beaten—whether Bert himself had told Dora about the kissing, or that she had heard about the charge of the bull.

But in the city, Papa had gone away in vain, because Mama saw Mr. Gericke.

The little boy cried out, "Don't hit her any more!" Dora had picked up an iron poker, and Bert thought, "She can't *mean* to hit her with that and hurt her forever." He stepped between, intervening, and hid behind his forearm and cried, "You're bad, Auntie Dora. You made *The Lucille Waltz* and you hit Lucy."

But Papa's sister brought down the poker on his arm, then dropped it and slapped his head from side to side. There was an unfillable void in his wail.

He implored, "Don't hit me any more. You meant it."

Little Bert, or The Intervention

His sore eyes covered with a gritty dust the flirtatious smiles and the flowers of the field. This dust lies there opaque between the eyes and their objects, intervening, rescuing us from the vividness of what is *meant*.

Little Bert's forearm was as if breaking with fatigue as he masturbated, offering himself the day's images unmeant. They made threats about his naughtiness, but he willed not to take them seriously.

He wailed at midnight, just to make it impossible for the others to sleep.

In the morning they were shouting in the next room about money and the crying child. Narrowing to a pointed grin the wide quadrilateral mouth of pain, Bert stretched his happy grin taut from ear to ear.

Auntie Dora came in and at once opened the drawers to pack the clothes. Lucy's movements were unwilling. The boy was not unwilling to return home, to surprise Mama. He did not like the milk warm from the cow.

So they made preparations to go. But now they were going indeed—away from the serious theatre where alone the flowers sprang alive. The horse was harnessed to the trap. The sobbing child stretched out his arms in longing. Auntie Dora sat stiff and their hostess was thin-lipped, but the farmboy helped with the valises with the dumb willingness of the baffled. The fat behind of the horse was the type of all things that hold back. Nevertheless they moved off.

Bert and Lucy silently stretched their necks to see back—in unison, but he could not touch her.

Bert was going back to the city.

Going to intervene, with a new insincere purposiveness.

So a man unwillingly (but why then does he do it?) boards the train that takes him from the place that promises a little comfort.

But to see the flowers is a little comfort.

His arms are lifted high: when will they come pounding down?

I cannot take your troubles seriously, as if they were meant; why do you tell them to me?

THE FACTS OF LIFE

Many the lovers I have brought together; then intervened like a physician watching the fever-chart—watching the progress of it like the figures on a fever-chart.

[*New York City*]
June 1946

Eros, or The Drawing of the Bow

Mesonuktiois pot' horais
—ANACREONTEIA

In the middle of the night
when the Bear already sinks
toward the hand of the Plowman,
and all the tribes that speak
lie overwhelmed in sleep:
then halting, Love did pound
upon my bolted door.
"Who bangs upon my door?
My dream you have divided."
But Love said, "Open up!
Only a child—don't fear;
I'm wet; I've lost my way
thru the night without a moon."
When I heard it I took pity
and taking up the lamp
I opened wide: a child indeed
I saw: he had a bow
and wings and a quiver.
He stood beside the hearth
warming the palms of his hands
and shaking the wet water from his hair.
But when the chill was past,
"Come," said he, "let us try
this bow, whether the string
is hurt by being wet."
He stretches it and smites me
full in the breast, and stings;
and now he leaps and laughs,

"O friend," he cries, "rejoice!
My bow it is unhurt!
but you will ache at heart."

So in these Trials of the Bow a man returns to his wound, both received and given; and joyfully puts his fear of castration to the test. In this first Trial he is a child again: to make all the world tiny, and be safe.

The History of Eros

This poem is the archetypal dream of the followers of Anacreon. It is a late dream, the result of a long repression. Eros has become a child again; he is no longer the powerful Archer of Homer. The older Desire was not helpless in the grown-up social world, but was one, not the least, of the forces of constructive and destructive action; his acts were so strong and direct that one did not need (to describe Love) to look for him in one's feelings, in the sting of the heart, but could depict an objective dramatic scene. But by the time of the followers of Anacreon the social action of Desire was moderated, kept within bounds; then one inquired into the feelings of this Eros. Nevertheless, there was as yet no illusion, for there was as yet no repression of the pleasures of Love, but only of all its grown-up social effects. On the contrary, the experience was nothing but pleasure (and pain), and was never released into constructive and destructive, and self-destructive, action. Clinging, all the rest given up, to this pleasure. Then speculating on the polymorphous pleasures that one felt, one came easily to discover the polymorphous child within.

Now later most of these pleasures themselves came to be denied, and even pleasure itself: then one ceased to picture Love as one's real self at all. Instead people developed the illusion of an ideal object, a Mother, close to the original object itself but forgotten and untouchable; then the boy Cupid shrank to the size of an infant, who still decorates our calendars. (And what shall we say of the most recent

years when a man, fostered in schools till his late adolescence, thinks that Love is an adolescent like himself, of
female sex?)

"In the middle of the night"—when business is intermit-
ted, especially the Anacreontic business of alcohol and
roses, and polymorphous pleasures; one is alone.

Then one does not speak, but instead dreams: images,
already the mode of thought of early years, but still concerned with grown-up business.

"Then on my bolted door"—for the mind is purposely
shut fast against its depths. Yet the child is halted there
behind: arrested.

"You have interrupted my dreams!" Surely! for this child
is not himself a dream, a dream-thought; but the fact itself,
the cause of thought.

It is only a child, no fear. It is the very child that one was.
He is wet: new-born. He comes from the dark night: one
had no acquaintance there. He was lost, but now he has
halted, arrested. In the Anacreontic day, many an experience might occur by which the child within might suddenly be summoned, and stand arrested.

"Pitying—" these are the idle tears, I know not what they
mean, that are shed for oneself. For whom else are idle tears
shed? But taking the lamp: now one will know.

So often, opening a door, one sees something framed in
the doorway.

A child indeed. The bow and darts are the small penis
erect. Winged: for easily a child soars aloft, borne in his
mother's arms. This is why the childish Cupid is winged.

Warming himself: for he has come from the cold world of
the dead. So it must always seem in the actual hour, that the
past is cold and dead. Now reborn dripping, so he must be
dried like a newborn child. Soon he is accustomed to the
warmth of the present hour, and he looks about.

We must think of this child as about six years old, in the
full maturity of childish sexuality, before that sexuality has
been blotted from the mind. Is his power lost? this is the
question. This is the trial of the bow.

His power is not lost: he stretches the bow. How easily

199

this experimental masturbation must become the rivalry, penis for penis, of the trial of the bow in the *Odyssey*! As yet it is the self-love of childhood; next the love of a man for this little rival within himself. Will he not discover rivals outside himself?

As for the child, he rejoices, says, "Rejoice *with* me!" as if, a new discoverer, he was the first to find how to give oneself pleasure.

But the poet returns to his wound. This is the deepest thing he wishes, to return to his wound. His wound is the weak-point in the armor of his ego: it is through the wound that stream the forces from the depths. To return and look into this deep spring. His wound is not the child, but that the child stands there arrested, that he could not merge into the present hour and vanish. That he torments one from the past. This sting leaves a rankling wound. It is a familiar experience, that we try to fill up this void, like a quicksand, with the pleasures of the followers of Anacreon. Also, on the contrary! there streams to us from this void such power and action as we do have. We loose another dart, and still the quiver is not empty.

2.

Toxou thesis
—ODYSSEY, xxi.

Penelope said that "whoever could easily bend the bow in his hands and shoot the arrow, with him she'd go, quitting her nuptial home so fair and full of the means of life (which she thought she remembered as in a dream)."

The suitors could not bend it, tho they warmed the bow at a fire and greased it well. But their hearts ached not because of the woman, they said, but because the people would call them feeble.

But Odysseus (disguised), when he took the bow, turned it all ways and tried it here and there, lest it had been harmed in the absence of the king. "See how he handles it, as if he had such a thing at home!"

This bow that his boyhood friend Eurytides Iphitus gave

200

him. He did not take it to the war on his black ship, but he kept it at home as a memento of his dear friend. There he used to carry it.

Taking the great bow, he looked about him on all sides, then, "as a man skilled in music and the lyre easily stretches a string around the peg, so hastily Odysseus bent the mighty bow."

He thumbed the string and it moaned like the swallow. A great ache entered into the suitors' hearts and their flesh crept.

This Odysseus did not have a wound, but the healed scar of a boar that attacked him when he climbed Parnassus with the boys of Autolycus.

Stripped of his rags, "Now this contest is over!" he cried to the suitors, "let us try another not yet proposed, so grant it me Apollo!" And he aimed the arrow at Antinoös.

It is the same penis-rivalry, play and earnest, that we met with in the poem of the follower of Anacreon. But now it is not the child who bends the bow, but the man himself. This is the heroic expression of Love in constructive and destructive action; it is not necessary to linger in the description of feelings.

The man carries not his wound, but the scar of his wound. By this we know him for the king. One has become a whole (scarred) man, with full power (such as it is). But it is worthwhile to mention also the hero Philoctetes, who was suffering a live wound, but then he did not shoot his bow.

"He looked about him on all sides"—posing: so the mutual contest turns into an exhibition of oneself. He exhibits first his scar, then his prowess.

The bow that his dear friend gave him, and the wound that he took in the company of the sons of Autolycus: we have not to do, as previously, with childhood, but with the sexuality of adolescence. From this wound one indeed recovers, and this bow can indeed be turned to slay one's fellows, after all have drifted apart.

At least Odysseus did not carry his bow off to the war: I take it to mean that Odysseus was not one of your vindictive warriors whose aggression is nothing but the result of homosexual frustration.

"As easily as a musician"—so says Homer! For Homer, to be sure, this prowess and this exhibition are very easy. This handling—this power to stretch as if lifeless the audience of the song.

> My hand is strong, has turned to fire
> the arpeggios of the lyre,
> and elsewhere we love carelessly
> who closely love Saint Harmony.

At the climax of his poem (we may picture the scene), the poet Homer compares his hero with—himself!

"Stripped of his rags"—Odysseus is not stripped naked; on the contrary, bristling with sword and spear. An armed love. And Antinoös, when the king looses his arrow, is about to lift the goblet to his lips to drink wine: "death was not his concern, among many feasting men," says Homer—these are the brothers sitting together, but no longer in trust and amity, but selfishness and greed.

"The doors were bolted"—it means that there is no opening into this conscious slaughter for any access of deeper love. For yes! there is a free and natural love, a mutual aid among all mankind, deeper than these Trials of the Bow.

3.

I have so far omitted the most striking passage.

The son Telemachus spoke up among them: "Zeus has made me crazy. My dear mother in her wisdom says that she will follow another and leave this house, yet I laugh and am happy, like a madman. Come, suitors, since this seems to be the prize, she's not the only woman in Greece. What difference does mother's fable make to me? But I myself shall try the bow, if I can bend it and shoot! Not to my sorrow would the lady my mother leave this house and go with another, when I'd be left behind alone to take father's prizes."

Eros, or The Drawing of the Bow

He stood on the platform and tried the bow. Thrice he made it tremble, straining with all his might. Thrice his strength failed him. But the fourth time, he strongly bent it.—But Odysseus shook his head and prevented him from shooting.

The prince mad, and pretending to be mad, at once puts us in mind of Hamlet. The difference is that Hamlet's father was dead and returned to him from within, to stay his hand. No longer a prince of epic destruction, but of tragic self-destruction, and then even, as Goethe said, a prince of feelings rather than acts. But Odysseus has returned alive to Telemachus: there he sits (the doors are not yet bolted), one of the suitors, just one of the suitors. Why should not Telemachus also try the bow?

We may say that Telemachus looked for his father in three ways: (1) in order to *find* him, so as to have a secure father instead of the rout of suitors among whom he grew up—and we may imagine his hostility; (2) in order *not* to find him, to be free finally to make up his own mind; and (3) to *hunt him down*—for the Trial of the Bow. Well, now he had hunted him down.

"She's not the only woman in Greece—" What an astounding statement for the son to make! what a lie of despair! Does he not hereby include himself among the frivolous suitors?

"When he should be left behind alone, in father's place"—blotting them out of the picture one and all, including Penelope, like a child affirming himself after he has agreed to take every fatal loss.

"Thrice he made the bow tremble!" So one grows up through childhood, boyhood, and adolescence. (By this time many sons have already won, or lost, the trial of the bow; but Odysseus has prudently absented himself for the full twenty years.)

"The fourth time he stretched it!" He is now twenty or twenty-one years old. It is a contest between grown men. This is the most unusual feature of the *Odyssey*, it is the essence of the *Odyssey:* that there is a father who has not struggled with and identified himself with, and succumbed to, his child at some childish age—two or six or thirteen—but he stayed away until it was a manly contest, in which a father has some chance of victory.

"But Odysseus shook his head and prevented him from shooting." So? Is this indeed what took place? And if Telemachus had let fly? And at what would the first arrow be let fly if not at Odysseus, the chief of the suitors?

What a surprise for Odysseus! to come home after twenty years to this young arrow! And as the blood gushes from his nostrils, is there not, nevertheless, a flashing glance of recognition, and love, from the eyes?

But Telemachus has not suffered a wound, therefore he lowers the bow.

These are the three trials of the bow. The trial of the child within; the trial of the boyish rivals; the trial of the father and the son.

The first is the lyric trial; the second the epic trial; and the third would have been the tragic trial.

But indeed, there is a free and natural love, mutual aid among all mankind, deeper than these Trials of the Bow.

[New York City]
[1946?]

The Legs of My Dog:
Some Notes on Gross Physiology
and Visible Form

The surface tells the deep secret. The figure breaks into appearance, or maintains itself in the conditions, by drawing on strong forces, from within and from the conditions.

Contrary to the usual opinion, the surface guards us against the plausible but irrelevant.

Water and Earth

Hamilton Falls: the abstracted interaction of water and rock, this is natural constructivism.

"Picturesque" is the emergence of a simpler physical force among the more developed. Thus "pretty places are always dangerous."

The great property of water is to be flat, seeking its own level. The effect is to conceal the variety beneath and also the variation in its own previous motion. From the rushing flashing falls to the flat plane in an instant still.

The property of earth is texture, that is irregularity and solidity.

Legged Things

Legs are standers in the solid and spanners of the irregular. The caterpillar is its own bridge. Man's Limbs are very free spanners in the six directions.

Flat roads belong to wheels not legs; walking on them

seems inefficient. This earth has solidity but no irregularity. (Problem in community layout on the "human scale": hills or even adobe-hut ladders, to exercise the powers of the animal.)

The Legs of the Dog Tinkerbelle

The legs of beasts, adapted to the hardness and roughness of earth, are flexibly posable spanners.

The extension of legs is to allow some space from the earth in order to fall by gravity to a position. Or better: a space to move the smaller part to position before committing the mass of the body; that is, to pose with a small effort and then to fall onto the support.

Joints are the way of being both flexible and stiff.

Our aim is to interpret the shape of things, the four legs of Tinkerbelle, by the interaction of the prevailing simple conditions. E.g. 1. Hardness and roughness of the earth, 2. Gravity. What can we say of the fourness of the legs and the bilateral symmetry? three points suffice to stand; with four it is possible to stand with three and alter the position with one.

In running, the dog seems to fall from diagonal (front-left, rear-right) to the other diagonal. This action relates to the chief parallelogram of forces in forward motion. I must someday study this closer to see what is the most efficient relation: the different gaits.

Right and Left, Forward and Backward

I see that the question of bilateral symmetry and forward motion forces me into a much simpler and more fundamental question. First, does right and left-handedness exist in space, or is it a condition of perception for any "center" (whatever that means)? Given the suspicious fact that the right and left-hand gloves are otherwise indistinguishable, we might like Kant (because of this very observation?) take the space as a form of perceiving. Or is the bilateral doubling the adjustment of the feet to the property of space?

The Legs of My Dog

That is, is it the nature of the desiring soul to protrude these doubles; or is this a necessity to get the food and love?

Here is perhaps a fruitful new approach to geometry: Let us regard, as is the case, the animals as more like ourselves than is the space; let us then look for the properties of space by inference from the locomotion of animals, instead of by pure geometrical speculation. "Less known by the more known."

Rightness-Leftness, e.g. similar triangles: this is embracing towards oneself as center, or pushing open a space for the center to live and move.

Likewise, we must ask of forwardness and backwardness: are the legs turned forward adapting to a forward-backward in space; or is this an effect of desire? The vast majority of species, down to the protozoa, seem to have a head-tail direction; yet pure geometry overlooks this differentiation in space. (Allowing for this directional differentiation one can easily prove the parallel postulate.)

The mirror-image is the true back image if our eyes were reversed (not rotated).

Motion without front-back or right-left: rings of a tree, amoeboid pulsation. Amoeboid flowing as pro tempore differentiating.

Libido and Space—Direction

Assume that front is desire. There is a psychological difference between backing away and turning to flee (= desire of another place). "Aversion" or turning is the transition.

Conceived backward (unpleasure), left and right are reversed. That is, apart from desire they are not yet determined. It would seem from this that left and right are the potentialities of the alternatives of *choice*. Starting with desire, and potentiating it as yes or no, doubtfully, not immediately, I can go forward or turn away, as well as simply backing away.

(Upright posture: quicker turn. Add this to upright posture: loss of smell, upright posture: ready hand, and upright posture: genitals exposed.)

Likewise with Up-Down: Up is a readiness to motion, by storing the potential energy of gravity; down is succumbing from local motion. (Succumbing, e.g., to pulsation of orgasm or to sleep.) In repose, the earth is less in potentia more in actu.

Amoeboid motion: its space is undifferentiated potentially but differentiated in act! Must we not draw the melancholy conclusion that all animals past the paramecium are already neurotically armored against many free possibilities? Endoskeletal is terrible, exoskeletal the worst!

I read that amoebae encyst in danger situations. The next stage of neurotic armoring is to conceive a *wary attitude* toward the environment, and this means to develop a head-tail disposition. Conversely, head-tail means a neurotic seeking out of the desirable, rather than a natural fulfilling of desire.

Gaits

Swinging arms is a vestige of the four-legged gait, but the arm, properly going back with its diagonally opposite leg, does not exert a forward push. Except in swinging.

Trotting of the dog: the advantage of the four legs is that the alternation of the diagonals cuts down the mean body-fall, correspondingly increasing the frequency.

Dog loping and jumping: forelegs and hindlegs alternate in parallel rather than diagonally. The body-mass falls further, the push-power is greater, the forward motion is therefore greater; but the frequency less. It is especially for these gaits that the hind-legs are heavier, the front legs seeming to serve mainly to regain altitude, but the hind legs to push front-up.

Stages to repose (with Freud regarding repose as the end): 1. From up to down. 2. From forward to being in position. 3. Amoeboid pulsation in position. 4. Repose in undifferentiated space.

South Windham
Summer 1946

On the Question:
"What is the Meaning of Life?"

Happiness is the action of the soul.

1. We must assume that to the happy man this question would not arise. For each activity to which he gives himself or is given, by desire or situation and for joy or grief, is viewed on its merits; its problems are calculated by him specifically, its means and usefulness for a specific end. Thus, asked, "What is the meaning of life?" he says, "I am hammering together this table; is it worthwhile to make a mortise and tennon, or shall I use a dovetail joint?" (But I, who am not quite happy, do not offer this example specifically but probably as a symbol for positions of love.)

Very few of us are happy in such a way that the question does not arise. (Many to whom the question does not arise are also not happy, but they do not pose the question for other reasons.) Nevertheless we recollect such and such activities of ours that, in act, were self-justifying without question, altho now when in a moment of misery we question them they do not justify themselves. Some then try to repeat the activity, but this attempt is an illusion.

We generalize from such recollections that to a happy man the question does not arise.

The outgoing of love is a type of such activity self-justifying without question; then it is said that "Love is the meaning of Life." But this is true only in the formal sense that "action is the meaning of life," for happiness is the action of the soul. But if love is sought concretely for this formal reason, the sentence is a terrible illusion: it is the outcry, the begging, of one who does not love, needs to love and cannot love. Also, pleasure is said to be the meaning of life, truly enough because pleasure accompanies action, so that it is indifferent whether we speak of the pleasure or the action as satisfactory; except that—at least on crude analysis—the action is more specifiable and therefore its problems are more soluble. But it is quite beyond our experience to think of happiness as the accretion to a general sum of pleasure; on the contrary the thought, "I do it to have a good time" belongs to the search for a distraction from misery.

Psychologically, the happy action is a specific opening out of the ego to the deep soul and the world. Therefore the question cannot arise, for it is a question posed by the ego just in so far as it is closed against the deep soul and the world: it wonders about its resources, or what next step to take. To answer the question would demand that the problem, the relevant evidence, and the demonstration be held together in the attention; but it is not a property of happy action to be attentive to the goal, the way, and the satisfaction all at once. The soul is absorbed in the happy action, the attention is limited to specific tasks of providing, taking care, etc.

Concerning the past, so long as the past is not considered as creating the present, the question could perhaps be asked even by a happy man, as an historical question—tho it is a usual opinion that the happy do not ask historical questions.

It is distressing for misery to confront happiness with the question. For the reaction of happiness is to snub the question and apparently the questioner by failing to take seriously the heavy import of the terms that weigh so much for misery. Such a snub is the necessary answer of the happy, as the strong seem (to the weak) to snub the weak. It is not a snub to the questioner, to whom the happy one might perhaps be giving close attention and offering much material help—only the help is not relevant to the heavy terms of the question. The miserable is offended, torments the happy with reproaches, and often stirs the fellow-feeling of the happy to grief; and this triumph is an evil solace to misery.

2. At the other extreme from the question not arising, is its arising and getting a definite answer, such as "The social advantage is the meaning of our lives," or the sum of pleasure, or the Superman. Now such an answer, given and proved before the attention, is a construction, a "second creation" of experience, that combines the unities of both art and science. It is scientific in that its material—our lives and their justifications—is the reality unbracketed: not postulated or projected in imagination. It is artistic and practical in that all this material is erotized, not simply observed: it is all regarded as object of desire and aversion. That is, the condition for an answer to the question is: *a construction of at least the predominant parts of experience erotized and held before the attention.* This is a waking dream, fully analyzed. Nothing important is thought of as extending into unconsciousness, for this would cast doubt on the answer. The ego is not potentially but actually adequate to its soul and world.

Such a condition, if it existed, would serve as the definition of perfect misery. In general, we find strength, for invention and even to persist, by giving-in to or going-out to dark impulses and dimly guessed objects of love, daring, and exploration. "We live by faith," and "faith is the substance of things unseen." But in the condition of an answer to the question there is, ex hypothesi, no reservoir of strength not already before the attention.

This is the non-existent extreme of a situation that is commonplace: to defend against the anxiety of giving in to a measure of happiness that we dare not admit to attention by holding before the attention some distracting purpose of will or pleasure.

Yet on the other hand, as we read in the biographies of fanaticism, great strength and a measure of happiness are given to those who seriously answer the question. How is this? A certain part is given by the form and condition of any answer, a certain part by the particular answer itself, whatever it happens to be. To fulfill the condition of any answer whatsoever is to distract the attention effectively from half-guessed contradictory motives; then it is not surprising if, free from surveillance, these motives should well up unrestrained—falsely recognized as the strength precisely of their opposites that fill the attention (as witness the hostility with which is preached the gospel of love). And again, to fulfill the condition of holding before the attention the whole of one's erotized experience is par excellence the means of defensively shutting out forever the deeper eros and the dangerous possibilities of the world; but such defense requires heroic vigilance and ingenuity; the more "proved" the construction the more precarious it is and the more searching and deeply symptomatic (therefore deeply tho ignorantly satisfactory) each new stroke of certitude. Such heroism releases endless strength; a man faced with such heroic tasks permits himself absolutely anything (consider Luther).

These are the means by which *to maintain* any answer at all releases happy action, altho the condition of any answer at all is the definition of misery.

3. But in fact no such answer is ever given simply but always in relation to a struggle against circumstances that would disprove the answer. The scientific theory is in fact a polemic, as in Augustine's great title "On Genesis, against the Manicheans." This is the part of strength and happiness that is given to the answerer by his particular answer, *what* it is that is the meaning of life. He holds to be the meaning of life that which in fact he longs for and does not have, or has insecurely and is threatened, that which is frustrated by the sociopsychological arrangements of the entire community (for it is unlikely that accidental biographical frustrations would be apotheosized to be called the meaning of life).

We have now left the ideal realms of no question or a proved answer and have entered the mixed realm where most of us dwell: the realm of sporadic questions and dubious answers that have still to be proved.

When the people are truly political, that is when they initiate policy in a forum where there is no cleavage between the personal and the official environments, then it will not be said that "the social advantage is the meaning of life." But when there is such a cleavage and the political

212

eros is frustrated, then it will more and more be said, as by Cicero, that "the social advantage is the meaning of life." This will be said for reasons of policy by both the exploiting and the exploited classes; but it will be said also, more especially by the exploiter, for the unconscious reason that just the social eros is frustrated by the existing circumstances, to their advantage, and the situation is intolerable. The answer is one means of partly satisfying the repressed instinct. So pleasure is philosophically proved by the anxiously moderate who cannot give in to pleasure. And the birth of a superior mankind is proved by the ill and childless man disgusted with the universal social dispiritment and philistinism.

There is a return of the repressed. But alas! our misery is that when such and such a natural power was frustrated, and repressed, it was one of a community of many natural powers, corresponding to the potential infinity of the world; but when it returns it has become "the meaning of life."

So, inspired and in knightly fashion combating for some natural good that they have dared to deprive us of, we both neglect the other goods and struggle for the one good in an isolation in which it is unattainable and likely evil if attained. And the knight is lucky who does not waste his life writing tracts on one theme (as I seem bent to do).

4. I am at present in the following not unusual plight: that the question recurs to me even obsessively (here I am writing about it), "What is the meaning of Life?" But I cannot find an answer to it; or even, I prove to myself that an answer is impossible. This plight, of the obsessive question and the impossible answer, is the expression of self-hatred, of hostility directed against the self.

It is the plight of the Dostoyevskyan suicide who says, "There is no God, no immortality—*therefore* I must kill myself." As usual with Dostoyevsky the terms of the analysis are correct but the connection is inverted: it is because he is about to kill himself that the suicide finds there is no God, no meaning in life, and obviously no immortality. For we do not see ordinarily that a man who has no answer kills himself, but only one to whom the question persistently poses itself, that is who cannot help posing to himself the question. It is a fatal and ominous question. All his conscious experience, memory, prospect, feeling, and will, is gathered before his attention in the form of a construction, but there is no content to it; that is, the worth of the ego is problematical: he is about to commit suicide. More deeply: the force of his closed ego does not weigh against some unknown demand, and this unknown appears to be ferocious.

The moment at which the closed ego is stripped of its defenses and symptomatic satisfactions, its possible answers: there are two possible outcomes. Either the unknown will prove to be some original power, a burst of happiness without a question; the ego opens out to this strength and there is an answer but no question. Or it is the unknown inhibitor itself that manifests itself, the dread super-ego, the castrator knife in hand; a question but no answer.

At this moment there is no effect, therefore there is no possible answer. Either the defenseless ego is temporarily holding back in fright from giving in to a terrible effect, which will then (but perhaps not at once) prove to be superabounding joy. Or with a frozen face he deals a fatal stroke as if it were of no significance; he does not know what moves his hand.

There is no answer, but the question poses itself obsessively. This too offers two possibilities—but between them there is an observable difference, so that one may know whether to predict happiness or misery. Either (with great hope so I read it for myself!) the question poses itself as restlessness—"Is *this* justified? Does *that* make any difference?"—trying to force feeling experimentally, holding the breath lest feeling rise, about to burst, obsessed with death, hateful of what one has been—then will he not release his breath, not burst but melt in present love, and cease, as Spinoza bade us, uselessly to upbraid the past which after all was one way of coming not too late to happiness without a question? Or the question poses itself with a stern singleness: "How are *you* justified?"—Please!

let him stay his hostile hand against himself and turn the anger outward, saying with a violent oath, "Damn you! who took from us children our natural good."

A question without a possible answer: such a question is meaningless, say the logicians. Nevertheless, as old Kant showed long ago, we are compelled to ask the question. Woe if it does not resolve into the opposite: many possible answers but no question.

Again and again we must repeat what Franz said: "There are questions that we could never get over were it not for an operation of nature."

In every work I return to the one theme, of disparaging the ego; shall I not direct it home, to hatred of myself? and stop escaping into generalities? Everywhere death and the praises of violence!—But softly, softly: do not hate myself; heaven forbid that we side with those animal-trainers mis-called our educators and grown-ups! But softly—there is no resentment against these either.

Question, no answer: it is nothing but the case of a child commanded to do his duty, for instance to shit, but he cannot produce anything because he has been well trained to hold back. What! is it for this reason that a man is supposed to hate himself, feel unjustified, and commit suicide? the colored flowers spring unadmired by him in the field? Or every beloved prove unpleasing because an aunt once made an idiotic threat against our exhibition? Should one not rather laugh?

First it is necessary for me to come to cry.

5. The small child is grieving:
"What is the use of *living* if they are so *mean* to me?"
—"I do the best I *can* but now I *can't!*"
—"*They take everything away from me.*"
He is stiff with fright, for she has hit him with an iron poker, going beyond any limitation, so that he can sob only, "You *meant* it!" clinging so desperately to life that it is impossible for him to loosen his grip and live. That was the last bit of meaning.

"What? . . . what?"
A question without any possible answer: such a question

is meaningless, but the fact that the meaningless question poses itself is not meaningless. It means that his ego springs alive in a continuum of love and of the potentiality of the world, but now there is a cleavage in the continuum. Because of the continuum he is now ready poised for an actual movement; but because of the cleavage, where is there to move? The arrested motion turns back into consciousness: "What is the meaning of Life?"

He is unwilling to revive those times. Then, concerning all the past rushing to the threshold of the present and arrested, he asks "What is the meaning of it?"—there is no answer for it cannot enter the present. Or contrariwise, he looks about at the present and asks what is the meaning, for all feeling is bound to the past.

The world is kept at arm's length, a good distance to ask a vain question of it. Is it not being measured for a blow?

Because such a questioner—and the questioner of such a questioner—is implacable. His jaw is well hardened. He is predisposed not to be answered, for it is too late. "Not another word!—" it is said warningly, with the right hand half raised; and the gesture completes itself by waving and brushing aside. It makes no sense. Or brushing it aside: he defies it.

He wants implacably to be pleased—with all proofs.

He sees that he is implacably attentive; implacably he watches for a moment of inattention. He watches implacably not to watch. And oblivion fells him at a blow.

6. We are no longer thinking of the structure of the question but of the character of the questioner. As I consider myself, I see that I am pleading, a beggar. Pleading with the reader, begging the question (avoiding the terms of the question).

Begging for what? For the least something—but on my own terms. A token satisfaction. Or even to be snubbed, but faced—on my own terms.

The trembling uplifted clutch of begging—the shaking fist of defies and curses—pounding blows—the panic hand as the face tries to avert itself: all these, given and taken, pass into each other, shuttling, blurring. Has not the rapid

vibration the terrible pitch of a scream? Is this an answer?
But softly. Let me come to say:
"Give me this."
Or "Here is what I made."
"I love you."
Or even, the blinding tears flowing down, "This is horrible the way I am treated."
"No! I will not stand for it."
Then perhaps I can assay the question, "What is the meaning of Life?"

7. It is reproached against me that I avoid—"it is the one thing that you avoid"—the question, "What is the meaning of Life?" What I write here is an instance of it, for I do not ask about the meaning of life but about the question, What is the meaning of Life?

It is a true reproach. I do avoid it. But how far does this avoidance belong to my happiness and how far to my misery?

In several ways the avoidance of the question belongs to misery. For instance, a chief part of my conscious desire has been for sexual love, a desire never adequately satisfied which is partly why it has loomed so large. (It is also a defense against hatred.) At the same time—no doubt both because of the frustration and as a cause of it—this desire has been guilty. Therefore I cannot ask what is the meaning of Life, because what I would likely materially take, from my desires, to be the meaning of life, I dare not formally, because of my guiltiness, raise to the dignity of saying, sexual love is the meaning of life. Now let me assume myself less miserable: I desire without guilt, then I could dare to say that sexual love is the meaning of life; but surely at the same time (both as cause and effect) there would be less frustration and less preoccupation, and I doubt if I should then consider that sexual love is the meaning of Life.

In another way, too, the avoidance of the question belongs to misery: there is hidden from me the full extent of my misery, plenty of rage, fright, boiling tears, and I know not what. I know that when the full extent of my deprivation, destructiveness, and waste of years becomes known to me, I shall cry boiling tears. But as yet I am afraid to reveal it, and this fear is also my avoidance of the question. For who can dare to say with Shakespere that Waste is the meaning of Life? or that Disgust is?

Or again, if I should answer to myself what is the meaning of my Life, I should be committed to this answer. But such a commitment would at once test me and bring to light the terrors from which I now shield myself by not committing myself to the question, or the answer, or to Life.

There is truth here, but my bother is: to *what* should I commit myself if I do not know the meaning of Life?

—Commit yourself to Life! then you will know the meaning of Life.

No no, the reverse will follow, if I may judge by the past. In many cases I do not commit myself not because of ignorance but because I am afraid. Sometimes however I take courage and commit myself to such and such an action. What follows is my partial happiness—but without a question and without an answer. It is this experience, as I said at the beginning, that makes me think that what here seems to be avoiding the question is really snubbing the question.

But perhaps there is a middle ground: if to avoid the question is undoubtedly misery and to snub the question is happiness, then to ask the question is transitory between happiness and misery. Is it advantageous or disadvantageous? to ask and find an answer or to ask and find none? Let us explore the possiblities:—

8. No need to explore, for I have—this very night—made an important discovery. (What is to be done?)

: That I am the meaning of Life! (What is to be done?)

Crowding my attention with my experience, to frame the question, looking at myself in my mirror, but then remaining with the question itself instead of looking for an answer: obviously no answer is to be found, I am the answer (what is to be done?); also I avoid this answer, until the thirteenth page. And what is to be done?

So. Is it terrible? I carry on a conversation with myself.

—But I am so boring! (What is to be done?)

218

"What Is the Meaning of Life?"

I avoid the question, what is the meaning of Life?—"it is the one thing you avoid"—because I am envious that something else than I should presume to occupy the sum of attention. So. Then let me gratify my desire to occupy the attention. I am the meaning of Life: for instance my self-hostility, my watchfulness. But it is so boring. Am I the meaning of life?

What is to be done?

"What is to be done?": that is to say, where is that external face, out of which so smoothly flows the talk, that I am going to strike with a blow of the hammer with which today I vigorously nailed together the table? I say, "I cannot find an answer to the question," but this is a euphemism for saying, "I take away the life" because I hate it that you should be alive.

Speechless, to answer; but it is not because I have nothing to say, but because my fingers are clenched around a throat.

The new philosophers say that Death is the meaning of Life; yes, but not *my* death.

9. But my life, my life. I do not mean to say that the meaning of my Life is my life—but to save my life, to regain my health. Not that health is the meaning of Life; health is the same as life; and for the happy the question does not arise, what is the meaning of Life? But I am sick and miserable, and to regain my health is the meaning of my Life. This is a small object of concern, but it cannot be helped; it is the penalty of long neglect.

This is the transitory meaning.

It is a small object for a small concern. What would one expect? Where is the energy for a great concern? (But the happy draw on the strength of the soul and the world.) Nothing is disproportionate.

We distinguish between "life" and "Life" with a capital L. The former is the give and take of the organism and its world, actualizing, with the novelty of the present, the latent powers in things (unknown till they are actualized). But of this life, altho I can see thousands of lovely acts in each nature, I cannot conceive the question of the "meaning." But Life, with a capital L, is an idea of the anxious ego;

now we know that every anxious symptom is both a defense and an expression. Then Life is a defense against the felt danger that the organism will disaggregate into parts, the limbs separate, the affects explode, the mind wander; and it is an expression of the vitality of the attention trying, in a closed ego, to increase eros, otherwise cut off, by collecting its memories and prospects. (Eros is "otherwise cut off" if the anxious ego will not allow impulse and affect except under the surveillance of attention: this is the condition for posing the question.) The tension of this straining of the attention is the obsession of the question. The meaning of the question "What is the meaning of Life?" is the possible action that will give orgiastic release to this tension: and this is the answer to the question. (The special case of "justification of the ego" is release of a tension that contains also a demand: it is a sado-masochistic orgasm.) Now such an orgasm is partial: it will not lose the tension of the impulses of life.

As for me, obsessed by the question and looking for its answer, I feel myself standing on the brink of a chasm of grief. Into this chasm I toss exploratory stones and the echo answers "Death Death." The grief is for castration. The chasm is the vagina unknown. It is armed with teeth and exhales an odor of death. The stones are masturbations with a hostile image. Where I hear "Death" with a capital D, I understand "life" with a small l.

10. The chasm is in the pit of my belly and in my chest. The property of this chasm is to be empty and not fillable.

The meaning of the question "What is the meaning of Life" is that I experience an emptiness, e.g. the loss of father, the separation from my friend. If I could answer the question, I would borrow from the world somewhat to fill it, but I must fill it from within.

Into this emptiness I have thrown twenty-five books, the praises of my instructors (sucked from them by complaisance), crimes of love, irregular learning and observation; but these do not fill it.

Likewise I have eaten 10,000 midnight snacks, confitures, beer and pretzels, bunches of grapes, my brother

"What Is the Meaning of Life?"

Arnold, many imagined boys. But these do not fill it.

I suck in smoke, I suck in the approval of folk by inviting smiles, I suck in painful pleasure of love, and gasps of forced labor. These do not fill it.

It is impossible for the little chasm in my breast to be so vast as it seems. It must be that I renew it, that with the other things I also suck in emptiness; the emptiness is continually renewed.

[New York City]
September 9, 1946

221

Incidents of the
Labyrinth

"There is no Minotaur after all!"—So the hero pauses, in a blank square.

The rooms of the Labyrinth are enclosed like the plazas of ancient towns, where one slips in back of the Statue of the Commendatore and out by an archway between the apse and the butcher-shop. Each place seems to be the heart of the community.

Suggestible. With upraised sword advancing tentatively—the light is always dim at the turning—Theseus imagines that here is the lair of the original beast. Lurking, looming, springing to him as he comes. Then the hero is not ashamed to shriek it out and let his knees knock, also whispering to himself "Courage! courage!" But it proves to be an illusion of the hangings or a picture on the wall. A shape cast into the darkness or leaping from the too bright.

In the quiet light these errors are often comical. (In principle they are all comical, but the animal spirits fail.) At least always interesting. But the passage itself is boring. Boring or recklessly empty of either prospect or dread. It is like the day before the day before the Day: when there is no longer any use of the old life, yet it is too early to make final preparations. I suppose that this is the time to put things "in order." What things? in what order?

With upraised knife one turns into the room that is perhaps the lair of the original beast, etc.: this moment is the day before the Day. Alas! how tight we live, in hope, and tightly defending ourselves against surprise; we intellectu-

223

als are too wound up. The clock does not tick for us. Shake it.—An alarm clangs in the stillness; but it is not *therefore* the Minotaur in the chamber. The day will not break just because the alarm wildly shakes the clock.

This room, however, is bare and brightly lit. One slips into it in the crevice between the slabs of insomnia and waking-sleep. Here the Minotaur does not seem to spring at me; there is no image on the wall to study; there is no darkness to cast a shape into the darkness. Nothing here.

Caught by the throat, as Pascal said. When the reckless boredom of the day before the day before has by custom become the old life; and one is always on the eve; wound too tight. He is caught by the throat. Can he breathe? (*This* is where we live who think too much, too close to the heart to breathe. How they misjudge us!)

The room is bare: it means "mustn't tell, mustn't tell."

"There is no Minotaur after all!"—so he ends. (It means "I am caught by the throat.") "Now to wind up the spool."

Aiiiiii!

—No no! let us end a little longer. And wind up the spool a round. Let us end a little longer and wind up the spool a round or two. Once I felt myself to be—do you know how once I felt my body to be?—a *Lute!* My straight back was the neck of it and my knees akimbo formed the belly; my fingers were taut in the crotch to be strings over the hole. Listening for the song to arise—

Aiiiiii!

"I am the Minotaur" cries the choking hero in a cry from his bursting temples.

The room is not bare but panelled with mirrors. In the mirrors, whichever way he stares, he sees the sword drop from his hero-hand weaker than a girl's.

So. This is not boring. Look quickly at the hero—quicker than those mirrors can dart it back—will you not see a smile flash? such a smile as of the points of the original fire: tiny spangle-caped ballerinas with pink bodies and star-wands. So a man woos himself with thoughts. (He does not see the smile, he thinks his face is serious.)

"Now for the second moment of my life—but the other was long ago forgot—I have a rival *worthy* of Theseus!

224

Incidents of the Labyrinth

"I came down thru these rooms pretending to be menaced by shadows, so eager to come to grips with the horror and try my courage again. I knocked my knees together and made the sweat stand on my face, and by such means one can awaken terrible fears. But mere feelings, not as a hero fears: that springs the wrists alive. For I have seen everything, I am not surprised by what I suggest to myself to see. I can easily conjure up animals behind the hangings, but I am nevertheless awake. But now, is not this the fact?"—Lays his hands on his bony ribs (concealing the secret of the heart).

This is the thought of the fourth generation of the creation: the heroes of Exploits. Their parents are the gods and giants, their children will be all tragic men, but themselves are imitators of the blood-greasy life in ingenious engines that do not break. Theseus, Daedalus, and my Orpheus: forest-purgers, town-planners, lutanists. (Also, let me say no evil of the creator spirit.)

(Seen in the mirror) his face is white, his knees are knocking, and the sweat stands on his face, and the sword has fallen from his grip weaker than a girl's. (He does not see the dancing grin.) Next, the tears are coursing down his face and he says:

"Theseus, pick up your knife. For pity's sake, in good order; see that the blade is sharp; proceed like a surgeon; and do not hack away. I am a subtile fencer. My wrist is very strong. I know as well as you which are the vital parts."

The Duel of Theseus and Himself as Minotaur: Variations.

(Soldierly. In Decent Order.)

The image in a good mirror is faithful, tho it reads in the opposite direction. But the image in the consciousness is opposite in intention. It means to lie. The amiable grin is an unfriendly bite. The man's shoulders are serviceably bent and he is choking with the sadness of the rejected; and he has stiffened his back like a soldier and is presenting you a grim smile: "I won't give you the satisfaction."

225

This is the suspense of the duelling of Theseus with himself: Can the ego counter *every* motion of the soul with a feeling, an interpretation, an action that is opposite in intention? Both champions have equal knowledge of the vital parts; the soul is more indefatigable, but the ego can retreat into diversions (but the soul presses close, or is there beforehand).

To counter with a feeling is easy for the sufferer; for the soul wants only to be happy—this simplicity is her weakness in the battle that we see everywhere raging—the ego can counter it by any species of misery as occasion arises: it can counter appetite with nausea, speedy ease with dizziness, eros with a shrinking midriff. These ripostes are vulgar; I do not need to read them off from the heroes of the fourth generation of heaven.

But to counter impulses to action with false action! As the struggle becomes tight, it is only a hero that can successfully carry thru the catastrophic enterprises that will be opposite to the joyous hints of rage and pleasure. For instance: in feeling a man turns simple longing into a scalding fire; good! but he then has the impulse to flee from this fire; only a hero will now turn not his back but his face to it, and blindly *pursue* he knows not what into the curtain of flames (behind which, to his surprise, lies sleeping the beauty).

Another instance: the anger of Hercules is serviceably turning Omphale's spinning-wheel.

Another instance: the great midriff of divine Prometheus that loves our human race, is concerned only for itself on the lonely peak.

Countering every divine impulse with an heroic mis-exploit; this is a hard duel. Sometimes the attention fails a moment; one finds nothing to hand. Then there is a bloody cut.

The body is muddy with it; the silence is heavy with breath.

Even so! so far the duel is easy enough. One does not need to be the Labyrinthine hero to wage it. But now he must also counter interpretation with misinterpretation. For the Labyrinthine man is quick to discover that what he feels hides what he feels and that what he pursues rushes toward what he flees. What he destroys is establishing itself. What he shuts his eyes to is ablaze in the dark. Having discovered it, is it so easy for him to counter action with action like a fool?

Here there is a bad error of misjudgment; he suffers a deep wound across the very mouth.

He lowers his sword. (It is time for a diversion.) Rest!

—I am not speaking of a systematic error of interpretation (for this one does not need to be the Labyrinthine hero; it is sufficient to be ———— ————). But of a systematic error of interpretation revised with every stroke of life, and also knowing itself to be in error. Is it so easy to save the appearances?

—It is not even clear to me which champion I favor in this combat that is fought not without my concern. As one looks at the sore-pressed hero, so evilly hurt, it is the soul of Theseus one sees—for the struggling body is the soul: so sober, frank, and brave a hero, doggedly trailing a thread, seeking only to release the seven youths, and to re-emerge to love. But the other! the self-conscious Knight! entangler! I do not see him but I know him well. I confess that I am breathless with admiration for him—in fact, choking . . .

Nay. Soldierly. In decent order.

Time. Theseus throws down his sword. (In every mirror, whichever way he looks, he sees the sword fall silent to the ground.) "I do not touch him. Let me come to grips."

His fingers are wrapped around his neck, and his eyes are wide. But he will not speak and tell.

How can he tell if he chokes off his voice? This is a typical incident of the combat of the self and the soul.

Again: presumably Theseus loves his dear soul and he would embrace her; but he cannot conceive of this except as choking himself to death. (But they say that a man cannot choke himself to death.)

—Another instance: When we artists will to immortalize ourselves, we make an abstraction from the animals and plants, we enclose the loose space with a form and we bring the time to a periodic close. We dig a grave and say a dead-prayer. But lo! the abstract forms—they are nothing but the breathing and the pulse-beat and the lively staring of the eyes—prove to be only the clearer symbols of desire. Yet we will not surrender to it; we ask: what elements of the elements have betrayed that growth and circling that we do not intend? let's bring these also to a pause! A despairing artist makes a thousand studies to conceal better what he needs to say.

—Still another instance: By their institutions the Americans deny themselves happiness, but they manufacture commodities to awaken and satisfy the sum of desires that could be called happiness. We see that these things make it difficult for people to love, eat, and move; yet with heroic inventiveness and industry they manufacture the equivalents of desire, flavor, room.

This clock is too wound up. It will not go.

At other times there is a momentary failure of attention: then a bloody gash.

He is strangling himself before the mirror. His eyes are great and his tongue is hanging out; no doubt that he has seen something. But he will not tell, he cannot tell. It is *I* who cannot bear it. My soldierly courage fails.

For pity's sake, Theseus! You are not the Minotaur. You are your friend. This is your dear soul. Embrace. Are you not in love?

There are too many whispers. Who can choose among them for a true clue? Also, all are true clues. Whispering:

"Courage! courage!"

"Rest."

"What did she whisper in your ear?"

"Nay! Soldierly! In decent order!"

"What will the Athenians say when the ship returns with black sails?"

"Perhaps it would be better to turn and wind up the spool."

The butterfly goes a zigzag way; one cannot avoid the illusion (it is an illusion) that she intends to deceive.

What on earth is it to me what the Athenians say?

Incidents of the Labyrinth

In the next plaza sits Daedalus, creator of this sad maze.

Says: "Among the vanities I have noticed, this is one of the gloomiest: that clever persons who think hard impose on themselves a subtility of conscience in conforming to crude laws. Men whose sensibility and self-discovery are the creators of ethics and decorum torture themselves in nice subservience to hand-me-down standards that were hardly fit for loose reckoning among their fathers.

"It is the cursed effect of having by nature a quick mind. For such a boy, crossed like any other by strength to which he is not yet equal, does not simply brood rebellion and give in or identify himself with the grown-ups and give in (oh, he does both these), but he also thinks out an evasive trick. For he is clever and inventive. When the trick is foiled, he gets around them by another. His rebellion becomes razor-sharp: it can no longer hack away. But in so far as he identifies himself with the oppressor, the effect of clever-ness is even worse. For now he prognoses the indefinitely numerous evasions that might be practiced but that he, having agreed to be well-behaved, does not practice. His fancy is the more fertile because the imaginary satisfaction is all that he has. Likewise as the judge-accuser he devises new traps for his conscience.

"Meantime the original law, like the original punisher, is massive and crude. It was not meant to crush these finesses. It would not, if only because of a sense of humor, have laid on them so awkward and heavy a hand. But these hard-thinking persons lay on these grace-notes, these ornaments of eros, a heavy hand.

"Also—because a clever and hard-thinking man cannot fail to realize that it is he himself who is the creator of the good (for the good is what it is human to be)—he now expends his creative force on the far-fetched, too difficult, too strange to be possible. But the possible, to which he is now perfectly equal, to compel it—and that many a fool achieves by luck—this he imagines that he no longer wants!

"So it is that, little by little, I have made this Labyrinth.

229

Long ago there was—I suppose, for it was long ago and forgotten—a Minotaur. Whatever it was. I doubt if it was savage; more likely an inconvenience of that family. I myself devised the machine for the copulation of the Princess and the Bull, and that was nothing but crude lust.

"See how cleverness has tangled up the space! Can you move? Believe me, it is not the Minotaur that devours them; they are devoured by my Labyrinth.

"I hoped to lay out a city for people. Do you know, to get a little comfort from each other? Each one of these plazas was supposed to serve a useful function. *The soul writ large!* Look! look! I left rich clues, as that you slip in behind the Statue of the Commendatore and leave between the apse and the butcher-shop—thru a covered way—But I have forgotten the sense of it.

"It is too late. I am lost here too.

"I do not see images in the shadows; I would not be afraid of the thing itself. Nevertheless these are solid walls."

—The old man is pounding on the wall in pain.

When I have better news to report from the Labyrinth, I shall again write to you of Theseus. Perhaps he may come on the monster and re-emerge to love by following the thread. As for me, I think it would be better for me to forget the maze altogether, but this is just what I cannot do, for the hero bears with him my soul. I cannot foresee anything that is not boring and sad.

3. *To Ariadne*

Woman eternal my muse, lean towards me
from ideal heaven, for these
comforters upon the earth have died
or left me, and none others please.

230

Incidents of the Labyrinth

Aren't you "Ariadne" my leader
to where the monster lies
(is he nearby?)—and you will bring
me forth unscathed under the skies.

Three-person'd Fate who draw my thread
and measure out and cut the length,
passing along from hand to hand
I rest assured in their strength.

*New York City
December 1946*

Two Political Fables

The Wisdom of Solomon

The two women claimed the baby boy and King Solomon commanded it to be cut in half and distributed. Then one woman said, "Good; let equal justice be done!" and the other said, "I cannot bear to see the infant slain, let her have him rather."

The King said: "This first woman is bloodthirsty. Plausibly it is her child that gave her pain to bear. She cries for equal justice because she cannot reconcile herself to the unequal lot of our women, and on this baby she is taking vengeance on every penis. And on her own penis, for so the baby is; for she indulges the fantasy that she had a penis that was cut off, and now she wants the King to repeat the incident and hack away. But why should I gratify this woman?

"Now the other woman seems to be indifferent to the infant, she is eager to give it away. She would prove to be a cold nurse. Yet plausibly it is her child, for it fits these cold characters, women of Gomorrah, who cannot admit to their monthly bleeding, to fantasy that they have a penis whole, only it is not in evidence. She repeats this fantasy by protecting the child whole and still not keeping it with her. The question of fact is how she came to sleep with the man in the first place. It is to a woman that she wants to give the boy.

"What!" cried King Solomon. "Is it on such considerations that I am supposed to assign the boy a home? These are the homes that reproduce the people's misery generation by generation. Now I am the King. I have great enter-

233

prises in hand, to prove that, whatever people think, my penis is as large as the Pharaoh's (never to mention that amazon of Sheba). Greater than father! more glorious than Absalom for all his golden hair! This child I shall rear in the palace, for a soldier. To a death in war—my vengeance on this hateful species."*

*Explaining his decision to the jurists, the King said: "Excited litigants do not speak for the objective interest of some third party. You must interpret their words literally as the wishes of their characters. These two women are concerned not for the child but for their relationship to it, and very likely to each other. Now one says, *"Hack away"* and the other says, *"Give it away"*; these are the literal wishes to be interpreted, you may disregard their motives as rationalizations (tho it is wise to consider why just such and such a rationalization). Further, you will recall that it was I, the King, who caused the sword to be brought in the first place. This was my literal wish: to destroy the infant—which I shall do eventually in a kingly way.

"What does a judge want? to *dispose* of the case.

"If it is justice you seek, you must consider the objective good of the third parties rather than the claims of the interested parties or of the judge. As a general rule, lay less weight on personal intentions and more on social consequences. Since the King is always an interested personality, with his private intentions, you would do better not to have a king. I can give you this advice because I have a cohort of soldiers in the courtyard. I *do* give it to you because I hate myself."

234

Two Classical Draft-Dodgers

Achilles and Ulysses, the heroes of the two Homeric epics, were unsuccessful draft-dodgers. The strategems they used are still familiar practices of men unwilling to be involved in wars against their interests. Achilles pretended to be not a man, Ulysses pretended to be psychotic. Achilles hid among the girls (in our mores, played homosexual) but was discovered. Ulysses yoked himself with an ox, but they found him out by laying his baby son in front of the plough. So these two were conscripted.

These incidents are deeply appropriate to the epic roles of these heroes. Their unwillingness to go to the war marks their independent spirit, they are personal heroes; but their failure in evading means that they share in the general infatuation of the war. Achilles asks continually, "What am I doing here?" and threatens to go home—obviously he will get himself killed. Ulysses, a less open temper, chooses rather to get what he can in booty and glory; he will survive. Neither for a moment lends himself unthinkingly to valor, like Diomed or Ajax. But besides this, the particular dodges that they chose in the beginning spring from the hearts of their characters and foreshadow their fates.

Achilles pretends to be a girl, weak and unwarlike, precisely because he is the strongest and most warlike; he tries to disguise himself in the opposite. But we know by psychoanalysis that just these pretenses are the underlying reality. The doom of Achilles proves to be his friendship for Patroclus, in which relation he, as the younger, played the passive, that is feminine role, the dependent and presuma-

235

bly the admired. So long as he could narcissize in his tent he could preserve himself; but as soon as his male-half, his ego-ideal (for Patroclus wears his armor), has been pierced, then he must turn for help to his mother and go forth to the battle. His savagery to Hector is unbalanced, sadistic; it is, to compare great things with small, the violent reaction of the castrated figures of Hemingway. He is killed as if by chance by Paris, as if to say: The cause of the war has nipped him because he could not follow his rational judgment to go home.

The psychology of Ulysses is more interesting. Being the canniest of the Greeks he tries to disguise himself as being demented. We may then, as above, take the dementia for granted and ask what is the form of it. Now the crude fact of the *Odyssey* is that the hero cannot manage to get home, and he has such erotic adventures by the way as other men have who cannot manage to get home, especially when a grim Patience sits waiting. This at once casts light on the trial of the baby before the ploughshare. Ulysses is every father displaced, forced out of his home, by the coming of the child. His impulse would be to plough the baby under, or disguised as an animal to devour him (at least so the child's nightmare says it). But he suppresses the impulse; he does not repress it but makes a canny compromise: I'll go and stay away 20 years, that is till the boy is grown, then I can return and fight on equal terms. Meantime Telemachus, cast too soon into a father-identification, has to combat the usurping suitors whose side he partly espouses (for he too is an usurping suitor); divided against himself he is put at a disadvantage. Wily Odysseus!

The greatness of Homer—only the Old Testament is a rival in this respect—is that such analytic considerations do not add anything to the stories, but seem already to be taken for granted by the poet. The psychoanalysis of modern writing, even Shakespere or Dante, is in part a psychoanalysis of the writer, (just as I shall soon analyze even these notes and surprise myself): much is in them that the writer did not "intend." But in those ancient tales, every detail of the legend is assimilated.

New York City
December 1946

Likely and the Dragon

Stand still, Texas!" they shouted at the horse.

"Stay, Texas!"

"Good Texas!"

The three of them—Matty, Laura, and Likely—kept shouting at the old horse. The field was full of flowers, in white and orange patches. The horse stopped walking and stood for the children to climb on.

They brought the ladder. "Stand still, Texas, so we can climb on," they said.

The patient horse stood and let them lean the ladder against him. One by one—Likely first—they climbed up and jumped off on the other side.

Likely sat on Texas' neck. Matty followed her up the ladder and he was the first one to dare to jump down on the other side into the grass. Laura, who was smaller, climbed halfway and clung to the horse's mane.

With a groan Likely saw her little brother Larry coming across the field. He was a pest, always following.

Old Texas was a pinto horse, white with great patches of brown, like maps. There were patches of white and orange on the field and patches of white and brown on Texas.

Larry was a pest because he couldn't do anything, he could hardly talk, yet he wanted to play in the games of his sister and her friends. He began to scream, "Yeow! Up! Me! Up! Me!"

"Scram, Larry, you're a pest," said Likely crossly.

The little boy began to cry.

237

But the others climbed up the ladder onto Texas' back and jumped off on the other side. Larry kept on crying. The three friends kept on screaming with excitement. The colors kept on shouting.

Suddenly the horse moved forward and the ladder fell. Texas took three steps forward, but he was too old and tired. With a sad whinny he fell over on his side in the field, and died.

The children were suddenly quiet. Except for Larry who kept saying, "Yeow! Up! Me! Me!" But the other children stood around Texas and said fearfully, "Good Texas! Stand up, Texas!" But he couldn't stand up any more.

They were going to run away but they didn't.

Suddenly they knew that he was dead and they began to murmur.

It turned into a sad song, which they sang over and over,

> "Texas is dead!
> Poor Texas!
> He can't get up any more!"

They picked some of the field-flowers, the white-eye-lashed daisies and the devil's-paintbrushes dipped in fire, and threw them on the dead horse, singing,

> "Texas is dead!
> Poor Texas!
> He can't get up any more."

The farmer came across the field to see what was the matter with the horse.

2.

In September, Likely and Larry came back to the city.

Sometimes Likely thought about Texas. She remembered—she could not forget—how he walked forward three steps and gave a whinny and fell down on his side in the field, and died.

Her eyes became hot and she said angrily, "Everything I love is going to die! Texas has died already. The summer flowers are gone and the autumn leaves are beginning to fall."

The sycamore leaves were falling slowly into the street.

"Mommy is going to die. Larry too. But I'm going to die before Larry, because I'm older than he is."

When she said this, Likely burst into tears.

Aunt Liz, who was her father's sister, tried to cheer her up and said, "Don't cry, Likely, God isn't going to die."

"No!" said Likely. "Everybody is going to die."

"No!" said Aunt Liz. "God is and God always was and God always will be."

"Oh, how awful!" said Likely, who did not want to be cheered up, "God doesn't have a birthday! He never had a birthday-party."

She didn't want to be less sad, and she began to cry out, "Ow! Oh-ow!" until she was screaming.

Aunt Liz was at a loss what to do.

3.

But by afternoon Likely was happy again and forgot about Texas and that God had no birthdays.

Everybody went for a walk in the sunshine, Mother and Aunt Liz and Larry and Likely. Likely wore her skates and Larry sat in a red wagon, but the grown-ups were only walking.

Likely skated ahead—she was always the leader—first on *this* foot, then on *that* foot. *This* foot, *that* foot, this foot that foot, faster and faster. She liked to go like the wind.

"Look!" she cried, "there's the redbird again."

"Where?" said Mother.

"There! it's a tanager."

"How do you know it's a tanager?" asked Aunt Liz.

"By the black wings. Can't you see it's a tanager?"

"I can't even see the bird, no less the markings," said Aunt Liz.

"Yeow! yeow!" crowed Larry, standing up in the wagon.

"Little brother can see it," said Likely. "Only he thinks it's a tomato. Zip! there it goes to *that* tree."

The streak of red burned in the sky and sat in the golden sycamore.

"I'll draw a picture of it," thought Likely, "with Larry standing up in the wagon."

"I still can't see it," said Mother.

"Now you can't see him because he flew away."

"Oh."

"Don't be disappointed. He lives in that nest—see? He'll surely come back."

"I see the nest. I can't see the bird."

Likely saw her friends skating around the corner. "Hi!" she shouted, and flew like the wind to catch up.

"Bye, Likee!" called Larry, standing up again in the wagon.

"Sit down, Larry," said Mother.

After a moment Likely came back around the block. She had gone all around the block. "There are five ways of going places," said Likely. "Walking, running, skipping, and jumping, that's four. Rolling on wheels—*this* foot! *that* foot!"

4.

Mother said, "Watch Larry a moment, while we go into the tailor's. It's steamy there."

"But I'm *skating*," said Likely. Her friends vanished around the corner like leaves blown by the wind. It was fall, and the leaves that had fallen in the street were blown by the wind.

"We'll be only ten minutes," said Mother. "If you don't want to, I'll take him in. I thought you might *want* to take care of him."

"All right," said Likely, and Mother and Aunt Liz went into Mr. Abrams'. "Sit down, you," she said to her little brother.

"Larry stand! Up! Me up!" said Larry.

"I hate you, lousy Larry," said Likely. "Why do I have to

take care of *you*? But if I don't, Mother will be angry."

She hated him because he was messy when he ate.

Larry could hardly even talk. He was contemptible. He kept shouting, "Yeow! yeow!" and bouncing in the wagon.

Sometimes she didn't mind taking care of him. Other girls had only dolls.

The wild race of her friends again came around the corner. They were skating round and round the block.

"Hi!" cried Matty, as he flew by.

"Hi!" cried Likely happily, because she loved Matty. She could skate as fast as he. Sometimes she wished she were a boy, like Father. Other times she was glad she was a girl.

"Hi!" said Laura, her best girl friend, and neatly stopped by dragging her left skate and swinging in a circle, ending in front.

"Let's drag Larry in the wagon," said Likely.

"Horses! I'm Texas!" said Laura.

"I'm Texas," said Likely.

"*I'm* Texas!" said Matty in a terrible voice.

"We'd better go slow or he'll fall out," said Likely.

"Roger! Texas will go very slow!" said Matty.

They grabbed the rope of the wagon and began to drag it. *This* foot. *That* foot.

"Yeow!" cried Larry happily.

"Giddyap, horsey!" said Likely.

Soon the three horses were dragging the wagon as fast as they could go.

"Yeow!" cried Larry, for everybody likes to be dragged in a wagon.

"He'll fall out and hurt himself," thought Likely frightened.

"Larry's not afraid! he loves it!" said Laura.

Their iron skates made sparks on the pavement and a terrible noise.

"Heigh-ho, Silver!" cried Matty.

This side, *that* side—the wagon careened.

BANG! The wagon crashed into a hydrant and Larry fell out.

He was so surprised he didn't even cry. His nose was bleeding and made spots on his clean suit. Then he screamed and Mother rushed out to see what was the matter.

Likely said to Mother, "It was my fault. I knew he'd fall out and get hurt."

Mother and Aunt Liz looked at her.

"I'm not angry with him any more," said Likely surprisingly. She was frightened at what she had done, but his nose stopped bleeding. "He's brave," said Likely. "He didn't cry once. He gave only two screams."

Mother was displeased at how Likely took care of Larry. "Now you can go skating if you want," said Mother, in her tone when she was displeased.

"I don't care if I do," said Likely, dragging her feet.

5.

Mother was not displeased for long, and at night, when Likely went to bed, she sang her some of the old songs which Mommy loved and Likely was learning them too.

She sang the old Scotch song, *Annie Laurie*, explaining the words of it, especially the strange Scotch words. If a song is beautiful, it is twice as beautiful if you understand the words and sing them with the tune.

The song *Annie Laurie* has three parts, and first Mommy explained the first part.

> Maxwelton's braes are bonny
> where early fa's the dew.

"Maxwelton is a place in Scotland across the ocean," she explained. "It's named after some old family Maxwelton that lived there. *Braes* means fields in Scotch, and *bonny* is the way they say pretty. And in these fields, the dew—you know what dew is—falls early in the evening, because it's cool and shady. Anyway, it means that those fields are very nice."

"*Fa's* is Scotch for falls," said Likely, who was smart.

> And 'twas there that Annie Laurie

242

gie'd me her promise true
that ne'er forgot shall be.

"This man who is singing the song," explained Mother, "is in love with Annie, and she promised to marry him or something, and he won't ever forget it. *Ne'er* means never, in poetry."

And for bonny Annie Laurie
I'd lay me doon and dee.

"Bonny is Scotch for pretty," said Likely.
"*I'd lay me doon and dee* means I'd lie down and die. He says this because he loves her so much."
"What a curious thing to say!" said Likely.
Mother then explained the second part of *Annie Laurie*.

Her brow was like the snowdrift,
her neck was like the swan,
her face it was the fairest
that e'er the sun shone on.

"He says her forehead, that's brow, is white and smooth as a snowdrift. And her neck is pretty as a swan's—he doesn't mean it's as long as a swan's."
"Of course not," said Likely. "I catch the rest. *E'er* means ever. In poetry."

And dark blue was her ee.

"Her ears!" cried Likely in astonishment. "Her ears were dark blue? That *is* curious!"
Mother laughed. "No no! *Ee* is Scotch for eyes. Her eyes were dark blue."
"So what?" said Likely. "Mine are blue too."

And for bonny Annie Laurie
I'd lay me doon and dee.

"I'd lay me doon and dee—same foolish remark as be-

243

fore," said Likely.

Then Mother explained the last part of *Annie Laurie.*

Like dew on the gowan lyin'
is the fa' o' her fairy feet.

"*Gowan* is a grassy meadow."

"That's light!" said Likely. "She walks along like dew on the grass, shiny and hardly touching."

"Exactly."

And like winds in summer sighin'
her voice is soft and sweet.

"Yes, I get it," said Likely drowsily.

And she's all the world to me.

Mother did not explain this, but kissed Likely goodnight.

Likely was fast asleep. Mother turned out the light and left.

6.

While Likely was lying there in the dark, she heard an awful voice. The sound of the voice was so frightening that her eyes stared and her tongue stuck in her throat. But what the voice said was even more frightening than the sound of it.

"*Likely,*" said the voice, "*you killed your brother Larry. Anyway, he's not here any more.*"

She moaned in her sleep. "I didn't kill him. He's inside in the next room." She called out, "Larry! Larry!"

But there was no sound, because she was asleep.

She lay there, covered with a cold sweat, and she moaned, "Help! help!"

To her help, in walked an old friend.

It was Texas!

He was changed. He was not pinto now but all white, except for his warm friendly eyes. And he had blue ears, which would have made Likely laugh if she weren't frightened.

"Don't be afraid, little Likely," said Texas, in a rich baritone voice. "Larry isn't dead, but he *has* gone away. We'll go and bring him back.

"Also," said Texas, "you didn't do anything especially terrible when you let Larry fall out of the wagon. All girls and boys hate their little brothers and sisters. It can't be helped. They're messy, and Mother has to take care of them because they're so little and can't do anything for themselves. Then, of course, she can't pay as much attention to you as she used to. Don't worry about it. Mommy understands how you feel, and she loves you the same as ever."

"Where *is* Larry?" asked Likely. "I called and there was no answer."

"He has disappeared over the horizon, and we must go and fetch him back. You know what the horizon is, but let me tell you about the Dragon."

"Dragon? I don't like Dragons. Yes, I know what the horizon is. It's the circle all around, where the sky comes down to the earth."

"Correct," said Texas. "Around this circle lies a Dragon who bites his tail with his mouth, so he makes a big circle. He is and always was. Now that Dragon—don't be frightened—has swallowed up Larry, but we'll go and fight him, and cut him open! And out will step Larry, better than ever!"

"Let's go!" said Likely, springing from bed. "How do we get there?"

"You may ride on my back," said Texas patiently.

Likely looked at him—embarrassed. "Won't you fall down and die?" she asked at last.

"No. I'm not going to die any more," said Texas.

And he stood against the bed and Likely climbed up on his back.

7.

Although he had no wings, Texas could fly like the wind. He had roller-skates on, which Likely hadn't noticed before. In a moment they were flying through the clouds and across the black and starry sky, for it was night.

Round them was falling the gentle dew.

When you look at the stars you can see that, if you draw lines from one star to another, they form the shapes of animals or giants or whatever you imagine. In one part of the sky is a quiet Lion. In another part is a giant Hunter who never catches what he is hunting. Among these shining shapes rode Likely on the back of Texas.

Texas pointed out the sights in the sky. "Here's the Big Bear, and here's the Small Bear. And there is the starry Crown, overhead for us all."

Then Texas said something so curious that Likely hardly knew whether or not to believe him.

"Do you play the game of Hopscotch?" said Texas.

"Of course," said Likely.

"Well," said Texas, "listen to this. You see how the sky is divided into the houses of different starry animals and giants. There's the Lion's house, there's the Crab's house, and there's the Ram's house, and the rest. Now these houses are the same as the squares in the game of Hopscotch! each one of which has a different number. But you must be careful and throw the little stone into each numbered square in turn, and visit all the houses!"

"Yes, that's how we play. Why must I?" asked Likely.

"Then you will have crossed the sky and you can come home and be happy. This is why children really play the game, but they don't remember any more."

A shooting star fell close, across Likely's left shoulder.

"Don't be alarmed," said Texas. "People say that's good luck."

Likely was riding on Texas' back. But somehow, at the same time, she could also see them both riding across the sky, and the stars shone through the horse's sides.

246

8.

Thus, they came to the Horizon. There, sure enough, was the ugly Dragon with his tail in his mouth, enclosing the world in a circle.

"Let me out! let me out!" cried voices, but nothing was to be seen but the endless Ocean. That was the dragon's name.

Likely climbed down from Texas' back.

"I'm ready," she said. "How am I supposed to fight him?"

"I'll dress you up as a knight in armor," said Texas, "and I'll give you a sword and a shield."

She knelt.

"Likely," said Texas, touching her with the sword, "every girl and boy must fight with this dragon. Do not be afraid."

And he gave her armor to put on. But this was a mistake. Her open face disappeared in the iron helmet that had a black plume. On her shield was a picture of the Winter Sun trying to shine through a snowfall. The armor was too heavy to wear, and Likely began to shake inside of it and be afraid.

And when, in the heavy armor, she went up to the ugly Dragon's head, he spat smoke and fire at her, as dragons do, and gave forth a bellow. He struck her with his claw and knocked her down.

"Oh-ow!" moaned Texas. "All is lost."

"Nothing is lost!" said Likely. "It's the armor that is too heavy!"

She stepped out of the heavy armor, and she took off the iron helmet so that you could see her face again. She threw away the shield, but grasped the sword.

Then she easily stepped up to the Dragon and cut his head off.

"I'm sorry to hurt you, monster," she said, "but you must give me back my brother Larry."

"Don't be sorry," said the Dragon's head. "Thanks! I'm glad at last to be able to let go biting my tail. Now I can go swimming, which I enjoy."

And the head dove into the sea and disappeared.

Likely cut open the body and out stepped Larry, happy

and new, and able to talk very well.

"Hi!" said Larry. "It's God's birthday. You know, God has a birthday every couple of weeks. Sometimes, when all's well, He has a birthday-party every morning at sunrise."

Likely was glad to hear it. She had never learned anything from Larry before.

She helped her brother up onto Texas' back, and she climbed up herself, and off they flew across the sky.

"Texas," said Likely, as they moved across the sky toward dawn on their homeward trip, "you are old and wise and we love you, but you don't know how to fight dragons. You must never wear heavy armor, but just swing your arms with all your might."

9.

The sunrise came into Likely's bedroom and she woke up.

It was the world's birthday. The world has a birthday-party when all is well. That happens sometimes, and it happens more often if you let it happen. Likely did not hold herself back with foolish fears. She could, if she wanted, fly into the very next moment; or she could sometimes sit still and let the next moment come to her. So she sang,

> Happy birthday to you!
> happy birthday to you!
> happy birthday, dear world,
> happy birthday to you!

The question is, how many candles are there on the world's birthday-cake? The answer is, One. It is the *extra* candle that they put on birthday-cakes, the one to grow on. That's really the only candle you *need* to have a birthday-cake.

Aunt Liz and Mother and Father and Likely and Larry sat down to breakfast and ate the birthday-cake. Since it was breakfast, the cake was toast. For it's not the chocolate icing that makes a birthday-cake, but the shining candle in the middle. You can make a fried egg into a birthday-cake by lighting a candle on it.

"Put a birthday candle on the heap of toast," said Likely.

"Why on earth?" said Mother.

"Because it's a bright sunrise," said Likely.

"It is. But we can't have a candle every time it's a bright morning, you silly girl," said Mother.

"No, but once in a while, for a change," said Likely.

"You're right," said Mother, and got a candle from the drawer and stuck it in the heap of toast and lit it.

"I want toast and cereal," said Larry in perfect English. Aunt Liz marveled that Larry had learned to speak so well. "It's as if he learned to speak overnight," said Aunt Liz. Likely knew why.

10.

Likely decided that it was better to have a real brother than a doll.

Matty and Laura came with their skates. You could first hear their skates clattering in the street. *This* side, *that* side. Then, after some scuffling, they came in carrying the skates.

Likely and Matty kissed each other because they loved each other.

"Is everybody here?" asked Likely. And she called the roll of the people in this story.

"Aunt Liz?"

"Here."

"Mother?"

"Here."

"Daddy?"

"Here."

"Larry?"

"I'm here," said Larry in perfect English.

"Matty?"

"Here."

"Laura?"

"Here."

"Where is Texas?" asked Likely.

249

"Texas is here in his absence," said Father.

"Yeow!" said Larry, to show that he could also remember his old words.

"I'm going skating," said Likely. "Larry can come along if he stays where we put him. As soon as he makes a fuss, he comes upstairs again."

"No fuss," said Larry. "Skate on sidewalk. *This* side, *this* side. With one skate. Yeow!"

Larry could skate with one skate.

"Do be careful, children," said Aunt Liz. "Don't go where the cars are."

"For heaven's sake, Liz," said Father, "Likely has sense and she can go wherever it's safe."

"Right," said Likely. There was nothing to argue about.

Soon you could hear their skates speaking in the street. *This* side, *that* side. This side, that side—faster and faster—then softly purring.

But Larry's skate said, *This* side, *this* side.

New York City
May 1947–[1968?]

Terry Fleming, or
Are You Planning a Universe?

I.

Mother told Terry that his father was dead. But when he grew old enough to read and to ferret in the trunk, he found newspaper clippings that his father was in jail. He was excited. His father was not dead but alive, not nothing but a person, not nowhere but in a place. He was angry with his mother anyway, now he was angry with her because she tried to hide his living father. She kept secrets from him, he kept his secret from her; but he had the advantage, because he knew.

His father and his father's plight seemed wonderfully interesting to Terry and he bragged to his mates in school. "*My* father is in a tremendous jail. It goes on more'n fifty miles. It's far away." His schoolmates were doubtful how to take this novelty. Those to whom the word *jail* meant something vaguely guilty and frightening were stirred to awe and envy, because what is guilty is forbidden and what is forbidden is delightful without limits. The thought of this ecstasy communicated itself from them to Terry. He radiated privilege.

He bragged to his teacher Miss Agostine that his father was in the great jail. She started and Terry was convinced that there was something unbelievable. So he insisted, to enjoy the reaction again and again. But when she showed signs of pity, he felt contempt and anger and said, "What do you know about jails, you old maid?"

To preserve his little glory he made a devaluating judgment of them all.

251

His schoolmates, fortified by information from home, conspired to take him down a peg, and at the corner after lunch they greeted him with the outcry, "Your daddy's a jailbird."

But Terry said serenely, "What do *you* know about jails? My daddy's alive. My daddy's alive and in jail. Even my Mom tried to keep it secret from me, but I found it out by reading. It's in the papers. He's not nowhere. Yeow! *My* daddy's alive, he's in jail."

2.

Terry's father, Dick Fleming, was inured. Whether in fear or perverse hope, he could not foresee any extraordinary punishment that they could inflict on him that would not be indifferent, indifferently sad, to him. When he first reached this condition, his attitude was exasperating to the prison authorities; it seemed to be insolent, defiant and provocative, a show of force to be met with new force. But there was no increment of reaction on his part and even a superficial observer could see that his expression was not a judgment of them nor of his relation to them, but of a certain relation to himself. To create such an inward-turning relation was the purpose of their reformatory, and therefore usually they now let him be.

Punished, or let be in his cage, Dick Fleming felt no anger. He had achieved a control of his feelings that prevented the fruitless anger from rising and disturbing the pleasure of surcease from pain. The worst pain would be to repeat the process of bursting with anger and swallowing the anger. Of turning four colors: red, black, white and purple: for there is the red anger of boiling anger, the black anger of settled wrath, the white anger of blazing fury, and the purple anger of suppressed rage.

The expense of soul in repeating this fruitless process was too exhausting to endure. Dick was preoccupied with avoiding the pain of the rising of the instinctive reaction of anger, and he was inured to the hurt, usual or extraordinary, that they inflicted on him. He did not fear anything but the obliterating fury itself, that would obliterate first himself.

But when he slept, he dreamed of the fire. We others dream of the fire with its features and colors and licking its objects: houses burning, explosions, and bolts of electricity. But the fire that Dick dreamed of was more like the dark fire of physics, an invisible mass not even hot because it touches no objects—the fire itself, filling a space, where nothing else can be, except that occasionally there is a white flash and annihilation because of some flaw in the perfect destructiveness.

3.

"My father is a king," thought Terry. "Enemies have locked him in jail. They have cruel guards and use heavy stone and iron to keep him unknown. But his dignity shines.

"They gave me to a gypsy. My real mother is dead."

Terry was too prudent to brag to his schoolmates that his father was this important person. But his knowledge of it enabled him sometimes to withdraw from stupid competitions with a distant smile. But the secret of it isolated him from his friends and he had no other confidants.

Terry did not let on to the woman he housed with that he knew she was a gypsy.

"Also, my father has a daughter, my older sister," thought Terry. "She is beautiful and she has let-down hair. She is not in jail, but she has a way of getting in to see our father. She works on the outside with our party. She is the one I must get in touch with, to know what to do next."

But it was not the case that Terry met his sister on any corner, altho he had a suspicion that certain persons, by their dignity, belonged to their party; but he was too prudent to be forward. Instead, what he recognized clearly, by their pretended dignity and their cruelty, were the enemies. He learned to mark how they usurped privileges and were abusing them. The enemies did not aim any special attacks at Terry himself because he kept his secret too well, that it was *his* father who was the king. Terry saw that most of the

253

kids were ignorant sheep who did not know what was going on, and they were the most abused.

Sometimes he was buoyed up by hope. At other times, especially in the anxious dark before sleep, Terry felt that the enemy regime was becoming the accepted order of things: the king was literally rotting away in jail and it was too late to rescue him. The world was closing in and there was no way of making a break-through, even if he met his sister.

Most of the day he was neither elated nor anxious but masturbated with dogged courage.

4.

Are *you* planning a Universe? Are you thinking of creating a *Universe*? Here are some *do's* and *don'ts* to bear in mind. If you follow these simple suggestions you will have a better chance of being content with your Universe.

Don't have any "chosen people." The fancied advantages of such an arrangement are found to be far less than the complications that arise.

Do have a good supply of material on hand, so that at the last moment you don't have to skimp on whole realms of being.

Don't try to settle everything beforehand, but *do* have a reserve for unforeseen changes, so that you don't end up stuck with an undesirable scheme and hating it.

Do show a little pity.

If you're planning a Universe. If you're thinking of creating a Universe.

Do show a little pity.

Don't hide your face too completely, because you might as well get some satisfaction out of your handiwork.

Do give the souls a little substance along with their necessary flexibility, or they will become complicated to the point of monotony.

Don't have any "chosen people."

If you follow these simple suggestions, you will have a better chance of being content with your Universe.

Terry Fleming, or Are You Planning a Universe?

Do try to keep it clear what is nature and what is violence.

Don't hurry, putting in a week's work and thinking you can have something to be proud of.

But *do* let yourself go, according to your whim. Remember that it's your show from the beginning to the end.

But *don't* have any "chosen people."

And *do* show a little pity.

If you're planning a Universe. If you're thinking of creating a Universe. Here are some *do's* and *don'ts*. Follow these simple suggestions and you will have a better chance of being content with your Universe.

Don't forget?

New York City
June 1, 1947

The Midnight Sun

Pytheas determined that the Pole Star is not at the Pole, and that there is in fact no star located precisely there. But he did find three stars in that vicinity so placed that if you were to imagine a fourth to complete the rectangle, then this imaginary star would be approximately at the North Pole.

—STEFANSSON

I.

If I had had a banner, I used to have embroidered on my banner a Wintry Sun, of white cotton thread on a milky sky (soon became dirty).

Because we poets make emblems, to recognize how it is with us and to reconcile ourselves to it, and then to blazon it out that "This is how it is with us," I unskilfully embroidered this blobule with weak rays.

This Wintry Sun meant that I recognized that I would not be happy, and I reconciled myself to it by no longer *wishing* to be happy, and then I blazoned it out to you saying: "I will shine nevertheless! you may rely on it! altho in my country there is little animal heat."

And I have been visited in my country by sundry polar bears and angry penguins. Our group in the snow, thru the shortening days of the year, my imaginary flag playing in the real sky, by day and night.

By day and night? Oh! as I stare hypnotized at my gray flag, which is the needlework of a small child whose fingers are none too clean, I see my emblem has become the Midnight Sun.

This makes a difference, makes a difference. Because we poets make emblems how it *is* with us, they are not lies.

Either that the weather of the world is changing or that, as I have heard, before freezing to death the numb body feels warmer—but such a hunger and thirst and lust for happiness is burning me that I shall go mad with it, go mad with it.

2.

I have awakened into midnight, and I see that: Along the walk in the park, thru the leaves of the trees overlooking the Harlem River, the midnight sun is rolling on my left. The sun is traveling with me, slowly, as I go. We do not hurry to hunt and pounce, for the daylight is not pouring away. It is pouring a golden dew but it is not pouring away. I notice that the shadows of passersby do not alter so rapidly about their feet. I have even been able to collect some of these bronzed objects, such triangles with an arm akimbo, or a yellow oval slanted on another oval.

And from the glen below is pouring the burden and the endless drone of a bagpiper. He's around a turning, and I cannot see him yet, but his song sings down all the paths.

> Listen! for the vale profound
> is overflowing with the sound!

I must sail to that land of the Midnight Sun like Pytheas of Marseilles. Pytheas heard tales of such a region where the sun does not set. Indeed he reasoned it out astronomically that such a region must be. He sailed there and he returned to tell tales of his own.

"Listen to me," I imagine that I have already returned, "I have brought objects. Here is some golden-leaf that I snatched up, the shadow of a passerby. The shadows there do not alter so rapidly about the feet. Neither are the substances so stony hard. The daylight is pouring a golden dew, but it not pouring away."

258

The Midnight Sun

3.

It is dark, there are hardly outlines of light around your gloomy faces. (I am waiting for the ship of Pytheas of Marseilles to put in for me here.)

These people do not seem to understand how wan the light is; they see each other in an illusory light. But as I listen to them, I see the shadow on their faces and hear the muffle in their words. My long discipline as a knight of the wintry sun has made me fearfully canny in perceiving the shadow behind the overt gesture, the repressed thought underlying the speech.

The unknown thought underlying the speech. The resentment behind the kindly advice. The anger behind the impartial judgment. The shadow behind the gesture. The nausea underneath the kiss. The indolence underneath the poem. The unknown thought behind the speech.

There is not one person here who is addressing himself to the sweet objects of the world.

On this porch my friends are carrying on a family quarrel. The brother is angrily speaking of the dangers of the company his sister keeps, that he long ago turned from reluctantly. The mother complains that the young people do not undertake responsibilities because suddenly she is face to face with the calamitous effects of old errors. The girl keeps the peace with a murderous smile. I assert my better judgment because I am again and again living in a stranger's home.

All this is usual with us, it is too ordinary to be fearful. What is fearful is my plight: that I can perceive nothing but these shadows. How am I to take part in the social intercourse, such as it is; such as it is it is all the social intercourse that there is. There I sit back in my chair, deep in my own shadow.

This is lonely. Am I to say "we are in deep shadow" and nevertheless take part in the bright social intercourse?

Oh, I am longing for the ship of Pytheas of Marseilles, to sail to where the sun of evidence shines night and day.

Here my friends are deceiving me, I cannot believe in the sweet love that they offer, and is not this the long shadow

259

that *I* am casting night and day? And perhaps all this shadow is my shadow, and every other countenance is bathed in light. No no; for I loyally lift up my Wintry Sun to see by, and I see that it is also they who are in shadow.

I for my part have remained loyal to a wintry sun, and by this light I have grown fearfully canny in perceiving the shadow behind the overt gesture and the forgotten thought underlying the speech. It is hard for me to take part in the bright social intercourse, such as it is, altho such as it is it is the only social intercourse that there is.

But oh, I am longing for the ship of Pytheas of Marseilles to put in for me here, and we shall sail to where the sun of evidence shines day and night.

4.

"Aboard! Aboard!" And now look! where we come! on the ship of Pytheas of Marseilles.

On the galleon of the Greek, with its hundred legs crawling on the swell and its great sail swelling in the south wind, we are flying three colored pennons whose tongues are reaching north in desire, in haste. As we crawl in haste thru the long arctic dawn let me inspect at leisure these fiery designs; for I am a connoisseur of such flags.

The aft pennon is two flat bands of blue: sky and navy. Between these two would be the line of the horizon, if this were an horizon, but the sky is the boundary of the sea and the sea is the boundary of the sky. There is no horizon, depth; there is nothing behind the scene. In all this world there is no rip or rent. All right! I am loyal to this flag, to the limited territory of visibility. This adequately fills the field of vision, and I touch it lightly with the palps of my eyes.

(But if, on the contrary, you look too curiously at the line of the horizon, the thread of it is tightening around your throat. Your eyes are going black and your hands are groping in impalpable depth.)

The flag atop the midmast flapping and snapping in the wind, is the four vertical bars of anger: red, black, white, and purple. The red flush of anger, the black beetling brows of wrath, the white flaring nostrils of fury, and the purple temples of suppressed rage. Flapping and snapping in the south wind, presenting first one then another color to the view, and tearing themselves to tatters.

To while away the dawn—to while away the dawn—as we all are crawling with our legs, in desire, over the swell—

Well! on the fore-staff is wagging the bold and wished-for Midnight Sun that bathes us already in its aureole light and casts our shadow. I see that something has been added to the flag, or I notice it the first time: The sun is riding above a wavering line that one takes to be the horizon, carelessly or mystically embroidered. But no, more closely and curiously observed, the line is a curling comber breaking from end to the end of the world.

The sun rises at a bound, on our faces of surprise.

Is wheeling long hours of the night and day above the horizon on a tilted track.

With blowing locks, as if he had never lain, nor would ever lie again, in bondage to the gulf.

As we communicate directly with one another and address ourselves to the sweet objects of the world.

I do not mean (God forbid) that the unconscious is transparent or visible to us, but that there is no need to puzzle it out. There is no use to puzzle it out. Clear enough as the occasion arises; for the occasion; that is, if we address ourselves, etc.

There is the sun of evidence.

It rises at a bound on our faces of surprise, and is wheeling long hours of the night and day a yard above the horizon, with blowing locks. It is the sun of evidence. There is no hope to puzzle it out.

In these waters, I see, there are no less shadows to things; every face still has a shadow, and there is an unknown motive underlying the speech. But the substances are not so hard as stone, and also the shadows do not flit so rapidly away. Now I have caught him! my hundred-legged Eagerness crawling in desire, in haste.

What! is it only this? But I expected to be *happy* when the sun would light my midnight soul at least clear enough for etc.

But I was sad without knowing it; now I know that I am sad.

Thru the blinding sheet of tears, a hundred suns have disposed themselves around the collar of heaven—each with blowing locks, as if he had never lain, and would not lie again, in bondage to the gulf.

Great sighs of breathing are making the cords tremble.

Fires (I have squeezed shut my burning eyes) are streaking from the horizon to the pole.

(It is the same if I open my eyes or squeeze them shut. No doubt they are shut and I think they are open, or they are open and I think they are shut; but I dare not alter it because of the burning.)

The black gulf opens in a blink from the horizon to the pole.

Now I am somewhat afraid. (Courage!) The darkness is warm and friendly; but vegetation is stretching its muscles with a terrible noise, like the breakup of the springtime ice; there is a rush, like the torrents of the spring.

The midnight sun rises at a bound on our glad faces of surprise. The world is black and we are enlivened—or consumed—it comes to the same thing—by a black power. It is the sun of evidence, and there is no end to puzzle it out.

The heroes of science and art explain and shape the objects to which they address themselves, as they rise from utter darkness. They themselves are not afraid to rest in darkness; the light is clear enough as the occasion arises.

Also, we are loyal to our dear flag of sky and navy, whose flat bands are the boundaries of each other and there is no invitation into depth.

Owow! our Captain is angrily whipping the sailors. He wants to go further.

Why does he? As for me, I'd be content to cruise awhile, under the midnight sun, pressing no further. Acting and speaking, and at the moment of doing so recognizing the unknown motive of the action and speech; sometimes thereby acting and speaking more powerfully, at other times (when the unknown and the known are contradictory) disastrously inhibited in action and speech: my arm falls limp, the tongue cleaves to the roof of my mouth.

Yet always finding a proof, of something or other (for I am not biased), when the unknown is called into recognition by action and speech.

Content (not very happy) with the security that there is in recognizing clearly enough for any action and speech a face of the utter darkness in which we are universally consumed. Sometimes also blinded with tears that streak fires from the hundred suns around, to the top of heaven, and there is no shadow anywhere till I dare to open my eyes and the gulf blinks from the horizon to the pole.

To continue another age, poor poet, recognizing how it is with me, and reconciling myself to it, and *blazoning* it out.

5.

No use. I am afraid of the impending wave breaking towards us from end to end of the world. It is angry. What? must we *dive* into it? The Captain is angrily whipping the sailors. To head, head first, into the comber advancing too swiftly anyway. He has broken a stick across a man's back. Row! row! for the gusts of wind are now coming from all directions.

He has torn down the aft and fore flags, both the mediterranean limitation and our paradise of the north. We are flying only the four bars of anger, ripped and rent. But I am not loyal to this flag; is it *my* flag?

I'd rather flee—but the wave will overtake us in any case. Oh, we'd rather land on the delightful shore we are even now leaving behind, where the flowers are exploding like thunder.

It is still. The breaker is uprearing his forebreast from the water. The sea and sky are gray. The swells are overlapping and there is froth on the lines of the polygons.

Is it "mine"? I cannot say "because." I cannot say "therefore."

263

Not "altho." Not "if I had."
Hardly "and—and—and."
Is it "there"?
"When" did it happen to me?
I am lost; I cannot say "it means."

6.

I have a certain courage, but have I the courage as a poet to do without my words "because" and "therefore" and "also" and "altho"; and "when" and "while" and "where"; and "whenever" and "wherever" and "always"; and "those there" and "here mine"? For these are the words with which I enchain the speakable world and immobilize it and protect myself from the onrush of anger and love. Causal clauses are my glorying power; when I utter them I am very safe in my strength. Concessive clauses are wrung from my weakness; by means of them I play dead and I am very safe. With conjunctions and disjunctions I stall for time. I assign times and places to build a wall of objectivity between them and me. With universal propositions I now advance to the attack and lay waste the world. In the emergency of dreaming, I say "it means."

(Let me say no harm of the faculty of reasonable speech, so subtilely and flexibly given for our advantage, and to me more than to most. God forbid. But the power is not intended to be used by me for my *dis*advantage.)

People protect themselves by verisimilitude from the simple outcries of invention, as if the new things of rage and love were like the familiar. But they are unfamiliar. I do not dare present them to myself, they are so strange; nor do I know the language to tell them, without comforming them to a reality less real than they.

Speech of direct anger and love is strange but it is not the imagery of dreams—tho dreams are nearer to it than my wan stories. The episodes of anger and love would have the closeness, horror, and pleasure of unbearable dreams, but would be as practical as waking experience. If I could feel those feelings I would know the episodes; and if I knew them I would dare to tell them in English.

Fire Island
July 1947

Little Brother

—for Naomi

Likely looked at Little Brother with anger, because he was wearing her red shoes and her green hat, and her golden beads. "Ha!" cried Likely, "I'll make him be *not* there!" She lifted the heavy sharp axe, and strong strength flowed into her arms. She swung round the axe, down square on his noddle, and she said "Ha!"

Blood gushed out of Little Brother and became a talking brook in the grass, talking to anybody and everybody. Lifting the heavy sharp axe again and again, Likely chopped him up into a hundred pieces, fingers, toes, eyes, ears, and nose; and she buried the pieces under a tree.

She tried on the red shoes, but they were too tight for her. She tried on the green hat, but it was too small and looked ridiculous. She put the golden beads round her neck and they choked her, but in spite she wore them anyway.

The talking brook said, "You had better look for the pieces under the tree and put Little Brother together again."

"Ha!" said Likely. "I won't."

The brook flowing in the grass was talking to anybody and everybody.

"Where," cried Likely in fright, "where is Little Brother? He is not there."

She began to look for the pieces, to put Little Brother together again. But the puzzle was too hard for her. The pieces would no longer fit together.

The fingers would not fit together to make a hand. The eyes would not look out on either side of the nose.

The pieces would not fit together because now some were too big.

They would not fit because some pieces grew into two pieces, and it was too confusing for her.

She made a botch job by joining the pieces in any which order, but this was not Little Brother. Besides, many pieces were left over.

Likely sat down on the ground and wept with frustration. It is called frustration that a person wants something and tries to get it, but cannot get it and comes to feel that she cannot get it.

"Ha!" said the laughing brook, "Ha! ha! ha! ha! ha!"

Worse and worse became the puzzle of putting the pieces together, and Likely sat down on the ground and wept with frustration.

A live thing, breeding and growing in the still depths of the brook, where the sun shone dimly, at last jumped out onto the bank. It was an ugly frog.

"Oh!" cried Likely, catching at her throat. But she was not afraid of the live thing, even tho it was so ugly. She took off the golden beads that choked her and threw them away.

"It is in this way and this way," said the frog, hopping and hopping, "it is in this way that you must put the pieces together. It is easy. It is very easy." He hopped about from piece to piece.

Likely listened. She was not afraid and disgusted, tho the frog looked so ugly, because it was a live thing.

As the live thing taught her, she put the pieces together without being puzzled. But she was surprised. She was not puzzled if the pieces seemed to fit into two different figures, because each piece had grown into two and some were small and some were big. She was not puzzled, but she was surprised.

She was surprised to see that from the pieces two persons sprang suddenly alive. One was Little Brother and one was Prince Charming, wearing golden beads.

The frog leaped into her open mouth and down her throat, and he became her pounding heart.

"Will you love me, Prince Charming?" she said, "because I love you."

Fire Island
August 1947

266

Raoul

The little old man used to pursue me, fearfully, through High Bridge Park or on the rocks along the river. At first I thought—for I have the opinion that I am not sought after—I assumed that he was following the same ones that I was following, and therefore he stuck so close. This annoyed me. But when it became clear that it was I for whom he panted along so wistfully, I stopped for him; I made it easy for him by asking for the match and remarking about the weather with a smile. I too shall one day be such an old one—I trust as innocent and cheerful—and I hope some one will stop for me.

Raoul—he could speak French of Quebec—was working for a syndicate of tailors; he did not overwork himself, being abroad on every fair day. If he was scouring the parks on the occasional days that I was, he was probably there almost always.

He was Raoul d'Anjou de Lys; I took an aspiring delight in this grand name, this Merovingian lineage, whose offshoots, long ago fled to Canada, were slowly decaying to perfection. An older brother was a prelate in a large western town and from time to time intervened with our Catholic police when Raoul's behavior got him into small troubles.

His particular perversion, that he compulsively at once tried to satisfy—though the October thickets had few leaves, and it was chilly—was "rimming," or tonguing the anus. Such tickling gave me slight pleasure but he snorted and wheezed with rapture, and comforted my sorry soul, as though I had to do with a dog.

267

He lived in a little hall bedroom on Broadway, whose rental was four dollars a week. Coming in, one was at once struck by the scores of pictures tacked and Scotch-taped on the walls. There were the usual aphrodisiac nudes (of women); but the greater number of the pictures were photographs, and these proved to be photographs of opera-singers of the decade 1915-1925, all inscribed *"à mon cher Raoul"* or *"à mon petit Raoul."* Some were posed portraits, some snapshots onstage. Dominating all the rest, and of course the first thing to strike the eye, was a full-length figure of the great contralto Mme. ——, blown up to heroic size, heroic size even for her.

On his bare chest Raoul wore a golden crucifix set with seed-pearls. By compunction of politeness, he would try to complete his rimming with fellation, at which he was rather inept (he had a few pointed teeth); or perhaps by pederasty, but he had no genital desires of his own. I myself was interested rather in his history, his family, and his charming personality. On Sundays he played the organ and led the choir in a small well-known church in the Village. It was his purpose, that he forwarded with cunning diplomacy and Fabian tactics, to elevate the taste to Gounod and Rossini.

He had been a singer, a lyric tenor; he had made his debut in 1919, after the war, at La Scala, in some medium role. He mentioned Turin, Salzburg, Montevideo, and Buenos Ayres.

When finally he had calmed his fears, had convinced himself that I was a good-humored brute who was not going to beat the shit out of him and rob him of the crucifix, that indeed I was not a brute at all but could speak French and hum the arias—when his lust was allayed and we smoked cigarettes, but he insisted that I smoke from his pack and not my own—he told me the following delicious anecdote:

Always he had loved to sing. (He did not say "wanted to sing," but he loved to sing and in fact did sing, trained or untrained.) He was brought up in one of the mill-towns north of Providence, where a number of French had settled. To his delight, I even knew the town, Woonsocket. At the age of nine and ten he used to walk along the road shouting

268

as loud as he could *Celeste Aida.*

For a mile, two miles, a barouche with two horses trailed him. The horses walked. At last it drew abreast and a great lady in a fur coat emerged.

"You sing so beautifully," she said, "I have been crying for two miles. What is your name, little boy?"

"Raoul d'Anjou de Lys," said the boy, proudly.

"That's a great name!" cried the lady. "Raoul, here is something for you—" and she wrote out a cheque for a hundred dollars and gave him tickets for a concert in Providence that evening. But when he returned home, his mother tore up the check and would not take him to the city to use the tickets.

Years later, 1917, he was in the Army, in training at Ft.—— in North Carolina. He had continued with his singing and at an entertainment given by his company, he appeared on the program singing *Celeste Aida.* Also on the program was the great contralto of the Metropolitan Opera Company, Mme.——; already at that time she was known as the "mother of the AEF." He recognized her, she was the lady of the barouche. She sang from *Huguenots* and also "Silent Night, Holy Night." He sang his best.

She said, "Don't I know you? Haven't I heard you sing before? I never forget a voice."

He told her of the incident of the barouche on the road, which he, of course, had never forgotten. And from that time on Mme.—— interested herself in him. On her tour of the camps in Europe, she looked for him especially; she arranged for him to study with the great E.P.; finally she had the satisfaction of hearing him at La Scala, in a medium role.

"I have so many photographs," said Raoul. "Would you like to see my photos of the war? of my Captain?"

He took a bulging envelope from the bureau-drawer. "My buddy George, this was my buddy George—this was my buddy Tonio—this was our cook. . . ." The photos were printed in sepia as was the custom at that time; they had faded. "*This,*" he said, still proudly and moved, "was my Captain. This was my Captain. Here is another one of my Captain."

One could not distinguish anything particular about this archetype of love.

"My Company—my Captain—our Company," he mumbled. The tears came to my eyes. I was terribly reminded of the military career of St. Loup in Proust and of that atmosphere of ending. I had cut myself off from that camaraderie of camps because I knew that those wars were evil and one must not collaborate in them.

There were many pictures of stage-plays, in which little Raoul had always impersonated the ingénue. His Company, his Company, amid the fierce war, was apparently a great group for amateur theatricals.

"Don't you sing any more?" I said.

"No! Never! Never since April 14, 1924."

"Why not? Why did you stop just that day?"

"All right, I'll tell you about that too," said Raoul and he laid his hand on mine, so that I thought his ardors were about to recommence, but it was for comfort.

Some time after the war he began to suffer from a difficulty of breathing, a kind of "phtisie" he called it—judging from his character and tastes I presume it was an asthma complicated by sinusitis. Since it was perhaps an effect of gas-poisoning (and to recapture the days of his Company), he had himself admitted to a military hospital in Maine. But there he was not recovering, till one morning, on a solitary walk, he came on a camp of friendly lumbermen. Then, as the result of daily walks, he began to improve rapidly. (All of his conversation was decorated with such cheerful little memories as we are wont to comfort ourselves with.) He walked to the camp of the friendly, and he sang loudly in the woods. Alas! the telegram came—

Mme.—— was dead. She was to be buried in Philadelphia. Would Raoul sing at the grave?

He had to. He ought not to have sung at that time. He had a laryngitis. It was a cold and rainy day. Nevertheless he sang at the grave, the *Inflammatus* of Rossini. Did I know the *Inflammatus* from *Stabat Mater*?

I hummed a bar. "You know it! you know it!" he cried. "Then you can imagine the whole scene! The guards shot their guns. I sang. My best. I sang my very best. I never sang

Raoul

that way. At the open grave. It was the end; I destroyed my voice forever. . . . Do you want to see a picture of it?"

This picture he kept in his wallet that he carried in the pocket of his leather windbreaker. (At a little distance, in the park, he might have been fourteen or fifteen.) A newspaper clipping, almost indecipherable: flags and a color-guard and a small fellow in a high-crowned corporal's hat, who might have been Raoul; a puddle of rain.

He used to lure me back by speaking of a neighborhood beauty who obeyed his every whim. No such person ever appeared.

One evening I found him in bed with the grippe, in his lonely little room. "You should have come this afternoon!" he cried. "You would have had a good time. The boys of the choir came to visit the old man. Ten—in this little room. All your type!"

I looked around at the pictures, the aphrodisiac nudes, and the photos of the opera, and the blown-up full-length of Mme.——. "What did they think of your pictures?"

"Oh? They don't pay any mind to what the old man does!" He referred to himself now as the old man.

Then if I read in the *Tribune*—for this is what they cover—that Raoul d'Anjou de Lys is dead, must I not mourn for him a day? Being today prepossessed by the thought of death: that we are dying in this senseless onrush of bright and dismal days—one cannot, not even with wilful invention, impart any sense to it.

New York City
November 1947

271

The Messiah-Blower

I have been given a horn and appointed to wait and blow it when the Messiah comes to our town. If I have been appointed? or have I appointed myself to this position? In any case I have a horn in my hand.

Naturally, from time to time, I cannot resist giving it an experimental toot. This makes a few (usually the same ones) prick up their ears and come running. But most people pay no attention to such a peep; they think, no doubt, that when the Messiah really comes, the sound will have a stirring unmistakeable appeal.

Really, with my tooting, I am trying to get a rise out of a person on the second floor there.

I am lying about those occasional toots. Actually I blow and blow my brains out. They are going to pass a decree to keep me off the streets.

Am I betraying my office by tooting at that second floor? But why shouldn't the Messiah come out of *that* window? If I don't rouse him, who will?

Questions. Questions. I whose vocation is for heart-easing hallelujahs, sound nothing but discordant blasts. Almost I could believe that the Messiah doesn't come just because I make such a damned racket! . . . Yet the Messiah will come anyway (I cannot prevent it either), and then shall I sound the heart-easing hallelujah.

[*New York City*]
March 1948

273

The Penny

*The privilege of coining has in all ages
and countries belonged to the sovereign.*
—BRITANNICA, 9TH ED.

The matter of the Coin is valuable: rare, got by labor. Densely valuable, so the coin may be small, to be carried and given and taken, fitting the fingers and the palm. It is durable, hard, able to go thru many exchanges. It is measurable, shaped in a regular geometrical figure. The coin and its value are identifiable, the auspices and value are stamped on it.

This is cold metal, warm in the palm because warmed by the palm. How do the *giving* fingers tend a coin? It may be pinched, held onto even while given; or as if disdainfully held away from the self; or flipped away, or rung down on the table, cast away. A coin is not given with a full-handed giving—the acts are sado-masochistic. How does one *take* a coin? Tentatively feeling, suspicious of counterfeit; or the palm and fingers fold tight around it; snatched, grasped, held onto. A coin is not easily received—acts of anxiety. The coin slips to rest, as foreign matter, in tiny crevices of the body, in purses and pockets.

The coin has a Head and a Tail, and we say, tossing it up, "Heads or Tails?" Coins and dice decide among alternatives by chance. The two-sided coin decides a conflict. This motion of the coin, to toss it up spinning, seems to me to be the original and natural one: the coins were first used to invoke Chance (I have no evidence for this). To find a way to proceed in a dubious crisis, rather than pause too long. One spins oneself around, to vertigo: one loses one's head and falls, with no more doubts. Then one has the God's head, or else the back of his head. In a conflict, the God faces toward A or toward B.

275

It is the decision of doubt that underlies exchanges: either of the exchanged goods is dubiously preferable. One risks and loses a part of himself, hoping it is for the best. Originally a sacred business of life and death.

The metal was at first a sacred metal. Perhaps this is why these metals have persisted as the media of money, tho they are no longer technically efficient. The labor-value is a rationalization of the inherent value. The unmixed, the unoxidized gold and silver, are reminders, as Plato would say, of the courts of Jove.

And it is primarily a God's Head, and the Back of his Head. Usurping the sacred right, the King or the State tries to assert that itself is the immortal thing among these changes and exchanges: the immortal stability of the world, the durable metal. The back of the God's head is darkness, night and death. The back of the King's head is a definite evaluation, 1 penny, a judgment that limits, not without humiliating, the infinite free giving and taking. "The King says that your love is worth a penny." The disfavor of the God is death (rejection).

But the counterface is also a Tail: that is, the coin is a little animal or homunculus. The tail with its grasped number is the anal holding and hoarding. The coin is a little idol: this is the grip of the ego to itself in the flow of the instincts. The Head is my public face of myself, exchangeable for other public things. The Tail is my saying to myself: "My love and anger are worth a penny."

The money is always alien to me. What is exchanged is not essential.

To put something up to chance, tossing the coin, is an imitation of spontaneity, after frustration and crisis, as the tragic hero who has lost his bearings cries out, "Come what may!"

The metal is not digestible, assimilable, but remains in the crevices of the body as foreign matter.

Yet the coin is our justice, such as it is: it is our medium of safe communication (calculated risk). Once we have admitted that we are isolated individuals and the continuity of love is lost, still we must somehow safely deal with one another, with a trust in the limits of the dealing: "I

276

The Penny

give you a penny's worth of myself." But this is *too* calculating: so we justify the justice of it by symbolically recalling the condition of unity underlying our isolations, and we embellish the piece with slogans and prayers: "In God we trust!"—"Liberty!" And with the faces and symbols of Gods and Heroes, eagles, crowns, owls, branched candlesticks.

The coin was an Idol. An idol is the illusion of a permanent good dreamed up by sorry creatures of loss and mourning. Handling money is idol-worship. They brought the idols to the Temple, and there also goods were exchanged, consulting the idols; eventually they exchanged the idols for the goods. Historically, the early media of exchange were such things as cattle and salt, consumptible, digestible, assimilable. This was technical exchange. It is not the same as the deathly exchange that occurs by means of the coins, the idols, the fatal lots.

And now—is my offering worth anything? What is it worth? The Head says, "It is worth what is back of the head" (rejected), or even "what is behind" (a lot of shit).

The sovereign ego says, "*I* have the right of seignorage" (anal retention).

But also, instead of reading the coin I can carelessly toss it up and clap it on the back of my hand: devoting myself to chance; and this too is economic history:

> When any person undertakes to work a new mine in Peru he is universally looked upon as a man destined to bankruptcy and ruin, and is upon that account shunned and avoided by everybody. Mining is considered as a lottery. . . .   —*The Wealth of Nations*

One does not mine gold, or hoard gold, as a calculated risk.

Gambling: the impossible attempt to stake oneself (adult masturbation).

Let us distinguish *secular alienation* and *sacred alienation*. Alienation is the isolation of the ego from the soul and the world: secular alienation is the calculated acts of the isolated ego; sacred alienation is the desperate act of the isolated ego. (Relation between Marx and Kierkegaard.)

South Windham
July 1948

277

The Lear Complex

Besides their concerted exhibitions, in chorus or conflict, the three little ones also daily stood forth alone. As in those books of the *Iliad* that narrate the Bravery of Ajax or Hector or Diomedes. Each shining in characteristic power: the boy who could talk a little whining "Mummy" and "Milk! milk!" clinging with tireless persistency, trotting with shorts steps of pursuit from room to room, or standing at the screen-door giving forth an apparently hopeless roar; the small girl shrieking "my" and "mine," controlling from the center of the floor her manifold possessions far as the eye and active memory could reach—and specializing also in spectacular night-terrors; or the boy who could not talk even a little, quick to be frustrated and imperiously screaming his anger, impetuously hurling the glasses from the table, standing at the bar of his pen with an accusing bellow not soon to cease. The lull during the evening hours was uneasy with the question: which display of *Areté* must one next expect?—the one beginning quiet as a mouse, "Mummee?" or the shattering wail of a sudden night-thought, or the sharp little outcry of turning over, premonitory of speechless rage. "Ach, it's he!" or "Dammit, she!" And one would rouse a second and all three take it up, together in sympathy and each one distinct.

We parents were terrorized, by these little heroes displaying their Bravery each his own. Fearsome clamor for attention and wreaking of rage. But perhaps we appeared more ignoble at that other moment, when they lolled at ease and uttered their commands like loathsome Byzantine emperors: the humorous one with a sadistic freak, or the Empress wilful-browed and stubborn-jawed, or the smirking one who had a fist of lead.

The analogy of the children is to battle-heroism inspired, and to the whim of imperial sway (just as at other happier moments, not now our concern, it is to the creativity of free artists).

From the exploits of the children one could not directly read off the characters, the errors, of the grown-ups, in our community of families. The *Areté* of each child fell from the blue, it did not seem to follow on such and such mishandling; therefore no remedies were obvious for our protection, one was at a loss. Perhaps the particular Byzantine complacencies bore some faint resemblance or reaction to the parents' ways, were confident expectations of accustomed surrenders, or triumphs won by tested means. But let us, for a change, overlook the failings of our grown-ups, whether or not, and to whatever degree, they were accountable for the punishment that all were now undergoing.

Rather, honor to the present generation of parents that has disarmed itself before the tyranny of natural force! Disarmed itself in the simple sense, of course, of renouncing the use of superior physical strength to punish and intimidate. Even the terrifying roar of the voice has been renounced (possibly we gentlefolk could not shout, bellow, or scream if we chose to). But disarmed, disarming ourselves, disarmed despite ourselves, especially by not knowing (or believing we do not know, whether we know or not). Not knowing what is best, what effects—talents, virtues— to aim at; nor again what means would lead to the ends if we knew the ends. Disarmed of anger and the spontaneous weapons of hand and voice; probably, therefore, disarmed of love and hatred. For how long can these last if we do not make a change?

Without doubt our withdrawal, grounded in self-diffidence, is part of the cause of the children's excessive demanding. Nevertheless this withdrawal, on the part of our present generation, at last lets us see the situation in its purity: *that the little children exhibit their prowess and*

280

the grown-ups who are strong do not destroy them with a blow. That is: in cramped quarters, during the hours of our possible leisure, lust, or needed sleep, they, making havoc of elementary grace and of the order of the space, affirm their principle, themselves, the life in them, and we do not refute them. Oh, as Yeats said,

> the best lack all conviction, and the worst
> are full of passionate intensity.

It is a paradox. On the one hand it seems that just because of an error, a lack of conviction or lack of knowledge, the strong are odiously subjected to the weak. On the other hand, it is always the free display of natural force that characterizes the strong and therefore proves the children to be the *justified* tyrants, no error.

Nietzsche was the historian of the domination of the weak over the strong, of the "slave-morality" energized by resentment. Evidently the strong have had some Achilles' heel that has made them succumb. Now the most universal tyranny of the apparently weak is the domination by the small children (perhaps this was not so obvious in Nietzsche's time and certainly not to him in his circumstances). These weaklings, at least, do not assert themselves by resentment but by free power. Why are the stronger subjected? Looking at the present generation of grown-ups, it leaps to the eye that *we* are holding back murderous resentment—we dare not growl or strike for fear of how hard we might. In former times, to repeat it, this repression was less obvious; it seemed that the children had everything to complain of; this is the theme of all the novels.

In general, given the cowed, domesticated state of the men we see about or have heard of, it is understandable that we cringe with guilt, fear and self-fear, in the face of any uninhibited display of force. In the face of creative spontaneity, revolutionary gestures of freedom, etc., men run for cover. This guiltiness before strange greatness and power, and really before our own freedom, is, roughly, the Oedipus

281

complex (introjected super-ego). Arbitrary force belongs to father and we fear it; and arbitrary force is our rebelliousness against father and we shun it. Yet it is conceivable, at least it is to be hoped—and this hope is the same as all our efforts in anarchist politics, progressive education, sexual liberation—that *this* kind of cringing may be radically cured: the father-like inner voice stilled or at least softened, so that a man can speak in his own voice, astonished at the sound of it. But what shall we say now of the cringing before the children?

This is the complex of Lear: the abdication of age and power to the demands of the new generation, the self-betrayal of strength to weakness because of some unknown drive to submit. What is this drive? A superficial but probably very important component of it has already been mentioned, the arrested motion to demolish the little brats: the motion turns against the self, and age and power abdicate to childishness. We become childish in turn, once more seeking dependency: this is a deeper level of Lear's story, the identification of the self with one's own childhood within, as projected onto the new children. One gives in to them, and makes demands of them, as if they were parents, just as the self-child depended on its parents. Partly because one's own childhood was unfinished, did not fulfil its powers, remains dissatisfied and autonomous (not integrated). This is the familiar story of the parents who wish every advantage for their children that they did not have, make every sacrifice, "live in their children," as we say. Every blasted hope of sorry age and power—i.e. weakness—is projected revived onto the children, who, to be sure, do not entertain these particular old-fashioned hopes and desires and are therefore all the more tormented by the sacrifices of age; but we project our lost lives on them because childhood does indeed display likely strength and possibility. Long ago, for various reasons of safety and love, we elected to renounce our powers and identify ourselves with the grown-ups (Oedipus complex); now, with Lear, we repent our former decision and choose the other way, becoming dependent and officious nuisances.

(The senile king gives way entire to what we, in our

The Lear Complex

so-called maturity, try to contain and combat. He at least reaches the infantile paradise and "enters fantastically freaked with flowers"; and the compassionate poet rewards him, for an hour, with one daughter who is also a good mother.)

Good; all these motives for the complex of Lear are conceivably eradicable. The pent-up destruction of the children (motive of Herod) turned against the self, might be moderated by lightening the parental burdens; in a rare quiet moment one sees they are not really devils, and the fact that one grows old is not really the children's fault after all (tho I do not deny that youth is hateful to contemplate). Also, if the present generation of children can fulfil more of their powers there will be less need for them as grown-ups to fall back into their unfinished childhood, nostalgically submissive to the new children (tho youth is indeed lovely to contemplate).

Yet let us not be too optimistic. It is a peculiar animal species, noted for its long childhood dependency—with or without a period of sexual latency—and noted, correspondingly, therefore, for a strong propensity of the adults to be depended on and to care for. On Darwinian grounds, survival by useful traits, we must assume that this eminently successful animal is by now inborn to tyrannize during its dependency, psychologically free, physically weak (thus the child exacts the conditions necessary for exercise, sustenance, and growth); and to submit during its competency, physically strong, psychologically servile. Perhaps a root of the Lear complex is in our natures and cannot be eradicated. It was long ago, said Kafka, that the dogs became doggish. Now it is too late.

South Windham
August 1948

283

Thoughts on Fever, and Thoughts on These Thoughts

The hypothesis of organic adaptation, nature as a symbiosis: We notice first the obvious adaptations—the animal drinks the water, the cat's tongue is apt for lapping it up; but then we must go on to ask about apparently accidental effects, incidental phenomena. For example, what is the purpose of the *sound* of the waterfall? It attracts the thirsty. Also, the sound of running water induces urination, so that the emptied animal can then drink his full afresh. The soughing of the trees? is no doubt a sign to the birds. But, given any functioning concretely in an environment, there will always be new incidental effects, indefinitely. Hence this rule of seeking the adaptation, and passing from the organism to the environment and back, leads the investigation infinitely onward. It produces a rich vision, admiration, stunning surprises.

Now fever is treated by the doctors as an accidental effect probably secondarily injurious; they drive high fever down with aspirin and cold compresses. Yet it is impossible that so universal and central a feature in pathology should not have some primary defensive (reactive) function of its own, as well as being symptomatic of other reactions. What function?

(In general, normal adaptations are investigated with relation to the environment; pathological adaptations as readjustment of the organism to relations with the environment.)

There is a presumed heightening of the chemism in

heated blood. Is this specific to the chemism of antibodies? Is the heat perhaps itself destructive of the invaders, as e.g. in induced fever cure of syphilis? If so, the fever should be "encouraged," that is allowed to reach its natural climax, rather than coddling with blankets, with rest even when there is no lassitude, etc. Fever has bad effects on the heart, this is indicated by the growing lassitude and aching muscles of the feverish; probably the fever would not injure the heart if we could give in to the tiredness. Let me make a conjecture of my own: that the *trembling* (of chills and fever) is a means of relaxing muscle-tension, in order to encourage curative vegetative flow.

We must picture to ourselves the chill and fever of a primitive man, naked, houseless: the high fever is strong medicine to effect a quick climax and cure. He has no time for long illnesses. Today doctors drive down the fever "if the patient is uncomfortable," but obviously the discomfort itself is functional, not accidental.

Yet why on earth must a layman make conjectures about so universal and central a phenomenon? Why has medical practice not long ago, as a matter of course, settled the whole theory? Perhaps the cultural conditions so long prevalent have made it quite impossible to observe fever with natural climax, so that its curative or destructive effects are not proved. (For instance, the danger to the heart: a typical modern disease: need to do business despite natural lassitude.)

Fever is just such a universal common occurrence unattended to as will make the fame of the man who attends to it. (As Freud attended to dreams or Reich to the orgasm.)

Now then, why do *I* take satisfaction in ferreting out such topics, but do not myself make the necessary observations and experiments? I seem to assign myself a peculiar role: to harry the scientists from outside, as a disengaged critic. As if to take care that the scientific enterprise is carried out in good form, well-rounded, without gaps.

I do it (1) to cast contempt on the physiologists, thru envy. (2) Still to take part in the play and work of my superiors, without undergoing the inferior labor of preparation or running the risk of being ridiculous. Indolence, inferiority. This makes me seek out especially the weak points. (3) I seem to find such points especially in the neglect of the macroscopic and obvious: I refuse, thereby, to recognize a discontinuity between the childish experience and the adult experience. I am a critic of the expert and specialist-technical. (4) As a boy I had a high general ability; I refused to commit myself to a specialty (adult adjustment). The same refusal is evident in my literature. I have also refused to become a specialist generalizer ("philosopher"). Choosing rather a "graceful" indefinite failure, in fear of competing. But unwilling to accept failure gracefully, instead I carp. (As a matter of fact I am generally right.) (5) Or on the positive side, I act so out of simple noblesse oblige, as an amicus curiae, since I do happen to see the points that are overlooked. (6) It is the materiality of the experiments that I avoid: avoidance of manipulation; keeping work at the level of speculation and talk: fear of masturbation, touching, of "coming to grips"—fear of aggressing, cowardice. This is related also to a contempt of labor, of the "lower classes." (7) I want complete, non-technical, understandable answers, those continuous with ordinary experience: this is (a) to satisfy safely my curiosity, without discovering anything radically new (infantile ignorance of sexual facts); (b) to isolate the external world, keep it "out there," as "nothing but that, after all"— without threat or mystery, protecting my own private secret. (8) My real interest is not in science but in magic; I refuse to renounce my childish omnipotence; I want only such causes as a child can magically make use of. Hence a deep contempt for the scientists—they will work no miracles; nor can I give up my great hopes by specializing and adjusting. (Lack of a father-identification.)

(9) I seem to myself to be quite lacking in "belief"—full of confusion, I am willing to say and think anything at all (except the plain nonsense that seems to satisfy most people). For conviction I substitute a flight to tangibility and ordinary experience. I have repressed my love and interest in the objects of the world: I do not touch them, I do not commit myself to their problems. Instead, since one

must have some contacts, I play it safe by making pot-shots. On the one hand I refuse to be overwhelmed by the admission of incompetence; on the other, I continually must prove my adequacy (fear of impotence).

(10) Positively, and simply, because I long to rest in my animate body and in the body of the world, to live and dance with it so and be happy; and these physicians and physiologists are indeed false because we are not happy.

South Windham
August 1948

Many Brothers

The two other brothers came while Don and Gordon were sitting on the wagon-seat eating, sandwiches and coffee out of a sun-warmed bottle. The brown horse was loudly munching hay out the back of the wagon. Most of the trees were cut. The gray horse was eating under a tree uncut. Neither Don nor Gordon spoke to the newcomers, who stood off among the stumps, the squat boy with the surly lip and the little scared one hanging behind. "I'll nail her shoe back after she's eat, least I'll *try!*" cried Don with an explosive laugh. His voice came always with an explosive cackle, no matter what he said. Protecting himself by looking at the humorous side of nothing, and ingratiating himself by sharing the joke. The explosions did not follow thru, but were like the handwriting that soars from the line with élan and drops suddenly with dispiritment, does not quite regain the norm. How long can we continue to gasp out a painful breath?

They were hauling out logs, pitiful spindles for pulp, that should have been left to flourish and grow great, even if one could not then print all of the *New York Times*. The heaps of red needles were fragrant in the dusty woods.

Gordon, who was thirteen, looked shyly, liquidly, at his older brother; it seemed to him mean not to say anything at all to the others, but it wasn't for him to take the lead.

When the horses had finished eating, the visitors gave up and disappeared in the brush. "Hey! did you want anything?" called Don. The squat angry boy reappeared and said, "Carvage is driving two fellows to Bellows Falls t'sign, and did you want to go along?"—to register for the conscription. "Hell! I don't read the papers and I don't tune the radio," cried Don explosively, "never heard nothing about it!" The brothers went away. "If they *want* me, let 'em come *get* me!" cried Don with a ringing laugh.

Gordon smiled with a wild light on his face, but with thin tired lips, to hear his brother carry on, to see him show a spark, anything.

"I don't give a shit if they take me or leave me!" cried Don. "Marching in the army or out here hauling timber every Goddam day. They can do anything they want with me, all the same." Speaking not especially to Gordon but to some ever-present person, ingratiatingly. "I once worked for a boss down in Grafton and Jesus he couldn't be pleased. I went down three years ago and tried to go in the army and they wouldn't take me. 4F. Wasted my trip! might as well stayed home! They can do anything they want to me."

He would see to it that it would not be any different.

"Are you finished eating, Mary? I'd better shoe the horse, least I'll *try!*"

There were still two or three other, older brothers, chopping, peeling, in the woods half a dozen miles away.

"I think I'll go down after all," said Don without a laugh. He had finished drinking the coffee from the bottle. The gray horse was also finished eating. "We can't do nothing today with the shoe torn off.

"Never do do a whole day's work!" he cried with a loud laugh. "Get right on in the forenoon, and afternoons there's always something."

Gordon managed to get the horses in the traces. "Take your bit, Mary," he said. But he lacked the authority to get their hind legs over to the pole. But Don authoritatively forced them over with the reins. The horses walked out onto the rough road and the wagon lurched, and onto the dusty road and the wagon bumped.

They pulled over and a car eased by. "We take just about as much room as a car!" cried Don. "Trouble is we can't turn in as fast. Well, they'll wait, they've *got* to." He exploded in a loud ingratiating laugh.

The strong-smelling horses hefted their haunches, side

to side. They were not prone to step lightly.

The next car was driven by Alan Chapin and it stopped. "Whoa," said Don, and he and Alan lit cigarettes. "Knock off so soon?" said Alan. "*Got* to!" cried Don, "I never do do a full day's work; start right off right in the forenoon and something always turns up." "Sure, keep out of bad habits!" cried Alan with an ingratiating but more self-assured laugh; he was five or six years older. "Got to go to Bellows Falls," said Don, "and register for Uncle Sam."

"Uncle Sam, he' a mighty powerful man."

"I went down three years ago but they wouldn't take me! 4F."

"Well, you gotta be near *perfect.*"

The horses moved forward a step and Don angrily cut them with the bit.

"Yes, I guess you gotta be perfect!" cried Don with a loud laugh. "You can't please 'em. They never told me what was wrong with me last time. Just 4F."

Alan tried to salve his feelings and said, "Might be just any little thing. For instance they figure you might have to sleep on wet ground so they look in your ears. You're strong enough to work but for the army you gotta be near perfect. Good luck!" He started his motor and eased by and sped away.

"There goes one swell guy," said Don, looking back over his shoulder, his black brows meeting in a point.

The ponds along the road were dry; the last lily-pads lay clung to the muck, gasping for a little moisture.

"I guess for the army you gotta be perfect," said Don soberly. "I don't give a shit what they do to me. All the same, hauling out pulp every Goddam day, one way or the other."

But Gordon, who was thirteen, felt hurt that his brother didn't show a spark, nothing, neither desire nor rebellion. Repeating himself, not bright. Gordon had a clear wide brow and liquid gray eyes, but thin care-worn lips. His uncut hair framed his face like an old-time scholar's, care-less of appearance. He went daily with Don on the wagon to keep him company. To get away. To talk to the horses. To be in the woods where the strong men handled their axes and big canting-hooks like light sticks (ashamed to work on such miserable timber). Where, tho it was early, many leaves had turned scarlet, yellow, and lilac.

South Windham
1948

The Bridge

You would have thought Rippy was a messenger between Dale and the next town, his green truck came by so often, on the road where there was little traffic. But it was that he had to keep passing the Wells house, thinking maybe he'd catch a glimpse of Dora, or maybe just to pass near her house. The house was across a bridge, in sight of the road, among its maples.

The green pick-up truck tended to miss on the third point and the sound of it was easily recognizable as it labored up the hill. Either way the Wells house was toward the top. Rippy was ashamed that his infatuated approach revealed itself so clearly; at the same time, of course, he wanted to be known, noticed.

"Here comes your boy friend again," said Wells to his daughter. They lived alone there and farmed fairly energetically. When the truck passed, Dora could sometimes be heard practising the harmonium. "Poor kid! shall I flag him down and take him out of his misery?" Wells offered as if to put on his hat and go out.

Dora sprang from the keyboard and cried, "Don't you dare! Just let him go by. What's that to me?—if he's not man enough to turn his car across the bridge. If he can't make up an excuse for calling, he's stupid, I don't want him. Why does he need an excuse?"

"He looks like a man to me," said Wells.

The truck dawdled by, still in second gear. The music from the house had stopped. The truck picked up speed down the hill.

"He's not stupid," said Wells, "but he ain't a mechanic. If and when he drives in, I'll put a file to those points."

Sometimes Rippy Neal dawdled by; other times—ashamed at being along there and as if he had to get back to work quick—he thundered by at forty-five miles, which was speed for that car of his. She shimmied and he gripped the wheel. So, one morning, tearing by bound for nowhere, he ran down a hen.

He saw her at the last moment, stopped the car and jumped out. The bird was dead. He picked it up—the feathers stuck to his sleeve; he held it gingerly away—blood ran down his fingers.

Holding the bird in front of him, he started across the bridge.

Dora came quickly down the porch-steps, down the path, toward him. She had no time, or else she did not bother, to fix her hair.

Two weeks ago, Old Wells had found Rippy on his knees, lining up the foundation of the Swede's new barn. He didn't want to create a scene, to embarrass the young fellow, and he waited till the Swede was out of earshot.

"Look, Neal, you keep away from my girl. She's too young for you, I know your type. What they say."

"Are you talking to me?" said Rippy Neal mildly.

"Yes, you. Don't be fresh, or I'll—"

"You and what uncles and brothers?" Rippy stood up, still holding the cord. They were both large men, but Rippy was young.

Rippy did not have the reputation of being bashful or backward with women. Yet it was not this that disturbed the father so much as the young fellow's present behavior. Dora could take care of herself. But he was puzzled. The fact was that he was fond of Rippy Neal and he spoke to him hostilely because he felt otherwise than hostile.

"Listen Wells," said Rippy Neal, dropping the cord and laying a hand on his sleeve. "I like you. And so I'll tell you this—" Suddenly his voice became dark and passionate, almost hoarse. "I'm sick and tired of playing a part, like a damned play. Either you have to be a lion-tamer and keep 'em in leash so they don't bite you, or you have to be pulling a rescue-act and save her from a dragon, her family or God knows; or you have to be a magician and wake up Sleeping Beauty. I'm fed up, I tell you. I want to be myself. I want your daughter; sure. But if she wants me she'll damn well have to give a sign, like I do. I'll go half-way, nine-tenths of the way, I'm damned if I'll go all the way, again."

The mason was pale. He had suffered, and brooded, making up speeches as he worked.

Tears started into the farmer's eyes. "You act awful peculiar, Rippy Neal, coming up that hill four, five times a day."

"Do you think I like it? I do it because I can't help it," said Rippy Neal.

He held out the hen.

"I'm afraid I ran over it."

"It's all right! that won't hurt her!" cried Dora Wells.

"Oh but it will! it did! I mean she's killed. How much do I owe you?"

"I didn't mean *that*," said Dora, blushing. "I meant I'll pop her in the oven and she'll brown just as good. Never know the difference. We'll have this week's chicken Thursday 'stead of Sunday."

"Oh. You'll have this week's chicken Thursday 'stead of Sunday," repeated the man mechanically; he looked stupidly at the dead bird in his hand.

They were standing on the bridge and the torrent of spring was boiling underneath.

"She's too big. Won't *you* come to dinner tonight and help us eat her up?" said Dora simply.

Rippy paused. He paused rather than hesitated. "Yes, I will come! I'd be *pleased* to come." His face broke into a friendly smile.

New York City
[1949?]

295

The Home-Made Sweater

Likely's mother was quietly hurt, terribly, as only a person can be hurt who has tried hard and done well and been refused, or again (but perhaps it is the same thing) as only a parent rejected by her child can be hurt. Skilfully and carefully, using magic colors, she had knitted for Likely's seventh birthday an Argyll sweater; and the sweater was a surprise of glory—it was like the coat of colors that Father Jacob made. But the small child would not wear it, she was not interested in it, she held it in contempt.

When she saw Likely hungrily staring at some rather trashy garments in a shop-window, mother quietly wept. Sometimes she wished that she could become angry, but it was not in her character. The child had recently become strange to her.

It was longer ago than recently; it was nearly a year, since Likely had started at school, that she had become strange. And the estrangement was worse than her mother feared. She did not even begin to understand in what contempt Likely had come to regard not only the Argyll sweater but many other things of her home. The girl was difficult at meals because the good food was "home-made."

On her way to school and from school, Likely used to stop and watch the construction-work in the big lot on 27th Street. First they had dug an enormous hole. The steam-shovels bit into the brown dirt and the dumping-trucks full of dirt climbed up a steeper and steeper slope from the hole. And now there were cement-mixers and they were building the "foun-dations." Likely kept hearing this word mentioned by the grown-up onlookers, those who know, and she knew that these white walls were the foun-dations.

On her way, early in the morning, the workmen were not yet there and the works seemed mysterious and vast. But when she returned in the afternoon, the scene was friendly and animated. The steam was blooming and screaming, a crane was swinging and trucks were moving, and everywhere were the workmen. She recognized some of the same workmen, the driver of the mixer who stayed near the hydrant, the man with the roll of paper white on the outside and blue on the inside, the three solemn old men who worked in a team. To Likely they were familiar figures.

She also was a familiar figure. The men recognized the small girl whose black hair fell to her shoulders but who swung her books in a strap like a boy. Because she waved and called to them, they called and waved to her.

Soon there was a forest of steel beams, that sprang up as if overnight.

She stopped at the hydrant for a drink. "Soon," the driver said to her, "soon you'll be going to this new school instead of the old one."

She stopped drinking. "School? What school?" said Likely. "I go to school."

"This is going to be a new school; that's what we're building. Didn't you know that?"

"School! don't be silly. That's foun-dations and things, that's not a school," said Likely positively and moved away.

But already as she walked away, she walked away with wonder; and she looked back once with amazement; and as she walked the rest of the way home she was thunderstruck. So!

Her busy wits leaped like lightning, and—she was quite bright—whole realms of experience fell together and were clear in a flash. So! You would not have thought on the calm fall day that such an electric storm was walking along the pavement. So a school was something that was *built!* it was *made!* by *men!* It had not been always. It was made by workmen whom she knew and who talked to her; and what

298

they were doing was not strange or hard to understand; they made mud out of sand and piled it up in forms and reenforced it with iron stakes. All that was familiar, and out of it came a school! Not only *this* school. That is, the *other* school had not always been there either. It had been *made*. By people. *This* one was not even finished yet; after a while the teachers would come.

That is, the teachers too were people; they had not always been there.

The light of it was so strong—it was so simple—that she was nearly blinded by it. Lucky she didn't have any dangerous streets to cross for she didn't look where she was going. Her wits leaped again and again. Not *only* the school, but the other buildings, all the things in the city, had been made! by people! The lamp-post, the railroad-tracks, the stores, the things in the stores, the trains that ran on the tracks, the pipes under the street that they got at thru manholes. All made, by persons like herself. Likely was far from stupid; in a way she had known all this before. But never until that afternoon was it *clear* to her.

As she came home and went into her own room, the very first object that struck her eyes was the Argyll sweater, shining under the chair where she had impatiently flung it. Tho it was under the chair, it magnetically drew her eyes. She picked it up. It was a surprise of glory (as well it might be, for it was made with the magic colors of love and care and skill and birthday). It was plaid. She put it on, climbed on a chair, and looked at herself in the mirror. The our-guy sweater was pretty.

Her mother came into the room and saw her standing before the mirror, wearing the Argyll sweater. Likely's mother was pleased and the tears wet her eyes, but she did not say anything. (She was a quiet woman and found it hard to say anything whether she was hurt, or angry, or pleased.)

So! thought Likely matter-of-factly, the sweater was not just an imitation sweater after all, made at home to imitate a sweater that ought to be bought in a shop. It was a *real* sweater, it was *made*, just as the sweaters in the shop had been made. They were made by people, but this our-guy sweater was made by a person too, by mama. She looked critically at the knitting—she was a judge of such things—and she saw that it was a better sweater than any she had ever seen.

She noticed her mother. "Thank you, mamee, for the sweater," said Likely, "it's very nice. It's well made." She held her mother, but only for a moment, for she wanted to look at something in the big room.

At the bookshelves that papa had recently built, that she had regarded with contempt. As a matter of fact, she saw, they were very ingenious, they hung from the woodwork on thin wires; you would not imagine that such thin strings could support such heavy loads of books; it was interesting.

All at once a tension within her dissolved and the little girl began to bawl and at the same time to clap her hands for joy; and she began to burst with pride for her dear people who had made not only the glorious plaid sweater and the wire-hung bookshelves, but also, no doubt, the house itself, and the street, and the street-cars, and the city. Her own father and mother, and she herself, could make them if they had the time.

... At school, even if they made you stand in straight lines and keep quiet, and the place was so big and strange and formal, and the teachers were forbidding and powerful, not like persons at all—nevertheless they were persons after all; the school was made! ...

Still another thought struck Likely; she remembered that her grand-uncle Ben, daddy's uncle, sometimes carried a roll of paper white on the outside, blue on the inside. (He was an architect.) "Mamee," asked Likely, "is Uncle Ben building the new school on 27th Street?"

"Why no, I don't think so," said mother.

The fact, unknown even to Likely's mother, was that Uncle Ben had designed that *other* school.

[New York City]
[1949?]

300

Two Methodical Pieces *

A Governor

When Luke stood in the doorway, his wife and a stranger-man were seated at the deal table having coffee; and he paused in the doorway to take in this cheerful scene.

A scene of theater, to be regarded for itself. That is, there was an absent-fourth-wall between the spectator and the scene, the wall one could see thru but not go thru. But the *cheerful* scene, of persons socially drinking coffee together, as it is said. "Lo how good and pleasant is the sitting down together—"

He loomed in the doorway out of the indefinite darkness of another space. In the room the space was sunny and a blue Delft clock ticked on the plaster wall. He was framed in the doorway, claiming attention, altho the high-light was in the room.

The floor supported him as he advanced.

The shudder of fixity of an unfinished situation, for ordinarily a man does not pause on the threshold to take in the scene but he takes part in it advancing. The clock ticked a little loudly as they turned to him their soft smiles which

Note: The first of these pieces is an exercise in naturalism in the light of character-analysis and psychosomatic physiology. The various ambivalent and past-fixated and purposeful meanings of a behavior are narrated as simultaneously occurring, as is indeed the case. The action of opening the door and advancing to the table is repeated in its analyzed elements, and a gesture, the smile, is narrated as acting independently. All this is analogous to portraying the profile and full-face in a single image.

The second piece tries to narrate with the attitude involved in certain primitive languages whose unit-words are concrete and particular in expressing relations, rather than analytic and general like our words. Each phrase between colons is to be read as a single word-notion, as if the words were connected by hyphens. The parentheses are connectives from our point of view.

he answered with a broad smile advancing. Often his mother used to bring a beggar-man or woman for a sandwich and coffee. People of that generation did not find it so hard as we do to enter into friendly contact with one another, and if a man was hungry they gave him food instead of money. This was a cheerful scene.

So he reduced the stranger to a condition passive and inferior; he kept the situation under control in his golden grip; the floor did not fail to support him and a shaft of sunlight made brilliant his outstretched hand.

As he came in with white clenched fists, never before had mama dared to bring him home. He knew that she was seeing the gaunt man with the blue jaw that could never be shaven clean (he was so sad-faced and homely), but to sit with him at the very table feeding him cake and coffee: The child noticed that they had eaten most of the cake. He did not hold back his flaring anger but at once came on making apposite remarks. They rose to their feet, to their great height.

At this moment occurred a pause. They stood in a Byzantine fixity: two looming figures in mosaic, complexions of purple and brows scored by black horizontal furrows, in a streaming aura of gold. But the Emperor had a golden fist.

For the murderousness was frozen out of the scene, or frozen in the scene (it comes to the same thing). And the darkness on those frowning brows was perhaps not wrath but perplexity. *What* was the puzzle in the sun-washed kitchen? The table was tan deal, the little circles of coffee were black in the white ironware cups, and the Delft clock ticked on the plaster wall.

Likely the stranger was an angel, as it is said, "Blessed is he who comes!" the missing father of the fatherless. When the angel came to announce his good news, and he was the good news, surely he would be invited to sit down and share a meal. But what would father be like after so many years?

There was plenty of reason for laughing, for often there used to be jokes. "For God's sake," mama would say, "don't always take the bigger piece of cake, it's not polite." "If you had your pick," said Luke, "which piece would you take?" "I'd take the smaller one of course." "Well you've got the

302

smaller one, what are you kicking about?" And why shouldn't the beggar-man that mama invited turn out to be an angel, with the gold and jewels of the Creation pouring in thru the window?

But therefore he paused and inquired. It was a scene. He came forward with clenching fists. Stood framed in the doorway and they turned to him their guilty smiles. He opened his weaponless hands and came forward imploring for friendship and protection. The floor failed to support him and he fell but did not land. He was falling. He stood in the doorway about to turn and flee into the outer waste. He was frozen in murderousness.

What attitude *should* he have when the dreaded longed-for moment arrived at last? When father was *sitting* at the table when he burst into the room? No pause! A boy of four does not pause but shrieks with fright and rushes into the loving embrace, as he shyly stands his ground and turns his right toe inward and looks up thru lowered lashes perplexed.

He recoiled and stood his ground. A man (whoever it was) was giving him a single blow and then, abashed, withheld his hand. But a single blow ought not to be given: it outrages pride and does not penetrate to feeling and action. If he had beaten him, as the unmannerly youth deserved, provocative and longing to be touched even tho hurt, in order to discover some meaning in the ungoverned waste that was merely free, as Franz said, "nothing more senseless, nothing more hopeless than this freedom, this waiting, this inviolability"—surely they would have come to a kind of love; or better (for the boy was a little old to be mastered), they would have entered into complicity laying siege to the woman (whoever she was).

As it was, by shuddering in fixity he achieved three things: he was fleeing into the waste world, blotting *all* that and *all* those persons from his concern, to start a new life of vengeance against them; and he was flinging himself down gasping, beaten, mastered, and in love; and he was advancing to deal the murderous blow that would rid him forever of any danger of loss. He was lording it peacefully over the devastation. He was used to keeping the situation in control, without risks or surprises.

Hungry for the cheerful matter-of-fact poverty of the good coffee with friends at the plain table, that in fact he enjoyed—

The half-cups of coffee looked cold and bitter, a gray cigarette was floating in the scum and the rim of one cup was stained with lipstick. A smoke-haze hung from the ceiling. His gorge was rising because this was practiced with guilt, hastily gulped down before it could surprise us, oh trying to cram the hole that they tore from his breast. The clock was stopped two years ago.

His eyes were close-set with envy: all others have a satisfaction but he was in a waste and could not return from it, only peer in, not break in. Withdrawing in pride. He was good at surprising, suddenly springing the door and standing in the threshold; but then they started guiltily apart, when what he longed for was for them to continue right on, so, watching the show, his desire could learn to mount while (they were contemptuous of him) his claws advanced—He kept a good watch; but he was blinded with grief, the legs of the overturned chairs stuck into the air, she was gone, that is blotted from existence.

"You have been fighting again!" he cried. "You mustn't do that, you nice people. Can't I have peace in my own home? Now what's the trouble? let *me* straighten it out." And with keen reason and large goodwill he took his seat in the not-overturned chair and embraced them in his loving understanding, holding his right arm on the chair-back with the right hand hanging behind, not to deal the blow. "Why did you let the clock run down?" he began inquisitorially; but he said, "I am above these jealousies, and further, how can I live myself if I'm not just and equal, and I take my pleasures where I find them, *if* I find them. Ow! Don't imagine for a moment that this loss will crush me; I have lost a hundred times and better than this. *I* am left. The reason in me, by which now I judge and do not, after all, fly into the fragmented parts." He brought his strong right from behind the chair and pounded on the door before opening it and pausing on the threshold, as if to give one and all due notice of surprise and an added moment of pain.

He advanced with an *inquiring* smile, for of old he was one to be interested (erotically excited) only by the causes of things. The pornographic pictures and stories of the other boys did not arouse him much, but he masturbated to etiologies. Hot to ask and know, and subdivide, and penetrate.

The parts were held together by reason, here, and the clock was softly measuring the now lapsing into the next.

The inner door sprang open and Jane jumped upon daddy crying "Daddy!" There was an instant that both doors were open. He closed the outer door.

The stranger half-rose and said, "My name is McHale."

He lifted his shoulders against the weight of duty and at once he felt the joyless spot in his chest. He was not dropping the child. It is by the primary growing (*nature*) that the parts of the world cohere and do not fragment; but to a man who cannot know this joyous power as it bursts and blooms, the sense of it is patience, duty, relying on the *underlying* energy, but it is underlying. His world did not fragment and bring on death and woe; he felt this as not neglecting his duty. He closed the door. That is, he did not like there to be two openings, one of which he could not survey.

"Please, keep your seat. Have you been waiting long? I'm sorry." McHale was a young man with the usual problem and would make of him again a father.

He was sorry because he was not merry; he was sad because he was not glad. Not pain is the opposite of pleasure, but unpleasure; the pain follows, it is in the chest. Therefore it was impossible not to give in, in everything, to the small girl, because she was still merry. *She* was the primary nature as it burst and bloomed. During the instant that the both doors were open he escaped howling into the outer waste carrying the child. But he experienced the streaming primary space as his fatherly duty, a heavy garment on the shoulders that stood up by itself. He slipped out of it—it stood there of its own weight—and he ran howling into outer space.

He closed the door.

It was a single smile that empathetically communicated itself, fleetingly defined itself by being communicated, in the room. For tho there were several persons and the smile was coming differently to each, the social trust of mankind was an overpowering influence—and drew each smile, also, to a little skeptical point at one corner. They were hungrily sucking consolation from one another.

His smile relaxing into the lovely social smile was drawn back above the canine teeth; but this snarl was quivering unable to hold under the wide circle frighteyes masked by close-set *in*-looking (invidia). With a smile of relief as one says Oof, the smile descended the flowery slope to the safe general smile: the general smile that did not dare to bare its teeth because it did not believe in itself, and *nevertheless* it was truly radiantly smiling. (For the surface expresses the deepest secret.)

One looks, in dangerous liaisons, for this lovely persisting smile that is a guarantee that, however the next passions mismatch, it is unlikely that there will be violence within the limits of the present felt space and hour, for this smile is a flag not of truce but of the indissoluble alliance of mankind. It is embarrassing to untwitch the face from it—and during this interim of effort, who does not have time to take to his heels out of the place becoming charged with menace?—unless he *wants* to suffer.

He bit his lower lip and closed the door.

In control. And now it was in control. It was not in his control but it lay here of itself, gasping. There was no surprise but the expected (tho momentarily he had been threatened with a surprise). That is, he was in its control. At last!

At last—a situation that occurred, comfortingly enough, most of the time—he was overpowered, fixed, in love: overpowered by its control, in love, without joy or surprises, with its control. He sat down gasping. He was not smiling, he was serious in love, but it was smiling. He had long ago, as Franz said, "fallen under the wheels, comfortingly enough."

A Governor

Safe in its control, he let rise a little the soft feelings of complaint.

He noticed that with his golden grip he was holding the wrist of the other hand. Thus in control there was no danger that he would strike in vengeance for not getting what he wanted which also he did not reach for. But he paused—one keen to analyse—and subdivide (oh, into small pieces)—and penetrate—and by this wrack his joy.

At the table, but, one was too close to the scene, that advanced itself as the reality, blurred somewhat by tears. A wife bonded to a governor: let her go free! What was the use of vindictively preventing the chance of joy improbable in the world (it was almost indifferent to him whether she did or not once he had surveyed the scene and knew the probabilities)? He kept a good watch; and if one time mama brought him home, he slyly knew the apposite remarks provocative—How he hated himself for this, he could not keep down the loathing.

"God damn stepmother nature!" he was waiting in the outer waste, safe at home but what was the use of it, since they merely hid themselves elsewhere?— "It seems that there is every chance of joy: beauty there and the season and the parts of the soul and body reaching inquiring for more. Should it be difficult to sit down to a cheerful cup of coffee?" He sent his shadow-self abroad.

And easily she walked the street and had the delights that his substance was afraid to take (which the world with almost no derangement of its order could afford us all). But his shadow-self kept returning to him. "*Why* do you return and not abandon me for dead with this body that I cannot use?" But so it was, that she returned.

"Why am I bawling? D'ye think I know? Bawling because the coffee's spilling in the saucer. It keeps spilling over (d'ye think I know?) If I make a swan's neck I can hardly swallow. No more! No more! Can't take it down. Bawling because the doughnut's on the floor. If I look up—d'ye think I know? Can't keep it down if I look up."

He unclasped his restraining hand from the other wrist, leaving both fists free.

307

THE FACTS OF LIFE

"And what can I do for you, young man? What's *your* trouble?"

New York City
May 1949

Daylight and
Adam Naming the Beasts

1. *Daylight*

Crashes softly the slow avalanche snapping trees the penis
beginning to grow radiates delicate feelings unevenly: (also)
haul and pull of a rope between two centers resisting it but
not failing to approach: (as) with a frantic itching and
scratching till they melt and uniformly burn

(the Sun daylight) primary of what is out there hungrily
appropriated: O! the "the" respectfully considered as with a
capital letter but not addressed: (also) there is none other
one is lost when this is lost

Found with such finding that perplexity and anxiety dissolve into unprovable confidence: (the sky and Adam are as)
when the breathing regularizes after climbing a steep:
greeted by eyes that relax their scrutiny and see color-forms

(the panorama) pauses over the whole extension so no
motion is possible not by constriction but desireless: as
food is inwardly absorbed without putting oneself to it

(Adam and the Sun) stare at one another each waiting for
the other to volunteer to do what both wish but are not able
to begin.*

---

*"The Fuegian soars above our analytic wisdom with a 7-syllabled word whose
precise meaning is, 'They stare at one another each waiting for the other to
volunteer to do what both wish but are not able to begin.' In this total situation the
persons, as expressed both in nouns and pronouns, are embedded, still only in
relief and without finished independence. The chief concern is with the lived
relation."—Buber

2. *A Meeting*

Face to face with a face surprisingly present claiming attention and fulfilling expectation: (suddenly as) one leaps to his feet inquiring: being electrified with shaping power in the blue field that accompanies ordinary (heroic) action accurate and irresistible.

(Adam) approaches the similar with all sensitive surfaces moistening in order to melt in touching: with the tautness of the awareness narrowing concentrating crystallizing to a definite figure that is urgent: as one comes to a decision to plunge into an abyss hoping it is a cooling pool

—the eerie of unresponsive eyes hypnotic wells to the bottom of life but not flashing a present message!: (he steps back) with revulsion from the unlike that attracted as the like: (as) one notices unlikeness in the set of the teeth making it hard to empathize.

(Adam is) disdainful as only the assured user confronted by other customs: as a man beats about for refuge when he is unaware of danger because he has never experienced fear

(They) stare at one another each waiting for the other to volunteer to do what both wish but are not able to begin.

3. *The Tiger*

One holds something at arm's length (and is thereby) apprehensive of a crack of the branch in the wood: (also) when the reaching out of confident self-giving and appropriating is arrested and there is vertiginous spiralling of the incomplete: (but Adam) slowly comes to a pause at the center of spiralling breathless

safe (in the fact that) what is held out there at the end of touch and sight-touch is the self holding it out there and it is an "it": smiling the secondary friendly smile of safe examination opening the eyes blinding wide: "Aha!" greeting with contempt what is only that "it" a toy of attention not advancing.

Flushing with the glory of being about to initiate and be an unmoved mover: confirmed in the sense of the soul

310

growing daring the confused unknown yet instantaneously crystallizing into the definite: (and) deciding with the gracious ease of the ordinary (heroic) to do the unique as if there needed no decision

("Is it a tiger?") not quite yet but expected as in the interval between the lightning and the thunder: (Adam names it) "the tiger" easily as sweet rain falls as semen spurts plenteously.

They stare at one another each waiting for the other to volunteer to do what both wish but are not able to begin.

4. Forepleasure

With the grateful secondary love for what has caused one's pleasure

as one notices pleased and afraid (like a poet) fearful symmetry burning bright.

5. Guilt of Having Created

> *The universe is my temptation*
> —BUBER

Flaming with the self-love of the instant of initiating the definite (when one is) calmly open to the favor of the unnoticed creator spirit all-pervasive of the world: thankful aware of nothing but his own grandeur yet resting easy in the creator spirit: aware that what is created in recognizing what is held out there is I

"You!" thing given in the Six days not made by me: humiliated you and I we in our relation thrown: (yet safely) upheld as a babe who does not fear to fall in the continuous generation from the beginning to this moment and a little beyond

(Adam is) dizzy with the self-joy of grand achievement that makes one sense within the abyss of unsuspected power: shuddering with the arrested embrace: frightened at (an erotically-fired memory image of) the unlike set of the teeth (he feels) the guilt of having dared to beget something in blinding forgetfulness of who and where one is: "Lo!" there abides the thing and must henceforth be reckoned with

(Adam and the name) stare at one another each waiting for the other to volunteer to do what both wish but are not able to begin.

6. *The Snake**

Alert at the noise of a snake in the grass: in flight from guilt to a contrary place where one can repeat the guilty deed: seeking out what is unlike in order not to repeat the reaching out arrested

(Adam is) yearning with joy that the snake has come to his water-trough on the hot day: (but) patiently waiting not to disturb a guest quietly drinking: with aching soul because the loved one will depart peaceful and unnoticing into the burning bowels of the earth

(succumbing to the suggestion of) slow eyes most like slow motion most like oneself thrice adream: frigid with horror confronted by a spirit inaccessible to material embrace: awesomely loving an equal lord and king of another realm when one is oneself a fearless lord and king

"It is the snake": owai! vanished into a black hole and one is left with an empty thought.

(Adam and the black hole) stare at one another each waiting for the other to volunteer to do what both wish but are not able to begin.

7. *The Tree of Knowledge*

Feeling the cold sweat of warding off the world (the feeling we others have domesticated as security)
    entangled in ramifying branches (of the names)
    as colored-birds hop about in fright peeping and grieving.
"Do not eat of this tree," utters the warning Voice.

*After Lawrence.

312

(the Voice) all Thou only Thou deeper than my next wish and providentially calamitous to me: (to which one is) so turned as not to notice that one's feet are not on the ground: (altho) one's legs are planted in the rock and aching with the vegetative currents: a communication not pleasant painful violent nor peaceful but promissory

(Adam) lowers his stare as one wooing met frankly gaze for gaze.

8. *The Dog*

(He and the dog) stare at one another each waiting for the other to volunteer what both wish but are unable to begin: With the sadness felt for a trusting limited gaze: noblesse oblige

Stretches out his hand as one offers a great hand: weeps the boiling tears whose meaning is unknown but they are for oneself: touches with the despairing grip that is meant to indicate not what it does but something else.

Teasingly moving this way and that to see if a gaze will doggedly follow: (Adam says) "You are the dog" as if giving not an objective name but presuming to say "my" as an essential relation: exasperated by having one's mere whim complied with

feeling the loneliness unmixed with fear of a person so superior that few understand him: feeling the need to subserve in order that one's nobility may not lose contact with the continuum of life

beginning as one gives oneself wholly but without confidence to what cannot eventuate.

9. *The Names*

The passionate use of a new tool for the sake of using it till one is overcome with meaninglessness!

wild with success until stupefied

(Adam) shakes the dream out of his hair and notices he is alone.

Notices that the milieu is apt for steps to be taken when one is no longer taking the steps.

10. *No Helpmeet*

Lonely with new experience one cannot communicate: as a surface expands meeting no resistance and is dissipating itself: aging with committed powers that do not eventuate

Thoughtful without puzzlement at a disproportion in the nature of things: (Adam) frowns a great frown

as one spreads one's fingers and unspreads them clenches the fists and unclenches them

hates the self for senseless excellence as tho this were boasting.

Naming things in order to tell them off: expressing without communicating in order to exhaust the soul and sleep.

Crying himself to sleep: becoming healed and solid in contact with the rocks gravity the rolling earth.

New York City
May 1949

Sailor's Money

He loudly clinked the coin on the counter, and did not reckon the change. "Set 'em up again!" It was a seaman.

A sailor does not keep a city, a domestic budget; it's indifferent to him whether the 'bus-fare is a nickel, or seven cents, or a dime. The mother-ship provides security.

Tommy, who had little lines of care about his eyes, watched his bravado with a certain admiration.

"Set 'em up." The sailor was high.— A sailor's money is loosely exchanged for pleasures for which he has a secret contempt. He does not calculate to have so many drinks for so many dollars, but he drinks until the money runs out, leaving a dollar to get back to the ship.

He clinked the coin loudly, throwing it away defiantly and with contempt, as tho it were foreign money—*all* money was foreign money. "Set 'em up for my friends."

He was a merchant sailor, with dark trousers and a black leather jacket, brown eyes, Pennsylvania Welsh, a big coal-miner. By now he was setting them up for a little knot of five or six of the convivial.

With appreciative eyes Tommy estimated the money in the sailor's billfold as above two hundred dollars. This sailor, he figured, could not blow more than a quarter of it before he staggered away. Tommy would get the rest. Tommy practised little unarmed stick-ups, a clean, safe, hardly illegal trade that increased the total good in the universe, for he made better use of money than a drunken sailor did.

But his eyes narrowed and he frowned when the number

315

of the convivial suddenly increased at a bound. "Set 'em for everybody here!" cried the sailor. At this new rate the roll would melt away fast.

"The son of a bitch is spending my money," thought Tommy.

With mounting euphoria, the seaman, a runaway boy, was finding the world repeopled with friends. No more loneliness. Everybody together. "You too! Whaddye drink? Have another."

But Tommy noted with approval that the sailor did not particularly encourage the couple of girls. They did their best, but he wasn't having any. These girls Tommy despised. They stole money using sentiment as a bait. His own trade wasn't dirty; he didn't offer false joys (he didn't offer anything). Tho it was difficult, he steadfastly refused to let the sailor pay for his beer; he insisted that the barmaid take the toll from his own few coins, of which he kept a careful reckoning. He didn't want to be friends with this sailor; he didn't want to be beholden.

"Take his out too!" cried the sailor angrily.

"Uh uh. Sorry. I can't drink 'em down that fast," said Tommy imperturbably.

Whether because of Tommy or because this was his characteristic next phase as he went under, the big fellow began to sense an edge of hostility in the atmosphere. He shouted, in a resonant, arresting voice:

"You think I'm just a drunk. Well I'm drunk, but I've seen the ports o' the world. The seaports! The seaports o' the whole world. And what did you see? You didn't see nothing. Has anybody here ever been to Bangkok? *I've* been to Bangkok. I've seen the ports o' the world and I've seen Bangkok. Nobody else here was ever to Bangkok."

He was indeed remembering Bangkok, with joy, with satisfaction, with an edge of sorrow, loss, hostility. And indeed nobody there had ever been to Bangkok—they choosing their land-ways, such as they were, with a careful reckoning of money, and he choosing his sea-ways and orphanage, and Bangkok, such as it was.

"What the hell!" said the sailor, "we're friends, no? Set 'em up. Nobody else been to Bangkok, so what? we're all

316

friends. But you just remember, I been to Bangkok. Don't you believe me?"

"I believe you," said Tommy.

Suddenly the sailor knocked down his stool and lurched away from the bar and made for the door. He was through. In Tommy's experience this usually happened suddenly. It did not seem to him that the sailor was going to be sick, but he had received his internal signal to get out. He was very drunk. Tommy had counted fourteen shots, and for this seaman that was, evidently, enough—enough if he was going to get back to his non-home under his own steam.

But surprisingly, the sailor turned at the door and announced, "I don't have any more money. All blown. Take it easy," and he went out into the night. They all saw that he had a good deal more money.

He went out into the cold night and reeled and dropped to one knee, like a boxer who takes a short count. Then he moved off.

Tommy followed him up three or four streets, slowly, for the seaman made slow progress. He figured that there was a hundred and a quarter left. The sailor had blown about seventy-five dollars—sixty dollars for drinks, and about fifteen that the barmaid had short-changed him. Tommy kept close tabs.

Then the street was dark and empty. Lightly the thief seized him by the collar and drew him into the alley and dug a stubby finger into his spine.

"Stick 'em up, sailor."

Slowly the seaman raised his arms and Tommy groped for the wallet.

"'Ts no use. 'Ts all blown. Just enough to get back to the ship."

"Hell it's all blown. You walked out o' there with more'n a hundred dollars. Don't you worry, I'll leave you two bucks to get back to the ship."

The Pennsylvanian was stone sober. With one terrible blow he laid the thief on his back. Lucky the alley was unpaved or Tommy would have had a broken skull.

"You son of a bitch, that's *real* money!" cried the Pennsylvanian in a new voice. "I make it when I'm on the

317

beach, like anybody else. Washin' windows, twenty thirty floors in the air, with a four-cent bonus and time and a half. That's money I send for the kids, do you think I'm gonna give it to *you*? Holy smokes! You *dirty* son of a bitch!"

He made as if to give the fallen thief a kick in the teeth, but he thought better of it and proceeded slowly down the street, apparently as drunk as ever.

"A schiz'!" said Tommy half-aloud, rubbing his jaw. "How should I figure it's a schiz'?"

New York City
December 1949

318

Textual Note

Goodman published four collections of stories during his lifetime, *The Facts of Life*, *The Break-Up of Our Camp*, *Our Visit to Niagara*, and *Adam and His Works*. The last was a collected edition and included most of the stories in the other three as well as a few "new" ones. Many other stories appeared only in magazines, and still others were never published at all. When he reprinted a story in a collection, he usually revised it, often extensively. Others were tailored to the needs of novels in which they were to be inserted.

In preparing this complete edition of all of Goodman's stories and sketches, I have returned to the earliest printed versions for my texts. Much of Goodman's revising was done twenty, even thirty years after first writing, and his style had changed enough to put his revisions at odds with his original conceptions. The general effect was to make all the stories, early and late, share a diction and syntax that is mere patina, spread thin over the variety of literary voices and manners he explored during a long career. His last and fullest revisions—for the majority of stories in *Adam and His Works*—were undertaken years after he had stopped writing fiction altogether, and after his style had undergone a journalistic refurbishing for his mass audience as a social critic.

I think that in every case his original stories are better than these later revisions. Moreover, since this is to be the definitive edition of his short fiction, there is good reason to represent his career as accurately as possible in its range and

319

its development. The revised versions mask and blur the relevant distinctions. And in any case they are already widely available in *Adam and His Works*, whereas the original texts are scattered among dozens of ephemeral magazines, and in books published in tiny editions, long out of print. Moreover, it would make little sense to print side by side stories written in the same year, one as it first appeared, the other as it was altered after decades had elapsed. Many of Goodman's stories did not find their way into any collection, and so were never revised. This edition includes twenty previously uncollected stories, nineteen never before published, and two dozen others that have appeared only in the special issue of *New Letters* magazine I edited in 1976. The establishment of an historical canon for all of these will make it possible to study the unfolding of Goodman's career by bringing together works that although written in the same period, repeating the same motifs, and even referring to one another, have never been available within the covers of a single volume.

(In the case of *The Break-Up of Our Camp*, I have used the text of the first publication of the entire work, rather than of the individual stories, to preserve its overall unity. In order to sustain similar values in *Johnson*, I have accepted the manuscript version as my basic text. Only two of the *Johnson* stories were published at the time of composition, and while retaining the substantive changes—not many—of those, I have emended the spelling and punctuation of the published versions to conform to the manuscripts. Still another chapter, "Martin, or The Work of Art," was published many years later, greatly altered, and since the original manuscript no longer exists, it has been treated here as an appendix.)

One further principle of selection needs to be mentioned. As the title of this collection suggests, it includes a number of works that are not strictly speaking stories, though they are not quite essays either but something in-between. A comparison of "The Father of the Psychoanalytic Movement" and "Golden Age" (see the edition of Goodman's psychological essays, *Nature Heals*, Free Life Editions, 1977), will illustrate the shading of one genre into the other,

and my cut-off point: the former I include here among his
fictions, but not the latter. On a slightly different basis I
have excluded "The Diggers in 1984," a political tract disguised as fiction; Goodman himself so regarded it, and did
not include it in *Adam and His Works*. I have also excluded
separately published chapters of novels unless there is good
evidence that they were originally intended as stories. Thus
there is nothing here from *Parents' Day*, although some of
it was first published in a magazine, as if a story; contrariwise, "Eagle's Bridge" and "The Continuum of the
Libido" are included because they were conceived as separate works. The two adventures of St. Wayward and the
Laughing Laddy, from the abortive fifth volume of *The
Empire City*, represent still another category, works that
were intended as parts of a novel but became short stories
instead—as indicated by Goodman's including one of them
in *Adam*. And of course I have included his two novels-in-
stories, *Johnson* and *The Break-Up of Our Camp*.

Of the unpublished stories I have printed all that cannot
be classed as unfinished or juvenilia. This is a matter of
judgment. My own conviction is that Goodman's maturity
came at a normal age for writers of fiction, about his
twenty-fifth year. Anything written after *The Break-Up of
Our Camp*, his first major novel, I have regarded as mature
work even if Goodman never published it; stories written
before 1936 have been considered on their merits. A few
pieces published in high school and college periodicals have
been omitted, but otherwise I have included everything of
his apprenticeship that saw print, as well as several that he
tried to publish, unsuccessfully. The manuscripts for a
couple of dozen others, chiefly exercises of his under-
graduate days, survive among his papers.

In editing this large body of work, I have tried to preserve
Goodman's original intentions so far as they could be determined. Publishers took various liberties with his texts,
and where I am sure Goodman preferred some other reading, I have adopted it. Thus I have restored "obscenities"
censored by cautious editors, and have rescued the ending
of "A Prayer for Dew" from the hell-box where its first
printers dumped it when it would not fit the page.

Goodman's spelling and punctuation were somewhat idiosyncratic, especially during the first two decades of his career. Some publishers made his prose conform to their own style-books, others did not. I have not attempted to sort out his usage from theirs, for there is nothing to go by, case by case; he usually discarded his manuscripts as soon as a work had appeared in print. In most of the early stories "though" is written "tho," "through" is "thru," etc., according to Goodman's habit. Exceptions probably represent editorial changes, to which he may or may not have agreed. Punctuation is even more difficult to deal with, for his own practice was sometimes inconsistent and careless, sometimes purposeful if eccentric. I have regularized a few recurrent patterns according to the modern usage that he himself sometimes followed, changing the old-fashioned "such-and-such,—" and "so-and-so;—" to "such-and-such—" or "so-and-so—" and sometimes "so-and-so;" depending on the sense. And I have made the use of quotation marks consistent, dispensing with them entirely for passages already marked as quotation by indenting. I have printed such indented passages in the roman font, even though Goodman often sets them off by italics. (In making such emendations I have been instructed by particular instances of regularization in *Adam and His Works*.) Aside from these, and the correction of obvious typographical errors, the texts are as they first appeared.

Goodman ordinarily entered the place and date of composition at the end of each story. I have included these whenever I could find them appended to any version of the text, and I have supplied them in brackets for those stories that must be dated by extrinsic means.

The following is the publishing history of the stories included in this volume; reprints in magazines or anthologies are not listed unless of special interest. I wish to thank those publishers below who have given their permission, or otherwise facilitated the publication of stories which first appeared under their imprint. Admirers of Goodman's work should be grateful to David Ray, editor of *New Letters*, for first making so many of the unpublished stories available. I also want to thank my co-literary executors Sally Goodman, George Dennison, and Jason Epstein for their help, and my friend John Dings, and my wife Ruth Perry.

Collections

The Facts of Life (New York: Vanguard, 1945).
The Break-Up of Our Camp and Other Stories (Norfolk, Conn.: New Directions, 1949).
Our Visit to Niagara (New York: Horizon, 1960).
Adam and His Works (New York: Vintage, 1968).
The Writings of Paul Goodman, New Letters, XLII (Winter-Spring 1976).

Publishing History

The Facts of Life (1940), *Partisan Review*, VIII (September-October 1941); *Facts of Life*, 1945; *Adam*, 1968.

On the Rocks Along the River (1941), *New Directions in Prose and Poetry 6* (ed. James Laughlin, Norfolk, Conn.: New Directions, 1941).

A Parenthesis (1941), *New Letters*, 1976.

The University in Exile (1941), *Facts of Life*, 1945; *Adam*, 1968.

Sailors (1941), unpublished.

The Commodity Embodied in BREAD (1941), *Facts of Life*, 1945; *Adam*, 1968.

Alcestis [1942?], *New Directions in Prose and Poetry 7* (ed. James Laughlin, Norfolk, Conn.: New Directions, 1942).

Fights

    A Statue of "Strength and Weakness" [1942], *New Road* (ed. Alex Comfort and John Bayliss, London: Grey Walls Press, 1944).

    A Page of Sketches of Fights [1960?], *Our Visit to Niagara*, 1960; *Adam*, 1968.

Kennst du das Land? (1943), unpublished.

A Fire on Our Street (1943), *University Review*, X (Spring 1944); *New Letters*, 1976.

The Dream of a Little Lady Painter (1943), *New Letters*, 1976.

For My Daughter on My Birthday (1943), *New Letters*, 1976.

The Knight (1944), *New Directions in Prose and Poetry 9* (ed. James Laughlin, Norfolk, Conn.: New Directions, 1946); revised version "The Old Knight" [1961?], *Fresco*, I n.s. (Winter 1961); *Adam*, 1968.

The Father of the Psychoanalytic Movement (1945), *Kenyon Review*, VII (Autumn 1945).

Handball Players (1945), *Chicago Review*, II (Winter 1947); *Break-Up of Our Camp*, 1949; *Adam*, 1968.

The Emperor of China (1945), *Possibilities*, I (Winter 1947-1948); *Our Visit to Niagara*, 1960; *Adam*, 1968.

The Formulation of Freedom (1945), *New Letters*, 1976.

Little Bert, or The Intervention (1946), *New Directions in Prose and Poetry 10* (ed. James Laughlin, Norfolk, Conn.: New Directions, 1948); *Adam*, 1968.

Eros, or The Drawing of the Bow [1946?], *View*, VI (May 1946).

The Legs of My Dog: Some Notes on Gross Physiology and Visible Form (1946), *Instead*, No. 3 (April 1948).

On the Question: "What is the Meaning of Life?" (1946), *New Letters*, 1976.

Incidents of the Labyrinth (1946), *New Letters*, 1976.

Two Political Fables
> The Wisdom of Solomon (1946), unpublished.
> Two Classical Draft-Dodgers (1946), *New Leader*, XXX (September 20, 1947).

Likely and the Dragon (1947–[1968?]), *Adam*, 1968.

Terry Fleming, or Are You Planning a Universe? (1947), *New Directions in Prose and Poetry 10* (ed. James Laughlin, Norfolk, Conn.: New Directions, 1948); *Break-Up of Our Camp*, 1949; *Adam*, 1968.

The Midnight Sun (1947), *New Letters*, 1976.

Little Brother (1947), unpublished.

Raoul (1947), unpublished.

The Messiah-Blower (1948), *New Letters*, 1976.

The Penny (1948), *New Letters*, 1976.

The Lear Complex (1948), *New Letters*, 1976.

Thoughts on Fever, and Thoughts on These Thoughts (1948), *New Letters*, 1976.

Many Brothers (1948), unpublished.

The Bridge [1949?], unpublished.

The Home-Made Sweater [1949?], unpublished.

Two Methodical Pieces
> A Governor (1949), *New Directions in Prose and Poetry 13* (ed. James Laughlin, Norfolk, Conn.: New Directions, 1951).
> Daylight and Adam Naming the Beasts (1949), same.

Sailor's Money (1949), unpublished.

Printed November 1979 in Santa Barbara & Ann Arbor for the
Black Sparrow Press by Mackintosh and Young & Edwards
Brothers Inc. Design by Barbara Martin. This edition is
published in paper wrappers; there are 750 hardcover trade
copies; & 200 special copies have been handbound in
boards by Earle Gray.

Photo: Ruth Staudinger

Paul Goodman (1911-1972) the well-known social critic (*Growing Up Absurd, Compulsory Mis-education, People or Personnel, The New Reformation,* and many other books) had several careers before his fame in the Sixties. He was trained as a philosopher at the University of Chicago, taught literature in various colleges, became an expert on community planning with his architect brother Percival Goodman, taught ninth-graders in a progressive school, founded with Fritz Perls the Gestalt Therapy Institute and practiced psychotherapy, married and raised three children—all while living on an average income about that of a Southern sharecropper (when he started doing therapy in the early Fifties, his income jumped to $2,000 for the first time in his life). But these were really just his sidelines, and the reason that he lived in voluntary poverty rather than following one of the more lucrative callings open to him was that he regarded his work as a creative artist as his true vocation. Among his thirty-odd books his novels, plays, short stories, and poems would fill a shelf by themselves. His masterpiece is *The Empire City,* a comic epic written in the tradition and with the zest of *Don Quixote.* His *Collected Poems* contain, among hundreds of fine poems, the extraordinary sequence he wrote in mourning for his son Mathew, *North Percy,* probably the most moving elegy in American letters. Even though they never made much stir during his lifetime, Goodman knew the worth of these works, and yet he himself spoke of his short stories as his personal favorites. He gave one of his volumes of stories to a friend in the mid-Sixties, and wrote in it that it was his best book. When asked why he preferred it, he said, "That's the book I think is lovely—*Our Visit to Niagara*—I just like it, everything in it. That last story—'The Galley to Mytilene'—it's enchanting, I love to read it."

The present four-volume edition of *The Collected Stories and Sketches* includes all of Goodman's previously collected stories, plus dozens that have never appeared in book form, and twenty pieces, written during every stage of his literary career, published here for the first time.